Two Truths and a Lie

Two Truths and a Lie

KATRINA KITTLE

WARNER BOOKS

An AOL Time Warner Company

Grateful acknowledgment is given for permission to reprint the following: *Animal Speak* by Ted Andrews © 2000. Llewellyn Worldwide, Ltd. P.O. Box 64383, Saint Paul, Minnesota 55164.
All rights reserved.

Warner Books, Inc., 1271 Avenue of the Americas, New York, NY 10020
Visit our Web site at www.twbookmark.com.

 An AOL Time Warner Company

Printed in the United States of America
Originally published in hardcover by Warner Books, Inc.
First Trade Printing: June 2002
10 9 8 7 6 5 4 3 2 1

The Library of Congress has cataloged the hardcover edition as follows:
Kittle, Katrina.
    Two truths and a lie / Katrina Kittle.
       p. cm.
    ISBN 0-446-52487-5
     1. Truthfulness and falsehood—Fiction.   2. Married women—Fiction.
   3. Actresses—Fiction.   4. Ohio—Fiction.   I. Title.

    PS3561.I864 T88 2001
    813'.54—dc21   00-050347

ISBN 0-446-67851-1 (pbk.)

Cover photo by Patricia McDonough/Photonica
Cover design by Brigid Pearson

For Scott
In celebration of ten years of
"a nonstop slumber party with my best friend."

Acknowledgments

This book would not have been possible without the inspiration of my dear friend Judy Keefner who introduced me to horses when I was in the fourth grade. The ideas in this book were discussed on many an autumn trail ride and over many a Klondike bar. Thank you, Judy, for teaching me to listen.

For her belief in me, her directness, and her sincere love of books, I'm forever indebted to Liz Trupin-Pulli, my agent and friend.

Diana Baroni is the sort of editor I always dreamed of having: passionate, committed, always helpful, and so much fun. Thank you for making this a better book.

Thanks to Tina Andreadis, publicist extraordinaire, and to the rest of the Warner family. I feel in very good hands.

I thank the magical Hedgebrook Retreat for Women Writers for the gift of those weeks in Cedar Cottage and for the greater gift of introducing me to five women who still enrich my writing and my life—Karen Wilson, Kate Boyes, Aurora Agüero, Bridget Hughes, and Barbara Earl Thomas (special thanks to Barbara for allowing me to steal the name of her art installation, *What Is Found, What Is Lost, What Is Remembered,* for a dance piece in this book).

Many people helped with research and details. The reference librarians at the Wright Library in Oakwood, Ohio, are my heroes. Thanks to Sharon Leahy, great choreographer and friend for the post-aerobic breakfast meetings; to Nate Cooper for the words for the steps and the sounds of tapping; to the incredible dance and music company Rhythm in Shoes for the inspiration for my fictional dance company. Chad Yelton at the Cincinnati Zoo, and Gloria Neuhaus, and Joe Thomas at the Aronoff Center for the Performing Arts, answered countless bizarre questions. Kathy Tirschek and Joni Sherman gave hours of their time, driving me around Cincinnati in search of the "jumping off point." My wonderful husband, Scott Rogers, supplied aikido demonstrations. And many cherished friends and new acquaintances shared their stories and offered me insight into the worlds of alcoholism and addiction—my life is forever richer from knowing of your struggles, strength, and perseverance. All errors, exaggerations, and misstatements are mine alone.

I am indebted to the work of many authors whose books provided new ways of looking at our fellow animals, especially Penelope Smith's *Animal Talk* and *Animals: Our Return to Wholeness*. Huge thanks to Llewellyn Worldwide and author Ted Andrews for their gracious permission to quote from the book *Animal Speak*.

I owe great thanks to Mark Metzger and the staffs of Town Hall Theater and WTRC for their continued support and long-suffering patience every time I blew one of their deadlines to meet a book deadline.

For their comments, honesty, and loving care on various drafts of the manuscript I thank my talented, generous writing groups. Both groups are now in new incarnations but at the time of this novel's writing they were, in Yellow Springs: Suzanne Clauser, Charles Derry, Lee Huntington, Sandra Love, Amy Pendleton, Julia Reichert, and Barbara Singleton. In Oakwood: Ed Davis, Nancy Jones, Suzanne Kelly-Garrison, and Nancy Pinard.

Thanks to Mom, Dad, Scott, Monica, Rick, and Michael, who read early drafts and asked the right questions. Add to them my larger, sprawling extended family—Donna, Tim, Nana, and all the aunts, uncles, and cousins—and they become the most loving group of cheerleaders I've ever witnessed. Your boundless belief in me overwhelms me with gratitude. I am lucky.

Note: While the places I name in Cincinnati are real, all characters are entirely fictional, *including* the animals at the Cincinnati Zoo. For example, Cincinnati Zoo has Indian elephants, not African elephants, and their elephant calf, Ganesh, is not an orphan but lives happily with his mother. Also, Queen City Shakespeare is in no way meant to represent the real, wonderful Cincinnati Shakespeare Festival that now has its own theater on Race Street.

Chapter One

Dair was a habitual liar. Not pathological or anything, just . . . recreational. As she drove through Cincinnati on her way to Interstate 75, she mulled over the lie she'd tell her husband when she reached the airport. So often the truth needed a little spicing up.

What lie would she tell Peyton today? Traffic crawled on Clifton Avenue, and she cursed, realizing she'd forgotten about the University of Cincinnati's football game. She glanced at her watch; she'd be cutting it close. What could she tell Peyton had made her late?

Dair knew the secret to a good lie was to include as much of the truth as possible. This meant, however, that she had to be sure to remember which part was the truth and which part the lie. Forgetting or, worse—believing her own lies—was a dangerous line she feared to cross.

Sometimes, though, she lied because the truth was already so amazing that no one believed it. Sometimes the truth needed to be tampered with just so people didn't assume it was a lie.

She checked on the dogs in the rearview mirror. They rode contentedly along in the backseat. The car windows were up, the air-conditioning on, the day unseasonably hot for this late, drought-dry October. Blizzard, their imposing Great Pyrenees, licked Dair's sleeveless shoulder, leaving a string of drool. "Our guy is coming home," she said, reaching back to pet his long white hair. "We gotta share the bed again."

Shodan, their black Doberman, looked out the window and yawned at the Victorian homes passing by, the avenue lined with stately trees and old gas streetlights.

What were the true things she'd actually done today that she could shape into a more interesting story? This morning she'd taught her acting class at the Playhouse in the Park. Then she'd been to the liquor store, but she didn't exactly want to tell Peyton that, because he might ask why she hadn't just bought the celebratory champagne at the grocery store. He wouldn't be suspicious, he'd just be curious, and it would make her feel too small to explain to him that she'd also had to buy a bottle of wine to replace the bottle of wine she'd *already* replaced five times since he'd been on tour. Dair worried that the same pink-faced high school boy would be her cashier at the grocery, a boy who'd taken one of her acting classes, who might someday make an innocent reference about her wine purchases in front of Peyton.

Dair drove under I-75 and inched toward the entrance ramp to the notoriously gridlocked highway. Some damn event always snarled up the traffic: a Reds or Bengals game at Riverfront Stadium or some concert at Riverbend. . . . Dair wanted to kick herself for not opting to go through downtown. In the car ahead of her, some college-age kids passed a beer around. She thought longingly of that replacement bottle of wine.

The bottle was from their party stash—the gifts people brought to gatherings at their house that never got opened before everyone went home. Dair and Peyton kept them in a cupboard with the bread machine they rarely used, and it gave Dair great pleasure every time she drew attention to them, as they left for this cast party or that season opener, announcing, "Hey, there's still wine left from the New Year's party. Let's take a bottle with us." She felt such satisfaction handing Peyton a bottle identical to the bottle that Craig, perhaps, or Marielle had brought to their house. Peyton didn't guess that it was the sixth such bottle that had been there, the original and all its substitutes wrapped in newspaper and tucked into someone else's recycling bin down the street.

So . . . she could tell Peyton she'd been to the grocery store and develop her story from there. What could've happened? An armed robbery? No, too much follow-up. Maybe someone had an epileptic seizure? Hmm . . . that had promise, but why would she have to stay once help arrived? Ooh, the ambulance just happened to park in front of her car. No, something about that scenario wasn't grabbing her. For a lie to work, she had to be committed to it. Could some-one have gone into labor in the checkout line?

"C'mon," she muttered to a driver studiously ignoring her as she tried to merge. "Let me in, you jerk." He did, and she nosed her red Saturn into the sluggish stream of cars heading south on 75.

Blizzard whined.

"I know, sweetie," she said as traffic came to a complete stop. "What's the deal?" Northbound 75, across a concrete barrier to her left, seemed to be moving without a problem, cars zipping by as if to taunt her. She thought about telling Peyton she'd been stuck in traffic. Ha. Too lame to even utter.

A little girl in the car beside Dair smiled and pointed at Dair's dogs. Maybe . . . maybe Dair's shopping got disrupted by a hysterical mother screaming that her kid was missing. They'd locked the doors to the store, not letting anyone in or out while they searched. She practiced the story, talking aloud: "The mom kept screaming that Katie was a little blond girl. 'She's in a pink dress!' she kept saying. 'She has ponytails.' So, I'm helping look around; none of us know what to do, really, and I step into the corner by the wine racks. You know how it's kinda dark back there? The only real light is from the freezer where the drink mixes are? Well, back there, I see a cloth on the ground. I pick it up and it's a dress, and as I lift it all this long blond hair falls to the floor. I run out into an aisle to tell someone, and the first thing I see is this woman with a stroller, and in the stroller is a little blond boy, sleeping, and he's got a buzz-cut, and he's wearing overalls, and I know it's the little girl; it's Katie."

Dair jumped when Blizzard growled behind her head, a sound that never failed to tighten a fist around her heart, even though it wasn't directed at her.

"Hey, hey, what's the matter?" she asked. She put the car in park and twisted around to face him. Shodan growled, too, baring her teeth, her sweet Doberman face transforming into a werewolf's—lips curled back, ears pinned flat, eyes hard and hateful. Both dogs stood, hackles raised, staring out the side window. Dair turned in time to see a woman in a purple dress burst out of the trees flanking the northbound side of the highway. Dair blinked. Had the woman come down the hill from the fancy homes on Clifton Ridge above the high-way? The homes, obscured all summer, were now visible through the autumn-thin foliage.

The woman waved her arms at the northbound traffic and stepped out onto the interstate. Dair cringed as cars honked and tires squealed, and a minivan swerved around the woman, almost sideswiping an-other car. The minivan slowed, but when the woman ran to it and pounded on the window, it peeled away.

Did the woman need help? Or was she drunk? She wore no shoes and weaved in a weak-kneed sort of way toward the concrete di-vider and the already stopped southbound traffic.

Blizzard and Shodan barked—predatory, savage sounds that dropped ice down Dair's spine. Dair hit the automatic lock as the woman climbed the divider and stumbled between the lanes of cars, yanking on door handles. Dair could see only the woman's torso as the woman came close to the Saturn. The woman's head came into view as she drew back from the snarling dogs hurling themselves against the window, but Dair still didn't see her face—the woman looked away, across the highway from where she'd come, her shoulder-length black hair obscuring her profile.

Some northbound traffic had pulled over, and other people crossed the interstate toward the woman. Some got out of cars on the south-bound side, too, holding cell phones to their ears. The woman scram-bled across the hood of Dair's car. Dair glimpsed hairy legs, bare feet, broad hands with fine black hair on the knuckles. As the woman ran to the guardrail to the right of Dair, Dair saw that the purple dress wasn't zipped up all the way, didn't meet or fit across the back.

That was a man. A man in a dress.

And Dair recognized the dress. She'd worn that dress.

The dogs stopped growling and instead yipped eagerly as if greet-ing someone.

The man looked over his shoulder again, panic in his eyes—the only part of his face Dair could see through his blowing hair. He flung one leg over the guardrail.

Oh, God. He couldn't climb over from there—it looked wooded and shrubby, like the Clifton Ridge hillside he'd just come down, but it wasn't. He was directly over Clifton Avenue, where Dair had been just moments ago. "Don't!" Dair yelled. She lowered the passenger window. "Don't jump!" she screamed.

But he did. He threw his other leg over and disappeared as if yanked from below.

Car horns and screeching tires filled Dair's head.

She yanked the keys from the ignition and threw open her door. She ran to the guardrail, the first to reach the spot, other drivers crowding around her, all of them peering through the trees at the glimpse of purple on the road below, the traffic there stopped, too, horns blaring, car doors slamming, as people surrounded the body.

"Holy shit," said the man next to Dair.

"Do you think she was on drugs?" a woman asked. "Or was it a suicide?"

"She was saying, 'Help me,'" another woman said. "She pounded on my window and said, 'Help me.' Only it sounded like a man. I think that was a man in a dress."

"It *was* a man," Dair said, pulling away from the crowd. Had she really seen that? Her limbs felt heavy as she contemplated what she'd had to drink that day. She'd seen a man, wearing a dress she recognized, fall to his death. Hadn't she? She took off up the highway shoulder, checking over the guardrail until she found the place where land came up to meet it. She climbed over and nearly fell down the steep incline. She scooted on her butt, dodging trees and shrubs, gravel and broken glass skidding down the hill ahead of her. Blizzard bounded past, followed by Shodan. *Oh, God.* Dair realized she had left the door open.

"Hey, you guys, wait!" she called, imagining the dogs darting out in front of traffic. They stopped and looked back at her, tails wagging, tongues lolling in their laughing mouths, then bounded farther down the hill. Panic sent Dair sliding. When the ground leveled out, Dair stood on Clifton Avenue, dusted her butt, and called, "Blizzard! Shodan! C'mere!"

Fortunately traffic had stopped. The dogs materialized from the center of the hushed crowd under the overpass. One woman's hysterical voice rose from deep within the huddle, crying between hyperventilating gasps, "I didn't see her! I didn't see her! She was just *there.* Oh, God. Oh, my God." A different woman at the back of the crowd turned toward Dair, her face chalky, set. "I think she's dead,"

the woman whispered, pressing a hand to her mouth. A siren sounded
a few blocks away.

Dair sat on the weedy, little-used sidewalk and said, "Blizzard, come."
He did and sat beside her. Shodan followed. Dair grabbed both their
leather collars. Their leashes were in the car. She looked up at the
overpass. Her car. Her car was just sitting up there, driver's door open.
People still stared over the edge; others scrambled down the hillside
as she had. The siren began to drown out the crying woman's voice.

Dair's hands shook. She released the collars and hugged the dogs,
on either side of her. Shodan whined as the siren grew closer. Blizzard buried his face in Dair's armpit.

The ambulance pulled up, cutting off its siren with an abrupt yelp.
Dair stood when the crowd parted. She saw the crying woman near
a car with a shattered windshield, the broken glass patterned in a
red-and-white kaleidoscope. The man sprawled in front of her car,
facedown, legs and arms doing things human legs and arms weren't
meant to do.

That was the dress. She hadn't imagined it. A dress identical to the
one she'd borrowed from Gayle, the artistic director of Queen City
Shakespeare. Saying Dair "borrowed" it wasn't an outright lie, just
some truth withheld. Dair took care of Gayle's cat whenever Gayle
was out of town, which she'd been for the past three and a half
weeks, guest directing a show in Chicago. Gayle had told Dair to
make herself at home and use anything she wanted. She hadn't specifically said clothes, and Dair didn't specifically plan to tell her she'd
borrowed any.

Dair had searched every catalog and store, but she hadn't been
able to find that dress anywhere to buy for herself. Yet here it was,
on a dead person.

An EMT knelt beside the man, reached under the neck, and paused
a moment before shaking his head at the other EMTs, who then
slowed their actions. Someone in the crowd said, "He was trying to
get into cars, someone heard him say, 'Help me.'"

"He?" the EMT asked. He frowned and looked down at the body,
as did several others in the crowd.

"It's a man," the onlooker said. "A man in a dress. He wasn't trying
to kill himself, he was running from something, he—"

A man behind Dair snorted and said, "I'd run, too, if someone caught me in a dress."

Some others chuckled, and Dair's pulse doubled its beat. Someone was *dead;* there was nothing funny. She turned to look, to locate the jerk who'd spoken, wanting to kick him. A bearded man grinned at the crowd's response. Next to him stood Dair's new friend, Andy Baker, the recently hired light board operator at the Aronoff Center for Performing Arts.

"Andy," she said.

Andy blinked, startled, and for a split second appeared not to recognize her. Then he walked toward her, his short blond hair lifting on the breeze. They stood before each other, unsure what to do. He turned to stare at the body.

"This is weird," Dair said. "I never expect to see you except outside the stage door."

He nodded, pale and obviously shaken. He pulled a pack of cigarettes from his shirt pocket. Dair often followed her fellow actors outside the Aronoff for smoke breaks during rehearsals, and since he'd arrived in town in August, Andy was inevitably out there, smoking with the union guys. Andy held a cigarette out to her now, but she shook her head no, and he lit one for himself.

"Hey! Whose dog is this?"

Dair turned quickly. Shodan nosed near the body, and the EMT seemed afraid to touch her.

"Shodan!" Dair called. The Doberman lifted her head and trotted back to Dair with blood on her nose and snout. Dair's stomach heaved, and without thinking, she knelt and wiped the man's blood from the dog, then stood, staring at her red-smeared palm and fingers. Her first instinct was to get it off her, but she stopped. The blood itself posed no danger to her intact skin. The dark burgundy fluid was the proof of the man's life, his existence. And Dair didn't know what to do with it. It seemed somehow wrong, irreverent, to just wipe it on her jeans. She held her hand in front of her.

"Shodan?" Andy asked. "What kind of name is that?"

"It's a rank in aikido." Dair couldn't take her eyes from the blood.

"Aikido?"

"It's a martial art." She pulled her gaze from the smear on her hand.

The EMTs hadn't touched the body, but a young woman now photographed it. She took shot after shot, her face grim.

"So, what rank is a shodan?"

Dair stared at Andy. Who cared? A dead body lay a few yards from them and he wanted to chat? "Black belt," she said.

"You're a black belt?" he asked with admiration.

Dair paused, considering the lie, but shook her head. "I don't study aikido. Peyton does. My husband."

Peyton. Oh, shit. She looked at her watch.

The photographer finished, and at her nod, the EMTs rolled the body over. The dead man's blood-caked face moved and shifted, like a ceramic mask that had been cracked, his nose a gruesome, gaping hole. Dair's eyes burned, and she had to turn away. Andy did, too, the hand holding his cigarette trembling.

They stood shoulder to shoulder. He smelled like warm apples. "I've never seen anyone die before," Dair whispered.

"Me neither," he whispered back. Dair was glad he was there. Witnessing this event with someone she knew comforted her in a strange way.

"I wore a dress just like that," she said, gesturing over her shoulder toward the dead man. "At *Othello* auditions."

Andy turned and squinted at the dress. "Oh, my God. You did."

"I borrowed it from Gayle," she said.

Andy shivered and took a long drag from his cigarette. Dair felt the smoke in her own lungs but longed for the gentle warmth of wine in her throat instead. She turned back to the street as the EMTs lifted the body to a stretcher. Some of the dead man's long black hair, those strands not heavy with blood, lifted on the wind and floated above his face. The brittle autumn leaves rattled in that same wind and fell down around them like confetti, one yellow maple leaf sticking to the man's dented forehead. The EMT didn't remove the leaf when he pulled a sheet over the man's face.

At the hollow clunk of the ambulance doors closing, the crowd shifted and began to drift away, as if it were the audience at a play and those doors the final curtain.

Dair looked up at the remaining observers on the overpass a moment, then turned to Andy. "I've gotta go."

"Need any help?" he asked.

"No, but thanks." They hugged, clumsily, embarrassed, then she clambered up the steep hill, grabbing on to thin tree trunks and branches for handholds, pleading with the dogs to stay with her, and held their collars as she walked back to her car. Someone had closed her door so that traffic could move around it, which it now did, albeit slowly.

She got the dogs situated, and as she dug her keys out of her pocket, she realized she'd wiped most of the blood off her hand, probably as she'd crawled up the hill. A faint stain remained, as if she'd held a leaky red pen.

She called Peyton on her cell phone to warn him of her now true delay but got only his voice mail. She didn't leave a message. She couldn't think of what to say. She crossed the Ohio River to the airport, too numb to come up with a lie but knowing the truth was too outrageous to be believed.

Dair wanted to cry when she saw Peyton. He'd wandered down to baggage claim and sat on his duffel, wearing a headset, his bag of dance shoes beside him.

When he saw her approaching, he grinned and stood, unfolding his long frame like a cat stretching. "Well," he said, talking over the constant banging clatter of the baggage carousel, pulling his headphones off his neck. "This is gonna be a good one." His dark brown eyes sparkled.

She hugged him, nuzzling her nose into the hollow between his collarbones at the top of his T-shirt, breathing in his clean leather smell. She lifted her face to his. His shoulder-length black hair was pulled straight back into a ponytail. She kissed his high cheekbones, the small, crescent-shaped scar outside his left eye, his slender Roman nose.

"Dair? Aren't you going to play the game?"

"I just saw a man die." She moved her hands to the sinewy muscles in his shoulders.

He grinned. "Oh, this *is* a good one."

"I'm serious. We were stopped in traffic and a man in a dress jumped off 75 where it crosses over Clifton."

He shook his head and bent to pick up his duffel bag. "God, I've missed you," he said, smiling.

"He got hit by a car when he landed." She stood still as Peyton hooked the strap of his dance bag to her shoulder.

"He was in a dress? That's a good detail." Peyton started walking, holding her hand. She allowed herself to be led. "That's just weird enough that people would think it has to be true, because why would you muck up a story with some bizarre twist like that?"

Dair said nothing.

"So, what color was this dress?"

"Dark purple." She reviewed the video in her head. "Really a deep plum. Velvet bodice with a V-neck, flowing skirt. The skirt wasn't velvet. It was some sort of crepe, textured with teeny-tiny tone-on-tone swirls—"

"Okay, now see, that's too much detail—"

"—but there's more of that plum velvet around the hemline."

Peyton slowed to where he was almost not walking at all, searching her face.

"It zips in the back, only it wouldn't close all the way on this man. It was open almost down to his waist."

Peyton frowned. "You auditioned for *Othello* in a dress just like that."

Dair nodded. "I borrowed it from Gayle."

Borrowed it, dry-cleaned it at the same place Gayle had cleaned it last, and replaced it in Gayle's closet. Her basement closet, where Dair remembered it hung with only two other gowns—both very formal, with sequins and beads—and a short fur coat.

Dair had felt gorgeous in that dress. It'd brought her luck, too, although she hadn't told Peyton this yet.

He stopped and faced her. "What happened, Dair?"

"I'm not playing the game. On my way to the airport, honest to God, a man in a dress just like the one I borrowed from Gayle jumped off the bridge and died right in front of us."

He opened his mouth to speak, but before any sound came out, a girl's voice shouted, "Hey, Dair! Dair!"

She turned, startled, to see redheaded twins running toward them. Sixth-grade girls with identical faces, round blue eyes, same height, same build, same hair length and style. The sight of twins, as usual, made Dair's mouth go dry and her internal organs shift. Peyton, guessing what she was feeling, squeezed her hand, which stirred her insides even more.

"Remember me?" one girl challenged.

"Of course. Hi, Kelly, Corrie. How are you?"

The girls' mother caught up to them, looking harried and irritated, her face flushed under her own frizzy red hair.

"Hi." Dair held out her hand. "I'm Dair Canard. I had the girls in class at the Playhouse."

"Oh!" The mother sounded relieved. "They adored your class. They learned so much. And we just loved you in *The Taming of the Shrew* last spring."

"Dair taught us that lying game," Corrie said. "'Two truths and a lie.'"

The mother rolled her eyes, and Dair had a feeling she'd created a monster in their home. "Two truths and a lie" was her usual icebreaker in a first class, but also her first exercise in the most basic key to acting: passing off something untrue as believable.

"Dair's was good," Corrie said. "She said: 'I'm a twin, too; I got my first role in a suntan lotion commercial when I was five; and I've been kissed by a walrus.'" Wow. The girl's memory amazed Dair.

"Guess which one is the lie," Kelly challenged her mother.

The mom's sigh spoke of a weariness with this game. And she answered quickly enough for Dair to recognize that the mother had learned it was easier to guess than protest. "Well . . . I doubt she's been kissed by a walrus."

Peyton chuckled.

"No, that's true," Kelly said, grinning. "She works at the zoo."

The mother looked quizzical, and Dair nodded. "I'm an audience interpreter. Lots of actors in town are. I do the walrus show three times a week."

"So which is the lie?" Kelly prodded her mother again. "You get one more try."

"My guess would be . . . the twin," the mother said.

"No!" Corrie said. "That's true, too! Isn't that cool? She had a twin sister!"

"Identical?" the mom asked.

Dair shook her head. Peyton squeezed her hand.

"I've never been in a commercial," Dair said with a smile, eager to change the subject.

"You know why you thought that was the truth?" Corrie asked. "Because she gave details—her age and that it was for sunblock. That makes it seem more real."

But the mother didn't care; Dair could tell. "Is your twin an actress, too?" she asked.

"No. My sister passed away."

Peyton put an arm around her shoulder.

"I'm so sorry," the mother said, pressing a hand to her heart.

"It's okay." Dair smiled. "It was a long time ago." She put her arm around Peyton's waist. "This is my husband, Peyton Leahy. He dances with Footforce."

"Really?" The mom eyed him with new interest. "I've heard of them. You're like a little Riverdance, right?"

Dair laughed out loud. Peyton grimaced. "Not exactly," he said. "We've been around longer. We do contemporary choreography based on the traditional forms. You should check us out sometime."

"Oh, I will," the mom said. The way her eyes lit up, Dair knew she was expecting Peyton to be shirtless in leather pants. As they talked, Dair looked at her husband through this woman's eyes and felt lucky and lustful.

"We just came off a short tour. We've been on the road for three weeks."

"Oh, well, then, we should let you go," the mom said, shaking his hand again. She turned to Dair. "Are you in anything else the twins could see?"

"Actually . . ." Dair smiled at Peyton. "I'm going to be in *Othello* for Queen City Shakespeare. It opens in November."

"Marvelous! We'll be there."

"We signed up for another class," Kelly said as her mother tried to pull her away. "The audition class."

"Oh, that'll be with Craig," Dair said.

"Craig MacPhearson?" Kelly asked. "Who was in *Shrew* with you?" Dair laughed and nodded.

"He's *cute!*" the twins said in unison.

Peyton and Dair laughed at that.

"You'll like Craig," Dair promised. And the mom succeeded in dragging the girls away.

Peyton took her face in his hands. "You got cast in *Othello?*"

She nodded, grinning. "Yup. I'm Emilia, the bad guy's wife."

He kissed her. His familiar flavor flooded her body like a long swallow of port, soothing and dizzying at once. He waltzed her down the concourse, his duffel bumping them, marking the time.

"Peyton! Stop it!" Dair laughed.

He did, eventually, as they reached the exit and stepped out into the ovenlike air.

He kissed her hand. "Congratulations, love. Did Craig get cast?"

"Yes! He's Iago, my husband."

Peyton laughed. "Again? People will start to think he's your real husband!"

"I won't," she said. "I promise." They kissed again, and she felt tipsy.

"We need to celebrate. Should we get something to take over to Marielle's tonight?"

"I already got some champagne."

Dair heard the dogs barking through the car's half-open windows. They'd seen, or smelled, their guy, their Peyton, and were beside themselves at his return.

He jogged the remaining hundred yards to the car. "Hey, you guys," he said, letting them out. Shodan greeted him first, since she was his. She wriggled with joy, her little stump of a tail waggling. He bent down and hugged her, and she licked his ears and face, whimpering as if she couldn't stand how glad she was to see him. Once she calmed, he said, "Hey, Blizzard," and the Pyrenees shuffled shyly to him, then stood, his front paws on Peyton's shoulders, in one of his bear hugs. He added a few licks to Shodan's. Peyton took Blizzard's paws and lowered them to the ground, laughing, then wiped his face with his arm. The dogs danced little jigs of happiness at his feet.

On the way home, traffic still crawled on both north and southbound 75 over Clifton. Peyton stared at the flashing lights, the yellow tape, and the news vans.

"I told you. I wasn't kidding. We got stopped right back there, just under Gayle's house." Dair took the exit and wound her way back onto Clifton, waiting for the police officer to wave her through the now one-lane traffic under the overpass. "The dogs knew something was weird before I did. Blizzard, especially, seemed disturbed."

Peyton swiveled his head from the accident scene to face her, grinning, "You sound exactly like your mom."

Dair's spine stiffened. Her mother believed she could telepathically communicate with animals and was always telling Dair and Peyton that Blizzard thought this or Shodan felt that. Peyton was sweet about it, but it made Dair impatient. Her mom was an otherwise reasonable, intelligent woman, and Dair wanted to shake her when her mother ruined this impression by blithely blabbing about what someone's dog "said" about his treatment or home life. It had been the source of much embarrassment Dair's entire life. "Please," Dair said, rolling her eyes. "There's nothing telepathic about it. You just have to pay attention. Anyone would've been able to tell that Blizzard was bothered. And . . . speaking of my mother: She's coming over tomorrow. I hope that's okay. She says she has some news she wants to tell us in person."

Peyton frowned. "Is anything wrong?"

"No. I asked, of course, but she says not to worry. You know she'll probably tell us that Blizzard feels threatened by another dog in the park, or that Shodan desperately wants to have puppies." They laughed.

Dair pulled onto their street, high on its hillside overlooking the Cincinnati Zoo. She parked across the street from the purple Victorian house they lived in. The huge house wasn't entirely theirs; it was divided into three apartments—the main house split into a two-story duplex, with an efficiency apartment on the smaller third floor. The third floor came complete with a turret.

"Ahh, home," Peyton said with a sigh. "God, I miss you when I'm gone." He touched her cheek with the back of his hand. "I love you."

"I love you."

Shodan whined, then barked. "Okay, okay!" Peyton said as if answering her.

Dair got out of the car and carried Peyton's bag of dance shoes up the steps that climbed the steep, ivy-covered hill of their front yard. Living here kept them all in shape.

Inside the house, their cat, Godot, sat in the middle of the worn Persian rug, awaiting Peyton. Completely buff colored, with no markings whatsoever, Godot reminded Dair of a miniature lion cub. He fixed his golden eyes on Peyton and mewed. "Well, hello," Peyton answered, sitting on the floor.

Godot had earned his name by making them wait for his appearance the entire first two months they had him, hiding so completely that Dair would've blamed the dogs for his empty food bowl and sworn he'd run away if it weren't for the daily deposits buried in the litter box. Eventually their wait was rewarded, and he emerged to join the family.

Godot examined Peyton's legs, lips parted, taking in the smells of Peyton's journey. Then he rubbed his chin repeatedly on Peyton's knees, purring audibly. Once he'd marked the man as *his* again, Godot approached the dogs with his tail high.

The cat batted Blizzard's nose, then took off, leaping over the still-sitting Peyton toward the kitchen. In a flurry of barking, the dogs were after the cat, also clambering over Peyton, but not as gracefully. "Hey!" Peyton yelled, rolling out of the way. He ended up on his back, looking up at Dair. He raised his eyebrows.

She lowered herself and straddled him. She slipped her hands under his head and undid his ponytail, running her fingers through his straight, silky hair. He reached up to her head and unclipped her own tangle of dark brown curls. As she leaned down to kiss him, she heard the approaching stampede, toenails and paws clacking like pony hooves on the hardwood floors. Godot used Dair's back as a springboard. "Look out!" Dair said, arching herself over Peyton, sheltering his head in her arms. Blizzard tried to leap off her, too, and knocked her sideways. Laughing, Dair and Peyton watched the dogs corner the cat under a chair. Godot lay belly up, batting at the dogs around the chair legs on either side of him.

"Better than TV," Peyton said. He still lay on his back, head turned to watch them. Dair lay beside him, on her side, propped on one elbow. Peyton stretched out an arm and playfully squeezed Shodan's back foot.

With his arm outstretched, Dair noticed a greenish gray bruise inside his elbow, the size of a thumbprint. She leaned across his torso, chin resting on his sternum, and touched it with her fingertips. "What's this?"

When he didn't answer, she lifted her head to look at him, tucking her hair back out of the way. He gazed at her, his face blank.

Their eyes met, and when she realized what he thought she was asking, her heart wanted to slide up out of her mouth.

"Looks like a bruise," he said in a careful, even voice.

Dair wanted to erase the moment, change the subject, anything
but make him think she questioned him, but she knew that to drop
it now would only make him doubt her belief in him.

"Duh," she said, straddling him again, poking him in the ribs. "What's
it from?"

She felt him breathe again beneath her. "I don't know." He lifted
the arm and examined the bruise. "Probably that *Vestiges* piece. You
know, the one with the fire and drums? It sometimes gets a little out
of hand." He dropped the arm back down.

She leaned over, her loose hair falling all around her, and kissed
the bruise, lingering. She felt his pulse under her tongue.

And, as often happened with them, they articulated the same
thought at the same moment. "I'm sorry," they whispered. Then they
smiled.

Dair sometimes felt so close to this man, she pushed her hair back
because his was in his eyes.

He pulled her face down to his and kissed her. She could get drunk
on his kisses alone.

"I'm sorry I didn't believe you," Peyton said. "About the guy on the
bridge."

"Why should you? Too weird that it should happen on the way to
the airport."

Peyton looked at his watch. "I wonder if it'll be on the news."

Dair climbed off him to reach for the remote on the antique Japa-
nese trunk that acted as their coffee table. They snuggled into the
couch, legs entwined, and she clicked through several news programs,
settling on one that promised local news after the national weather
report. The dogs and Godot continued boxing, and they watched
them until an anchorwoman announced, "A thirty-four-year-old Cincinnati man jumped off the I-75 overpass over Clifton Avenue—near the
Mitchell Avenue exit—today, and was hit and killed by traffic below.
The man first disrupted traffic by running at approaching cars, attempting to get inside them. Adding to the bizarre scene was the fact
that the man was dressed in women's clothing, wearing a purple velvet gown. Many witnesses at first believed the jumper was a woman."

The camera swept the cluster of onlookers.

"Andy was there, too," Dair said.

"Andy?" Peyton asked.

She nodded as a reporter interviewed a distraught-looking woman. "You know—the new light board operator at the Aronoff. He's been here since August."

"That guy you and Craig smoke with?" Peyton teased. "I don't know him."

"I bet you'd know him if you saw him. Maybe they'll show us."

But they didn't. Peyton leaned forward as the distraught woman said, "I just assumed it was a woman when I saw the dress, the long hair. I didn't get a good look. I was stunned when we found out it was a man."

The anchorwoman returned. "The man has been identified as Cincinnati actor Craig MacPhearson."

"Oh, my God," Peyton and Dair whispered together.

Dair felt her lungs deflate, as if drained, and refused to refill. The woman couldn't have said Craig's name. But then she said it again: "Fellow actors interviewed in the last hour at the Playhouse in the Park say MacPhearson gave no hint he was suicidal, nor had any reason to be. They also claim they have never seen him wear female clothing."

Air finally filled Dair's lungs with a gasp.

The boxing match stopped, and all three animals looked at them with wide eyes.

"You didn't know it was Craig?" Peyton asked as if in disbelief. His eyes shone with tears.

Dair shook her head, her own tears burning hot down her cheeks, feeling as though she'd killed Craig herself. "No. His face . . ." She touched her cheekbones and nose, remembering how the broken face had moved like red puzzle pieces. "It—it happened so fast. And it was out of context—Craig doesn't live in this neighborhood. I—I really thought it was a woman at first. I wasn't thinking of Craig . . . or looking for him. I thought . . . Oh, God, I thought it was some crazy person."

The room slowly rotated around her like a bad, bed-spinning drunk. That body *couldn't* be their Craig. Oh, please, why couldn't this be some stupid story she'd made up?

Blizzard approached and put a paw on her knee. Dair stared at the TV, where the footage showed them loading a covered stretcher into an ambulance. She remembered the yellow maple leaf stuck to Craig's shattered forehead. Watching the footage felt like déjà vu. If only she'd known. If only she'd recognized Craig, let him into her car.

The anchorwoman said, "The Hamilton County Coroner's Office will perform an autopsy tomorrow morning. Authorities want to rule out the use of drugs before declaring the death a suicide."

Blizzard burrowed his snout under Dair's arm. She tried to pet him, but he kept his nose glued to her hand. She pulled it away from him and opened her palm. The blood—Craig's blood—was no longer visible, but Blizzard didn't need to see it to know it was there.

She brought her palm to her own nose, trying to smell what Blizzard smelled. A faint mineral odor, like an empty bottle that once contained vitamins, lingered there, but other than that, nothing. She envied Blizzard his ability to conjure up a whole person with just that odor. A whole, healthy, laughing person. Their best friend.

A person cast to play Iago to her Emilia.

A person who'd fallen in love with their next-door neighbor, Marielle.

A person who knew more about Dair's lies than anyone in the world.

Chapter Two

We have to tell Marielle," Dair whispered.

Peyton nodded, but they didn't move. They held hands, and stared at each other, at the room's intricate wooden moldings, at the fireplace's carved mantel, at the TV, which had moved on to a game show. No matter what Dair stared at, she saw Craig alive in her mind. Craig smoking with her and Andy at rehearsal, his script folded in half in his back jeans pocket. Craig kissing Marielle as she and Peyton watched rented movies and ate popcorn with them next door. Craig's eyes alight as he talked about Marielle at their kitchen table.

He *couldn't* be dead. And he wouldn't be dead if she hadn't locked her car door. If he'd opened it, if she'd seen his face, she might have pulled him into her car, to safety. What had he been running from?

Finally Dair stood, unable to sit still with these thoughts. Peyton did, too. Still holding hands, they stepped out onto the porch they shared with Marielle, where a fat pumpkin Craig had selected sat waiting for Marielle's son to carve it into a jack-o'-lantern. They knocked on the front door next to theirs, the wood already covered with Matt's construction paper ghosts and black cats.

A hand parted the curtain in the window, and Marielle's cautious eyes appeared. Then the curtain was flung open. Marielle smiled and held her free hand up by her face, fingers spread wide, shaking the hand back and forth—American Sign Language for applause. She was saying, "Yea!" with her hand, and Dair doubted she even knew she did it. Marielle wasn't deaf herself, but she sign interpreted for many schools and colleges in town. They'd met her when she'd been a substitute signer for one of Dair's productions. The locks clicked in the tumblers and she opened the door. "Welcome home, Peyton! Hey, Dair."

They stepped into her apartment, standing at the bottom of the stairs to the bedrooms. Marielle wore a crisp white T-shirt and tan linen shorts. She had a wide-hipped grace, an ampleness to her muscular thighs that always reminded Dair of a mare. Her honey blond hair was clipped loosely at the back of her head, her straight forelock of bangs nearly reaching into her eyes. She hugged them both. Dair had almost wanted to find her weeping over the evening news, so they wouldn't have to be the ones to hurt her.

"Hey! How was the tour?" Marielle asked Peyton, kissing his cheek.

"Oh. Um, okay. . . ."

"Are we celebrating tonight? Your return? Craig and Dair's success?"

They paused.

Marielle frowned, looking at their faces. "What's wrong?" she asked.

Just then Matthew cried out, "Hey, Peyton!" His white blond lamb curls bounced as he ran down the stairs. "I've been working on those steps you taught me before you left. You wanna see them?"

"No, Matt," Marielle said, hands on her hips. "You're supposed to be in your room."

"But, Mom—"

"Upstairs." Marielle pointed.

Matt tightened his mouth into a furious pinch and narrowed his eyes at her before stomping up the steps. He slammed his bedroom door, and Slip Jig, his slender gray wisp of a cat, came flying down the stairs. Matt had named her after seeing a pretty girl dance a slip jig at one of Peyton's Footforce shows.

Marielle stared after her eight-year-old and shook her head. "Matt got in trouble again at school. He says the other kids are mean to him, but the teachers never see anyone else start anything. I don't know what to do . . . but I won't have him hitting people."

She sighed and smiled weakly at them, but their faces reminded her of another worry. "What's the matter?" she asked. "Here. C'mon in, sit down." Dair and Peyton followed her into the living room, Slip Jig bounding onto the striped sofa ahead of them. On the coffee table stood a beautiful, beckoning, open bottle of Chardonnay and two glasses.

"Craig'll be here any second. What's going on?"

Dair and Peyton looked at each other. Marielle had just made their job easy, if cruel.

"Um, Craig *won't* be here any second," Peyton said gently, shaking his head.

Marielle's gaze traveled back and forth between their faces, searching for a clue.

Dair took one of Marielle's hands and led her to her couch. "Sit down," she said. Marielle did, but her eyes widened as Dair sat right beside her, still holding her hand.

"Oh, my God, what's wrong?" she asked, her voice shrill. She squeezed Dair's hand tighter, instead of pulling it free as Dair expected her to.

"There's been an accident," Dair said.

Marielle exhaled as if someone had punched her, then said in a flat, dull voice, "He's dead." Her green eyes were hard and feverish as she stared at Dair, waiting to see if Dair protested, if Dair corrected her. Dair couldn't.

Marielle yanked her hand free and stood. "He's dead," she repeated. "If there was an accident and he was just injured, if he was in the hospital, if he was alive, you'd be saying, 'Come on, let's go,' not telling me to sit down. Oh, my God. Tell me I'm wrong. Please, please tell me I'm wrong." Her graceful hands, her long fingers, signed some sort of begging as she backed away. She seemed to be waiting for Dair and Peyton to tell her no, no, that's not it, and when they didn't, she backed into the wall and slid into a heap as if someone had kicked her behind the knees. Slip Jig darted from the room.

Dair crouched at Marielle's side, hugging her. Marielle didn't embrace her back, and she didn't cry. They all seemed frozen, stunned. "What happened?" Marielle asked.

Dair told her. She told her everything, including how she and Andy hadn't recognized Craig, what the news had reported. Every detail.

Marielle pressed her hands to the sides of her head, fingers entwined in her hair, as if this information threatened to burst her skull apart and she needed to hold it together. Telling the story again, saying the words out loud, felt to Dair like rehearsing her way through a new scene. She was only beginning to believe it herself. This was real.

Marielle stood up, took a few steps, then reeled. Dair rose to steady her, but Marielle shook off Dair's hands and wandered around the room. "He wasn't suicidal," she said.

Dair sat on the ottoman. Her throat and chest ached as though she'd been screaming. She craved the Chardonnay's golden coolness. She wanted to soothe the parched throbbing, the unbearable thirst that had materialized the second she saw it.

Marielle stumbled and sat herself down on the couch across from Dair. "Are you *sure?* Are you sure it was him? It doesn't make any sense. He wouldn't jump. Because . . ."

"Because what?" Peyton asked, his voice full and swollen as if it came from the bottom of a well. He finally sat, in the beat-up armchair at the head of the coffee table. The coffee table, with a full bottle of wine sitting on it. Waiting.

Marielle slumped her shoulders and stared at the wine. Dair willed Marielle to pour it, and she did. She poured for herself, then scooted the bottle toward Dair. Gratitude flooded Dair's body. Marielle stood again. "I'll get another glass—" she began, then stopped and scrunched up her face at Peyton. He shrugged, and she waved a hand around her face as if irritated that she'd forgotten he never drank.

Dair filled her glass and raised it to her lips, where it poured down her throat like relief itself. This was her third and final drink of the day. An AA test she'd read had challenged her to limit herself to three drinks a day for six months. It was very specific: You couldn't go over three no matter what special events or tragedies planted themselves in your life. The test included the explicit instruction "Even if someone dies, you can only have three drinks."

Even if someone dies. Someone had died. Dair kept needing to remind herself. Craig had died. Craig, who'd been Cornwall to her Regan in *King Lear,* who'd kissed her passionately onstage and only six times offstage, at midnight on the last six New Year's Eves. They'd had countless beers together after rehearsals, had napped together on the greenroom floor on double show days, had confided in each other like siblings. Craig knew the truth about Dair's biggest lie. That thought made her want to chug the whole bottle of Chardonnay. Her throat constricted so she could hardly swallow.

"I have to show you something," Marielle whispered. She slipped into the kitchen.

Dair set down her glass. Peyton stared after Marielle.

She came back cupping something in her hands, her face blank, vacant. She sat again opposite Dair and opened her hands to reveal a small, gray velvet jeweler's box. Dair already knew what was inside—Craig had told them. "He wouldn't have killed himself," Marielle said. "Something else happened."

She lifted the lid and started to sob at last. Dair and Peyton both moved to sit on either side of her.

Inside the box was a tasteful diamond ring. No mistaking its intent. "He told us he was ready to do this," Peyton said, touching Marielle's blond hair. "We just didn't know when."

Dair and Peyton had never played matchmaker in their lives, but ever since they'd accidentally brought Craig and Marielle together, they'd been delighted by what had developed. They'd giggled like little kids the first time his car stayed parked out front all night, when Matt was gone at summer camp. They'd noted all the firsts—the first time he'd introduced her as "my girlfriend" at a party, the first time they'd grocery shopped together, the first time Craig did a "guy's job" around the apartment, trimming the bushes on her side of the house. Peyton once commented that when Marielle and Craig were together, they were almost always laughing.

Marielle sniffed. "He—he gave this to me yesterday."

Dair couldn't help but smile that he had asked her. "But . . . then why—?" She gestured to the ring still in the box.

Marielle's mouth crumpled. "I hadn't told Matthew yet," she said, sucking in a sob. "W-we were arguing, and I didn't want it to be . . . spoiled. Tomorrow, we had an evening planned, just me and him. I was, I was going to tell him then. . . ." She looked up at Dair, her eyes bloodshot. "That's the only reason I didn't tell you," she whispered, grasping Dair's hand. "I wanted to be able to tell him he was the first to know. It was so important for him to be happy about it."

Dair held her and rocked her and whispered, "Shhh," into her hair. Marielle smelled clean and fresh, like a hay field.

A car door slammed in front of the house. Dair turned her head toward the street. Another slam followed. She heard Shodan and Blizzard through the wall, barking in their living room. Peyton stood and peered out the window. "It's the police."

Dair's heart lifted—perhaps they had some news, some explanation—but she realized it wouldn't matter. No matter what the police told them, Craig would still be dead.

"Are they coming here?" Marielle asked, shrinking back into the couch.

"Looks like it." Peyton went out her front door to meet them.

"I wonder . . . I wonder how they knew to come here." She drew her legs up, arms wrapped around her knees.

Dair shook her head, her mouth suddenly dry. "I'll clear this for you." She scooped up the wineglasses with one hand, their stems sliding through her fingers, their bowls resting in her palm. She grabbed the bottle with the other.

She headed for the kitchen, passing the front door, where Peyton talked to the police on the porch. She turned and glanced up the stairs toward the bedrooms. The hall above was dark and silent. Was Matt asleep? Or sulking? Could he hear the dogs? The police?

In the kitchen Dair set the bottle on the counter, then shifted the glasses so that she held one in each hand. She swallowed her remaining wine, reveling in that sensation, icy and warm at the same time. She looked at Marielle's still full glass and paused. This was breaking the rules. Or was it? In her three weeks of the AA test, she hadn't always had three drinks a day. On two days she'd had only two drinks. And once, only one. So, technically, she had four extra drinks in the bank. She downed Marielle's, too, the tingling warmth spreading through her chest. She rinsed the glasses and set them in the drainer as Peyton and the officers came through the front door. Before shoving the cork back in the open mouth of the bottle, she tipped the bottle back and took a long slug, then laid it on its side in the fridge.

She heard the officers' voices in the living room. Heard a man say, "His apartment manager said you were his fiancée?" She knew she should join them.

As Dair passed the stairs again, she noticed Slip Jig, halfway up the staircase, staring at something on the top landing, tail twitching as if she were playing or stalking something. Dair followed her gaze and inhaled sharply as she saw Matthew standing there in shadow. Had he been there when she'd looked before?

She opened her mouth to speak to him, but he backed out of the faint light, into the darkness. The cat bounded up the remaining steps and followed him. Dair heard Matt's door softly close.

In the morning, when Dair woke and didn't know where she was, a heavy weight settled on her, like someone sitting on her chest. The weight lightened when she realized it was Peyton's head between her breasts. Dair and Peyton were entwined on Marielle's couch, both their long bodies finding the necessary configurations to occupy this small space together. She heard his gentle, wheezing snore, like the purr of an asthmatic cat.

Then she remembered *why* they were sleeping in Marielle's living room, and the heaviness returned. The police hadn't been any closer to knowing what had happened to Craig. They'd only wanted to know the last time Marielle had seen or spoken to him. She'd met him for a picnic lunch at the Krohn Conservatory, where he'd given her the ring. That left approximately twenty-eight hours since she'd seen him and approximately nineteen hours since she'd spoken to him—he'd called her at ten Friday night.

"And what was the nature of that call?"

Marielle blinked. "The nature? To tell me he loved me."

The officer looked at his feet. "Did you ever know him to wear women's clothing?"

"No."

"Do you yourself have any dresses missing?"

"No."

"Will you contact us if you find that you do have clothing missing?"

A nod. She took their card with trembling hands. The police offered no encouragement, no hope, no promises.

Dair and Peyton helped Marielle tell Matt. Marielle reported the news to her son in a dull voice and halting sentences. Dair gently filled in the gaps whenever Marielle stopped speaking. Matt listened with little emotion, his eyes wide. Dair figured he was more concerned about his zombielike mother at the moment than about Craig.

Dair and Peyton stayed while Marielle made some phone calls and watched the eleven o'clock news. The news was what finally blew her wide open. They ended up staying all night after tucking her shell-shocked body into bed.

Dair thought about their dogs next door. They'd need to be let out soon. She slowly slid herself from beneath Peyton, lowering his head onto the cushion she'd been using. He inhaled and yawned but didn't open his eyes. She kissed his forehead, then stood and tiptoed to the kitchen to leave a note on the pad by Marielle's phone, in case anyone woke while she was gone. She jumped to discover Marielle sitting at her table, staring at the wall before her. Without breaking her gaze or turning her head to Dair, she said, "I can't sleep."

Dair stood behind the chair, rubbing Marielle's shoulders. Marielle had her hands on the table, one palm face up, one palm down. She rolled her wrists, reversing her palms. "He can't be gone," Marielle said. She rolled her hands in front of her again. Dair wondered if it was the sign for death. Her throat closed. When Marielle repeated the gesture a third time, Dair reached down and stopped her. She kissed the top of Marielle's head.

"I need to move," Marielle said. "Can we walk the dogs?"

"Okay."

Marielle stood, as if to follow Dair out the door that very moment, barefoot in the nightgown Dair had helped her put on last night. "You get dressed, Mare," Dair said. "I'll go feed the gang and make us some coffee." Marielle nodded but didn't move. "You want me to help you?" Dair asked, the weight on her chest growing heavier.

Marielle shook herself and rubbed her forehead. "No. No. I'll meet you out back." And she went up the stairs, moving like a regular person again. Dair wrote Peyton a note and left it tented on the coffee table beside him. She also left one for Matt in the kitchen before stepping onto the porch and unlocking her own front door.

The dogs bounded and jumped at her return. She opened the back door to let them out in the picket-fenced backyard while she filled their food bowls and started the coffeemaker. She brushed her teeth and dressed in shorts and a sweatshirt, then let the dogs back into the kitchen. They snarfed down their breakfasts while she poured a cup of coffee. She uncapped her bottle of Kahlúa but stopped, remembering her fourth drink last night. The aroma of the rich coffee liqueur, with its hint of vanilla, was so intense that she could taste it. The idea that the tiny shot she slipped into her coffee counted as a whole drink was absurd. But she capped the bottle, put it away, and let half-and-half suffice for this morning.

She carried two mugs out to the back porch—a wooden deck they shared with Marielle—and let the dogs caper about the yard. She shivered at what finally felt like autumn weather. Still no sign of rain, but cooler temperatures might at least take that baked, desperate edge out of the air. She raised her eyes to the narrow metal staircase snaking up to Mr. Lively's apartment on the third floor of the house. She rarely heard Mr. Lively—a wheezing, frail old man, who in no way lived up to his name—but she often heard his damn bird, an African gray parrot named Captain Hook. Captain Hook shrieked and squawked and took great pleasure in imitating the train whistle from the zoo down the hill. The actual whistle was annoying enough, but the parrot's endless repetitions of it were somehow even more grating. He also imitated a ringing phone so convincingly that he'd fooled Dair more than once. And she'd heard him sing out, "Hey, Peyton!" mimicking Matt's voice with eerie accuracy. Once he'd called the dogs in her own voice, and they'd loped over to her even though she sat studying a script and hadn't said a word. This morning Captain Hook was mercifully quiet.

Just as Dair was about to go check on Marielle, she appeared, moving like a sleepwalker but locking her back door behind her. She'd managed to dress appropriately in jeans and a sweater, but nothing she put on could mask the devastation cloaked around her.

Dair handed her a mug, but Marielle didn't drink. She held it between both hands as though to warm herself and watched the dogs with expressionless eyes. Dair's own eyes stung just to look at her. It seemed unfair that someone as generous as Marielle should be asked to suffer such loss twice—she'd already lost Matt's dad in a car accident before Matt was even born.

An elephant trumpeted. Marielle didn't flinch, but the sound raised the hair on both dogs' spines as they faced the front yard, noses in the air, growling low in their chests.

This house overlooked Cincinnati Zoo property, and the dogs marveled at the odd sounds and exotic smells that wafted up to their street. They'd grown used to it, Dair guessed, figuring these strange animals never vied for their territory. The dogs barked back at the howler monkeys but were always a bit cowed by the elephants. Blizzard looked up at Dair, brow furrowed, tail and haunches low to the ground, his face beseeching her, *What the hell* is *that?* She had to smile.

Dair leashed them and petted Godot, who'd slunk out of the cat door and sat on the back porch, his nose lifted, sipping the elephant smell, too.

"You ready?" she asked Marielle, who put down her mug and followed. Normally when they walked the dogs together, Marielle took one leash, but today she didn't reach for one, and Dair didn't offer. They went through the gate and around to the front yard, where the dogs picked their delicate way down the steep stairs to the street. Marielle walked with her arms crossed over her chest, chin jutting forward, not looking at scenery, not looking at the dogs, her eyes straight ahead, as if simply walking took every ounce of energy and concentration she had. Dair stopped attempting conversation when a few of her questions were met with nods or ignored. They just walked together.

The grass was dry, bleached brown and white. It crunched under their feet, and dust billowed in the wake of the dogs' paws. Dry leaves skittered across the sidewalk and flavored the chilly air with the faint sweetness of an old tea bag left to decay in the sun.

They walked fast enough to warm themselves, but the loss of Craig dragged on Dair's legs like the weight of shin-deep water. Poor Marielle. God, what would Dair do if Peyton died? She almost couldn't breathe for a moment, imagining that loss.

They entered Burnet Woods, where Dair had met Peyton eight years ago. For twenty-seven years of her life she'd survived without him, functioned in the world, laughed, smiled, talked. How strange that eight years changed so much, made the thought of living without him seem like paralysis.

She led the dogs past the Spanish-tile-roofed pavilion, the picnic shelters, the normally lovely lake that now held only one or two inches of stagnant water and some miserable-looking ducks who muttered and eyed the dogs with suspicion. The dogs knew the way down a hiking trail into the dry, crackling woods—a place Dair would never walk at night—to a clearing enclosed by maple, oak, and sycamore trees, the unofficial dog run for the area. Technically dogs weren't allowed off leash within city limits, but every dog owner Dair knew indulged in it here, deep within the eighty-nine acres of the park.

She unclipped them and led Marielle to a dusty ledge, where they sat to watch the dogs run and play. Dair put an arm around her, and Marielle dropped her head to Dair's shoulder.

"How did you survive it?" Marielle whispered.

"What?"

"Losing your twin. Someone so close to you. Part of you. Tell me how to do it. . . ."

Dair leaned her cheek against Marielle's hair, feeling sick and miserable. "You know how," she said. "I can't tell you anything you don't already know. You survived losing Matt's dad. You're strong, Marielle."

Marielle tensed against her and began to cry. Dair held her and rocked her slightly, watching the park fill up with people. Most glanced at them, then looked away, wary of their sorrow, as if it might be contagious.

Peyton hadn't been wary of sorrow. He'd been drawn to it. The first time Dair met Peyton, she'd lied to him, just as she lied to everyone she met in the park. She'd had a puppy, a conversation magnet, so she got a lot of practice. She'd bring Blizzard, a chubby white ball of fuzz, and create answers to the question "Where'd you get your dog?"

"From one of my dad's clients" just seemed too dull. So she made up stories about how Blizzard found her, arriving on her porch one morning. A story about her best friend who'd died of AIDS and made her promise to take care of his puppy. A story about how she stole him out of some jerk's car who'd left Blizzard baking in the hot sun with no water.

And if the conversation moved beyond the dogs, Dair made up stories about herself. Sometimes she was a medical student, or a social worker, or a musician. Once she worked for the FBI. She often pretended to be the character she currently rehearsed.

Then she met Peyton. Peyton was with Shodan, a sleek streamlined seal pup to Blizzard's clumsy polar bear cub.

Dair liked the easy, catlike way Peyton walked and climbed the hills. She liked his height, his slight yet muscular frame, his pecs cut and defined under his T-shirt.

When they'd used up all their small talk about the dogs—Peyton hadn't asked where she'd gotten Blizzard—he said that his sister didn't like Shodan.

"Does that matter?" Dair asked.

He shrugged. "It did. I was living with her for a while. When she complained about the dog, I moved out."

He looked out over the field, watching their puppies wrestle each other, tumbling in the grass. Dair wondered why a grown man had been living with his sister and figured he was unemployed, or unambitious, or unappealing in some way that didn't show on the surface.

That made the lie easier when he asked, "You have any brothers or sisters?"

Dair paused, got sad and serious, and said, "Not anymore." She lowered her gaze to the ground and said, "My sister died."

Peyton made a small sound, and she looked up at him, into his eyes, and it popped into her head. "My twin." She said it for no reason. She felt obligated, as in an acting exercise, to look for the most interesting option. And she stuck to her rule: The lie did leave her an only child, which was the truth.

Dair's mind raced with the challenge, filling in the story, imagining the questions he might ask. She knew her twin's name, when and how she'd died. But Peyton only looked pained and said, "I'm sorry." He sighed in a way that suggested the loss was his and whistled to his dog. They walked on, but then he was back the next day at the same time.

"Hello, again," he said with that slow, unfurling smile of his. A cautious smile, as if he wanted to be happy but wasn't sure he deserved it. The flutter in Dair's chest surprised her.

Then he wasn't there for two weeks.

She told herself she'd forgotten him. She'd pretend she wasn't combing the hillside every morning for his fit, slender form. And then, one day, he reappeared.

"Hey," he called, changing direction to come toward her. Another flutter in her chest.

"Haven't seen you in a while," she said as casually as she could muster. The dogs touched noses, sniffed each other's hind ends. She and Peyton watched, and she blushed, thinking how pleasant it might be to get close enough to this man to smell him.

He blushed, too. "I've been out of town."

Dair sat on a rock and he sat beside her, thrillingly close, the small distance between them charged with possibility.

He nodded toward Shodan, shining black in the sun. "I miss her when I'm gone, you know? Okay, I know this'll sound corny, but she's helped me through some . . . stuff, some hard stuff I've been working on." He made a face as if mocking himself, and Dair sensed him deflecting attention from a subject too raw.

She nodded, hating to think of this beautiful man suffering through any kind of "stuff."

"I can tell you and Blizzard are the same," he said. He looked at her a moment. "You know what I mean. You've been there."

She stared at him, confused.

"Did Blizzard help you when you lost your sister?"

Shit. Her heart dropped. "N-no . . . ," she stammered, remembering the elaborate back story she'd created. "That was . . . before. A long time ago."

She liked this man, and she wanted to erase her fictional sister. But she couldn't very well say, "Actually, I never had a sister. I just made that up." She couldn't think of any reason, any motivation, she could give for the lie that wouldn't make her now seem like a freak.

He nodded and dropped the subject, looking back at Shodan.

"Where do you go?" Dair asked. "I mean, why were you out of town? Is it business?"

That's when she learned he was a dancer. She'd figured he might be, based on his body. But she was thinking a ballet dancer. She'd never known a tap dancer, only knew "tap" as that arm-swinging, show-choir-looking stuff in most musicals.

The next day in the park, Peyton asked her if she wanted to grab coffee with him. She held the dogs while he ordered for them in a coffee shop. Their fingers touched when he handed her her cup, and a pink flush spread across his high cheeks, no doubt matching her own. It felt as daringly intimate and arousing as if he'd touched her breast.

The day after that they met for lunch, without the dogs.

They met at a crowded, noisy deli, both of them seeming to sense that if they were to do anything besides rip the clothes off each other, they needed a very public place. The cashier asked for their names at the counter and seemed especially vexed when they told him. He made them spell both names for him, but he mispronounced them anyway when he yelled out their finished orders. Peyton brought their food to the table, laughing.

"We both *do* have uncommon names," Dair said, unwrapping her egg salad sandwich. She felt uncommonly happy sitting with this man, embraced by the cozy aromas of fresh bread and rye.

"How do you feel about your name?" Peyton asked.

She smiled, surprised. She was used to questions about her name—was it short for Adair? Daria? What did it mean? But how did she *feel* about it? That was new. "I like it. I like what it implies—it's like a directive from my parents: Dare. You know? It's permission to risk, to be different, not to be afraid."

He nodded. Dair was pleased they had to lean close over the plastic gingham tablecloth to converse without shouting. She couldn't help but be aware that their faces were within kissing distance. "Peyton's a family name. I'm always getting jokes about *Peyton Place* and crap like that. It's Irish. It means 'soldier's estate.' "

"Ooh, so you're housing a soldier in that dancer's body?" Dair stopped herself from saying "that hot, sexy dancer's body," but he blushed anyway.

"For many lifetimes, I think," he said. He looked down and stirred his potato soup.

Curiosity swelled within her. "What do you mean?" She lowered her voice. "Like reincarnation?"

Peyton made a face. "Is that too weird? Have I just ruined my chances?"

Dair laughed. "No, not at all." She wondered just what it would take to ruin his chances at this point. Maybe serial murder. "I just don't know much about reincarnation. I've never thought a lot about it." She stared into his open face, at his slender, arched nose. That little scar by his eye.

He stared back at her, and she had an image of them both rising, leaving their barely touched food behind, and walking wordlessly to whoever's apartment was closer.

Gales of laughter from a nearby table jarred them and made

them break their gaze and return their attention to their lunches. Peyton raised a spoon of soup to his mouth, blowing to cool it. Dair couldn't pull her eyes from his lips.

After a few moments of awkward chewing and swallowing in silence, as if they'd already had sex but couldn't recall each other's names, Dair cleared her throat and asked, "How do you know . . . I mean, what makes you think you've been reincarnated?"

He cocked his head, reminding her of her mother. He seemed to be considering something, weighing a possibility in his mind. He looked down and stirred his soup. "I've always known. And I mean *always,* like from the time I was little. My family tells stories about it. I don't really remember the early stuff, but my parents have no reason to make up these stories—"

"What? What stories? Tell me."

He traced the red and white squares on the tablecloth with the handle of his spoon as he talked. "Well, apparently when I started talking, my first word was 'home.' I kept saying 'home.' And later that I wanted to *go* home. They said I was three or four before I'd call my parents 'Mom' and 'Dad.' I'd tell everyone that they weren't my real family. I'd tell my sister, 'These are your parents, but they're not my parents.'"

"Oh, my God," Dair said. "So, were they curious? Are they the ones who thought—"

"Oh, *no.*" Peyton laughed. "They never considered reincarnation— they don't believe in it at all—they were just pissed off." He shrugged. "Like I said, I don't remember this. They tell it today as proof that from the day I was born, I've tried to alienate and embarrass them."

That slow smile unfolded, prompting warmth to unfold in her belly.

"So, what else? Were there other things that made you believe?"

He stopped tracing the gingham checks and squinted at her, as if he suspected she were making fun of him. "Have you ever had a recurring dream?" he asked.

Dair nodded.

Peyton smiled as if relieved and scooted his chair forward. His knee touched hers and stayed there. "Well, Freud once said that a recurring dream points to a repressed memory of a real event. Most psychologists agree with that." He took a deep breath. "So . . . what if you have a recurring dream that's vivid and real, even though the dream has no basis in reality in your life? You consistently dream a setting that as far as you know, you've never really seen, but it returns again and again, until you'd recognize it if you ever stumbled upon it. And then . . . you do."

Dair shivered. "Where? What was it?"

"A training place for samurai in Japan. I'd dreamt about it since I was ten. On tour in Japan last spring, I went on a walk, and all of a sudden I knew where I was. I followed streets, not getting lost, until I came to it, the gate looking just like I'd seen it. And even though I couldn't speak the language, this old man nodded at me and let me in. He didn't watch me; he just let me wander this courtyard. And, Dair, I knew where everything was—storage drawers for weapons, a box with mats in it . . . every last detail. I *knew* I'd been there before."

Dair exhaled some small sound. As strange as the story was, she believed him.

Peyton studied her, as if he were trying to determine how much to reveal. "And the old guy, he hands me a sword. I'd never held a sword in my life—this life, anyway—but it felt so at home. It felt like *coming home,* actually. And my body just started doing these moves, holding the sword, going through this slow series of strikes with this sword."

He paused, but Dair nodded at him to go on. "When I got back to the States, I started studying aikido, and I already knew how to do it; I knew the techniques. But I had to learn it backward. It was like . . . like finding yourself possessed of the knowledge of how to dance the entire *Swan Lake,* but having to go back and learn what each individual step was called."

"Wow," Dair whispered.

He sipped a spoonful of soup, which by now was probably cold. "Yup. But that's just one example. There's an Irish thing, too, but I don't know if it's just genetic, you know, 'in the blood.' The first time a teacher turned me on to Irish step, that spoke to me, too. But, I tell you, those drums, the bodhran, sure spark a totally different desire in me than to *dance.*"

She raised her eyebrows.

"I think, in this lifetime, I'm supposed to learn how *not* to kill someone."

She swallowed.

"I've killed a lot of people in my past lives," he said. "And wasted some time in this life trying to kill myself." He made that self-mocking face again and touched the scar at the corner of his eye with his fingertips.

This fascinated her. *He* fascinated her.

"So . . ." He looked at her, forehead wrinkled. "Am I a freak?"

She shook her head. "Do you like Shakespeare?" she asked.

He looked startled. "Uh-oh. Is that a requirement?"

She laughed. "No, I just . . ." She quoted, "'O, day and night, but this is wondrous strange!'"

Peyton grinned and answered, "'And therefore, as a stranger, give it welcome.'"

Dair's mouth dropped open. He winked at her.

"You know your Shakespeare!" she said, delighted in the way some women might be to discover their date was a doctor or a millionaire.

"Well, yeah," he said. "I mean, I *should*." He bit his lip, then leaned forward and whispered, "I *was* Shakespeare. In another life."

Dair froze. Her heart slid into her shoes. He'd been way too good to be true.

Peyton cracked up, clutching his chest. "I'm *kidding,* Dair. Look at you. It was a *joke*."

She breathed again, wadded up a paper napkin, and threw it at him.

"What? You think I'm some dumb dancer jock who doesn't *read?*"

She just shook her head at him.

"And you said you had a recurring dream?" he asked, still chuckling.

"Yeah, but not like that. Not of a place, just . . . it really is a memory, I guess."

"Tell me. What was it?"

"Oh, it always starts with this chickadee tapping at my window with its beak, and a little girl, this little dark-haired girl, shows up and she always presses her face up against the window, all silly, and we kiss each other with the glass between us." Dair shrugged and pulled another napkin from the dispenser. "I dream it every now and then."

Peyton's face lit up. "So what's it a memory of?"

"Well, I had a little chickadee when I was a kid. I found it in our yard, injured, and my dad taped its wing for me—he's a vet—and I nursed it back to health, and when I let it go, it used to hang around and tap for me at my window."

Peyton grinned. "That is so cool. And the little girl, she's your twin."

Dair coughed, almost choking on her sandwich. She hadn't made the connection, hadn't made up the dream or told it deliberately. She really did dream the little girl. And she kept forgetting about the damn twin. The weird thing was, the day she'd met Peyton in the park, she'd decided to call her twin Sylvan, if he asked, which was what she'd named the chickadee. So now she needed yet another lie: What was she going to say was the chickadee's name, if Peyton asked? She'd have to remember to keep the real Sylvan and the made-up Sylvan straight in her head. The egg salad was suddenly too thick to swallow.

"There's a reason you dream about her," Peyton said. "Recurring dreams, déjà vus, gut feelings, phobias, impulses—those are all messages from our soul, the part of us that's been through all our lives. There's something to be learned from that dream."

She looked at his earnest face. She couldn't imagine feeling so sure of something. Well . . . actually she could. She felt very sure that she loved this man sitting before her. She had this sense of finding someone after being lost, this great connection, a spark of "So, *there* you are." If holding a sword felt like coming home for Peyton, holding Peyton—which she did that very day—felt like coming home for Dair.

But she knew she had to come clean about the dead twin. A week later, the night they officially became lovers, an opportunity to tell the truth presented itself. They were at Peyton's narrow, downtown apartment, and Dair and Blizzard had been invited to spend the night. Peyton had only one room, nearly empty—the double bed the centerpiece that Dair found impossible to avoid looking at or thinking of. They'd just finished dinner and had finally moved to that bed when she felt Peyton's body change, felt a tightening within him. He stopped kissing her and cleared his throat. "Look, there's something I need to tell you."

Those words floated in the air around her. At first she felt cheated: Those were words she was supposed to say, had rehearsed saying. Then relief washed over her. He had something to confess, too. They could both start over, with no lies. But, in a delayed fashion, she won-dered what *he* could have to tell *her?* Oh, God—was he bisexual? HIV-positive? Married? Did he have a kid? Had he been in jail?

And would any of those things matter?

"Dair . . . I, look I've done some things in my past that I'm not really proud of."

She took a deep breath. "That's okay. So have I."

He smiled, grateful, but pained. "But . . . my past is kinda present, too, I . . ." He saw her confusion and blurted in a rush, "I have a drug problem. I don't anymore, but . . . you need to know about it . . . be-cause, well . . . I mean, I don't use right now, but it's still a . . . it's something I struggle with, and . . . I just wanted you to know that. To know . . . me."

Before her sat the most together, centered man she'd ever met. He'd been a drug addict? No way. He might as well have told her he was a vampire.

He continued talking, his words tumbling over each other, need-ing to tell her more than she needed to hear it. He'd been out of rehab a little over a year. He'd used for two years, injecting both heroin and cocaine, and had been fired from the New York City Bal-let. He'd lost his phone, then his electricity, eventually his apartment. His sister had come to New York and brought him home, paid for his rehab, and had never forgiven him for going back to the City. Even though he was finished at the ballet, he took classes, watched the street tappers in Central Park, asked them to teach him, followed them to where they studied, made his rounds at auditions. The Cincinnati-based company he was with now knew all about the drug years. He went to NA—Narcotics Anonymous—meetings usually three times a week, sometimes every day, occasionally three times a day.

"After rehab, I was suddenly this different person, my identity was gone, I felt like part of me had been cut off. . . ."

She murmured something, fighting not to cry.

"It's like it must've been when your twin died," he said.

Dair winced.

"That's how I knew you'd understand. You've been there. You've lost a part of yourself, too."

And in that instant she knew that part of their coming together was because of this lie. That he'd been drawn to her because of her loss, her tragedy, her sorrow.

"That's why I knew I could tell you this. You know what it feels like to be split in half."

And she knew she had only this moment to say, "It isn't true." But she looked at his face and knew she couldn't tell him then.

And she knew if she didn't tell him then, she could never tell him. She said nothing.

So Dair accepted Sylvan into their lives, naming her after her pet chickadee. Sylvan Nicole Canard, her twin who died of leukemia when they were ten. She told stories, when asked, of their childhood together, the clothes they wore, her favorite games, how she was pathologically afraid of slugs, how she loved sunflowers. How Dair's bone marrow didn't match hers. How Dair destroyed all the photos of Sylvan in a gray haze of depression when she was sixteen. How it still killed Dair's parents to talk about her. Dair knew the anniversary of Sylvan's death and now dreaded her birthday.

Sylvan wasn't the sole reason they stayed together, but Dair knew it was why Peyton came back to the park. It was the reason he believed that she was someone who could possibly dare to take this journey with him.

Here, back in Burnet Woods, watching the dogs, Dair started to cry. Marielle lifted her head from Dair's shoulder and sniffed. "I want to go home," she said.

Dair nodded. She did, too.

Because the first time she and Peyton had made love, he'd whispered, "Ahh . . . I've been looking for you." And she'd known just what he meant.

Chapter Three

Peyton felt it the second Dair slipped away from him on the couch. Somewhere deep in a movement of his dream, he knew it was happening; some part of him felt her leaving, her absence. He didn't have to be conscious to recognize the return to empty sleep, as he thought of nights on the road. He'd slept better crammed into this couch with Dair than he had for the last three weeks in deluxe hotel beds. They had the choreography of sharing a small space down pat; they always had.

A ringing intruded on his dream. Harsh. He thought it was a school bell and he'd fallen asleep in class and some nun was about to smack him in the back of the head. Then he realized it was his alarm and he had to get up and make it to rehearsal. He had to; they were on to him, they were watching. No, shit, it was the *phone.* It might be his dealer, it might be—

He found himself standing in Marielle's living room, drenched in sweat, panting. Oh. Relief, then sorrow flooded his veins as he remembered all that had happened and where he was, here and now. It was *Marielle's* phone. He guessed she'd turned the machine off, because it rang and rang, and he limped into the kitchen, the one day of travel, of not dancing, already rusting in his joints and muscles.

"Hello?" he croaked, finding rust in his throat, too.

"Um . . . hi . . . ," a woman's voice stumbled. "I was trying to reach Marielle Evans?"

"She can't come to the phone right now. Could I take a message for her?"

"Oh." The voice sounded relieved. "Yes, please tell her Bethany Butler called and—"

"Bethany, this is Peyton."

"Oh! Oh, God, Peyton, how is she?" Bethany was another actress in town, who'd been in lots of shows with Dair, cast as Desdemona in *Othello*. "I just wanted to check on her. Is there anything she needs?"

Peyton thought about an appropriate answer to that question but couldn't find one. She needed Craig alive, but instead he said, "No, but thanks. I'll tell her you called."

"Peyton, what happened?" Bethany sounded on the verge of tears. "Why did he jump? Why was he in a dress?"

Peyton began to zone out, only halfway listening to her. And then he felt it. For the first time that day, he felt the craving. He wanted heroin. He'd been waiting for it. It happened every day, sometimes fifty times a day. On a bad day, maybe a hundred. The first time, there was always that clean slap of recognition, that stomp of a tap shoe on a hardwood floor, a stinging sound, the announcement of its presence. Today it had taken what? Five minutes? Even that? On a good day, he might get a few hours.

"Peyton?" Bethany asked.

"I don't know," he said. "I have no idea."

"When did you get back? You've been on tour, right?"

"Yeah. I got back last night." A rush of adrenaline jolted him at the lie. Damn. It didn't feel half bad, that rush, but then it soured into a bitter taste. Dair lied all the time, but she was better at it than he was. If Bethany could see him at that moment, he bet she'd know he was lying.

She sighed. "What a welcome home, right?"

Peyton didn't know what to say. He looked around Marielle's kitchen and knew that all four of them, five counting Matthew, would've been eating pecan pancakes on any other first morning back from tour. He felt a spinning, like dancing too hard on not enough food. That light, out-of-body feeling, halfway between nausea and exhilaration, like you're either going to pass out or fly.

"The paper says he might've been a cross-dresser," Bethany went on, losing her fight against the tears. "That's absurd. He wasn't, was he?"

"I don't know . . . I don't think so," he said.

"And they're doing an autopsy for drugs."

"He wasn't on drugs."

"Oh, God," Bethany said. "It's so . . . it's so awful. None of this makes sense. It doesn't fit him at all. I keep hoping it's all some big mistake."

Peyton nodded, which was useless on the phone. He hated talking to people when he couldn't see them. It was like suddenly being blind. And the blindness made him almost deaf and mute as well. He needed bodies to talk to people.

"Okay," she said finally. "Tell Marielle I'm thinking of her. Dair, too."

They hung up, and he wrote Bethany's name on the message pad. The phone rang again, but when he answered, whoever it was hung up.

Before he could turn the machine on, the phone rang a third time. And, again, his voice caught the caller off guard. "Uh . . . hello, I was, uh, calling for Marielle?"

"Malcolm?" Peyton asked, recognizing the voice with another rush. Another actor. A man Peyton had recently, reluctantly, formed a tenuous friendship with. "It's Peyton. Are you okay?"

"Oh, hey, Peyton. *Yes,* I'm okay," he said with an edge of irritation. "Jesus . . . what happened?"

"I don't know."

"How's Marielle?"

Why did people ask that? How did they expect her to be? "She's got a lot to deal with. It's not just like he's gone, but there's all this stupid shit dumped on top of it. All this cross-dressing crap, and doing an autopsy for drugs."

"He didn't do drugs," Malcolm said. "What the hell is that about?"

Peyton shook his head, saying nothing, listening to that steady background whine of wanting a fix slicing into the back of his head. The whine that rarely sounded in Dair's company. He wondered if Malcolm heard it, too—his own whine, not Peyton's.

"So, did everything work out yesterday?" Malcolm asked. "You got back to the airport in time for Dair to think you flew in with the company?"

"Yup, no problem. My luggage came in with the rest of the Footforce stuff, and I was there waiting. She never thought twice about it."

"Thanks. I owe you, man."

"No, you don't," Peyton said. "You owe somebody else. Your turn will come."

Malcolm paused a long time. Peyton wished he could see him. "It's hard to believe right now," Malcolm said.

"I know."

Malcolm paused again, and Peyton heard a toilet flush and the sounds of movement upstairs. Matthew was awake.

"Listen, tell Marielle I called," Malcolm said, changing the subject, as Peyton hoped he would. "Most of the theater crowd knows, even Gayle, who's still in Chicago. Tell her everyone is thinking of her and we're ready to do anything if she needs help."

When he hung up, Peyton turned on the machine and thought about the ripple effect already spreading. How that ripple would be felt in all who'd known Craig. Like on tour, when Maggie sprained her ankle and they reworked *Predilections,* a four-person a cappella tap piece, onto just three of them. The show went on, sure, and they called the piece the same thing, but it wasn't. It was a new incarnation. It had the same bones, the same muscles, but its pulse, its heartbeat, was different.

They would all be different now, too.

That thought broke something open in him, and he let it inside—the loss. He'd already missed Craig these past weeks, had looked forward to returning to the rock of his presence, his friendship. But that rock was gone, the foundation of Peyton's fort, his protection, weakened. Threatened. Wind howled through the empty hole remaining. Howled and whined.

He shoved the thought away and quieted the goddamn whine with a little barefoot soft shoe, transforming that three-person piece into a solo. He got the rhythm set in his head, enough to block up the gaping hole, but got distracted on the groove of Dair. He wanted her here with him.

He walked back into the living room and picked up her hand-written note, just to feel a connection. She was the tune that stuck in his head, that he wanted to follow in the dance music, that he found himself humming when she wasn't around. It'd been a nameless tune most of his life, one he'd heard once but couldn't remember. When he saw her that day in the park, though—the minute he spoke to her, looked into that somehow familiar face—it all came back to him, the words, the music, that sense of *I've known you before*. Like comfort or ritual. Like belonging at long last.

The phone rang again. He listened for the click of the machine, put the note back on the table, and went upstairs. Matt's door was ajar, so he knocked, then pushed it open. Matt sat on the edge of his bed, a framed photograph in his hands. Slip Jig lay beside him, licking the bottom of one back paw.

"Hey," Peyton said.

Matt nodded and stood to put the photograph back on his dresser. It was one of a young Marielle and a blond, bearded man Peyton didn't know.

"That's my dad," Matt said.

Oh, man, Peyton felt out of his league there. "I've never seen this picture before," he said, bending over to look closer at it.

"I usually keep it in my desk," Matt said. "It makes Mom sad."

Peyton nodded and put his hands in his pockets. "Your mom and Dair are walking the dogs."

"I saw them leave," Matt said, nodding toward his window, which overlooked the backyard. He sat back down on the bed. He looked across at the photo.

Peyton sat beside Matt and ruffled his hair with one hand. Matt had been on the verge of finally having a father. Close enough that he probably felt that now he'd lost two. "I know," Peyton whispered. And he did, sort of. He knew what it was like to want one, anyway, at least a different one than he'd had. He hadn't been abused, or neglected, or starved. Not in the literal ways. He'd never belonged to the family he was born into. So he did starve, kind of. Spent his life fighting a hunger. A hunger that existed long before the first needle.

He felt it again, that yank throughout his body, a giant suction happening, as though his veins themselves had hunger cramps. Even after ten years.

"How 'bout some pancakes?" Peyton asked.

Matt looked up, his smoky eyes the same color as his cat. "Craig would've made some this morning," he said.

Peyton wrapped an arm around his shoulder. "Yup."

"I'm gonna miss him," Matt said, leaning his head against Peyton.

"Me, too." The tug in his veins changed, centering in his chest like something wanting to get out. Peyton breathed deep. He hugged Matt to him and looked across at that photo. It was of a Marielle who smiled with eyes that couldn't imagine she'd see such sorrow and the familiar face of a man Peyton had never met. Whom Matt had never met. Peyton could look at that photo and feel he'd known him, though. He seemed familiar, maybe because he saw the hints of him in Matt's face, could project Matt into that photo in fifteen years or so.

Above the photo, over Matt's dresser, hung the framed poster of a pack of timber wolves that Peyton and Dair had given him for his last birthday. Matt loved wolves, had been obsessed with them ever since Craig and Peyton had watched an *Animal Planet* wolf special with him one night while Dair and Marielle had a girls' night out. This pack sat at the edge of a snowy forest, all six heads lifted in a communal chorus of howling.

Matt followed his gaze and said, "Now there's too many."

"What?"

"There was one for each of us," he said, pointing to the poster. "Now there's one extra."

"But . . . six? Who—?"

"Mr. Lively!" Matt said, almost scolding him. "Remember how the pack took care of the old ones and the babies? Even fed them?"

Matt's stomach gurgled loud enough that Slip Jig stopped her grooming and looked, curious. Matt clutched his hands over his stomach.

"Speaking of feeding," Peyton teased.

"I haven't eaten since lunch yesterday."

"Lunch? What happened to dinner?"

Matt looked down so that all Peyton saw was the top of his head. "Me and mom were fighting," he said. "And I wouldn't eat."

"Why were you fighting?" Peyton asked as casually as he could. When Matt didn't answer, Peyton stood up and headed for the door. "C'mon, let's go make pancakes."

Matt followed him down the stairs, admitting, "I got in trouble at school," quickly adding, "I didn't start it! The other kids are mean to me. Nobody likes me."

Peyton wandered into Marielle's kitchen. "Why not?" he asked, knowing it was useless to say, "Of course they do." He remembered those days well enough.

"They make fun of me. They call me a runt. They say I'm a freak."

Peyton laughed. "I know all about that. I took ballet, remember?" He heard the crunch of metal in his memory, felt the sensation of being slammed up against those tall, gray green lockers. He blinked, trying to see what was in Marielle's cupboards. He was sick of eating in other kitchens, in restaurants. The phone rang again. "Let's go next door, okay?"

Matt looked at the phone with wide eyes and nodded. Peyton scribbled a note on the back of the one Dair had left and put on his shoes. They went out Matt's back door and in through Peyton and Dair's. Peyton hated not being greeted by the dogs. It felt wrong.

But it helped to be in a room where he knew where things were, where there were signs and reminders that he belonged. The cupboards he'd helped paint himself in purple, yellow, red, and lime green. The red-and-white Mexican-tiled table that they'd picked out together. Dair's seven wooden birds that he'd hung from the ceiling, painted in the colors of the seven kinds of chickadees, all with their black caps. The birds stirred in the draft from their opening the door. These reminders helped dull that shrill whine in Peyton's brain.

Godot slunk into the kitchen and yowled a hello. He helped, too. Peyton picked him up, and from his shoulder Godot reached for the gently spinning chickadees, his golden eyes bright, his paw extended. He couldn't quite reach them, though. He never could, but he tried every time as if he'd never failed. Peyton loved that.

Matt did, too, and it was good to see him smile.

Godot squirmed to be put down, so Peyton obliged, bending over in time for the cat to spill out of his arms from not too great a height. Godot promptly stalked to his cat door, batted it open, and leapt through it before it swung shut.

Matt giggled.

Peyton opened a cupboard and found a box of Bisquick. Craig would've made the pancakes from scratch, but this would have to do. He set the box and a mixing bowl on the counter in front of Matt. He pointed to the recipe. "I'll get the stuff out and you measure it, okay?"

"Cool," Matt said, opening a drawer for the measuring cups.

Peyton handed him the eggs and milk from the fridge, then searched for some sugar. "So," he said, checking the sugar bowl, which was empty, "you're getting into fights?"

Matt cracked an egg on the side of the bowl. "I have to! They shove me and stuff. Did you ever get in fights?"

"Oh, yeah."

"Mom says I shouldn't fight back, but that's stupid. What did your mom say?"

Peyton crouched down at a lower cupboard, rummaging past the party wine for the sugar canister. "Not much. She just nodded when my dad said I deserved to get beat up if I was such a pussy."

Matt's eyes about bulged out of his head. "Your dad called you a"— he lowered his voice to a whisper—"a *pussy?*"

Peyton found the canister and stood up. "Yup."

"Why? 'Cause you took ballet?"

"Yup. Gymnastics was bad enough, but ballet? As far as he was concerned, I might as well wear a dress to school."

A shadow crossed Matt's face, and Peyton wished he hadn't said that. It made them think of Craig. Matt turned his face to the Bisquick box and looked at the recipe for lots longer than he needed to.

"He wanted me to play sports," Peyton said, trying to think of something to say to slice through this awkward silence. "Like 'normal' people did. I wrestled for a while. He liked that."

"Really? Did *you* like it?" Matt poured some milk into a cup.

"Not really." That wasn't true. He'd loved the discipline, the rigor, how hard it was. All his life he'd known his body was a tool for something, that needed training. He quit wrestling because of the dreams he had of breaking necks and snapping spines. It got to where he had a sense of déjà vu every time he came to touch an opponent, and it scared him. By that time he'd studied enough about reincarnation to know those urges, those memories, were left over from his previous lives and clues to what his soul had chosen to work on in this lifetime. Matt poured the milk into the mixing bowl, then measured out the cups of Bisquick. "Do you think you could teach me how to fight, like teach me some of your karate stuff?"

"I don't do karate. I do aikido, and aikido won't teach you how to fight."

"C'mon," Matt said, taking the sugar canister from him. "Can't you teach me some kicks or punches?"

"There are no attacking moves in aikido. It's useless until someone attacks me first."

Matt stared at him.

"I know. Sounds pretty wimpy, huh?"

Matt just shrugged and scooped out a tablespoon of sugar, his answer clearly being yes. Peyton smiled. "Remember what the TV special said: Wolves avoid confrontation if at all possible."

"Yeah, but if you corner them, they'll attack."

Peyton sighed. "It's good to know how to defend yourself without hurting anyone else." A throb started somewhere beside his left eye.

"But if they started it, don't they deserve to get hurt? They asked for it."

"That's too easy," Peyton said. "And there are bigger things to worry about. I can teach you some aikido if you want, but it takes a lot of practice. It's not flashy or fun."

Matt stirred the batter with quick, stabbing strokes and didn't answer.

Peyton took the canister and crouched to put it away. The throb by his eye intensified, and he touched the old scar with his fingertips. "I don't want to hurt anyone," he said into the cupboard. "And I'm sure not killing anyone, no matter what they do to me." He hoped those words were true. He closed the cupboard and stood up.

The throb disturbed him. Reminded him of when the wound was fresh. He listened to its beat and found it similar to the drum, the bodhran, in *Solstice,* a piece the company did. In his mind he arranged the fiddle, the accordion, the penny whistle. He turned it into a reel and danced to it, making the dishes rattle in the cupboards and the wooden chickadees spin and clack together. Matt laughed and rolled his eyes. There. If anyone thought Matt was a freak, Matt surely thought Peyton was. And that was okay by Peyton.

Feedback marred the music, though. A piercing, prolonged tone, like from an amp. Oh, the whine. That's all it was. The wanting. He needed to eat—feeding one of the hungers helped pacify them all.

He stopped his reel and selected a skillet. "'Bout ready?" he asked. Matt nodded, and Peyton dropped a hunk of butter in the pan and turned on the burner. When the butter melted, Matt poured two cups

of batter into careful circles. He pulled a spatula from their orange
vase of utensils.

"When there's bubbles in the batter, you flip them," Matt said. Peyton nodded, and Matt added softly, "That's what Craig says."

Said, Peyton corrected, but only in his head. He got out two glasses,
opened the fridge, and poured orange juice for them. He opened the
freezer for some ice. Dair's bottle of Absolut stared back at him. Making sure Matt didn't notice, he turned the bottle so that the front
faced him. He measured against the letters. The clear liquid still stood
level with the middle of the line *Country of Sweden.* Well, well, well.
She hadn't had a sip this morning. Of that, anyway.

He grabbed a handful of ice and closed the freezer, then dropped
two cubes apiece into their glasses.

Peyton had come back early Saturday morning to help Malcolm,
but he'd kept it a secret because he'd wanted to check on Dair. Peyton had snuck into his own house yesterday while he knew Dair
was teaching at the Playhouse. He'd checked the Absolut bottle, the
Kahlúa, the party wine, and the bottles in Marielle's trash.

Dair drank too much. Peyton knew that. And he knew she did it
for a reason. And he knew that until she figured out the reason, she
wasn't going to stop. He didn't judge her for that. He couldn't. She
did that herself, protesting too much, rationalizing, stretching the truth
about how much and when.

And lying. She lied about big things and small things. She lied without thinking about it, for no real reason. She'd lie to other people,
to anybody, really, but she always shared the lies with him.

Except for the drinking. Peyton wasn't sure she knew she lied
about the drinking.

And the drinking was the only real thing she lied about to him.

Chapter Four

Dair and Marielle walked the dogs home. Dair regretted skipping her Kahlúa and imagined the glorious glass of vodka and orange juice she planned to savor once they parted ways at home. Marielle went into her back door, and Dair entered her own, eager, expectant, ready to welcome a long-lost friend.

Her reunion was postponed by Peyton and Matt at the kitchen table, eating pancakes.

She froze in the doorway. Her neediness felt visible, as if they'd caught her swilling from a bottle in a paper sack. The dogs shoved past her, and the caught feeling shifted into something like missing the bus by less than half a block.

"Hey," Matt said. "It's the alpha female."

Peyton grinned at her. Ever since the guys had watched that damn wolf special, that had been Dair's nickname. Peyton and Craig had behaved themselves when Matt told her all about the wolf's strong family loyalty, their carefully defined rules and rituals. When Matt wasn't around, though, they got a lot of mileage out of calling her the alpha bitch.

"Hey," she teased Matt back. "It's the runt pup." He didn't smile; he scowled, and she remembered that he'd been fighting again at school. He was small, even for his age. And there was a pecking order, a herd mentality, no matter what the species.

Marielle came through their back door, looking panicked until she saw Matt at the table. "Sit down," Peyton said to both women. He stood and served them pancakes from the plate by the stove. Dair eyed the heaping stack. Why had they made so many?

She buttered one and poured syrup on it, but the pancake was doughy and hard to swallow. She wanted a drink.

Dair looked at the clock. She'd slept late and lingered at the park. She had to think a moment to figure out what day it was. Sunday. "Oh, no," she said, remembering. "My mother is coming today. It's too late to call her, to tell her . . ." Dair looked at Marielle, unsure what to call it—to tell her mother their friend had died and they didn't feel like chatting about the dogs? "She's already left." Her parents lived two hours away.

Marielle didn't respond. She just looked at her pancake.

Peyton watched Marielle, then looked at Dair. "It's okay," he said. "It'll be good to see Cass."

Dair wondered what it was Mom wanted to tell her in person. "I better go feed Gayle's cat before Mom gets here."

Marielle gasped. "Oh, my God. Do you think Gayle knows about . . . ?" She couldn't say it.

Peyton nodded. "You got a lot of calls this morning from theater folks wanting you to know they were thinking of you."

"A *lot* of calls," Matt said. Dair figured these phone calls were what woke the guys up and brought them over here.

"I talked to Malcolm Cole," Peyton said. "He mentioned Gayle—she's been notified."

"Malcolm Cole?" Marielle asked, cocking her head.

"Yeah," Peyton said. "He's an actor, friend of Craig's." He stopped after saying Craig's name, and they all stared at the space before them, as if Craig's name hovered above the table in neon letters.

"What's he been in?" Marielle asked. "Have I seen him in anything?"

For a split second Dair couldn't think of a single show that both Malcolm and Craig had been in. They were such similar physical types and often up for the same roles. And, at least in Gayle's theater company, Queen City Shakespeare, Gayle's preference was so obvious that it inspired jokes: Malcolm rarely got cast if Craig auditioned.

"*Richard III,*" Peyton said. "Malcolm was Richard the summer before last."

Marielle's eyes brightened briefly with recognition. "Oh. Jimmy's boyfriend. I don't really know Malcolm, but his boyfriend took my signing class when he got cast in *Children of a Lesser God.* Malcolm called? That was sweet."

Malcolm generally was sweet, in a shy, geeky sort of way, but he'd been strange lately—fidgety and absentminded. Dair worried about him. He'd recently broken up with Jimmy, after they'd been together for five years. Rumors circulated that Malcolm had been evicted from the apartment they'd shared.

"Hey," Peyton said softly. "Did Malcolm get cast? When I talked to him yesterday, he didn't know."

"Yesterday?" Dair asked. "When did you talk to Malcolm yesterday?"

Peyton shook his head. "I meant this morning."

She knew how he felt. She couldn't keep track of time, either. Everything felt surreal.

"No, he didn't get cast this time." She didn't add that he might very well be cast *now*. He'd read for Iago every bit as well as Craig had. The pancake stuck in her throat.

She stood and put a hand on Marielle's shoulder. "You gonna be okay if I go over to Gayle's and feed Tuxedo?"

Marielle nodded and squeezed Dair's hand. "You don't have to baby-sit me, you know."

"I know." Dair kissed the top of her head.

Peyton mouthed, "I love you," at Dair, and she mouthed it back. "I should get going."

She showered and dressed, stalling a bit, hoping they'd leave the damn kitchen so she could get a drink. They didn't, so she kissed Peyton good-bye and drove to Gayle's, feeling put upon and cheated. Her skin itched.

She drove the mile or so down Clifton, approaching the very spot where Craig had jumped. Thankfully she didn't have to cross under the overpass, since the turn onto Gayle's street was just before it. Dair paused, though, before she turned. Today the only sign remaining was a strip of yellow police tape, one end tied to the guardrail up above, the other flapping in the wind. Not even twenty-four hours had passed, and traffic moved along on 75 as if the life that had shattered on the ground below meant nothing.

A car tooted its horn behind her, so Dair turned right, climbing up to Gayle's elegant stone house on Clifton Ridge. She picked up the Sunday paper in the driveway and unlocked the front door.

"Tuxedo," she called, walking down the hall. Gayle's house was decorated entirely in black and white, from a zebra-print couch to the white marble bust of Shakespeare wearing a black velvet beret. She unrolled the rubber band on the newspaper and laid it on the flat, tidy stack on the dining room table next to the accumulated mail. Alongside today's headline, MAN'S LEAP FROM OVERPASS A MYSTERY, a black-and-white photo of Craig smiled up at her. One of Craig's résumé head shots. Craig with his whole, unharmed face. Craig in his little wire-rim glasses. His photo blurred before Dair's eyes.

Tuxedo nudged her shin. A fat, black-and-white cat—even Gayle's pet matched her decor—he was marked with four white gloves and a white bib with a crooked black bow tie at his neck. He mewed at her. His meow was always a coy question, like a person saying, "Hmm?" She leaned down to pet him, but he strolled away down the hall.

The 75 overpass over Clifton Avenue stared back at her through Gayle's entryway window—visible through the autumn-bare trees on the hill. Poor Gayle: She'd have a permanent view of the site of Craig's death. Dair walked toward that window, and, feeling sheepish even as she did it, she locked Gayle's front door. She'd never locked herself in while she'd been there before.

But from up here on the ridge, she saw that yellow tape struggling in the wind from the traffic. Why had Craig even been in this neighborhood? And why was he in a dress?

She froze, hands on the door latch. The newspaper reported he'd been in "a purple dress" with no real description, but she saw again the details of the dress as Craig had clambered over the hood of her car. Had it actually *been* Gayle's dress?

She went to the top of the basement steps. The purple gown was down there in a closet in the guest bedroom. "C'mon, Tuxedo," she said, hoping for some company, her tight voice a feeble invitation.

She started down the steps, and the cat followed her. The door to the guest bedroom stood open, as always, but she jumped at the sight of the stripped-bare mattress on the bed. A stripped bed was no cause for alarm, but it startled her, the way walking in on a naked person might. Had the bed been stripped before? She tried to remember the house when Gayle had first left for Chicago, but most of those days Dair had come down the hall to the kitchen only to feed Tuxedo, never even glancing into other rooms. She'd only been down here the day she'd taken the dress and the day she'd returned it. Had the bed been stripped then? She would've noticed it, remembered it, wouldn't she? Tuxedo padded into the room behind her, and Dair watched him circle the bed, finally jumping on it and moving his head stiffly over the mattress, the hair raising on his arched back, his tail ballooning to three times its normal size. Dair saw Craig's face in her mind. Why hadn't she recognized him on the street? An image came to her of his dark hair spread on striped pillows. She shook her head.

She watched Tuxedo and for no apparent reason found herself thinking of Malcolm again. That self-effacing sense of doomed world-weariness he lugged around, prompting Craig once to call him Eeyore. And that was *before* Malcolm had actually played Eeyore in *The House at Pooh Corner* for Cincinnati Children's Theatre at the Taft. Dair had been Tigger. Craig hadn't been cast; he'd been in something else at the Actor's Theatre of Louisville.

Craig. Her eyes stung again. She focused on the cat to keep herself from crying but couldn't help herself from seeing Andy. How she'd stood beside him, chatting, never dreaming the death they'd witnessed was of someone they knew. She wanted to talk to him. Would he be in the theater tomorrow for the *Othello* read-through? No. Why would a light board op be there for that? But what show was currently running? Was there any other reason he might be around? She tried to picture herself at the read-through. Who would be the replacement Iago? Malcolm? God, why was she thinking of something so ridiculous? Did she really care? She couldn't even imagine herself in rehearsal without Craig.

Tuxedo abandoned his inspection of the bed, jumped down, and sniffed around the bottom of the closet, shoving a paw under the crack.

Dair cleared her throat as if about to do an audition monologue and took the three steps to the closet on trembling legs. She opened the door, pulled on the lightbulb chain, and stared. Stared at only two gowns—one blue sequined, one a beaded, black floor-length—and a fur coat.

She moved the dresses apart, absurdly checking to see if the purple one hung between them. It didn't. Her heartbeat hammered in her ears.

On the floor of the closet was a large clear plastic bag. She reached down and picked up the bag. A Jerry's Valet bag, ripped into halves, barely connected at the top around the neck of a wire hanger.

Tuxedo sniffed the floor where the bag had been, then lifted his pale green eyes to hers.

An image of Craig's feet flooded her mind. His bare feet. Only she didn't see them on a car's hood. She saw them on white carpet. White carpet like this. She blinked, hard, and opened her eyes again. God, she was losing it, seeing things.

She wadded the dry cleaner's bag into a tight ball and tossed it into the back of the closet. Then she moved the gowns again, checking, double-checking.

She closed the closet and leaned against it. Had someone broken into Gayle's home just to steal that dress? Why would anyone do that? She moaned. What had she been thinking, skipping her drink this morning? She *owed* herself drinks after all. She ran up the basement steps to Gayle's kitchen.

The fridge stood nearly empty, except for condiments, bottled water, and a jar of olives. The freezer was full of frozen pizzas and ice-cube trays, no vodka. In a cupboard Dair found a beautiful bottle of Merlot sleeping on its side. She reached for it as for a lover, but it hadn't been opened; the cork was still embedded deep in the bottle's neck. She checked the label—expensive, good wine, a bottle Gayle wouldn't forget she had. If she were anything like Dair, in fact, this was a bottle she looked forward to returning to, one she'd never stopped thinking of while she drank what she drank in Chicago. "Shit." Dair slammed the cupboard.

Dair sat on the tile floor, begging her breath to catch up to her heart. What if she *hadn't* returned the dress? Could she have forgotten?

Tuxedo approached her, one cautious foot at a time. "Hmm?" he mewed.

She took a deep breath and held it. She wanted to drive to the corner grocery store and get some wine or beer, but she looked at the clock and knew that she didn't have time. She had to get home before her mother got there. She'd spent eight years nervously managing the logistics of Peyton and her parents, making sure they were never alone together lest dear little Sylvan came up in conversation. She couldn't forever expect her mother to think Peyton was talking about her pet chickadee on those rare occasions he mentioned the name.

Her mother. Her mother was coming. Dair exhaled and breathed deeply again, picturing herself in the wings about to step onstage. She could do this. She'd never gone onstage drunk.

She blinked and frowned. She rarely got drunk, *ever.* She couldn't remember the last time. Well . . . that would be back, four, almost five years ago? She'd had one of those unrealistic diet moments, where she'd promised herself she wouldn't drink at all. And she didn't during the weeks, but she made a habit of getting looped at weekend parties. She'd feel greedy, as though she needed to "stock up." All it took was for Peyton to say to her, as they stepped onto Craig's porch, "Take it easy tonight, okay?" He was too sweet, too generous, a man to tell her she'd embarrassed him. Dair didn't drink at all that night.

She stood up. See? She hadn't drunk that night, and she hadn't been drunk ever since. She hadn't been drunk, or tipsy, or giddy from alcohol in almost five years. Well . . . except for that night just three weeks ago, with Craig, when she'd told him about the lie. That was the night that had inspired her to try the AA test. But even so, there was no way she hadn't returned the dress. She remembered doing it, remembered how the bag had bunched up as she carried it, remembered tugging the bag down smoothly. She hadn't made that up.

So . . . someone else had moved the dress since she'd returned it.

She wanted out of this house. She wanted to call the police. But to tell them what? To report that one dress was missing?

From where she stood, Dair could see into Gayle's living room and dining room. Nothing had been disturbed here. No sign of a break-in. Dair fought the urge to go check the closet again. "It's gone," she told herself.

"Hmm?" Tuxedo asked.

Dair walked around the kitchen island, stopping at Tuxedo's still-full food dish. "You didn't eat, Tux," she said. "What's wrong? You miss your mama?" His water dish looked untouched as well. "C'mere. C'mon. Eat a little," she coaxed, although it would hardly hurt him to miss a few meals. He obliged her, and she stood watching him eat, willing herself to think of something besides Craig and the dress—*anything* else.

Why was her mother coming here? "I have something I'd like to tell you in person," she'd said. But she'd said it breezily, casually. It hadn't sounded ominous.

Peyton was bemused by Dair's mother's belief that she could talk to animals, but other than that, he adored her. If Dair said that her mom was strange, he denied it. As a kid, the reverse was true—everyone else thought her mom was strange. Dair didn't deny it, because for the longest time she didn't know. She'd never questioned her mother's ability, her gift. Dair hadn't even thought of it *as* an ability or gift. She'd accepted what her mother did as normal. Dair had once believed that everyone could talk with animals.

People used to come to her childhood home to seek animal advice from both her parents. They came most often to see her dad, who was a veterinarian. He also did chiropractics on horses and dogs and massage on any kind of animal, once even a llama. A pale blue barn out behind the house contained his practice.

"Hmm?" Tuxedo mewed, pulling Dair back to the present. Dair walked down Gayle's hallway to clean Tuxedo's litter box in the half bath, but she stopped, looking at the cast and crew photos framed and matted on Gayle's hallway wall. It was odd to see pictures of herself in someone else's home.

Odd, too, to see photos of Craig. So *many* photos of Craig. Perhaps the jokes about Gayle's feelings for Craig were true—as talented as he was, he was cast a disproportionate number of times in Queen City Shakespeare productions.

Dair took their *Shrew* photo down and rubbed a smear off Craig's face with the bottom of her shirt. She rubbed his picture gently, as if wiping her own tears from his face. This beautiful person was dead. And not just gone, which hurt enough, but stolen from them in this undignified, almost sordid way. The dress, the running—it didn't make sense. It wasn't fair that those were the details the police, the media, were focused on.

She tried to set the photo back on its hook, but her hands trembled, and after several attempts she burst into tears and sat on the floor with the picture in her hands. Stop it . . . stop it, she scolded herself, wiping her nose on her shoulder. Think about something else.

Tuxedo nudged her elbow. What would Dair's mother claim Tuxedo had to say? People brought their animals to her to find out because they believed she had that ability. Dair had once believed it so entirely without question that she completely humiliated herself in fifth grade. That was the day she told her first lie.

She remembered it in vivid detail—the fifth-grade classroom too hot, the windows steamed over, the red-and-tan tile floor, her corduroy jumper and white turtleneck. Her excitement and anticipation. Even then, she loved to be onstage.

They'd been encouraged to investigate what their parents did for a living. They had to stand up in front of the class and give an oral report, sort of like a show-and-tell. And Dair told what she believed to be the truth: "My mother talks to animals and helps solve their problems. She's like a translator for people. You can call her or come see her and she'll tell you where the dog is that ran away or why the cat is eating her kittens or why the pony is afraid of men."

At first a small spark of energy ignited in the classroom. The energy of amazement and expectation—that moment in mob mentality when the herd looks to see who will lead. Dair talked on and sensed her classmates shuffling in uncertain confusion, each one of them poised and ready for one cow to bolt so the rest could follow. They looked at each other. They looked at the teacher. When Mrs. Corcoran finally pursed her lips and said, "Dair," that one word, she was the cow that bolted. The class stampeded into giggles.

Mrs. Corcoran said, "You can't stand up here and tell fibs."

Dair's face stung as if the teacher had slapped her. Fibs? Someone in the back of the room said something about "Dr. Dolittle" and another rush of laughter trampled her.

"But it's true. Some of them know it." Dair pointed to the class. "Some of their moms and dads have used my mom to help them." Those classmates shrank down in their seats, their expressions of horror like another slap.

Only one other girl said she knew it was true. Darla's dog had been sick and dying, and their vet—not Dair's dad—was at a complete loss. Dair's mother had been able to pick up from the dog where he felt pain, and the vet had then discovered a tumor he'd never suspected. But Darla was overweight and picked on in gym class. One boy said, "Oh, Darla *would* believe it. She *is* a dog, so of course she can talk to them."

Laughter ran Darla over along with Dair.

Dair slunk to her seat. Teresa, a popular girl, made eye contact with

her. Dair's mom had found Teresa's lost dog by "seeing" the dog's location through the dog's eyes. Rather than say a word in Dair's de-
fense, Teresa smiled at her, her eyes full of pity, then turned her head.
And Dair took her cue from Teresa: *No one* believed this.

At recess boys barked at Dair, and she walked the edges of the
foursquare games alone.

When she got home that day and Mom greeted her at the gate
with, "How'd it go, hon?" Dair smiled, and to spare her mother her
humiliation, she said, "Really good." Her mom hugged her, and they
ate oatmeal cookies together. And it dawned on Dair that Mom seemed
to think that Dair had talked about her dad. Dair let Mom believe
that, and even back then Dair recognized the distinction: that she
hadn't told an actual lie except for saying, "Really good." The rest of
it, simply allowing her mother to believe she'd talked about Dad's
practice, was an assumption uncorrected. *Mom* provided that, not
Dair.

And from that day on, Dair couldn't stop lying. She lied for no
other reason than to see if she'd be believed. She'd lie about ridiculous things, from a nonexistent spider she saw in the girls' bathroom
to the fictitious pizza they'd ordered for dinner the night before, as
if anyone cared. These lies weren't about anything crucial. They were
merely exercises.

She'd never again believed in her mother's ability to talk to animals. It shamed her to realize she'd accepted it stupidly, like the tooth
fairy or Santa Claus. If someone came to the house to see her mother,
it was because Mom was an expert in animal behavior. If Mom knew
that their rabbit felt sick, it was because she paid attention to the
beings in her house and was very aware of their normal actions and
appearance. How was that different from her noticing Dair's own
glassy eyes and hot cheeks before Dair ever said a word about feeling feverish?

Dair felt feverish now, just remembering that day. She stood, replaced the photo on its hook, then scooped out Tuxedo's litter box
and flushed the poop down the toilet.

She was done. She could get out of there, get a drink. But . . . it
struck her: Had she accidentally put the dress back in Gayle's own
bedroom closet upstairs?

She didn't believe it. She knew she hadn't, but she had to go look, she had to hope. "C'mon, Tuxedo," she called, and headed up the stairs, chattering nonstop to the cat, trying to fill the house with her voice, brave and cheerful.

At Gayle's bedroom door, she gasped, then felt herself tense to turn and run. A giant bouquet of magenta-and-white star lilies stood on Gayle's nightstand—the only splash of color in the black-and-white room.

The flowers were fresh. Their too sweet, head-clogging scent reached her from across the room. These flowers couldn't have survived three weeks, even if Dair *had* been tending them.

She stepped into the room, fear and adrenaline making her movements jerky. She approached the lilies as if they were a crate of snakes, ready to leap back from their strike. A card lay on the nightstand next to the black glass vase, stamped with the logo of Mount Lookout Sprouts, a florist shop over in Craig's Mount Lookout neighborhood. The card read only "Welcome home. I've missed you. I've missed us."

Hair on Dair's arms and the back of her neck rose as her skin contracted in goose bumps. The walls and floors rumbled with a low vibration, and for one confused second she thought it was part of her panic before she recognized the sound and sensation of Gayle's automatic garage door opening.

Tuxedo bolted down the stairs. *Oh, shit.* Gayle was home early. Dair looked around the room, feeling as though she needed to hide any signs of her being there.

No, that was ridiculous. She was *supposed* to be there. Gayle had asked her to be there.

Dair started down the steps just as the thought occurred to her: What if this wasn't Gayle? She wasn't supposed to be home until tomorrow. Who else would have her garage door opener? At the bottom of the steps, Dair stood poised by the front door, hand on the knob, listening to the car door echo in the attached garage, heard the door to the kitchen open. She didn't breathe until she heard Gayle's voice call through the house, "Hey, Dair."

"Hey." Dair's voice squeaked.

As she walked down the hall on rubbery legs, Dair heard Gayle say, "Well, hello there, Mr. Tuxedo." Gayle's voice sounded as off, as wrong, as Dair's own.

Dair stepped into the kitchen. Gayle's face was lined, haggard, as if she hadn't slept, her usually stylish mass of deep chestnut hair flat and dull. She held a paper grocery bag against one hip.

"Oh, God," she said, her chin quivering. "I'm so sorry about Craig."

Dair nodded, afraid she'd cry again if she spoke.

Gayle set down the bag and took Dair's hands in hers, a trademark gesture, one that drove Dair crazy. "Darling," she said. "Are you okay?"

Dair opened her mouth to speak, but Gayle rushed on. "You must be devastated."

Dair pulled her hands free and then had no idea what to do with them.

"You poor thing," Gayle said. "Malcolm says you saw it happen. You and Andy."

Dair nodded. "I was in traffic." She pointed down the hill outside Gayle's front door. "Right out there." Gayle watched her, her eyes unblinking, like a predatory bird. Then she walked away from Dair, toward the door, to look, as Dair had, out the entryway.

"Did you hear he was engaged?" Dair asked her. "He'd asked Marielle to marry him."

Gayle froze, her back to Dair, and put out her hands to the hallway walls on either side of her, as if she needed to be held up. She turned her body, her forehead against one wall. "I didn't know that," she whispered.

"I didn't, either," Dair said. "Nobody did. He just asked her, the day before . . . he died. That's why it doesn't make any sense for him to commit suicide."

Gayle put her forehead back against the wall with too much force. She didn't exactly slam it, but Dair heard the faint thump from where she stood. Gayle did it again. Always the drama queen, even in real moments like this.

"Gayle."

Gayle lifted her head and walked back to the kitchen. She looked around the room, as if taking inventory. "Did everything seem okay? Here, in the house?"

Dair swallowed, thinking of the dress and trying not to. "Yeah. Except . . ." She coaxed her heart down to a more collected trot. She found the lie easily, naturally: "Tuxedo didn't greet me this morning, and I went looking for him. Upstairs, I—I was a little concerned. Someone put fresh flowers in your bedroom, and it wasn't—"

"Oh, darling," Gayle stopped her. "I got back late last night. I left Chicago as soon as I heard about Craig. I should've called you, but it was *so* late . . . or so early, however you want to look at it. I'm sorry."

"Oh." Thank God Gayle hadn't caught her snooping. What if she'd gone up there and found Gayle asleep in her bed? But maybe . . . if Gayle had been home last night and this morning, she might've stripped the bed herself. But why would she sleep in her guest room? And it sure didn't sound as though whoever gave her the flowers slept in a separate room.

Gayle's eyes continued roving, searching. She shook herself, as if releasing some worrisome thought, then she snapped her fingers. "Oh, before I forget: Could I have that spare key back?"

The request startled Dair, stung her. Gayle had never asked for her key back before.

"Sure." Dair dug it out of her pocket and handed it over.

"Thanks." Gayle looked at it in her palm for a moment, then looked up at Dair with weepy eyes. "I think I may have some sort of gathering. After the funeral, or memorial, or whatever Marielle arranges."

Dair winced at the realization that Marielle really was the "next of kin." Craig's parents were dead, and he'd been an only child.

Gayle went on, "Something for our theater community to do together, to remember him. Unless . . . unless Marielle wants to do something herself."

"I think she'd like for you to do that," Dair said. "That would be nice. Would you like me to ask her?"

Gayle nodded. "I still can't believe it," she said, her chin quivering again.

"I should go," Dair whispered.

Gayle walked Dair toward the front door. "I'll let you know about the gathering once I find out the arrangements, darling." At the door, Gayle picked up Tuxedo, who'd followed them. "Thanks again for taking care of my baby." Her fondness for him was so clear, so real. "I'll be going back to Chicago next weekend, to see the second run of the show. The playwright's coming in. Would you mind looking after Tuxedo again?"

"Um . . . sure." Then why the hell had Gayle asked for her key? "So, you'll just give me a key later this week?"

Gayle blinked. "What?"

Dair pointed to the key Gayle still held awkwardly in one hand as she juggled the cat. "My key. I'll need my key back."

Gayle frowned, clutching Tuxedo to her chest so she could open her palm and look at the key. "This is *your* key?"

For a fleeting moment Dair felt they were speaking languages foreign to the other. She nodded.

"Oh, no," Gayle said, handing the key back to her. "I meant the spare key *Malcolm* was using. He was supposed to give it to you."

It took Dair a second to translate Gayle's words in her brain. "Look, I didn't know anything about a spare key. I didn't—"

"No, no," she said, waving her free hand as if to assure Dair this was not her problem. "I just, I'm . . . I told him to give it to you at the *Othello* auditions. I didn't want him to keep it." She seemed irritated.

Dair shook her head. This new information gave her a spiraling sensation. Why would Malcolm have a key to this house? And did this mean that *Malcolm* could've taken the dress? Malcolm occasionally took part in drag shows—at AIDS fund-raisers at a local gay bar.

Dair had read with Malcolm a million times at the audition. Shit. Would he remember the dress she'd worn? Did he know it was Gayle's? Would he mention it to her?

"Darling, what's the matter?" Gayle asked. She hefted Tuxedo up to her shoulder and reached out to touch Dair's cheek.

Dair shook herself. "Oh . . . I just—it creeps me out a little to know someone else had a key to your place. I would've flipped if he'd been here when I came over." She laughed, a hollow, unconvincing laugh. She wanted Gayle to tell her why Malcolm had a key.

"Oh, Malcolm wouldn't hurt a bug," Gayle said, smiling a tight smile. "But he's not the most . . . responsible person, you know."

Dair didn't know what to say. "I—I think he's having a rough time right now."

Gayle's eyes bored into her as if she were trying to glean some information. Dair shrugged. "You know, the breakup with his boyfriend and everything."

Gayle nodded and exhaled, as if relieved. "Still," she said, "I don't like the idea of keys to my house floating around. I told him to give it to you."

"Well . . . he didn't." Dair didn't know what else to say. She longed to ask Gayle outright why Malcolm had a key, but this felt too nosy, too forward, like asking about Gayle's personal life.

"Oh, well. I'll call him myself. I didn't mean to confuse you, darling. Thanks again." She lowered the cat into her arms, leaned over, and kissed Dair's cheek.

Dair stroked Tuxedo's head. He fixed those celery eyes on hers again, and an image came to her of Craig here at this door, panting, fumbling with the lock. What the hell was wrong with her? She was seeing things, going crazy. She turned away and burst out into the autumn air, grateful to suck the cold crispness into her lungs. She wanted away from that house.

And she wanted a drink before her mother got there.

Chapter Five

Dair drove away from Gayle's fearing for her own mental health; she'd been practically hallucinating. Her entire body—her chest, her muscles, her stomach—was wound way too tight; any second she expected to snap and fly apart.

Maybe Peyton and Marielle would be out of the goddamn kitchen by now. If they weren't, she'd just say she forgot something at Gayle's and turn right back around and head for the grocery store. Maybe she should stop anyway. . . .

But she found herself on her own street, her panicked flight leading her home by instinct just like a runaway horse or an abandoned cat.

Should she tell Gayle the truth? What would happen if she did that? And why should she? She'd taken the dress back, end of story. But if it meant that someone else had been in Gayle's house, shouldn't Gayle know? And if it in any way offered a clue to what had happened to Craig . . . Dair sighed. She tried it out, parked in the street in front of her house, as she often gave a lie a trial run. "Look," Dair said earnestly to the steering wheel. "You know how I told you I saw Craig die? Well, he was wearing your plum velvet dress. Not just a dress *like* that one. I'm pretty sure it's the very same one. You know how I know this? I did this incredibly irresponsible, tacky thing and borrowed it for the audition. You have such amazing taste, and the dress is stunning. And I'd never seen you wear it. If it was something you wore all the time, I never would've done it. I had it dry-cleaned even though I only had it on for about three hours. I even took it to the same place you had it dry-cleaned before. But today, when I came to feed

Tuxedo, that dress was gone. It had to be the same one Craig had on."

She rested her forehead on the steering wheel. Her own story lacked something. If someone delivered that monologue onstage, Dair wouldn't believe her. And if she told Gayle about the dress, wasn't she practically accusing Malcolm? Why would Malcolm have a key to Gayle's house? There's no way Malcolm and Gayle were lovers . . . or was there? Could *he* have brought the flowers? No, Malcolm was attractive enough, but even if he were inclined toward women, he wouldn't pick *Gayle,* would he? He was so quiet, so . . . dull, really, offstage. But maybe that's the kind of man Gayle liked, so she didn't have any competition for the spotlight. Maybe Malcolm was really, really in a mess after this breakup, and Gayle was desperate, and . . . Dair shuddered and begged herself to stop it.

A vehicle pulled up behind Dair and she lifted her head to the rearview mirror. A red pickup truck. Her mother.

Shit. She'd blown her chance for a drink.

Dair got out of the car. Her mom stretched her short legs down from the truck's driver's seat and stood, in faded denim overalls, hiking boots, and a long-sleeved navy T-shirt that made her look years younger than she was. The streaks of gray in her brown ponytail reminded Dair of a roan horse. Dair visually examined her mother for signs of illness or injury, but Mom smiled, offering no clue to her news.

"Hey, Dair." Dair looked at that round, outdoorsy face for some sign of herself. Like looking into a mirror of her future.

"Hi, Mom." Dair hugged her, noticing with the same strange sensation she'd had since seventh grade that she was taller than her mother. She always somehow forgot and found herself startled when they embraced. "It's good to see you," Dair said, thinking it was a lie but finding that the words, as she spoke them, felt true. She was surprised, and glad, to mean them. "Now, what's up? What's this important news?"

Her mother ignored the question. She put her hands on Dair's face, peering up at her daughter. Dair wondered if she was a mirror for her mom, too. "What's wrong?" Mom asked.

Dair's throat closed, and her nose burned with impending tears. "Craig died," she choked out. "Y-yesterday."

She watched her mother's face shift as she took in this information, felt it. Her pale blue eyes darkened. "Oh, no. Oh, Dair. I'm sorry. What happened?"

"H-he jumped off 75. Everyone thought he committed suicide, but really he was—"

"Good Lord, no—he wasn't the man in the dress! I just heard this on the rad—"

"Why is that all anyone wants to talk about?" Dair snapped, pulling away from her. "It isn't a joke, it isn't—"

"I'm sorry, Dair." Her mother grabbed her arm, preventing her from walking away. "I know it's not a joke, but . . . it's just what stuck with me, what I remembered from the story. I didn't pick up his name." They stood in the street, at the bottom of Dair's front yard hillside. "Do you know why he was in a dress?" her mother asked quietly.

Dair shook her head. "I'm sorry. I didn't mean to yell at you. I'm just upset."

Her mother hugged her again, and they climbed up the steps and around to the backyard, where the dogs rushed to the gate to greet Dair's mom. "Well, hello," Mom said as Blizzard embraced her in a bear hug. She turned her face, laughing, as he licked her cheek. She lowered his paws to the ground, then crouched to ruffle Shodan's ears.

The staccato, machine-gun-fire sound of Peyton tapping on his dance floor rattled up from the basement, faintly audible in the yard. He had nothing to rehearse the day after a tour ended, so Dair knew the punishing stomps reverberating through the walls and floorboards had to do with Craig.

Only when Mom stood did the dogs come to Dair, to check out her smells, to see where she'd been. Dair couldn't feel slighted, though, when Blizzard graced her with a hug, too. She bent and kissed Shodan on top of her head.

"Where's Godot?" Mom asked. The dogs trotted into the house when Dair opened the back door, and Mom followed them down the hall to find the cat. Dair heard clicking footsteps on the basement stairs and knew Peyton was coming to greet Mom. Dair took the opportunity to whip open the freezer, uncap her vodka, and take a gulp. It scorched her throat with its coldness, watering her eyes, but then it spread more gently through her chest.

She took one more deep slug, one that made her face contort and her lips pucker, then she capped the bottle and shoved it back in among the frozen peas and bags of stir-fry veggies.

"Hey, Cassie," she heard Peyton say. She walked quickly down the hall and into the living room in time to see him hug her mom.

"I'm so sorry about Craig," Mom said. "Are you okay?"

Peyton shrugged and shoved his hands deep into his jeans pockets. "We're pretty blown away," he said, staring down at his scuffed black tap shoes.

Mom touched his cheek, and he pulled his hands from his pockets to grab her hand and kiss it. "It's great to see you," Peyton said.

Dair should've been thrilled by how much Peyton loved her parents, but the diligence it required from her was exhausting. She had to always be "on," as in an improv game, to steer the conversation away from certain topics that might lead to Sylvan. And if the conversation did touch on her fictional twin, she had to manage to keep it making sense for both parties—Peyton thinking he was mentioning her sister, Mom and Dad thinking they were discussing her old chickadee. The day after she and Peyton spent any time with her parents, she always felt a bruised soreness, as if she'd done too many sets of sit-ups—probably from the held breath and the knot she clenched in her stomach as she waited for the truth to finally fly out.

"Sorry R.B. couldn't come," Peyton said to her mother. R.B. stood for Robert Barrett, but no one ever called her father that. And the initials were pronounced with the emphasis on the R, as though you meant Arby's, the restaurant.

"So, what's Dad doing today that he couldn't come with you?" Dair asked.

Mom cocked her head. "Oh . . . well. He was . . . working."

"On Sunday?" Dair asked. "What? Some kind of emergency?"

"Um . . . some follow-up, I think, yes." But Mom wouldn't look at Dair. She bent and too intently scratched Blizzard's ears.

A flutter of panic sputtered to life in Dair's guts. Was something wrong with her dad?

"So, what's up, Mom? What's this news you wanted to tell us?"

"Oh . . ." Mom hesitated. "This isn't a very good time for you guys . . .

with your horrible news. I wish you'd called me. I don't want to bother you right now."

"Hey, you're here now," Peyton said gently. "Sit down." He sat in an armchair.

Mom remained standing. Dair did, too. Mom looked at Dair and said, "Why don't I come back next week? You two don't need—"

"Mom, *what?* Just tell us."

Mom sighed.

"This isn't anything about the animals, is it?" Dair asked, beginning to suspect something more serious was going on.

Mom looked startled. "No."

"Then, what? You *have* to tell us now. It'll drive me crazy to wait a week. What's wrong? Is Dad okay?"

Mom paused a moment too long before she said, "Yes."

"Sit down, you guys," Peyton urged.

They did, Dair in an armchair, Mom on the couch. Godot walked the back of the couch and settled on Mom's shoulder, sniffing her hair. Mom smiled at him a moment, apparently stalling. "Everything's all right," she said. "Everyone is fine, healthy . . . it's nothing like that." She took a breath. "I'm leaving your father."

Peyton's head snapped up. Dair's did, too.

"Actually I *have* left him. Or rather, he left me. It was my decision, for us to separate, but he's the one who's moved out of the house. He only comes over for his clinic hours—"

"Whoa, whoa, wait a minute," Dair said. *"Why?"*

Her mother sighed. Godot slipped down her chest from her shoulder and curled up in her lap. Both Shodan and Blizzard sat at her feet, their heads on her knees. Godot touched Blizzard's snout with a paw and left it there, tan on white, as if saying, *"My dog."*

"He doesn't believe me," Mom said in a calm, clear voice. "He refuses to acknowledge my skill, my ability. I find myself trying not to bring it up around him, avoiding it in conversation. I feel like a person who can sing, but I'm not allowed to let anyone hear me."

"Are you talking about the thing with animals—?"

"About my communication, yes. Your father doesn't believe me. I can't be my real self with him, and it took me all this time to realize I'm tired of living like that."

Dair felt punched in the stomach. And she wanted to punch back.

How could her mother wreck Dair's memory of a happy childhood? How could she destroy the home Dair loved to return to? "Mom. You've been married thirty-six years. Something had to be right. Can't you guys work this out?"

"I've tried." She smiled sadly. "This isn't a rash decision. I avoided talking about it for far too long. It was like I became invisible."

Dair looked at Peyton. He stared at her mother, deep lines etched in his face.

"Invisible?" Dair asked, shocked at the scorn that hovered in her own voice.

Mom turned defiant eyes on Dair, but her voice was gentle. "I know you don't believe me, either. It's one thing for your child to be embarrassed by you." Dair's face flushed hot. "That's what mothers do: embarrass their children. But it's another thing entirely for the man you live with to feel nothing but irritation with your deepest belief. And it is my deepest belief. For him not to acknowledge that is for him not to acknowledge *me*. I deserve better."

Dair felt so small, so ungrateful, as if she'd been a horrible daughter all her life.

"When did you guys separate?" she asked.

"It's been four days, today."

Punched again. Why hadn't Dad called to offer her this information himself? "Where is he staying? Living?"

"He took an apartment in town." Mom shifted forward, careful not to jostle Godot, and pulled out a folded scrap of yellow notebook paper from her pocket. "Here's his address and phone number. He asked me to give this to you."

Dair stood up to take it so that Mom didn't have to move Godot. Peyton got up, too, and stood by her side. "So, you're still talking?" Dair asked.

"Good heavens, yes. I've seen him every day. We're perfectly friendly."

"But you're not living together."

"Right."

"For how long?"

Mom cocked her head at Dair again. "Maybe forever, Dair. We might get divorced."

Dair unfolded the notebook paper in her hand. Peyton put an arm around her shoulder and read it, too. What would they do for Thanksgiving? Would they have to have three different Christmas gatherings now? God, that was selfish, petty, but it seemed so absurd—her parents couldn't get divorced. Not after three decades. What couldn't you resolve in over three decades?

Dair exhaled. "Never in a million years would I guess that this is what you were coming to tell me." She blinked hard, willing herself not to cry. She sat back down and drew her knees up to her chin. Peyton hovered above her a moment, then sat beside her, on the arm of her chair, instead of returning to his own. He threaded his hand under her hair, gently rubbing the back of her neck.

"Why don't we go outside?" Mom asked. She picked up Godot and set him beside her on the couch before she stood. "Let's go for a walk, okay?"

At the word, both dogs rose to all fours, their faces expectant.

Dair sighed and nodded, unable to speak. She was such a mess today.

"Can you spare us, Peyton?" Mom asked him.

"Sure." He unfolded himself to standing. "And if there's anything you need, Cass—R.B., too—we're here for you guys."

"Thank you," she said. "I'll tell him. We don't want you two to feel you need to take sides, or anything ridiculous like that."

Peyton nodded. "You two go walk." At the repetition of *that word,* the dogs wagged their bodies and pranced in place with their front legs.

"Can you stay for dinner?" Peyton asked.

She smiled. "I'd love to." She turned to Dair anxiously. "Is that all right?"

"Of course," Dair said, knowing it meant more hours of concentration and energy.

"Cool," Peyton said. "After three weeks on the road, it'll be a treat to be in a kitchen, not a restaurant. I'll rustle something up for us."

"Let me hit your bathroom before we head out," Mom said.

Dair walked straight down the hall to the kitchen and opened the freezer. She made no attempt to hide her swig from Peyton, who actually missed it.

"Are you okay?" He came into the kitchen just as she shut the freezer.

She shook her head. The dogs bounced around her feet. "I can't believe this—" She nodded to the living room, indicating this recent news. "And then there's Craig. I—I'm just—"

Peyton reached out, grabbed one of her belt loops, and pulled her to him. Pressed chest to chest, his arms around her, she breathed in the warm leather smell of him, the slightest tang of sweat from dancing downstairs. So much bad news. This had been the sort of twenty-four-hour period that made her want to cocoon Peyton away someplace safe. Safe from himself. She didn't want to give him any more bad news, but to keep another secret felt way too heavy. She whispered against his neck, "Gayle's dress is gone."

He released the embrace and cupped her face with his hands.

"It's not hanging in Gayle's closet. The dry cleaning bag is still there, but the dress is gone. Does that mean Craig was at Gayle's the day he died?"

"How could he have gotten inside Gayle's?" Peyton asked, still holding her chin in one hand, pushing back her hair with the other.

"Well, she told me today that Malcolm Cole has a key! What if he had something to do with it, with . . . Craig's death?"

Peyton frowned, then snorted and looked up at the wooden chickadees. "Dair, come on. That's pretty hard to believe."

"I know, but the key, and . . . It's so weird . . . and I still can't believe Craig's really gone. And, and now *this*."

He hugged her again. Rubbed her back. He sighed so deeply that she felt it against her ribs. She looked up and saw his eyes wet, glistening. Her stomach fluttered. "Are *you* all right?" she asked him.

He nodded. "I just—I love your folks. This is so . . . ." He shrugged. "I like them better than my own parents."

"I know." She kissed him.

They heard her mother's footfall in the hallway and parted. Dair suddenly didn't want to leave Peyton, but she handed her mother Shodan's leash. Blizzard and Shodan crouched down, trembling with anticipation, fighting to stay still so they could be leashed.

As she clipped Blizzard's leash, Dair asked Peyton, "How's Marielle?"

"She's hanging in there."

Mom straightened up from Shodan's collar. "Marielle? Next door? With the little boy?"

Dair nodded. "Yeah. She and Craig were engaged."

Were. Past tense. She'd never gotten to say it in the present tense. Not once.

Outside, Dair walked beside her mother, retracing the steps she and Marielle had taken earlier that day. Mom was silent, as Marielle had been, but Mom's face looked peaceful, content, gazing up at the trees and their changing leaves—mustard gold, bright ragweed yellow, rust, eggplant. One maple's foliage shone neon orange, so bright that it took Dair's breath away against the cornflower blue sky.

"It's a crayon day," Dair said quietly, not looking at her mother. She'd said that once when she was a little girl, and she'd heard both her mother and father repeat it countless times since then.

Mom reached out and took her hand. Dair decided she wouldn't let go until her mother did. They walked down the street toward the park, holding hands, their outside arms reaching forward at the end of the leather leashes.

They entered Burnet Woods again, the dogs straining at their leashes, sniffing here, sniffing there. A breeze stirred the dry leaves, rattling them like bones. Dair led her mom to the clearing deep in the woods. It was more crowded now than this morning. "We can unleash them here. It's safe."

Her mother released Shodan. Dair did the same for Blizzard, and the dogs hopped around the women's feet for a moment, licking them, licking each other, as if to say, *Thank you, thank you, this is so fun!*

Dair and her mother sat on the ground at the edge of the clearing, both with their arms around their knees in front of them. Were they always these mirror images of each other? Dair looked at her mother's profile as she gazed up at a V of Canadian geese flying overhead, honking and babbling like a distant traffic jam. Would she one day have that soft, vague face, her cheeks drifting into her chin instead of her sharp jawline, angular cheekbones? Would Dair one day have that roan white speckled through her dark brown hair?

"Why *now*, Mom? Why after all this time? What was . . ." She wanted to say "the moment before," a theater term, the prompting incident before the scene the audience saw began.

Mom didn't answer or even turn her head. The dogs took off trotting toward some new playmates.

If Dad had always been skeptical, why had it taken her mother thirty-six years to get sick of it? Something wasn't right.

"Do you remember Bob Henderson's mare?" Mom asked in a small voice, still not looking at Dair but watching the dogs romp. Shodan ran the perimeter of the field with a German shepherd. Blizzard chased them, barking.

Bob Henderson's mare was a majestic Clydesdale named Bonnie. Bonnie the Clyde, Mr. Henderson joked. Every spring she had a baby, and Dair's dad would take her and Mom to see it. One February, the February Dair suspected her mother was thinking of, Henderson came to their house in the middle of dinner. Bonnie wasn't doing well, and since she was such an experienced mama, it had Mr. Henderson worried. He described the symptoms to Dair's dad over a cup of coffee and asked her dad to come take a look at Bonnie tomorrow if he could, although Dair could tell he really wanted her dad to come right then. A woman would've asked, but Mr. Henderson said tomorrow was fine, even though he fidgeted with his coffee cup, turning it around and around, and never did drink any.

Her mother gazed intently at Mr. Henderson, who kept stealing furtive little glances at her. Mom finally cleared her throat and said, "Bonnie's really worried about her filly; she thinks she's missing—"

"Cassie," Dad cut her off. He hadn't sounded angry, just exasperated, pleading. His embarrassment had a pinch like a terrier nip. More a surprise than a wound. But a surprise can *be* a wound, as Dair had discovered with Mom's news today.

"Whatever happened, that year?" Dair asked.

"What?" Mom pulled her gaze from the romping dogs. "What year?"

"Remember? When Mr. Henderson came to the house? You said Bonnie was worried, but Dad interrupted you?"

"Oh." An odd expression flashed over Mom's face. She'd been thinking of something else.

"The foal was fine, I remember," Dair prompted her. "And it was a filly, just like you said."

"Just like *Bonnie* said. If your dad hadn't done some bloodwork and discovered that the mare had a vitamin deficiency, she would've delivered a dead foal."

Dair tried to put it all together. "Did you know that? That she had a vitamin deficiency?"

Mom shrugged. "Her mineral block, in her feed box, was gone, and Henderson hadn't noticed. She'd eaten it, instead of just licked it, because she had this craving. Once the block was gone, not only was she deficient, she was also anxious about this craving she couldn't satiate."

Poor Bonnie. Just hearing her mother say that reminded Dair of the taste of vodka on her tongue. "So, you saw that her mineral block was gone?"

Mom closed her eyes and snorted a laugh, her shoulders slumping. "I've never been inside the Henderson barn in my life. I've only been in the pasture, like you, to see the foals."

"So, how . . . ?"

"How did I know that? Do you really want to know? I'm not interested in proving anything to anybody. If you don't believe me, there's no point in talking about it."

Dair studied her mom's face, the fine white lines in the corners of her eyes from squinting in the sun. The words stung her. Mom was right, of course. "No, Mom, I just don't understand it. I don't want to do what, I guess, Dad has done, or made you feel. I do want to know."

"You used to understand it. Don't you remember?"

Dair didn't want to hurt her. As kindly as she could, she said, "No. But I remember believing that you could do it."

Mom narrowed her eyes, then shook her head. "No, you could do it yourself. You still could, if you weren't so busy creating static."

"What do you mean?"

"With your drinking."

She said it with no judgment in her voice, but heat rose to Dair's cheeks and stirred in her stomach. "Excuse me?"

"I'm sorry. But I worry about you."

Dair laughed harshly. "Mom, you're the one divorcing a good man because he doesn't believe you talk to animals. You're the one people should worry about."

Her mother didn't even look angry. She looked sad for Dair. Dair's face burned. Blizzard and Shodan faced off, rears in the air, tails wagging, barking nonstop.

"Dair, I can divorce a man, but I can't divorce myself. That's what you seem to be trying to do. That's why I worry."

"You said you were worried because of 'my drinking.'" Dair repeated her phrase as though it were the most absurd thing she'd ever heard.

"Your drinking problem is part of your divorce proceedings."

"I don't *have* a 'drinking problem.'"

Mom looked at her a moment, then lifted her face to the wind, and Dair watched her nostrils working as if she were a dog or a wolf trying to catch some scent. What was she doing? Then she sniffed in an exaggerated fashion, and Dair recognized the childhood joke. *Sniff, sniff,* Mom sucked in through her nose, then said, "Hmm. I think I smell *pants.*"

Pants on fire, she was suggesting, as in "Liar, liar . . ." Dair couldn't help but grin, even though her mother had just slammed her. Mom used to do that when Dair started her lying career in fifth grade. That was before Dair developed her finesse.

She was grateful, though, that her mother seemed willing to let this slide. Dair could sense she didn't want to, but perhaps Mom felt they had enough issues for one day.

"It got cold," Mom said, hugging her arms across her chest.

"We should call the dogs and keep walking," Dair suggested, wanting to move, wanting out of this cornered feeling.

Mom nodded and stared intently across the dry field.

Dair opened her mouth to call Blizzard's name but saw him raise his head, look directly at them, and come running. She turned to her mother, who grinned and winked.

Shodan loped over, too, and the dogs rubbed their heads against the women's shoulders, threatening to knock them over as they sat on the ground.

"How did you do that?"

"I just pictured them coming to us, thought about our intention to go home."

"That's how it works?"

"For some people."

Mom didn't seem to need to have Dair believe it. Proving it to her, "converting" her, as it were, was not important.

"Can you get them to do something else?"

Mom sighed. "It's not a party trick."

"But, no, I mean, can't you just do something like that to prove it to Dad?"

Mom rubbed her forehead as if pained. "Dair—it doesn't work that way. I hate that word, *prove.*" She paused a moment and looked exhausted. "I'm not interested in making animals do what I want. That's not communication. And besides, you and I communicate, right? We even speak the same language, but does that mean you'd do anything I asked you to? That if I said, 'Stop drinking,' just because you understood the words, you'd do it?"

Dair clenched her jaw at her mother's example and said nothing. They stood up, and Dair almost lost her balance as Blizzard leaned against her. She caught herself, but she felt ten years old, afraid and uncertain.

They moved on, not saying much. A flurry of questions flitted around Dair's brain, but she didn't ask any. They walked the dogs the long way home, around the southern edge of the woods down by UC.

Several houses they passed had already been decorated for Halloween, just like Matt and Marielle's. Jack-o'-lanterns and cornstalks sat on porches, and white-sheet ghosts hung from a few trees, swaying on the breeze as if dancing.

October 31 was Dair's birthday, so Halloween, for her, was a holiday of mixed emotions. The weight of the lie settled on her the heaviest in the days surrounding her birthday. The insomnia, the sadness, the vague uneasiness, the feeling of teetering on a perpetual verge of tears, felt real, as if she'd convinced her brain the depression were genuine. She could no longer remember not feeling this way in late October.

Even in her childhood, her memory replayed her birthday as a quiet, somewhat solemn event. After trick-or-treating, Mom and Dad took Dair out walking, all three of them holding hands, listening to the wind rattle the leaves, looking at the moon. It was a magical night, a night when different things were possible, a night when it was okay to believe in things you normally wouldn't. That the dead might walk again. Vampires. Ghosts. Witches.

Dair looked at her mother. In another time her mom might be considered a witch, not a laughingstock. She might've been accused of consorting with the devil instead of just being the town's crazy cat lady. She might have been burned or hanged or drowned.

"Dair," Mom said. Dair thought her mother seemed afraid. Dair watched her take a deep breath. "I think I should tell you I'm not the only one who's worried."

Dair frowned, confused.

"Peyton worries about you, too."

Dair realized she was talking about the drinking again, but as her mother continued, Dair felt cold chills, not heat like before.

"He's talked to me about it, and he feels, with his history, that he's in no position to give you advice on—"

"Whoa. Wait. You talked to Peyton *when?*" She didn't even care about the drinking insult at the moment. She only cared that Peyton and her mother had conversed, apparently in some depth, without her. Had Sylvan ever been mentioned?

"He calls me from the road sometimes and—"

"He what?" Dair's heart slid into her shoes. "How often?"

"What's wrong? You act like this bothers you."

Dair opened her mouth, feeling that zip of horror, like blanking on a line in front of an audience. "Well, of course it bothers me, you two talking about me behind my back."

"Dair." Mom pursed her lips, looking at Dair as though she were seven. Dair felt it.

"What else do you two talk about? Or is my *drinking* the only topic of conversation?"

"Dair, please. This is important. I'm afraid of what I'm seeing you—"

"Look," Dair said with forced civility. "I don't know where you got this idea, but you're making a big deal out of nothing. I'm *fine.*"

Mom sighed and they walked in silence back to the house. For Peyton to have talked to her mother about a subject he'd never once broached with Dair felt like a sort of infidelity, but terror more than betrayal rushed through her. God, how long before he found out the truth? How would it come up? Some casual question about her birthday? Dair fought the urge to curl into a ball on the sidewalk. She kept putting one foot in front of the other.

But if he'd been unfaithful, so had she. She'd told Craig the truth about Sylvan. She'd told Craig three weeks ago, the night after Peyton left for this last tour. Marielle had one of her nights where just she and Matt went out, and Craig and Dair went to dinner. While she was with Craig, they'd split a bottle of Pinot Noir, but Craig didn't know she'd had three big glasses of wine already before they met in the bar at Palomino's.

She'd been drinking and crying because Peyton had left that morning for tour. She wasn't crying because she missed him, though; she cried because she realized, with nauseating horror, that she was relieved Peyton was gone—she needed room to move, to breathe, to set down the heavy load of the lie. It was too much. She was too tired. And it was her own damn fault.

So she'd gone to dinner with Craig with the lie fluttering against her ribs like the wings of some frantic bird in a cage—it wanted *out*.

And somehow she knew each glass of wine brought her closer to telling the truth. She felt it, and it made her both nervous and bold. She kept pouring more to drink, consuming two-thirds of the bottle herself.

That night their conversation over curried calamari had flowed from Craig wanting to marry Marielle to naming what they thought had been the smartest things they'd ever done in their lives. Over rotisserie prime rib they'd told stories of their greatest mistakes, and when Craig ordered cappuccino with dessert and Dair ordered Amaretto, Craig had leaned across the round marble table and asked, "So what's the worst thing you've ever done?"

And without hesitation she blurted, "Lied to Peyton."

Craig looked at her and must have known it was bad. He took her hand. "Oh, no."

She'd nodded, fighting tears, and the bird struggled against her ribs. It needed to be released. And she told him the whole hideous story of her made-up twin.

Dair remembered every detail. The aroma from the spit roaster. The neon sign for another restaurant visible through the window, the giant, red "ROCK BOTTOM" a magnet for her eyes. How appropriate, she'd thought. Craig's horrified expression. He'd paled to a sickly, shocked green when she'd told him that Peyton believed this was why they'd found each other. He'd kept saying, "Oh, my God. Dair. Oh, no."

And she remembered how good it felt to give some of it away.

Dair pictured the lie as real, visible weight, like those flat slabs of lead they slid into horses' saddle blankets at the track to even out the handicap. She couldn't help wondering if the added weight had sped up Craig's plunge off the overpass. Like shoving a brick into a bag with an unwanted kitten before you dropped it in the river.

She was back to square one. The burden balanced on her shoulders alone.

Dair thought again, as she often had, of telling her mother the truth and begging her to go along with the lie. But she couldn't bring herself to admit it. When she rehearsed it, the lie sounded so stupid, so neurotic—and it *was,* wasn't it? She didn't believe her mother would ever agree to lie to Peyton. It was even doubtful that she'd agree to remain silent on the subject. Dair couldn't bear to imagine her mother's pained disapproval, the endless pestering to come clean.

But, God, she longed to feel that release again. The sweet release that telling Craig had provided.

She shivered, now, wondering if Craig had wanted to unburden something, too, but she'd been too self-absorbed . . . and too drunk to notice. "What's the worst thing you've ever done?" he'd asked. "The thing you think no one would forgive you for?"

Why would he ask that if he'd had nothing to reveal himself? He might've been about to tell her something that would've prevented his death. Or at least ended the mystery of it.

"Dair?" Her mom reached out and took her hand. They were a block away from Dair and Peyton's house and smelled beef cooking. "Do you think that's our dinner?" Mom asked, trying to lighten the mood.

Dair made herself smile. "I hope so."

It was. Peyton stood at the grill on the wooden deck in the backyard, tending several luscious steak fillets. "That smells fabulous," Dair said, climbing the stairs and slipping her arms around him from behind, kissing his back. What would he do, this wonderful man, when he found out?

"Mmm. Thanks," he said. "I had a craving." He turned and motioned for them to move in close to him. "I invited Marielle and Matt. I hope that's okay; it just sort've happened—"

"Of course it's okay," Mom said. "Do you need me to go?"

Dair's brain screamed, *Yes! Yes, please leave.*

"There's plenty for everyone, Mom," she heard herself say.

Peyton nodded, looking relieved. "Did you guys have a good walk?"

Dair and her mother looked at each other. "Yeah," Dair said.

Mom smiled. "Yeah," she agreed.

They unleashed the dogs and Dair opened the back door, expecting Mom to follow, but she stayed by the grill with Peyton. Dair hesitated, knowing it would look stupid for her to turn around and come back out. "I'll be right back." The dogs pushed past her, snuffling and snorting through the house, checking to see if anything had changed in their absence.

She opened the freezer and grabbed the vodka, carrying the frosty bottle upstairs, the dogs following her. Lately it'd been tough to get a moment to herself in the kitchen. She needed a better spot. Look at her—what was she doing? Proving Mom right? No, if ever there was a day where she needed a goddamn drink, this was it. And for God's sake, if everyone was going to make such a huge deal out of it . . . She opened the hall closet. "To Bonnie," she said, taking a swig, thinking of that magnificent Clydesdale mare, "May all your cravings be satisfied." The dogs sat at her feet, attentive, thumping their tails on the floor.

Then she shoved the bottle between two stacks of sheets. Chills ran up her spine as she thought of the stripped bed in Gayle's basement. The reality kept smacking her square in the face: Craig was dead. It was a hard fact to keep hold of. It seemed so absurd, so wrong.

Dair went into the bathroom and flushed the toilet, although she hadn't used it, in case anyone questioned her being up here. Then she whistled for the dogs to follow her. She needed to get downstairs.

A realization stabbed her as she hurried out to the back porch: She'd created a life where the best thing about a visit from her mother was the moment she drove away.

Chapter Six

Peyton stood at the grill and searched for something to focus on other than the loss. Other than Craig being gone. He imagined he heard the aroma of the steaks—lingering notes, the languid pauses. Made him want to slow dance with Dair and forget.

He felt guilty rejoicing in anything at the moment, but he grooved on the growling in his stomach. He craved something, and here it was before him. Here he was able to share it with people he loved. People he considered family. He believed people were drawn to those whose paths they'd crossed in other lives. A peace and contentment came to him from finding their company again. He dreamed occasionally of a previous life with Dair. Sometimes he saw brief snippets triggered by the strangest things—once when they'd kissed underwater in a swimming pool; once when they'd crammed into the window box at Marielle's to hide for Craig's surprise birthday party; and once when he'd had the flu. Dair had leaned over him, putting a cold cloth on his forehead, troubled enough by his suffering that she had tears in her eyes, and it caused a rush of déjà vu. They'd done this before; she'd cared for him when he was ill.

For now, he focused only on being with her here. With Cass and Marielle and Matt. He felt almost high with the prospect of a need fulfilled.

Cassie stood beside him on the wooden deck. They'd talked of his beliefs often. He'd told Cass how he'd dreamed about armor—the weight of it, the bloody smell of rust. How men moved too gracefully in it in the movies. How he'd felt dizzy and disoriented, suddenly naked, the first time he'd seen the weapons display at the Met.

"I tried to talk to Dair about the drinking," Cassie said.

Peyton grew still.

Cassie shrugged. "Not great, but not *bad*. She was offended, but she didn't totally shut down. It's a foot in the door. It's a seed planted."

Peyton nodded, grateful, and stuck a fork into a steak. The last time he'd grilled had been with Craig in August. They'd grilled brats and burgers for a huge party, both of them preferring a purpose over aimless wandering and small talk.

Peyton flipped a steak. The fillets weren't ready to be turned over, but he liked the ritual. He liked to poke and prod at them and feel busy. It kept Craig out of his head.

Matt came out of his back door at the same time Dair came out of theirs, with the dogs, all of their feet thumping hollowly on the wooden porch. Dair looked hunted, worried. Peyton wondered if she knew they'd been talking about the drinking.

Matt looked hunted, too, his face drawn and tight, his gray eyes looking like smoke that might wisp away.

Peyton hoped Dair would forgive him for pestering her about her habit spiraling out of control. Did she know he'd talked to Cass? He felt sick and sleazy when he thought of lying to her yesterday, sneaking into the house before she even knew he was back in Cincinnati. But she hid her drinking so well, it scared him. Her habit was insidious.

Captain Hook, Mr. Lively's bird, squawked a series of short shrieks. Blizzard and Shodan glanced at the metal stairs leading up to his apartment and snorted.

Cassie followed their gaze, grinning.

"Can we invite Mr. Lively?" Matt asked.

Peyton groaned and Dair made a face, but Peyton pictured the old man up in his apartment and thought about his own dizzy, high feeling of happiness. Matt's wolf poster came into his head, and he remembered the wolf pack's dedication to family and tribe.

"We should," Peyton said, his voice low, knowing the old man could hear everything they said. "I bet he won't come down, but we should at least ask him. The rest of the house is eating together, and he'll know it."

"The more the merrier," Cassie said, shrugging. She didn't know him. Besides, tonight's dinner would be anything but merry.

Dair nodded at Peyton and turned to her mom. "Will you come with me?" she asked, as if about to go into a haunted house.

"Don't," Peyton warned Cassie, teasing. "He's a mean old fart."

"Oh, thanks a lot." Dair laughed at him, and as usual, her smile infused him with something, something he couldn't articulate, but it was like a drug, like a shot of well-being. She tossed her hair over one shoulder and pretended to scowl at him. "It's okay for *me* to go up alone, but you'll spare my mother?"

"I'll come with you," Matt said to Dair, and Dair went still. Her eyes moved from Peyton to her mom, her mouth open. What was she afraid of? That he might talk to Cassie about her drinking? He saw her catch him studying her, and a smile returned, but not the one he'd seen seconds earlier. "Okay," she said to Matt. "C'mon, let's do a good deed." They began to climb, their feet clanging on the metal steps.

Their noisy approach warned Mr. Lively, and he flung his door open at the top. "I already know about Craig," he said, scowling, his words booming down, as if he were body-miked, to where Peyton stood at the grill. "Not that anyone bothered to *tell* me."

Peyton paused with his fork over the hissing steaks. Dair said something that he couldn't hear.

"I saw the news," Mr. Lively said back. "I knew he was no good for that girl." He snorted. "Wearing a dress."

Peyton tightened his grip on the fork and stabbed a fillet with too much force, tearing the tender pink flesh.

"Just like I told *you*." Mr. Lively pointed at Matt, who stepped down one stair. "He just would've moved her off somewhere else, and who knows what kind of rabble would've moved in. It's bad enough to have you"—this time he pointed down, encompassing Peyton and Cassie in his accusations—"and your wild parties. And your damn dogs barking at all hours."

Peyton ground his teeth together so he wouldn't say something hateful about Mr. Lively's damn bird screaming at all hours. But, as if Captain Hook read his thoughts, from inside the apartment he shrieked an ear-splitting, *"Get away from there!"*

Peyton clutched the fork to keep from dropping it. That was Craig's voice. Slightly warped, as if on a tape recorder, but Craig's voice right down to his nicotine rasp.

"Hey! What the hell are you doing?" Captain Hook shouted, sounding so much like Craig that Peyton would've believed Craig was in that apartment if he hadn't seen Craig's dead body loaded onto the stretcher on the news. He handed Cassie the fork, afraid to hold it any longer, and climbed the stairs three steps at a time.

Mr. Lively looked alarmed, and Peyton half expected the old man to slam the door shut.

"Has he ever spoken like Craig before?" Peyton asked.

Dair put a hand on Peyton's arm, as if to hold him back. He welcomed the reminder.

Mr. Lively turned his head over his shoulder at the agitated parrot in the room behind him. Captain Hook bobbed his head and rocked from one foot to the other on his perch.

The old man stammered a moment before finding his usual sure footing. "H-he talks like anyone who goes around shouting. You've all given him a terrible vocabulary."

"What the hell?" the bird shouted again.

Matt looked up at Peyton with wide, frightened eyes.

"Have you ever heard him imitate Craig?" Peyton asked the kid.

Matt shook his head.

"He does all of us," Dair said, gesturing to the three of them hovered on the stairs before the old man. "But I've never heard him do Craig."

"What do you want?" Mr. Lively asked.

Peyton looked at the old man. He couldn't remember.

Dair took a deep breath and said, "I just came up to ask if you'd like to join us for dinner. My mother is—"

"No. Thank you." He shut his door.

"Hey!" Craig's voice yelled, as if in protest.

Matt ran down the stairs, his footsteps ringing on the metal. Marielle emerged from her half of the house, and Matt flew into her arms. She held him but looked up at Dair and Peyton, her face white, her eyes hopeful. Dair took Peyton's hand as they came down the steps.

"It was the bird," Peyton said. "I'm sorry. It was just the bird."

"Blizzard! Shodie!" the parrot yelled—in a tape recorder version

of Dair's voice this time—from behind the closed door. The dogs trotted to their people at the bottom of the steps.

"That is so annoying," Dair said, letting go of Peyton's hand and patting the dogs' confused faces. Released from her grip, Peyton's own hands shook. He balled them into fists.

Marielle's hopefulness settled again into that zombielike glaze. She looked down at Matt, who broke away from her. "You okay, sweetie?"

"That was just . . . creepy," he said, his face pink. He glanced back at Mr. Lively's door.

Peyton looked at Dair. Her face was pink, too. "Who would Craig have said that to?" Dair asked. "Did you ever hear him say that?"

Peyton shook his head. Craig's voice troubled him. Made him . . . uneasy.

"He probably said it to the dogs," Matt said. "Remember the time Blizzard stole his hamburger?"

Everyone smiled. Except Cassie. She frowned and said, "No, he was—"

"Marielle, this is my mom, do you remember her?" Dair interrupted.

Marielle smiled politely, but only with her mouth, not her eyes or cheeks.

Cassie said, "I'm so sorry." Dair's mom could say that clichéd expression and make it sound as though it meant something. Peyton took the fork back from her and returned to the grill, hoping to recapture that agreeable sensation he'd felt earlier. Trying to focus on the hunger in his stomach. The aroma of the beef. The hints of its taste in the grill's smoke. He thought he'd heard the whine faintly in the background and wanted to stave it off.

"The funeral is Wednesday," Marielle said to no one in particular. Today was only Sunday and had seemed to last a lifetime. Peyton couldn't bear the thought of existing through three more days like this . . . and who knew how many more. He couldn't imagine ever feeling right again, for this suffocating feeling to release its hold.

"You're the lady who talks to animals, right?" Matt asked Cassie. Peyton caught Dair's wince.

Cassie, though, smiled and nodded. "Yup."

"Can you teach me how to do that?" Matt asked, as if Cassie might be able to hand him a twelve-step instruction manual. Couldn't everything difficult on this planet be reduced to twelve simple steps after all? Peyton stabbed another steak, but it was further done and didn't rip. Twelve-stepping. Sounded like some hideous line dance. He tried to picture it in his head.

Cassie sat on the wooden steps leading to the yard and said to Matt, "You can probably already do it and just never paid attention. Most kids can do it, but the older you are, the harder it gets."

"Why?" Matt asked, sitting beside her. Peyton wanted to know, too.

"Small kids don't rely so much on language. Once you learn to speak, though, that's what gets all the attention and encouragement, and any other kind of communication gets scolded. If someone your age says, 'The dog says he's thirsty,' or, 'The cat says she wants her red mouse toy; she can't find it,' most grown-ups will say, 'Oh, stop fibbing; the dog didn't really tell you that.' Kids get embarrassed. They pretend they can't hear their animal friends in front of other people for a while, and eventually, they really do stop hearing them." She looked up at Dair, who turned away.

Cassie made it sound so simple and no-nonsense. It really was kind of cool. Jesus, Peyton's own mother couldn't even effectively communicate with other humans, so he didn't see what the big deal was about this.

Peyton prodded the steaks again. Matt chewed his lower lip and pondered what Cassie had said. Then he nodded as if he'd absorbed it and it met his approval.

When the elephant trumpeted at the zoo down the hill, Cassie chuckled at the dogs' typical reaction: They froze, hackles raised, noses to the wind. After twenty seconds they both went and busily peed in the four different corners of the yard.

"Ewww," Matt said. "Why do they do that?"

"They're marking their territory," Cassie told him. "They can tell that elephant is *big* and strange. And that it wants a different home. They want to make sure the elephant knows that this yard already belongs to somebody."

Peyton met Dair's eye again. He thought of Tibaba, the African elephant at the zoo. She'd just gotten a new home, a huge new habitat, called Vanishing Giants. Dair glared at her mom. Peyton tried to will her to lighten up.

Blizzard hiked his leg by the gate. Matt giggled. "If I were a dog, I could pee on my school desk to keep people out of it?"

Cassie nodded.

Matt giggled some more. "That's so nasty."

Cassie shrugged. "Not really. People put up fences, shoot each other, fight whole wars just to keep people out of their yards. If you look at it that way, peeing on the ground seems a lot more civilized, don't you think?"

Peyton snorted. "You've got a point there, Cassie." Now Dair glared at him. He looked down at the steaks and turned them over one more time. He dreaded going inside, imagining the pained silence at the table. The sorrow didn't feel as crushing out here in the open air. Thank God Cass was here. And thank God Matt was talking. Cass and Matt might make the dinner bearable. "Okay," Peyton said, closing the cover on the grill. "Let's get the rest of this show on the road."

He led them all into the kitchen and put Cassie, Matt, and Marielle to work setting the table with Fiesta Ware, each plate a different bright color. Marielle stood holding her silverware as if dazed, and Matt took it from her and set it himself. Dair helped Peyton make salads with avocado, tomatoes, and blue cheese.

"Do you have any wine?" Marielle asked.

Peyton went still but made himself say, "Yeah. Anyone want some with dinner?"

"Yes," Marielle said.

Cassie looked anxiously at Dair and said, "No thanks," but Dair didn't answer, didn't even look up from the avocado she was paring. Peyton examined their collection of party wine and selected a nice Merlot to go with the beef. He knew Dair wanted some; he set two glasses.

"Everybody, grab a seat," he said. "I'll be right back." He took a plate and went out to the porch to grab the steaks. They were perfect, juicy and tender. This was all it took to comfort him. A family sitting down to dinner. Everyone he loved gathered around him—or almost everyone. . . . He thought fleetingly of Craig but pushed the thought out of his mind, pictured it tumbling away in an aikido roll fall.

The dogs shadowed him into the house, whining. "Go lie down," Peyton said to them. They retreated to a corner of the room. Blizzard whimpered.

"I know it smells good," Dair said to Blizzard, taking the plate from Peyton. "But no."

Blizzard sighed and lay down, his face forlorn.

"Can you talk to animals, too?" Matt asked Dair.

She made a face and scoffed. "No." She began making her way around the table, putting a fillet on each colorful plate. Peyton caught himself watching her as if she were onstage. After tours, he loved to rediscover her, listen to her like improvised jazz—the notes were never what he expected, but always just right.

"Yes, she can," Cassie said. "She used to talk to her animals all the time."

"Really?" Peyton asked. "Like her bird?"

Cassie nodded, and Dair said to Matt, "I had lots of animals. I had a bunch of dogs, and one cat who slept with me every night."

"Snowflake," Peyton said, remembering the cat's name. "She could talk to Snowflake?" Dair had talked often of her white cat who'd lived to be twenty-something.

Dair rolled her eyes and put a steak on Marielle's turquoise plate.

"I'm not hungry." Marielle lifted her plate for Dair to take the fillet back.

Dair left it there. "You have to eat, Marielle."

"Why did you never mention that, Dair?" Peyton asked. "That you could talk to Snowflake?" He worked the corkscrew down into the bottle's neck.

"Because it isn't true."

"Yes, it is," Cassie said.

The muscles bunched up in Dair's jaw. It was as if her mom were telling them Dair used to wet her bed as a teenager or something. Peyton wondered why Dair seemed so angry . . . so pained by this.

The cork came free with that satisfying, sexual release, and Peyton poured Marielle's glass, the rich, woody odor of the wine reaching his nostrils, filling him with regret. It drained him, this constant vigilance against himself. This feeling that he was alien, incapable of enjoying, partaking in what normal people could without a thought. He focused on Dair, her face, her fabulous cheeks, those features sharp as her sense of humor. "I think it's cool that you could do this," he said, pouring the wine for her. He started to ask, "Could Sylvan do it, too—" but accidentally tipped Dair's glass and the Merlot rolled across the table. "Shit. Sorry."

"No, I'm sorry," she said, laughing. "Oops."

Everyone lifted their plates and sopped with their napkins. Dair grabbed a dishtowel and wiped up the mess. Peyton put the wine on the counter, disappointed his question would now go unanswered. Dair set her glass next to the bottle, kissed his shoulder, and said, "I didn't want any, anyway." Peyton raised his eyebrows in disbelief, and Dair turned away. He realized his expression had ruined the effect she wanted her comment to have on her mother.

Cassie didn't seem to notice, though. "What did you say about Sylvan?" she asked.

Peyton went still again. Pictured a wolf hearing someone step into his territory a mile away.

Dair walked back to her seat, talking too loudly all of a sudden, as if she were onstage. "I dreamed about her the other night."

"Really?" Cassie looked up at the wooden chickadees. Peyton watched to see if Cassie would flip out, as Dair had all but forbidden him to mention Sylvan around her parents. Marielle seemed to be watching, forehead furrowed, for the same thing. But Cassie seemed calm. "That's very interesting. You know, a dream is often a sign from your totem—"

"Peyton always says it's a sign, too," Dair said, winking at Peyton as though this were all a big joke. Her wink seemed obscene somehow, in front of Marielle.

"Well, it is, don't you think?" Peyton asked Cassie. "I mean, how old was Dair when she stopped communicating with animals?"

Cassie looked at Dair and pursed her lips while she thought. "You were in fifth grade. So you were, what? Ten? Eleven?"

"So, the connection seems obvious, don't you think?" Peyton asked. Marielle nodded, but Cassie's face went blank. A bit befuddled. Peyton didn't want to be totally tactless and blurt, "C'mon, her twin dies and she loses a communication ability?"

While Peyton searched for the right words, Dair turned to Matt and teased, "See how she's changing the subject? She never did answer your question, did she?"

"Yeah," Matt said, goaded on by Dair. "Teach me how to talk to animals. How do they talk back?"

"Oh, that's right," Cassie said, lifting salad onto her orange plate with tongs, looking anxiously at the rest of them, as if unsure whether to continue. Peyton felt sorry for her; she was suddenly on the spot, offering the only thread of conversation anyone could hang on to. "Well, animals use their minds; they don't have to use language like we do. They send pictures and impressions, and what I call intentions. It's not concrete, word-for-word conversation, although once I get an image or an emotion from an animal, then I do sort of put it into words because that's how humans communicate."

"So, it's like you translate it?" Peyton asked. Dair had never explained this much to him, and he found it fascinating. And Cass had never talked this freely about it. She was different tonight. Was this because of the separation? He looked at Dair, but her playfulness from seconds before was gone and she seemed irritated. He didn't understand and opened his hands to her, as if to ask, "What?" but she looked away, taking the salad bowl from her mother.

Peyton felt a misstep. A break in the rhythm.

Cassie paused, noticing this exchange, then nodded at Peyton. "Yeah, I guess you're right, Peyton: It's like a translation or interpretation."

It was nothing new to Peyton to have to defend his own beliefs from ridicule. He wished he'd asked Cassie more about this years ago. Wished he'd spent the time and effort to affirm and show acceptance for her opinions, as she always had for him.

Dair put salad on Marielle's plate. Marielle looked down at it as if she didn't know what it was.

"But . . ." Matt frowned, skeptical. "What is there to translate? They can't have much to say."

"Why not?" Cassie asked.

"Well, I mean, they're *animals*. They're not very smart."

Cassie smiled and didn't seem at all offended by this. From the twinkle in her eye, Peyton imagined that she encountered this attitude often. "What makes you think they're not smart?"

"Well . . ." Matt shrugged as if the answer were obvious. He looked at the dogs and chewed his lip as if searching for an example. "Okay," he said, thinking of one. "They can't open the doors to let themselves out."

Cassie snorted and waved a hand as if to say, "Oh, *that*." She leaned toward Matt. "That has nothing to do with *smarts*. That's just a physical trait, because they don't have hands with thumbs." She cocked her head at him. "Can you fly?"

He shot her a look of disdain. "No." The unspoken "duh" was loud and clear.

"So, you're not as smart as a bird?"

His mouth dropped open.

"Can you see in the dark?" she asked him. "Or run thirty miles an hour?"

Matt squinted but grinned at her. He got the point.

"Again, spoken language is a *physical* skill, not a sign of intelligence."

Hell, that was true. Peyton thought of all the idiot humans he knew. Sure, they could talk, but it didn't mean they ever said anything.

Cassie smiled and added shyly, looking only at her plate, "If you're really interested in learning more about it, I'm hosting a communication workshop this Saturday."

"Really?" Peyton *was* interested. He didn't care if Dair wouldn't go with him.

"I've got leftover brochures in the truck. I'll give you one before I go. The workshop is already full, but I'd make room for you." Cassie looked at the rest of the table. "For any of you, actually."

"So, like, show me," Matt challenged Cassie. "What is Blizzard thinking right this minute?"

Cassie laughed as Blizzard lifted his head at the sound of his name. "That's too easy, Matt. You know what Blizzard is thinking, don't you? Look at him." The Pyrenees sat up, eyes hopeful, expectant, tail thumping on the hardwood floor.

"That he wants some steak?"

"Right."

"So, it's not really telepathy," Dair said. She said it gently, almost apologetically. "We all know he wants steak from his body language. That just comes from looking at him. Right?"

Cassie blushed slightly and lowered her eyes. "You're right, Dair. The steak thing is obvious."

"I'm surprised you eat steak," Marielle said to Cassie, ignoring Dair's comment. "I would've guessed you were a vegetarian."

Peyton had never thought of this.

Cassie thought a moment, then shrugged. "I believe in the food chain," she said simply. "Most of our animal companions are also carnivores."

Marielle nodded, but Matt fidgeted, bored again. "Ask the dogs something else, then."

"Yeah," Peyton said. "Is there anything they want to tell us? Anything they want—besides steak, of course—to make their lives better?"

Cassie narrowed her eyes, as if accepting a challenge. While she paused, Dair muttered, "You all are usually such rational people." Peyton ignored her and leaned toward Cassie.

Cassie looked at the dogs briefly, and they both lifted their ears toward her. "Music," she said. "Peyton, you always have music on in the house, and they like that, but Dair, you never play any music, so when Peyton is gone, they really miss it."

When they turned to Dair, Peyton felt her defenses gathering. Sensed she felt accused in some way. What Cassie said was true, but he wondered how she knew that. Not from Dair's childhood, because both Cassie and R.B. had told him how Dair had nearly driven them crazy as a teenager, playing music all the damn time. Dair stared back at them, fierce and silent.

"What else?" Matt asked.

"When Peyton is gone, Dair lets them both sleep on the bed."

Peyton smiled. "I figured as much." Feeling bad for Dair, though, he added teasingly, "But that could've simply been a good guess."

"They think you're worried," Cassie said to Dair.

"Worried?" Dair asked, barely concealing her disdain.

"You're worried about . . ." Cassie paused as if trying to search for the perfect words. She didn't look at the dogs, but they kept their eyes on her. "Having to tell someone something important."

From across the room, Peyton felt the time step of Dair's heartbeat go into double time.

"Something about a . . . a . . ."

He watched Dair hold her breath. It made him have to inhale deeply for his own.

Cassie shook her head as if what she was picking up couldn't be right. "Something about a . . . a handkerchief?"

Peyton laughed, wanting to take that panicked look off Dair's face. "A handkerchief?"

Cassie nodded and continued watching Dair. "Sometimes you look for something around the house, and they wonder if you're trying to find it." She looked down at Blizzard, who wagged his tail, his broad face earnest and eager. "Hmm. He shows me you putting something in the closet upstairs. Is that where it is?"

Dair's face blazed bright red, and fast, like a reaction to poison. It looked so hot, Peyton brought the back of one hand to his own cheek.

"Nobody has handkerchiefs anymore," Matt said. "We use Kleenex."

"Do they even know what a handkerchief is?" Peyton asked.

Cassie leaned forward across the table. "Are you okay, Dair?"

"I'm fine," she snapped.

Cassie paused, and Peyton sensed she didn't want to continue in the face of Dair's obvious discomfort, but Marielle surprised them all by asking, "A handkerchief? Really?" Her face seemed suddenly alive, alert.

Cassie nodded, glancing anxiously at Dair. "That's what they're picturing. A white handkerchief. It's very specific. It has red strawberries embroidered on it. They seem to feel Dair is very upset about this handkerchief."

"Oh, my God," Dair said, all that red running from her face so fast that it made Peyton light-headed. She looked over at Marielle, who nodded—eyes sparkling, mouth open.

"It's from *Othello*," Marielle said. "Emilia steals the handkerchief for Iago, and he uses it to set up Desdemona."

Peyton's own jaw dropped. "Wow," he said, his brain spinning. "Jesus—can the dogs *read?*"

Dair eyed the dogs as if she'd never seen them before. "I—I've been reading my lines, thinking about the role. But I don't think I've *ever* said the lines out loud yet. I've only known a few days."

"Even if you've thought of it, they'll pick it up. Probably even clearer than if you said it out loud. Is this Emilia upset about the handkerchief?"

"Oh, yes," Marielle said, seeming more alive than Peyton had seen her since the news of Craig's death. "Emilia lies about it at first, but then things get out of control and she realizes she has to admit her part. She steals it for her husband, and—" Her rush of enthusiasm trailed off, and she swallowed. She blinked at them, as if suddenly unsure where she was.

Dair put an arm around Marielle's shoulder. "Craig was cast in it, too," she told her mom.

Cassie nodded. Dair tucked a strand of hair behind Marielle's ear, a gesture Peyton had seen Cassie do to Dair countless times.

"But what about the searching?" Matt asked.

The red flared in Dair's face again. The look she shot Matt cursed the curiosity of children, but he didn't seem to notice. "The dogs said you were searching around the house?"

Dair laughed lightly. "I'm not sure what that's about." She picked up her silverware.

Matt wouldn't drop it. "Blizzard said you put something in the upstairs closet."

"Well, I did some laundry," she said, poking at her steak with a fork. "That must be it."

Cassie frowned and shook her head. "No, it was . . ." She looked at Blizzard again, a blush spreading over her cheeks. She turned her face to Dair, and their eyes met. Something passed between them, a friction so palpable that Peyton almost heard it. "Hmm," Cassie said again, her voice pinched, nearly hoarse. "I'm not sure what he thinks it was. He might just be mixed up with the handkerchief."

Peyton didn't believe her. He could tell by her expression that she knew exactly what Dair had hidden in the closet. It took every ounce of his control not to run upstairs and look that very second.

They continued staring into each other's eyes until Matt asked, "What about my cat? Can you talk to my cat?"

"Sure," Cassie said, and Peyton sensed her relief at breaking her gaze from Dair's.

"I'll go get her!" Matt jumped up.

"No, sweetie," Marielle said.

"I don't need to see her. It's telepathic, remember?"

"Really? You don't even have to be able to look at her?" Matt was beside himself.

"What's your cat's name?" Cassie asked.

"Slip Jig."

Cassie grinned at Peyton. "That's a great name. What does she look like?"

"She's gray, with two white paws in front and light blue eyes."

Cassie nodded to herself, and her gaze shifted focus as she looked at their table but saw something else. It was subtle, but her eyes and expression mellowed ever so slightly like a person fighting sleep. To

Peyton, she looked like a lucky person feeling the peaceful waves of heroin lap against her brain.

Matt sat back in his chair, watching her. "So, what does she say?"

"Oh, she's beautiful and she loves you, Matt. You're her person. She adores you."

"Why won't she sleep with me anymore?"

Cassie frowned and pulled her eyes from the point of her focus to look at Matt. "She does. She did last night."

His eyes widened again. "Yeah . . . but before that she didn't for a long time. She always used to sleep with me, but not for like, a month."

"Hmm. She says it's too . . . windy?" Cassie cocked her head, her face dreamy again. "Are you leaving the window open or something?"

"No." Matt frowned. He narrowed his eyes at Cassie, as if she were a fraud.

Marielle's eyes flashed, snapping her out of her sorrow. "The ceiling fan!" she said. She signed the word as well, twirling one index finger of her long, slender hands. Peyton loved when she did that, like a bilingual person dipping into one language while talking in another.

Matt turned to her, nodding. "Yeah! Peyton and Craig helped us install ceiling fans in our rooms!"

"Well, that fan makes the room too windy. She doesn't like it."

Matt jumped out of his seat again, almost hopping with excitement. "And last night I didn't use it. It got cold last night. I even shut my windows."

"And she came in and slept with you," Cassie said simply.

Marielle leaned across the table toward Cassie. "Can you ask her why she's not using the litter box?"

Cassie frowned again. "She says she does. She's very offended by this question."

Marielle hunched her shoulders apologetically. "She's usually great. But every now and then, she poops in the basement. She's done it, like, four or five times."

Matt furrowed his brow, his smoky eyes darkening. Peyton knew Marielle hadn't wanted to get a cat at all.

Cassie looked down at her plate and closed her eyes, her expression tranquil. Peyton tried not to remember how good it felt booting the heroin, embracing the safest, sweetest sensation imaginable. Cassie lifted her head. "She's defining her territory. There's someone who comes over who she feels very threatened by. She thinks this person is a threat to you two, as well."

Matt looked perplexed, but Marielle sat up straight, frowning. "Who?" she asked.

"Um . . ." Cassie sighed. "She doesn't really want to give me anything else about it. It's unpleasant to her."

"She won't tell you?" Dair asked. She sounded curious, not disdainful.

Cassie shook her head. "When she showed me the image, though, it was someone tall. Tall, at least to Slip Jig. Dark hair. Long."

"But that's . . . Craig," Marielle said, faltering slightly over his name. "She liked Craig."

Cassie paused. "No, this isn't Craig. She flashes a different feeling of Craig, although her picture of him does look a little similar. But Craig was good and safe."

"Peyton's tall with long hair," Dair said, looking at him, her face no longer angry.

"Dair's tall with long hair," Matt pointed out.

Peyton nodded. "And I'm over there a lot. If she doesn't like the fan and I helped install it—"

Cassie shook her head, silencing him. "It's a man. But it's not you. I get good feelings about you and Dair." Peyton didn't like the look on Cassie's face. She blushed again, as she had when she'd kept to herself Blizzard's vision of whatever Dair hid in the closet.

The blush worried him. What had she seen? A throb thrummed in his right temple.

"What is it?" Marielle asked, her voice thin and fearful.

Cassie sat up straight, focused and alert again. "I'm sorry, I don't mean to upset you, but I get the impression from Slip Jig that this person comes into your house when you're not there."

Marielle looked as if someone had slapped her. Peyton wished there were some way to spare her from this day. He remembered how it felt to have all the misery in the world sliding down on him at once.

"Slip Jig only tries to define the territory when this man has been in the house."

Marielle let this information sink in. "But, like I said, she's done it five times! Oh, my God, are you telling me that some intruder has been in our house five—"

"Seven, really," Matt said quietly.

"What?"

"She's pooped in the basement seven times. I cleaned it up twice and didn't tell you because I knew it made you mad. You said we might have to get rid of her if she kept doing it."

Marielle covered her mouth with both hands.

"She did it this morning," Matt whispered. "I found it when we went home, after pancakes."

The throb hammered behind Peyton's eye. He clenched his steak knife in his fist, pictured slitting the throat of this intruder, felt his warm blood, just as in his dreams of battles and combat. "Why the basement?" Peyton asked. "If you were going to mark your territory wouldn't you do it more obviously, like at the doors?"

Cassie nodded, that faraway look in her eye, then she focused in on him. "It's where the man comes in."

"Oh, God," Marielle said, nodding, her hands dropping from her mouth to her heart. "She always poops under a window, by the table."

Peyton stood up, his chair legs screeching on the floor. "Let's go look." He still held the knife. Anger infused him, a yearning to destroy something. He didn't like it, that yearning, didn't want it, but nobody messed with his pack. Everyone looked up at him from the table, faces cowed and fearful. "Come on," he said, heading for the door.

"Wait," Dair said with too much urgency. Peyton looked back at their table, the barely tasted steaks, the eager dogs in the corner, their eyes full of disbelief at this luck that these people were leaving all this food. "Let me put up the steaks," Dair almost begged, and Peyton knew she didn't want to be left behind, even for the few minutes it would take to put the plates out of reach. The sound of fear, hers and everyone else's, rose like a sharp, sustained high note on a violin. The dogs must've heard it, because Blizzard whined and Shodan let loose with a short howl that made Dair jump.

Marielle hugged herself and said, "No, bring them. Bring the dogs. Please?"

Peyton nodded, and when they all went next door, he locked his own kitchen door behind them.

Chapter Seven

Dair stuck close to Peyton as Marielle led them downstairs, turning on every light she passed. Bare lightbulbs illuminated the basement's concrete floor, the washer and dryer in one corner, storage boxes, bikes Dair didn't know they had. A picnic table sat in one corner, covered with Matthew's paintings—startling brightness in the drab room. Five paintbrushes stood in a glass of murky water.

Slip Jig slunk down the stairs to join them and nervously held her ground in spite of the big, overexcited dogs. Mom crouched and stroked the cat's chin, but Slip Jig moved away from her touch.

"She always poops under that table," Matt said, pointing from the bottom of the steps.

Dair looked at the window above the table. The window sat on the surface of the ground and was maybe a foot and a half high, two feet wide. The sturdy wooden table beneath it offered the perfect step down without even the slightest risk of injury or noise.

She looked at her mother. Why did she have to know this? Why did she have to complicate everything and force Dair to dig up these long-buried bones—this disdain, this admiration, this confusion? But at least an intruder was better than Mom focusing on that goddamn vodka bottle. God, how could she even think that? Poor Marielle. This was serious.

Dair looked to Peyton, whose face was stony and set, like some furious statue. His anger made her feel safer. He stepped up onto the table and hunched over, his bent back brushing the ceiling as he touched the window. It didn't budge. He pressed the window's top, then its bottom. As he pushed against the bottom, the window shuddered slightly. "Oh, my God," Marielle whispered. She looked around, as if to double-check where Matt was.

Dair watched, enthralled, as Peyton wiggled the window side to side and shimmied it out of its casement. He laid it on the ground above him and stood up straight, poking his head and shoulders through the opening. Barely having to stand on tiptoe, he laid his torso on the ground outside, then scooted until his legs followed him through the square. And in spite of the tension, thick in the air, and her fear, thick in her throat, Dair admired Peyton's sinewy grace, the ease with which he accomplished this act. He was outside, vanished from the basement, in seconds. Dair stepped closer to her mother.

Peyton knelt and peered down at them, catlike. "I think we should call the police."

"And tell them what?" Marielle asked in a thin, shrill voice.

She had a point. They couldn't exactly report that a cat told them about an intruder.

Peyton said, "We could just tell them that you found the window open or something."

They stood uncomfortably, looking up at Peyton's face in the window. Dair craved him back inside, beside her. Blizzard and Shodan snuffled around, occasionally nosing too close to Slip Jig, who puffed up and raised a paw as if to strike but never did. The dogs were the only ones in the room who seemed unconcerned.

Marielle whipped around to face Dair's mother. "Can't you tell me who it is?" she pleaded. "Can't you get a description?"

Mom shook her head, looking at the cat. Slip Jig pinned her ears down flat. "I'm sorry. She doesn't want to give me any more."

"What do you mean? Why not?" Marielle asked almost angrily, as if she felt Slip Jig were simply being obstinate.

Mom sighed. "It upset her. Animals live very much in the present; they don't see any reason to return to unpleasant events. She's very relieved that you know about this intruder, but she won't tell me any more about it. I saw someone tall with long, dark hair. But I got the impression that this is someone who's been here with you at some point. It's not a total stranger to her."

"Really?" The relief in Marielle's voice made no sense to Dair. She examined her friend's face, but Marielle turned away. Wouldn't she rather have some unknown, random intruder than a *friend* breaking in, someone she thought she trusted?

Peyton slithered back in the window, feet flailing a moment before finding safety on the table. Dair breathed easier with him back in the room.

Marielle stared at Dair's mother while Peyton crouched over and fitted the window back into place. "I haven't had anyone over but Craig, and these guys," she said, pointing to them. "No one else."

"Wait," Dair said, remembering. "When did Slip Jig first poop down here?"

Peyton turned to her, nodding. "Yeah. Was it anywhere around the party?"

Marielle clapped a hand to her mouth, eyes wide.

"It was right after the party!" Matt said.

"You had a party here?" Mom asked.

"Actually, *we* did," Dair said. "But Marielle let people use her bathroom. People were walking back and forth all night."

Almost eighty people had come through their home that night. It was a combination party—a season opener for Queen City Shakespeare and a home-show celebration for Footforce. The actors, the dancers, the technical staffs, had danced, eaten chili—Cincinnati style over spaghetti—grilled brats and burgers, drunk beer, and played live music until three in the morning.

Dair fast-forwarded through the video in her head and hit pause: "Malcolm Cole."

Peyton hopped down from the table and turned to her, shaking his head, his expression suggesting she'd said something as inappropriate as "Mickey Mouse" or "my dad."

"What?" Marielle asked. "What about Malcolm Cole?"

"Malcolm Cole is tall and has long, dark hair."

Mom made a troubled noise and bent to stroke the cat again, but Slip Jig darted away, up the stairs. The dogs watched her flee, their ears raised. "Something's wrong about that hair," Mom said. "I saw him with short hair and with long hair, in different images."

"If you see different images," Dair asked, "could it be two different people?"

"Oh, shit! You're telling me there's a *parade* of people coming through my house?"

Dair and Peyton looked at each other. They'd never heard Marielle cuss. Matt moved close to Dair and took her hand, which made something melt within her.

"No," Mom said. "It was the same person, same smell, but he looked different. Do people ever dye their hair for parts? Or maybe he had long hair and now it's short?"

Dair's mind almost whirred as she cataloged the possibilities. She longed for the Merlot she'd intentionally spilled, saw it spreading its red wash across the tiled table.

"You have to call the police," Peyton said.

"But what does this person *do* inside? Nothing's ever been stolen! What do I report?"

Mom cleared her throat. "In the images Slip Jig showed me, he was looking around the house."

"Where? Where does he look?"

"At the fridge."

"The fridge? He takes our food?"

"No, no, not *in* the fridge. He was looking *at* the fridge. Is there . . . ?"

But Marielle stormed up the steps to the kitchen. They followed, Dair experiencing a troubling collision of emotions. She wanted Marielle to be more appreciative of what her mother was doing for her, and she wanted her mother to shut up, to stop freaking everybody out. In front of the refrigerator, they all stared at Matt's artwork, his grade card, Marielle's class schedule. "What else?" Marielle demanded of Dair's mother.

Mom took a deep breath and asked Marielle gently, "The big bed, with the rocking chair beside it, that's yours, right?" They were all too spooked to marvel at her knowing this. Marielle nodded.

"He looks in your top drawer, touches things, takes them out, it's your . . ."

"My underwear," Marielle said, her jaw tightening.

Dair's flesh crawled with goose bumps. She sensed Peyton's anger mounting, radiating from him. She reached out and touched his arm, felt the fury under his skin.

Mom bit her lip. "And he got in your bed."

"In my *bed?*" Marielle wheeled and ran up the steps to her bedroom. They followed again. She whipped back the covers as if expecting to find the intruder still there. "Wouldn't I notice? How could I not tell someone had been in my bed? I—I'd smell someone. Craig, he always leaves his scent." She touched a hollow in the pillow closest to her. "I can still smell him on my pillows."

Dair closed her eyes and thought of Peyton's comforting scent—those whispers of mesquite charcoal or smoked ham in his sweat after dancing, that soft leather aroma that clung to his clothes and pillow.

Mom turned and pointed to Matt's room across the hall. "And he went in there."

A growl escaped Marielle's throat. Her eyes narrowed, and her nostrils flared. "Oh, no. He better fucking not."

Matt, still holding tight to Dair's hand, dropped his jaw at these foreign words falling from his mother's lips. Shock zipped through Dair, too, and fear. She wanted everyone behaving as they normally did—Mom keeping her mouth shut, Marielle sweet and unflappable, Peyton calm and grounded, Matt too grown-up to hold her hand.

Marielle crossed the hall into Matt's bedroom, and Dair and the others followed helplessly. "What does he do?" Marielle demanded of Dair's mother, like a woman possessed. "What does he touch?"

Mom shook her head. "He sat on the bed. Slip Jig pictured him just sitting, looking around the room."

Marielle snorted, tossing that little forelock of her bangs. "So help me God, he better not mess with my son."

Who? Why did she say it as if she knew who it was? All the emotion in the room felt spiky and sharp. A few good swallows of that wine would soften these edges.

Matt pressed himself against Dair, and she put her hand on top of his lamblike curls.

"Peyton's right," Dair said. "You need to call the police."

Marielle opened her mouth to protest, and Peyton cut in: "You don't have to mention the cat. Think about it—we can say we found the window open."

"I don't want to call the police," Marielle said. She must've seen disapproval on their faces, because she rushed on. "I don't want to lie to them; it'll get messed up somehow."

"No, it won't," Dair said. "You're not lying by *leaving out* the cat." There was a huge difference between concealing and fabricating.

Every good liar knew that. She couldn't tell yet if Marielle was a good one or not.

Marielle frowned and looked around the room. "We don't have any proof. . . ."

That word again. Proof. Dair looked at her mother's face, but it showed nothing.

"I'll call them," Peyton said with finality.

"No, don't, I—" Marielle rocked from foot to foot, hugging herself, reminding Dair of the neurotic leopard at the zoo, pacing relentlessly, that cornered look in her eye. But what was it, Dair wondered, that had backed Marielle into the wall? How could she not want to notify the police? Dair didn't want to think these thoughts. She wanted to go back downstairs, to Marielle's fridge, to that bottle of Chardonnay Marielle had opened last night.

Peyton crossed the hall back to Marielle's room, and they followed him, standing like idiots, watching him dial the phone next to her bed as if they'd never seen anyone do this before.

When Peyton began to speak, Matt tugged on Dair's shirt. "Should we search the house?" he asked, his voice small and high-pitched. He'd told them that Slip Jig had pooped in the basement this very morning.

Dair hugged him tighter to her. "I don't think the person is still here, Matt."

He shrugged, a tremor at the corner of his mouth revealing his effort not to cry.

His fear changed something in Marielle, made her wake up. She knelt beside Dair and cupped Matt's face in her hands. "Would you feel better if we searched?" she asked.

He nodded, the tremor turning into a tic.

She stood up. "Okay." She took his hand and stepped into the hall. Dair followed and made a kissing noise, bringing the dogs trotting up the stairs to them. She thought that might make Matt feel better, too. She knew it made *her* feel better.

"You know, Matt," Mom said, "I bet Blizzard and Shodan would bark and let us know if someone was still here."

Matt frowned and thought this over. He shrugged but said, "We should make sure."

Dair felt that melting sensation again.

Peyton came to the door of Marielle's bedroom. "They'll send someone over, but it might be a while."

He joined in their search, standing in the hall with Dair and Mom
while Marielle turned on the bathroom light and pulled back the
shower curtain. She lifted the fabric skirt hiding the pipes under the
sink. "Nobody in here," she said.

Matt pointed. "The hamper."

Marielle lifted the lid. "Nothing but stinky towels." She tried to joke,
but Dair heard the strain in her voice, saw it in the rigid tendons in
her neck, her quick, too forceful movements.

In Matt's bedroom they looked in his closet, behind his curtains,
between the bed and the wall. Shodan plopped down and yawned,
but Blizzard got playful when Dair knelt to look under the bed, certain they were teasing him with some game. He pranced and lowered his front paws, butt and tail high in the air, then tried to wriggle
under the bed.

"C'mere, you silly," Dair called to him. He backed out snorting and
sneezing, dust bunnies clinging to his white snout.

Marielle smiled a tight smile. "We're not finding anything but my
bad housecleaning habits." She turned to Matt. "Downstairs?"

He shook his head. "Your room."

"We started in my room."

He fidgeted with a button on his shirt. "We didn't search." Poor
kid. He was spooked. Dair was, too. She might have to search her
own apartment when they went back. Searching. That reminded her:
She needed to move that damn vodka bottle.

They returned to Marielle's room. The second Dair got on her
knees and lifted the dust ruffle on Marielle's bed, Blizzard barked and
shoved his head underneath. He continued whining and growling
and scooting on his belly until all Dair could see were his back paws,
black pads turned up. "Blizzard," she scolded, "get out of there." She
grabbed a paw and squeezed. He barked.

"He's found something," Mom said. There was a weight in her voice
that made them all look at her. She'd turned pallid, as though she
might be sick. "He's picturing Craig."

Dair swallowed. For a split second she pictured body parts, then
remembered the paramedics loading Craig's whole body onto the
stretcher. Blizzard barked again.

Peyton dropped to his knees, grabbed Blizzard's back legs, and hauled him out from under the bed. Blizzard yelped in surprise but wagged his tail, more convinced than ever that this was a game. More tumbleweeds of dust clung to him, but in his jaws he held a slightly wilted bouquet of flowers—some snapdragons, some peachy pink gladiolas, and some pink-and-white star lilies. From Mount Lookout Sprouts. Just like the ones in Gayle's bedroom. The breath stopped in Dair's chest.

"Good boy, give it here," Peyton commanded, wrenching the bouquet from Blizzard's teeth. The green paper ripped, but the tiny white card stayed intact. Peyton held it up and away from Blizzard's happy, panting mouth. He read: "'Your "yes" made me the happiest, luckiest man in the world. Love, Craig.'"

Dair found it hard to will air back into her lungs and feared for a moment she would choke or pass out. What if . . . it couldn't be. Craig didn't leave those lilies for Gayle *himself*, did he? Mount Lookout Sprouts was in walking distance of Craig's apartment.

Marielle shook her head. "I never got those," she whispered. She took a step back when Peyton held out the card to her, then shook herself and took it from him.

While she read it, Blizzard tried to wiggle under the bed again. Dair grabbed his collar in time and leaned down to look. "There's still something under there," she said. "Hold him."

Mom knelt and took his collar, murmuring, "Good boy, good boy."

Dair lay on her belly and reached for the bundle she saw sitting alone, away from the plastic storage boxes. She shivered, not knowing what it was, but grabbed it and hauled it out.

Everyone gathered around her as she brushed the lint and a few flower petals from a neatly folded white linen shirt and a pair of jeans tied together with a black leather belt. The collarless shirt had red brown stains near the neck that looked like drops of dried blood.

Or Merlot. The drops were the exact color of the Merlot soaked into those dishtowels next door. God, she'd be willing to suck the wine out of the terrycloth right now.

"Are these Craig's?" Dair asked.

Marielle nodded. "I—I think so." She turned to Matt, one hand clutched to her heart, horror in her eyes as she looked at her son as if recognizing him for the first time. "Sweetie, why are these under my bed?"

Matt's pale face flooded red. "I didn't put those there!"

"Marielle!" Dair protested, unable to believe the accusation in her question. Dair kept looking at those flowers. What if Gayle and Craig were having an affair and Marielle found out and . . . Stop it. Stop it.

The bundle felt heavy, so Dair unbuckled the belt and found a pair of black Doc Marten's sandwiched between the shirt and jeans, black socks, and a pair of blue Jockey underwear tucked in the shoes.

Blizzard snuffled the shirt's collar with interest. Dair lifted the shirt from Blizzard's reach, holding it up, letting it unfold.

"Look," Marielle said, pointing. Deep grass stains and dirt marred the back of the shirt.

Marielle snatched up the jeans. The butt was marked with grass stains, too.

"Stop touching this stuff," Peyton said, taking Marielle's hand and guiding it away. He pulled Dair up from the floor by her elbow. "Dair, put the shirt down."

She started to, but something slid from the shirt pocket as she bent to put it back in the pile. A pair of wire-rimmed glasses landed softly on the jeans. They stared at the shattered right lens, the bent right arm.

Dair remembered Craig running down the highway. He hadn't had his glasses on; that's why he hadn't recognized her, or her car, or the dogs. He hadn't been able to see. He hated contacts, never wore them except onstage. Without them, or his glasses, he couldn't tell that he was climbing over the guardrail in a sudden spot where it dropped down to a road. The trees probably led him to believe he was going to slide down a hill and keep running to safety. But . . . this bundle of clothes was a long way from Craig in a dress falling to his death a mile away.

Again Dair pictured Craig yanking on her car door. Before she even knew it was Craig, it had been obvious the "woman" needed help. Why had Dair turned away?

"W-why are these here?" Marielle asked in a voice that must've been a second-grade version of herself. She blinked rapidly.

No one answered for a long time. Peyton whispered, "These are probably the clothes he had on . . . when . . . whatever happened to him, happened to him."

Dair looked up at Peyton, opened her mouth, tried to form words. What did he mean? It frightened her not to know; it felt strange and unfamiliar to be out of mental sync.

Marielle shook her head and sat on the bed. Slip Jig darted into the room, leapt atop the bed beside her, and rubbed her head against Marielle's elbow.

Relief coursed through Dair when Peyton looked at her. She took his hand, craving connection. "But . . . ," Dair said. "What happened to him was . . . I mean . . . he was in a dress. He—he jumped in front of twenty witnesses . . . I *saw* him, so . . . I don't . . ."

"Look," Peyton said. "We all know he wouldn't jump, right? Or wear a damn dress. . . . So maybe, this is . . . connected somehow." Dair looked at the clothes and swallowed.

Marielle clutched her skull in her hands. "But *how?* He changes clothes here, puts on a dress, and runs a mile down Clifton Avenue? What are you saying?"

"I'm saying maybe something happened to him *here.*" Peyton held Shodan's collar. Mom still held Blizzard. Marielle buried her face in her hands as Peyton went on. "I think he was bringing these flowers to you, and . . ."

Those flowers. It was too bizarre after seeing them in Gayle's bedroom. What if these weren't even *for* Marielle? What if "your 'yes'" meant the role in *Othello?* But Gayle hadn't cast Othello, hadn't even been in town. As artistic director, though, she would've been in on final casting decisions, would have had to stamp her approval before contracts were offered.

Her mind flashed on a thought. One look at Peyton's face told her he had grabbed hold of the same idea, and this comforted her. "Remember what Captain Hook said when he mimicked Craig's voice?"

Peyton nodded. "Yeah. He said, 'Get the hell away from there,' or something like that. Jesus, do you think Craig saw the person going in the window?"

Marielle moaned without lifting her face.

It was bad enough to have lost Craig, and bad enough for Marielle to have an intruder in her home, but Dair hadn't wedded the two horrors in her mind. She looked at Marielle, wondering if *she* had.

"That damn parrot yells all kinds of things," Marielle said.

Mom cleared her throat. "I used to have a parrot."

Dair looked at her. She'd never known that.

Mom nodded. "It was my grandfather's. I sort of 'inherited' it because they live so long—this one lived to be seventy. Anyway, when a parrot mimics a *voice,* it's repeating what a *specific* person said. It's nearly impossible to teach them to imitate a phrase in a particular voice unless they've heard that person actually speak those words. You heard him today. He mimicked Craig so clearly that you came out of the house."

Marielle stayed very still.

Mom went on. "And they usually mimic loud or startling sounds, like people shouting—the way he imitates Dair calling the dogs. I think Peyton's right. That bird heard Craig shouting at someone. Quite possibly at someone breaking into your house."

Marielle raised her face to them. "And then what?" she asked, her voice tinged with hysteria. "How do we get from Craig interrupting an intruder here to Craig ending up on 75 in a goddamn dress and jumping into traffic?"

They stood in silence. No one knew that answer.

"And how," she went on, "did these clothes end up under my bed?" She turned to her son. "Are you *sure* you don't know anything about this, because it isn't—"

"Yes, I'm sure!" Matt yelled, his face flushed.

"You didn't hide these flowers because you were mad at me?"

"No!"

"It's okay. You can tell me. I know you were angry. You've got to tell the truth before the police get here."

"No!" Matt yelled again, and turned to stomp from the room. But Dair reached for his arm, and he let her stop him.

Dair put both hands on his shoulders, hugging his back into her. "Marielle," she whispered.

"I'm sorry, sweetie," Marielle said to Matt. "I'm just—oh, my God, what's happening?"

Dair massaged Matt's shoulders, hard and tense beneath her hands.

"We can't stay here," Marielle said. "I've got to go to a hotel."

"You're not going to a hotel," Peyton said. "Sleep on our side tonight."

"I don't want to be in this house at all."

"Marielle," Peyton said gently, "it'll be all right. You'll stay with us."

She didn't look convinced. She looked down at the clothes again and repeated, "How did these get here?"

No one spoke. Blizzard sighed and sat down, Mom's grip still on his collar.

Matt's tension changed under Dair's fingers. "M-maybe Slip Jig knows," he said. "Maybe the person coming in the window put them there."

They all looked down at the sad pile of clothing. The way they'd been dropped back on the floor made Dair think of *The Wizard of Oz;* Craig had melted away before them, leaving only his clothes and shoes and glasses behind.

She wanted to scoop up the clothes and hug them, breathe in Craig's scent. And she wanted to hug Peyton and breathe in *his* scent and forget all this. She longed for the comfort of dismissing all this as ridiculous. People couldn't talk to animals. There was no intruder. She looked up at Peyton. His eyes were pink and watery.

"Why?" Marielle whispered to the pile, as if asking the clothing.

"Did Slip Jig see the person do it?" Matt asked Dair's mom.

Mom looked at the cat on the bed. Slip Jig stopped nuzzling Marielle's elbow and returned Mom's gaze. The cat's blue eyes were calm, her mouth open slightly. But she closed her eyes and turned her head away. She flicked the end of her tail. Mom shook her head. "No . . . she doesn't want to talk about it. I think she usually hid when the man came over. All the images she gave me of what she saw him do are views from around the corner of the door frame, like she was peeking at him. I didn't get any picture of him putting something under the bed."

"If there was shouting, wouldn't she have heard it?" Matt asked. "Can't you ask her what she heard? Ask her what happened after the shouting."

Mom's face was suddenly so weary that Dair felt protective and wanted everyone to leave her mother alone.

Mom sighed. "It's not that exact. It's hard to make them pinpoint days or specific events unless something particularly memorable happened to them." Her shoulders stooped. "I'm sorry. She doesn't want me to ask any more."

"It doesn't matter," Peyton said. "We can tell the police about the open window and this stuff. And we'll tell them about the parrot. They'll probably want to talk to Mr. Lively."

Dair met Peyton's eyes, aware that once again their minds had locked on to the same idea. "Mr. Lively," Dair said. "He would've been home when it happened!"

Marielle sat up straight, looking exasperated. "You guys, *I* would've been home when it happened, whatever 'it' is. I was only gone a few hours yesterday. Mr. Lively was keeping an eye on Matt for me. Did you two hear any shouting, Matt?"

Matt shook his head and dug the toe of his shoe into the carpet. Blizzard barked, tired of being held.

"I'm not accusing him," Dair said. "I just think he might know something that could help us. I'll go talk to him, tell him the police are coming."

"Could you talk to Captain Hook?" Matt asked her mom.

"Maybe. If he feels like it. I could try."

"Can I come, too?" he asked.

Dair looked at Marielle, but Marielle stared at the clothes, rubbing the back of her neck. Peyton gestured for them to go ahead. Dair knew he would stay with her. Dair didn't want to leave him, to be out of his presence, but their teamwork in this fueled her.

She led her mother and Matt out the back door to go pay a visit to their neighbor.

Chapter Eight

The dogs followed Dair, her mother, and Matt outside and scampered off to inspect the yard. Dair led the others up the metal stairs to Mr. Lively's door. Please, please let the old man know something, Dair thought. Dair wanted to believe this would be a comfort, although she suspected it wouldn't matter. Even if they knew *exactly* what happened, even if Mr. Lively turned over a videotape of the entire event, it wouldn't bring Craig back.

The metal rang beneath their feet, and when they were halfway up, Captain Hook shrieked and asked, *"Who's outside?"*

Mr. Lively flung open his door. "What's all this racket? I told you I didn't want—"

"I'm sorry to bother you again," Dair said, feeling the familiar surge of resentment the old man inspired in her. "I need to ask you some questions."

"You may need to ask, but I don't need to answer." Mr. Lively started to shut his door, but Matt spoke up.

"Please, Mr. Lively? It's important."

The old man paused, looked at the boy, then opened his door again. "What is it?" He was always nicer to Matt than to anyone else.

"Who's outside?" Captain Hook repeated.

"Can we come in?" Matt asked.

Mr. Lively frowned, practically blocking the door with his arms, but he looked at Matt, nodded, and stepped aside.

Matt led the way into the apartment. Dair and her mother followed.

In a sweet old voice that sounded suspiciously like Mr. Lively's, Captain Hook greeted Matt with, *"Hello, my little man."*

Mr. Lively's face colored slightly.

Dair had never been inside the apartment. It had a sloped roof on either side of its long rectangular length. The door led them into a narrow kitchen equipped with a mustard gold refrigerator and stove. Dair eyed the fridge and wondered if the old man drank. If he did, it would be something inexpensive. Boone's Farm, maybe. That would do. Dair didn't feel picky. Beyond the kitchen was the bedroom and living room. A television flickered soundlessly, illuminating the round turret. The turret offered a view of the steep front yard, Dair bet, and the street. Surely Mr. Lively saw everyone come and go.

"Mr. Lively, this is my mother, Cassie Canard." Dair wondered, as she said it, if Mom would keep her married name. Dair had never taken one.

Mr. Lively cleared his throat and shuffled his feet. "How do you do?"

"What a magnificent parrot," Mom said. She stepped toward Captain Hook on his perch in the middle of the kitchen. "He's remarkable."

Mr. Lively beamed, totally transforming his face. "He's my buddy."

The bird chirruped and puffed out his white chest. He squawked and said, *"Captain is a good buddy, best buddy. What a fine fellow."*

Dair had to smile. "That's right, Captain," Mr. Lively said, then looked at the others and coughed.

"Ohh," Mom said, peering closer. "What's going on with his chest? He's lost some feathers. Looks like he's plucking them—"

The scowl returned, and Mr. Lively fluttered his hands. "Yes, yes, that started yesterday. We came home and he'd had a fright. I don't know what happened, but he hasn't been right since. He pulled out lots of feathers. He's slowed it down some."

Mom turned to him. "Do you know what frightened him?"

"No, I don't." But Dair caught the cold glance he cast at her. "He gets upset when those dogs bark."

Dair bristled. Mom, however, murmured a sympathetic sound and said, "Did you take him somewhere?"

"No, no, I don't take him out, except on occasion in a warm rain."

"I bet he likes that. Don't you, Captain?" Dair liked how her mom talked to animals in an open, clear voice, not in that high-pitched, saccharine croon most people used. "Do you like the rain?"

The parrot squawked and spread his wings. *"Captain wants a bath, Papa."*

Matt giggled.

"Now don't get his hopes up," Mr. Lively scolded.

"It's raining! It's raining!" the parrot called, fanning his red tail feathers, stretching his wings and preening, as if he were getting a shower.

Dair wished the parrot were right: It hadn't rained in over two months. She sympathized with the dry, hard ground and brittle leaves—she felt their craving, felt that parched herself.

"He has quite an impressive vocabulary," Mom said. Again Mr. Lively grinned with almost childlike pride. Then, looking only at the parrot, Mom said, "I asked if you took him somewhere because you said '*we got home.*'"

Damn. Mom was good. Dair hadn't even caught that. Goose bumps prickled on her skin. The air nearly crackled as Mr. Lively and Matt froze, staring at Dair's mother. Matt shook himself, then stooped and busied himself picking up the seeds on the floor under the bird's perch. Mr. Lively glanced at the boy's sudden movement, and the alarm in his eyes affirmed Dair's first thought: Wrong move, Matt. Too nervous, too guilty. Exactly how she'd block a scene about someone hiding something.

"You were mistaken," the old man said curtly.

"Oh, I'm sorry, I misheard you," Mom said.

Matt and Mr. Lively went to the zoo together all the time, so why were they lying? The secrecy, the denial, made Dair uneasy.

"Captain wants a bath, Papa!"

"Now see what you've done?" Mr. Lively snapped as if he might throw them all out. In a totally different voice he said to the parrot, "No bath, Captain. No bath. Settle down."

The parrot folded his wings and shifted from foot to foot, turning his head sideways, examining Dair with one yellow eye. Dair wanted Mr. Lively to ask them to sit down, but there was nowhere to sit here in the kitchen. Only one metal chair stood at his tiny round table. That table was the only other piece of visible furniture between here and the bed.

"Mr. Lively," Dair said, "we're very concerned about the things we heard Captain Hook say earlier today, remember? In Craig's voice? We think maybe the bird, or perhaps you yourself, heard something that could help us understand what happened to Craig—"

"I told you, the bird repeats anything that anybody yells. All my training is for naught when he hears people shouting—"

"But Mr. Lively," she tried to copy her mother's gentle tone of voice, "when you think about *what* Captain Hook heard Craig shouting, it becomes very important. We wonder if he heard what happened to Craig. If he did, then he could be very valuable to the police."

"The police?" he asked, his forehead crinkling.

Dair jumped when Captain Hook burst into an imitation of a police siren. No one could continue talking as the parrot perfectly captured the ear-piercing rise and fall of a siren passing by. Matt covered his ears, grimacing. Mom grinned. When Captain Hook faded out the sound as if the cruiser had driven past, he squawked and said in Mr. Lively's voice, *"Just the police. Just the police. There, there, now."* Dair pictured the old man comforting the bird when such disturbing sounds threatened from the outside, as sirens often did, with Cincinnati's five biggest hospitals all clustered nearby.

"Yes, the police are coming over soon," Dair said. "We have some more information, and while they're here, we need to tell them about what the parrot said."

"Now why are you dragging me into this? What have I—"

"No, no, Mr. Lively, please. We think you can *help* us. We just want you to think about when you first heard Captain Hook say those things in Craig's voice."

He puffed out his chest, much as his parrot had earlier. "I heard it for the first time today, when you heard it."

"Did you happen to hear Craig shout those things himself?"

"He certainly never shouted them at me, if that's what you're implying."

"No, no, of course not. But did you hear him shout them at anyone else? Outside?"

"No, I never heard him shout. I would have shouted back, told him to be quiet."

Captain Hook shrieked, spreading his wings, then immediately reprimanded himself in his owner's voice, *"Be quiet, you. The neighbors will complain."*

Mr. Lively glowered at Dair when she laughed. "I don't take courtesy lightly. I try not to disturb you. I don't appreciate your dogs barking."

"Those damn dogs," Captain Hook said.

"I'm sorry if they disturb you," she said. "We try to keep them quiet. We really do."

Mr. Lively snorted and looked past her at the soundless television. "So there's no reason for the police to come up here. They'd just be wasting their time, and mine. And Marielle needs to rest. She doesn't need all this fuss, or the police nosing about."

Nosing about? Someone was dead, after all, wasn't a certain amount of nosing a *good* thing?

Dair's mother asked, "Could you tell us more about when you found him frightened?"

He turned to her, his eyebrows raised, as if he couldn't decide whether to be flattered by, or wary of, her interest.

"I used to have a parrot, too," Mom told Mr. Lively. "A blue-and-gold macaw, not an African gray. Not a master talker like Captain Hook here. I know it's common for birds to frighten easily. They can even die of fright from loud noises. You must take exceptional care of him if he overheard something traumatic and didn't cause himself serious harm."

Again Mom found the magic route. Mr. Lively softened at her praise. "Something sure scared the daylights out of him," he said. "We found him on the bottom of his cage, shaking and pulling out his feathers."

That "we" again.

Dair saw Matt nod and knew her instincts had been correct: Matt had gone somewhere with Mr. Lively yesterday. Marielle believed her son had been home all day. She'd just said it moments ago, and Matt hadn't denied it. He hadn't exactly lied yet, only left an assumption uncorrected, but he wasn't committed to his concealment and was leaking the truth all over the place.

"I wonder," Mom said, gazing at the bird. Captain turned his head from side to side, regarding her with first one lemon eye, then the other. "I wonder, Captain, did you hear Craig shout?" She faced the bird, exhaled softly, relaxed her body.

Watching her, Dair realized how tense her own body was. She tried to relax, too, but the effort only made her crave a glass of wine . . . or a vodka and lemonade . . . or Bailey's in an iced coffee.

She discarded those thoughts when Captain Hook ruffled up his nape feathers and spread his wings. *"Papa? Papa, where are you?"*

"Here, now," Mr. Lively said. "What are you doing? You're upsetting him." But really, Mom wasn't doing anything they could see. Dair realized, with a start, that she did believe her mother was doing something, however. That she was indeed communicating with this bird.

Mr. Lively pushed past Mom and reached for the bird on the perch, but the bird fluttered his wings, ducking out of the old man's hands. And again the bird spoke, as he had that afternoon, in Craig's voice. *"Hey! What the hell are you doing?"* he intoned with every inflection of Craig's voice when he was angry. *"Get away from there!"*

Dair held her breath and waited for new words, new phrases, perhaps the key to the whole puzzle, but that's all the bird said. Then he barked like the dogs—Dair could actually distinguish the difference between Blizzard and Shodan in his imitation. When the real dogs joined in the barking in the backyard, the parrot stopped and asked in a plaintive voice, *"Papa, where are you?"*

"I'm here, buddy. I'm here," Mr. Lively said. Dair swore the man had tears in his eyes as he tried to take the bird in his hands again.

Captain Hook shrieked and said, *"Who's outside? Who's outside?"* over and over again, and imitated the sound of someone knocking on a door. He plucked feathers from his plumped-up chest.

"That's what he did before!" Matt blurted out.

Mr. Lively didn't seem to catch this slip; he was too concerned with his distressed bird. But Dair did. Mom made eye contact, and Dair knew she'd caught it, too. "Here now, stop that, Captain," the man crooned. "Don't hurt yourself. Papa's here. No one's gonna hurt you." Mr. Lively finally got the parrot in his hands and held him to his chest. They stood in silence until the bird relaxed and said, *"So nice."* Mr. Lively stroked the parrot's white head. *"So nice. Isn't that nice?"* the parrot asked.

"I didn't mean to upset him," Mom said. "I'm sorry. Please forgive me."

Mr. Lively nodded, and a tear slipped down his cheek. Dair turned away, wanting to spare him, not wanting to watch him cry, but her gaze fell on Matt and her stomach somersaulted. Surely the old man didn't have anything to do with Craig's death? She couldn't believe that, but would he hide information about it? She could believe that, especially if it meant protecting Matt or Marielle. But . . . *Stop it!* There she went again. This made no sense. Marielle was crazy about Craig.

Matt was, too. Dair was just making stuff up, building a good story, a lie. *Stop it.*

The parrot chirred in Mr. Lively's arms, the sound the equivalent of a cat's purr.

"I'll tell the police everything you told us," Dair said. "But they might want to talk to you themselves."

He scowled. "When are they coming? I put Captain to bed at nine. He doesn't need to be more upset."

"I'll tell them. I promise." She felt tipsy on all this information: If she moved too fast, her head spun. And she longed for the tipsiness to be real, for that warm, bubbly sensation in her head, a glass of wine's special power to deflect her focus from something so troubling. She shook off an image of herself slurping up the Merlot she'd spilled intentionally, lapping it with her tongue from the table. "Thanks for talking to us."

They filed out. *"Good-bye!"* Captain Hook called. Mr. Lively shut his door.

They walked down the steps, not speaking, the ringing metal the only sound. Mom looked at Dair, those circles under her eyes deeper and darker. Matt kept his eyes on the ground, biting his lip. He walked quickly to his back door, ignoring the dogs dancing around him in the gathering autumn dusk.

"Matt, wait," Dair said.

He froze, then turned slowly.

"You went somewhere with Mr. Lively yesterday."

He stared into her eyes a moment, then nodded.

"Does your mom know that?"

He shook his head. "I'm grounded."

"Where did you two go together?"

Matt flickered his gaze to her mom, then back to Dair, and said, "To the zoo. Are you gonna tell my mom?"

"I think I have to."

He slumped his shoulders. "I'll get in so much trouble."

Dair looked at her mom, for help, for guidance, but Mom's gaze told her nothing.

"Matt, this is really important. If Craig came here and you were supposed to be here . . ." She shivered in the chilly autumn air. What if Matt *had* been here? Would he be dead, too? "Yesterday, what time was it when you found Captain Hook all scared?"

His eyes widened. "I had to be home by eleven because that's when Mom would be back. She was signing for some deaf guy's class at the college. We came home at ten-thirty just to be safe."

Dair thought about yesterday morning. She'd been teaching her Saturday class at the Playhouse in the Park. "So," she said, "you were only at the zoo a little while?"

He nodded. "Mr. Lively gets tired. And since we're zoo members, we didn't have to pay, so it didn't really matter how long we stayed."

"And Captain Hook wasn't scared before you left?"

He shook his head.

"So you went right when the zoo opened at nine and were home by ten-thirty." Dair paused. The zoo entrance was at tops a ten-minute walk from their street, maybe fifteen minutes with Mr. Lively. Dair had no idea how the old man handled the steep front steps, much less the walk down Vine Street. "So . . . ," she said. "We know Craig came over sometime during that hour and a half."

Matt's mouth dropped open. He nodded but winced as if he felt physical pain.

A lot of hours spanned from ten-thirty to shortly after four, when Dair had seen Craig fall to his death. Nearly time enough for a full-length play to perform twice.

"Let me tell her," Matt begged.

"Okay," Dair said. "But you have to *now*, tonight, when the police come."

He opened the door, stepped into his kitchen, then turned back to the women, pale. "I think they're here already."

"You'll be fine. We'll back you up."

He went inside. Dair started to follow, but Mom grabbed her arm. "The parrot heard it all," she said. "A scuffle, a struggle. Your dogs barking. He kept calling for his 'Papa.' When it quieted down, someone knocked on the door to the apartment. Kept knocking. I think someone may have heard him and thought he was a person."

"Mom, this is so . . . messed up." Dair leaned in the door frame. "If our dogs barked, can they tell you anything?"

Mom shook her head. "They won't latch on to language the way the parrot does. There's too many things they bark at outside. Squirrels, the mailman, people walking by. I can't get them to distinguish any one event in particular."

Dair nodded and watched Mom study her face.

"So you believe me?" Mom asked.

The knowledge that she did burned through Dair like a shot of tequila. "Yeah, I do. I—it's . . . amazing. Can—can I ask you something?"

"Of course."

"If you can get all that from animals, can you—can you read people, too?"

Mom cocked her head, then lowered her gaze and played with the doorknob with her fingers. "People usually have barriers," she said softly. "It's more difficult to receive. They're not *trying* to communicate telepathically . . . often they're doing the exact opposite. They don't say the same message that they think."

"You mean they lie."

Mom nodded.

"Animals don't lie?"

Mom laughed. "Oh, good heavens, *yes,* they lie. Haven't the dogs ever acted like Peyton hadn't fed them so you'd give them a second meal?"

Dair smiled. "All the time."

"Birds pretend their wings are broken to lead predators from the nest, possums pretend to be dead . . . animals lie. They just don't lie about *emotions.* It's the emotional honesty that makes them easier to read."

Emotional honesty. That sounded like dangerous terrain. "What do you mean?"

"A dog won't pretend to be happy to see you if he's not. He won't feign wagging his tail and dancing around if he honestly doesn't like you."

Dair thought a minute. "You never really answered me. Or . . . maybe you did. You can read people, can't you?"

Mom shrugged. "I don't choose to. Only occasionally do I get something, and it's usually something a person doesn't have guarded, something . . . vulnerable." Mom played with the doorknob again. "Now, can I ask you a question?"

Dair nodded.

Mom lifted her head, looked Dair right in the eye. She touched Dair's arm. "Why—if you don't have a drinking problem—are you hiding bottles in your closet?"

Dair tried to tug her arm away, but Mom held tight. Dair loved and hated her equally in that moment. Loved her mother for letting her off the hook, for not exposing her in front of Peyton and Marielle. Hated her mother for knowing this about her.

Dair jerked her arm free and walked into Marielle's kitchen. She could tell only so many truths in one day.

Matt appeared in the hall. "You guys," he said, "the police are leaving."

Already? What? Dair rushed down the hall to the living room, where two uniformed police officers and one man in a suit headed for the front door. They couldn't be leaving.

Marielle sat on the couch, her face worse than when they'd told her Craig was dead. Totally spent, drained, as though someone had pulled a plug on her.

Peyton's face looked as if he suspected someone were playing a sick joke on him, his shoulders tense, spine rigid, fists balled in his jeans pockets.

"Wait," Dair said to the officers. "Are you going to talk to Mr. Lively, our neighbor?"

"We have that information," the suited man said. He said it kindly, but a smirk played around the corner of his mouth.

Peyton shook his head at her, sending her some sort of warning.

The front door closed behind them. "But—did they get the clothes?" Peyton nodded and rubbed his face as if he'd been awake for days and days. Silence settled like dust in the room. Marielle stared at the floor. Matt looked up at Dair with his large, unblinking eyes. Mom hesitated in the kitchen doorway, Slip Jig rubbing against her shins.

Dair waited. Finally Marielle spoke. "They found heroin."

Dair blinked. "What?"

"In the autopsy," she said.

Chapter Nine

Marielle and Matt were tucked into Dair and Peyton's guest bedroom—Marielle having been convinced not to go to a hotel—Mom had called to say she was safely home, and Dair and Peyton sank into their own bed, reaching for each other.

Their bed was queen-size, but they usually occupied the space of a twin bed together, a lovely tumble of entwined limbs and long hair. They were too numb, too exhausted, to make love. They simply escaped to sleep.

Dair dreamed her recurring dream of being in her childhood bed, by her childhood window, and the tap tap tap of a bird's beak on the glass. Sylvan, the chickadee, fluttered at the window. Dair watched for the little dark-haired girl, but she hardly ever came anymore. The little gray-and-white bird with its black cap continued its tap tap tap as if it had something critical to impart to her. Dair tried to listen but heard only the *thunk*ing against the glass. The bird, in frustration, flew away, and Dair flung open the window to shout, "Wait!"

Dair jerked awake, the cry a garbled noise deep in her throat. She sat up. She was in her grown-up bed, her grown-up bedroom. She sensed, before she saw in the moonlight, that the bed was empty except for herself. She hadn't awakened Peyton because he wasn't there. Her heart *thunk*ed, sharply, like the bird's beak on the glass.

Blizzard lifted his white, bearlike face over the foot of the bed and yawned. "Hey," Dair whispered. He stood and shook his collar, tags jingling.

She got out of bed and stood naked in the moonlight. "Where's Peyton?" she whispered. "Where's Shodie?" Blizzard yawned again and sat at her feet, glowing as if the moon were black light illuminating his white fur. Dair tried to picture an image of Shodan, the way Mom had said she pictured them getting ready to go home at the park. "Where's Shodie?" she whispered again.

Blizzard stared at her blankly, and Dair turned away, feeling ridiculous. She pulled her purple chenille robe off the back of the door and put it on. Her mother might have this gift, but she was wrong when she'd said Dair had it herself.

Dair slipped out of the room and into the hall. The door to the guest bedroom stood slightly ajar. She peeked in and saw Marielle's and Matt's heads on the pillows—Matt's curls incandescent in the moonlight like Blizzard's fur. Marielle ought to sleep deeply. She'd polished off the rest of that bottle of Merlot pretty much on her own. Dair had drunk a glass and a half. She loved the soothing languor it wrapped around her brain, but here she was, now wide awake and wanting more.

She looked at the hall closet. Earlier, while Peyton had gone downstairs to make sure the doors were locked, and Matt and Marielle were already in their guest room, Dair had whisked the vodka bottle out of the closet and under the bed into a Capezio shoebox, stashing her now homeless character shoes in a drawer. She'd managed to be under the covers by the time Peyton came back up the stairs. That closet door was now open. Hadn't she closed it? Or was she just being paranoid?

After checking the bathroom, she tiptoed down the stairs, Blizzard following her. Faint light led her to the empty kitchen, where Blizzard stopped to slurp from his water bowl. The light spilled up from the open basement door. Fear quickened her heartbeat and made her consider calling Peyton's name to make sure it was he she heard softly rustling something.

But she feared something else more than an intruder, so she stayed silent.

She listened for a moment. The rustling wasn't rhythmic enough to be Peyton practicing his aikido walks—twelve measured, cadenced sets of movement, each eight counts. Dair had sat on these stairs many times watching the ritual, hypnotizing as dance, trancelike as meditation. But the sound she heard was not Peyton's bare feet whispering on the wooden floor.

She crept down the steps until she could bend and see into the basement. Only one lightbulb was on, creating odd shadows in the stone walls. Shodan was sprawled asleep in the middle of the dance floor. Peyton knelt at the old dresser in one corner, wearing a pair of loose black sweatpants. The battered dresser was from Dair's college days, relegated now to storage. She watched Peyton rummage through a drawer she knew contained wrapping paper and ribbon. "Peyton?"

He stood up abruptly, startled. He turned to face her, closing the drawer with one leg.

"What are you doing?"

He shrugged. "I couldn't sleep."

She came down the remaining stairs. Shodan lifted her head, blinking at Dair, and wagged her stump of a tail. Blizzard padded down the stairs behind Dair and went to Shodan, licking her face.

"What are you looking for?" Dair asked, gesturing to the drawer.

"Nothing. Wrapping paper. Stuff like that."

"Why are you looking for wrapping paper?"

He sighed and ran a hand through his hair, pushing it out of his face. In the dim light, the shadows defined the muscles in his chest and abdomen in clear, cut lines. Too late to be believed, he said, "Well, you know, your birthday's coming up." Dair stared at him. "Look, I'm not looking at wrapping paper," he said. "I told you, I couldn't sleep. I'm just . . . wandering."

He started to walk past her, and she took his hands. She stretched out both his arms, palms up, lifted his palms to her lips, and kissed them, slowly, taking her time. She studied the soft white skin inside his wrists and elbows, the map of blue veins, that one small bruise she'd noticed yesterday.

"What are you doing?" he asked in a flat, cold voice. His body had gone still as he submitted to her inspection. When she let go of his hands, he lowered his arms to his sides, controlled and deliberate as a choreographed movement. He kept his eyes locked on hers.

"Go ahead," he said, smiling a smile that scared her. He pointed to the dresser. "Go look. You know you want to."

Dair swallowed and shook her head. She didn't want to.

But he knew why. "You go look," he commanded her. "Because you don't believe me, and I won't have that. Go look in the goddamn drawer, Dair."

"I—I do believe you."

"No, you don't," he said so harshly that both dogs cocked their heads. "Here." In two strides he was back at the dresser. He yanked out the drawer in question and dumped its contents on the floor. He dropped to his hands and knees and shook through all the paper, tossing aside what he'd handled, spreading it all over the basement floor.

Dair went and knelt beside him. "Peyton, don't," she whispered. "Please. I'm sorry."

"See anything?" he asked. "Sure you looked carefully enough? Want to check the rest of them, too?" He stood and jerked another drawer out of the dresser.

She sat on the floor, her eyes stinging. "Stop it. Please? I'm sorry."

He looked down at her, panting slightly, the muscles across his flat, hard stomach rising and falling. He held the drawer, knuckles white, poised to dump it like the other.

"I'm sorry," she repeated. "I was just—I woke up and I was scared."

He sighed, and his face softened. He set the drawer carefully on top of the dresser. "Okay. Okay, fine. That's fair," he said. "Well, I'm scared, too, okay? So tell me something: I've looked in the hall closet, and I've looked through the kitchen and living room, and the basement. All that's left is the rest of upstairs. What am I going to find if I keep looking? If I keep searching through every drawer and closet and under every goddamn bed?"

She heard that tap, tapping again, only the bird's beak was in her chest, hammering into her sternum. "What are you looking for?" she asked.

"I'm looking, very specifically, for one bottle of Absolut that this morning was in our freezer and now is gone. I know you can put it away, my dear, but never *that* fast."

The cold concrete floor seeped through her robe, and she shivered. She pictured the bottle hidden safely under the bed and said, "What are you talking about?"

"I'm talking about this new, rather dangerous step you've taken." When she didn't answer, he crouched before her and took her face in his hands. "Dair," he whispered, "you never tried to hide it before. Don't you see what you're doing?"

She pulled her face from his grasp and scooted away from him, but he grabbed her ankle, preventing her from standing. A faint ammonia odor from Godot's litter box reached her nostrils. She jerked her foot free and stood. "This is such bullshit." She headed for the basement steps, but he was on his feet, quick as a cat, and blocked her.

"Is it? Then tell me, where's the bottle of Absolut?"

"It's gone," she said. "It's been gone, I just haven't bought more. What's the—"

"God, you're *such* a liar," he said with an almost admiring tone of voice. "You didn't even flinch when you said that. But it's only been 'gone' since this morning. You didn't drink any before you left with Marielle, but you had quite a bit before you headed out with your mom, and then, before dinner, the whole goddamn bottle disappeared."

"Jesus! Are you spying on me?"

He gestured toward the dresser and the mess he'd left. "Weren't you spying on me?"

"Please. The situations hardly compare."

He narrowed his eyes. "What's that supposed to mean?"

She didn't want to say it. But it felt like the only protection against the ice pick of that beak splitting into her bone. "You know what it means. *You* have some nerve. I hardly think you have the room to—"

His expression shut her up. She welcomed his anger, almost felt relief. He took a deep breath, though, and it faded. And the expression that replaced it finally splintered her sternum. She had to press a hand between her breasts. He sat on the stairs as if suddenly too weary to stand. "I knew you'd say that." His voice was almost emotionless, with a hint of sorrow. "I knew it. And that's okay. It's the easiest thing to say." He took another breath and exhaled slowly, with control. He raised his face to her, and his eyes glittered. "Dair, I know you too well. It's *because* the situations compare that I know what you're doing. And you're scaring me, love." He sniffed and drew his forearm over his face. "I know exactly what you're doing, because I've been there, too."

It scared her to see him cry. The dogs seemed to sense it, flanking her on either side, looking at Peyton on the stairs, whimpering their concern, raising their faces to Dair as if to ask, *What's wrong with him? Aren't you going to fix it?*

She cleared her throat. "When you say Craig wasn't a drug user, how do you know that?"

He stopped rubbing his face. "What are you asking me, Dair?"

"You told Marielle you knew Craig didn't use drugs. How are you so certain?"

He stared as if trying to see into her mind, something she felt he was frequently able to do.

"That's not what you want to know. If you want to ask me something, you're going to have to ask it."

"Why do you always back me into a corner?"

"Why do you always work so hard to change the subject? You're a master at that. You don't want to discuss what we're discussing, and presto, before anyone can blink, we've seamlessly moved on, haven't we? Don't think I don't notice."

The tap tap began anew. What was he saying? Had he noticed this with Sylvan?

"I asked you a question," Peyton said calmly. "And I asked it straight out: Where is the bottle of Absolut? If you want to know something, you'll have to ask it straight out, too. Only I'll answer honestly."

"Fuck you."

"Fuck *you*." They both froze, eyes wide with surprise and amazement. Dair wanted to suck the words back into her mouth.

"I can't believe you said that," he said. "You've *never* said that to me."

"I'm sorry," she said. And she meant it. The air in the basement felt tainted. "I'm sorry. But . . ."

"Where's the bottle of Absolut?" he asked.

"Now who's changing the subject?"

He laughed, and she wanted to slap him. "I'm *not* changing the subject. I'm trying to keep you on it. Where's the bottle of Absolut?"

"All right, fine," she said. "You want me to ask so bad, I'll ask: Are you using again?"

Without hesitation he said, "Nope."

Dair took a deep breath. She believed him. "Do you think about it?"

"Every day."

The certainty and speed of this answer saddened her. Made her feel she didn't measure up in some way. If she were perhaps a better wife or friend, he wouldn't have this need, this want. But that made no sense. If ever she'd found a soul mate, it was Peyton, but he didn't stop her own need.

He watched her carefully. "Dair, just because I think about it doesn't mean there's anything lacking in my life. It's like I divorced somebody. Just because I don't live with them anymore doesn't mean they cease to exist."

She nodded, hugging herself in her robe. "Do you think Craig was using heroin?"

He shook his head.

"How do you know that?"

He shrugged. "I can pick another addict out of a crowd, the way, I don't know, the same way I can pick out another dancer in a room of actors, or the way Malcolm or C.J. talk about picking out other gay guys in a crowd. There's something shared. It's like we speak the same language, like we're the only English speakers in a foreign country. We understand each other. Craig didn't speak that language."

Dair didn't think he did, either. She could tell by the infuriating way he'd nurse a beer, making it awkward for her to order another until he finished. The way he'd let a beer get completely empty before flagging down the waitress. He didn't need the insurance, he didn't feel the impending deprivation.

"You know he didn't," Peyton whispered. "For the same reason I know he didn't. And for the same reason that I know what you're doing, and it scares me. Please, Dair. Where's the bottle of Absolut?"

She felt the lie welling within her. She let it fill her eyes while it grew and took shape. Part of her wanted to squelch it, but she knew she wouldn't; it was instinct now, like survival. "I—I dumped it," she said, hearing the catch in her throat of authentic tears. "My mom talked to me in the park and I"—she sucked in a breath—"and I was so, so mad, but"—another sob—"I knew she was right. I was so . . . embarrassed that you knew . . . and I thought, I'll show them, I'll show them I don't have a problem." She turned away, wiping her runny nose and tears with her robe sleeve. And as she knew he would be, he was at her side in a second, his arms around her, his lips on her forehead, his hands stroking her hair.

"You don't have to be embarrassed, Dair," he whispered, holding her to him. "It's okay. You don't have to prove anything, or hide anything."

She cried into his neck. Her regret, her shame, at least, were true. She loved this man so much, felt dependent on him, as if her blood supply and ability to breathe and eat and function were somehow linked to him. She wanted not to hurt him. But he was wrong: She *did* have to hide, and she did have to be embarrassed.

And this little episode in the basement was a very close call.

They didn't make it back to their bed until nearly three in the morning. They got sidetracked in the living room, where they made love, urgently, quietly, because of their guests upstairs. Peyton sat on the couch and Dair straddled him, her open robe cloaking them, her breasts in line with his lips, his hands under the robe, on her buttocks, lifting her, moving her, her hands braced on the couch behind his head, fingers clawing, fluttering over the fabric every time she came. "Shh," Peyton said often, once even putting a hand over her mouth.

They eventually lost the robe, growing slick and sweaty. Blizzard, always one to join in any game, tried to climb onto the couch beside them, sniffling under Dair's arm, licking her shoulder. She laughed quietly and nudged him away and was vaguely aware of him following Shodan up the stairs to the bedroom. Godot held his ground in one corner of the couch but turned his back on them prudishly, ears flat, shoulders hunched.

When Dair heard the shift in breathing that signaled Peyton's impending orgasm, she watched his face and delighted in that expression of ecstasy. Afterward they grinned at each other, panting. "Beat ya," she teased. "Four to one."

He shook his head, chuckling breathlessly. "Not fair. Not fair at all." Without disengaging himself from her, he hugged her tight and lowered her onto her back on the couch. Lying under him, she wrapped her legs around his rib cage, locking her ankles together, reveling in that surge of warmth he'd released.

He rested his head on her chest, under her chin, and she fumbled on the floor with one hand for her robe, pulling it atop them. They lay there savoring the afterplay until they got cold and tiptoed up to their room, where the dogs had taken over the bed.

"Everybody out of the pool," Peyton scolded them softly. Blizzard and Shodan sighed and reluctantly dropped back to the floor as Dair and Peyton crawled under the quilts the dogs had left warm and toasty for them.

They interlaced their bodies again, and Dair whispered, "If Craig wasn't using heroin, what does this autopsy mean? Would he have . . . I mean, could he have tried it, just once."

Peyton shook his head and kissed her hair. "Hardly anybody just 'tries' heroin, you know? It's not like pot getting passed around at a party."

She thought about that.

"I wonder if they can tell if he smoked it or injected it."

Peyton tensed beside her. "What difference would that make?"

"Well, you couldn't make someone smoke, could you? That'd be tough. But somebody else could've injected him, right?"

"Jesus," Peyton whispered. "Yeah. But you can also snort it, or take it in nose drops or eyedrops, or, hell, even opium *suppositories*. There's a ton of ways someone could've given it to him. But *why?*"

"I don't know. I'm just trying to make sense of it. So, the cops think it was a drug deal . . . but that still doesn't explain the dress. Or what he was doing up on Clifton Ridge."

"I don't know," Peyton said. He sighed heavily, his rib cage rising, then sinking beneath her.

Dair hugged Peyton tight and kissed his cheek, his eyelid, that little scar she knew was there but couldn't see in the dark.

"Dair?" he asked. "How can your dad not believe your mom? How can *you* not believe your mom?"

This question frightened Dair for some reason. "I don't . . . I never saw her like this before," she whispered. "She never did that—talked to an animal like that in front of us."

Peyton made a troubled noise. "Your dad . . . this seems like something he'd accept. Hell, I think he'd welcome it. This divorce, it doesn't make sense."

Dair didn't think it did, either, but was afraid to say so out loud.

She remembered again Dad cutting Mom off when she tried to talk about Bob Henderson's mare. After the fifth-grade report, Dair had felt a new understanding of her father, and it pained her to think that he felt as embarrassed as she had standing in front of that laughing class. It helped Dair feel justified in dismissing her mother herself. But . . . what she'd witnessed tonight couldn't be dismissed.

Eventually Peyton fell asleep. She matched her breathing to his own, hoping to follow him into dreams. She stared at the fat white moon through the window and thought about that open closet outside their door. Peyton had checked there. Did he remember what Blizzard said at dinner?

What Blizzard said at dinner. How absurd. But . . . she tried to pare down her habitual resistance. How else could her mother have known about Slip Jig and the window? About the ceiling fan? About the vodka bottle?

And her mother had said Dair could do this, too.

Mom had said Dair talked to Snowflake. Dair pictured that cat with her long white hair, her eyes that blue green of a glacier pool, her nose and lips mottled in black freckles. She'd slept on Dair's pillow, purring, kneading her paws. Dair would wake up in the night and she'd have slipped away, so gently that Dair hadn't noticed the sound or the kneading stop. In the morning, Snowflake would slink back and sit on Dair's chest, telling her every detail of her night's adventures with those magical blue eyes. One morning, in her bedroom, Snowflake peered into Dair's eyes and Dair saw fat, grinning raccoons in the moonlit garden and later found the corncobs they'd devoured and tossed about the yard like vandals. Another morning, under Snowflake's gaze, Dair heard a rabbit shriek, felt it shudder. And later that day she found a baby bunny in the side yard, the puncture marks in its broken neck as neat as if it'd been taken by a vampire.

Was that it—communication? Is that how her mother had seen images from Slip Jig? But Dair's pictures from Snowflake just *happened;* Dair didn't ask for them. Dair thought about receiving those images, tried to recall what it felt like. Some vague alarm sounded somewhere within her and tried to nudge what felt like a recent memory into focus, but just as had happened when trying the communication with Blizzard earlier, her attempt produced only blankness.

Remembering those days made weight settle in Dair's chest. Those memories felt so lonely. That familiar sensation, of a burdensome yearning, mystified her.

Had she always felt it? She stared at the ceiling, confused. And what was it a yearning *for?* To fill some sort of loss. An emptiness. And had that yearning begun when she stopped listening to the animals? Or had it always been there?

After the report in fifth grade, the other kids tormented her for months even after the summer. The sixth-grade classroom gerbil fell sick and stopped eating, staring out of the glass with dull eyes. The kids joked, "Ask Dair's mom what's wrong with him. Maybe somebody hurt his feelings." The gerbil was a *she,* and she was depressed because she was lonely and bored—constantly pleading for attention, for play, for a friend—but Dair didn't volunteer that information. She just rolled her eyes and shook her head as she'd learned to do when they teased her, and because she was a good sport and didn't cry or fly into a tizzy, her classmates eventually believed she thought talking to animals was silliness, too.

And she started to believe it herself. It was important, that acceptance, that her classmates felt she was normal, she belonged. Something about her was incomplete; she'd sensed it way back then, and connection with those kids, however tenuous, took some—not all—of that ache away. Those were the worst years. Before junior high. In junior high, in a bathroom stall with Mandy at the holiday dance, she'd discovered alcohol.

There was something restful about that warm hum her first sips of sloe gin produced. That hum eased the ever-present sense of emptiness, of sadness. The hum allowed her to relax and her mind to quiet. Those images of marauding raccoons and dead bunnies stopped. Those forlorn and begging voices hushed. Not hearing them made it easier to deny. Was her mother right? Did the alcohol cause static? Had it created the emptiness?

But no . . . starting in junior high, her life got *better.* The emptiness existed *before.* In seventh grade she "came out" as a liar in a totally acceptable way: Mandy talked her into auditioning for the winter play with her. Dair ended up getting cast, and Mandy didn't. Dair walked into the first rehearsal and found the cast playing "freeze and replace," an improvisational game. She watched a few rounds, and when the director noticed her, she said, "Freeze! Dair, jump in," and some cute boy pushed her into the center of the circle, where two other kids stood frozen, holding crazy poses.

"Pick a person," Miss Perkins instructed her. "Tap one, take their pose, and, based on the pose, start a new scene." So Dair did. She tapped the girl who had her hands held over her face. In the seconds it took Dair to copy the pose, she ran through all the possibilities for this scene.

She could be weeping from the horrible news she'd just received—that she had cancer or her sister died or she flunked her math test; or she could be about to throw up—from the poison she just drank or the horrible food her hostess served her or from being in zero gravity in the space shuttle; or she could be praying, or sneezing. . . . Her problem wasn't finding a story to tell, but deciding *which one*. She decided to reveal her new face after plastic surgery.

Eleven more rounds passed before anyone replaced her in the circle, and then it was too late. She was high. No amount of sloe gin could match that hum.

And she got a bigger role in the next play. And the lead in the one after that.

And the emptiness sort of went away.

But not really. It had never *really* gone away until she met Peyton and had that feeling of finding something she'd lost.

She couldn't bear to feel that loss again. Would she, if she kept drinking? What would Peyton do if he found the bottle of Absolut? And what had their conversation accomplished, really, except yet another emergency thatch on her leaking roof of lies? Was it all right for her to drink as long as she didn't hide it?

Peyton snored, a gentle wheeze like a cat purring. She'd never told him she *wouldn't* drink, so why was this so humiliating? Didn't she hide her drinking to protect *him?* Keep *him* from temptation? He never seemed tempted, though. She envied his strength.

So . . . she drank a little. Big deal. She got through her days, she went to work. Where was the problem? Alcoholics were muddled thinkers, right? Surely not capable of juggling as many balls as she had in the air. No alcoholic had the memory it took to keep these untruths from crashing to the ground.

She drifted off, but it was hard to sleep with that damn chickadee rapping away at the window.

Chapter Ten

Knocking hammered in the back of Peyton's head. Someone pounded on a door. This had never happened before in this familiar dream. That dream of Dair in another life. In the dream he was sick. He knew he would die, but he was comforted by her embrace. No one had ever knocked before. No one else had ever entered the dream.

Dogs barked, and he struggled not to surface all the way, fought to will himself back under, into sleep. He liked the dream. It soothed him in spite of the sorrow.

The knocking sounded again, after a silence. Make it a drum, he told himself. Make it music. But it was short, staccato. Had no rhythm to latch on to. No meter he could identify. Barking and clawing accompanied it, and the dogs' nails on the bedroom door finally scratched his brain into the realization that the knocking was real.

He opened his eyes to a room flooded with daylight, felt Dair's limbs intertwined with his own, her hair strewn over his torso.

"Who's outside?" Captain Hook screeched from above them. Dair moaned, then laughed against Peyton's chest.

He turned his head to the clock. "Oh, man, it's ten. I didn't mean to sleep this late."

"Blizzard! Shodie! Hush!" Dair scolded, rolling away from him, reaching for her robe.

Peyton pulled on his sweatpants again. The dogs bolted past him when he opened the door, scrambling down the stairs, growling and snarling. He stepped into the hall and saw Marielle standing at the guest bedroom door, peering down the stairs.

He wished he knew how to wipe away those lines of worry on her forehead.

In the living room, he glanced out the front door window. Malcolm Cole stood on their porch, holding a white paper bag and some flowers wrapped in green plastic. The whine in the back of Peyton's head sputtered feedback. He wished he'd had the guts to tell Dair the truth about when he'd returned Saturday and why he'd come back to town early. But he remembered her inspection of his arms last night and didn't want her to feel that same horrible resentment; not even to show her what it felt like every time she did that to him.

Dair stood behind him, in her robe, and Marielle still hovered in the guest room doorway at the top of the stairs. "It's just Malcolm," he told them.

Dair suddenly looked worried, but Marielle looked relieved and put a hand to her heart. She looked down at herself in her nightgown, signed something—forgetting, as she often did, that they didn't understand sign—and ducked back into the room.

Peyton took a deep breath and prayed that his lie was not about to explode in his face. He opened the front door, blocking the dogs with his body.

"Oh, sorry," Malcolm said, a red stripe crossing his pale face as Peyton's appearance registered. "You were still in bed."

"Yeah, but it's okay. Don't worry. Are you all right?" Peyton squinted at him, checking for signs, for clues, peering into Malcolm's eyes for pinned pupils, at his skin for unnatural sweat on this cold morning. Malcolm stared right back at him—with normal eyes—and knew what Peyton was doing. A fist tightened somewhere in Peyton's guts. He'd been subjected to this very inspection last night. He knew firsthand how humiliating it was.

Malcolm lifted the flowers and opened his mouth to say something, but Blizzard and Shodan squeezed past Peyton's legs, and Blizzard jumped up, greeting Malcolm with a hug.

Malcolm held his bag and flowers safely away from Blizzard in outstretched arms, craning his neck to keep his face away from the Great Pyrenees's tongue. Peyton grabbed Blizzard's collar and hauled him off, but he'd left a wide swath of white hair on Malcolm's black leather jacket.

"Here," Dair said. Peyton grinned at her trying to keep her robe closed while she handled Shodan. "I'll put them out in the backyard." She took Blizzard's collar from Peyton's grip and lugged the dogs from the room.

"Sorry," Peyton said.

Malcolm looked stunned.

"Here, c'mon in." Peyton led Malcolm into the living room. "You okay?" he asked again.

"I'm fine," Malcolm said, tucking the bag under one arm and fussing with the bouquet with those weird little hands of his. They were too small, like a doll's, and they creeped Peyton out a little. "I . . . um, brought some things for Marielle, but I wondered if you—I mean, since I don't really know her, I didn't want to . . ."

"You didn't have to do that." Peyton tried to picture himself taking gifts to someone he didn't know. It felt odd, almost too familiar. If Malcolm died, would Peyton go take something to Malcolm's boyfriend, if he had one? But what did he know—maybe it was nice, a good gesture. He paused too long and made Malcolm paranoid.

"I mean," Malcolm said, "I didn't want to knock on her door. She wouldn't know me."

"She knows you," Peyton assured him. "And anyway, she's here, upstairs. She and her son stayed here last night."

Malcolm shuffled his leather boots, his sharp cologne reaching Peyton from across the room. Peyton couldn't stop looking at Malcolm's hands. Hands usually gave a drag queen away, but Peyton had seen Malcolm do drag at an AIDS fund-raiser once, and he knew that if he'd seen Malcolm anywhere but there, Malcolm would've fooled him. He and Dair had agreed that Malcolm was the best one of the night.

"If you could just give her these," Malcolm said. "You know, tell her I know Craig and—" He froze and winced but didn't correct himself to speak in past tense.

Peyton felt disgusting with his bed head and morning mouth. And he felt stupid, standing shirtless in front of Malcolm. Malcolm stood there, not moving for the door. Peyton sensed Malcolm didn't really want to leave. And although Peyton didn't want him to stay, he felt sorry for him; he remembered too well that sense of rebuilding his life, what it felt like to know that the few people who knew him didn't trust him.

"Want some coffee?" Peyton asked.

"Uh . . . sure." Malcolm said it casually, but his eyes were grateful.

In the kitchen, Dair turned around from the back door, having successfully herded the dogs outside. He watched her eyes sparkle at his bare chest, a twitch playing at the corner of her mouth. Heat spread in Peyton's cheeks.

"Hey, Malcolm," she said softly.

"Hey, Dair."

She opened her mouth and cocked her head as if to ask him something, but must've changed her mind. "I've gotta shower. I work at the zoo today."

Peyton nodded, and the room felt empty, as usual, when she left it.

"Can I leave these here for Marielle?" Malcolm asked, setting his bag and the flowers on the table.

"Sure."

Peyton opened the freezer—the frigid blast of air making him even more aware of his bare skin—and took out their bag of coffee beans, missing the familiar fixture of Dair's bottle of Absolut. Had she really poured it out? He wouldn't be surprised if she'd decided to pour out the bottle, and told him she had, but actually hadn't done it yet. She told "chronological lies" like that all the time. That was okay, but he worried she might change her mind.

Malcolm moved beside Peyton at the counter, glancing toward the hall. "Um . . . Bethany saw us downtown Saturday."

Peyton froze with one hand in the bag of silky beans. "What did she say?"

"She just wondered what we were doing."

"What do you mean?"

"She just asked, real casual, 'Oh, I saw you and Peyton Saturday. What were you doing?'"

"And what did you tell her?"

"I just said I was out and ran into you and we were grabbing lunch."

The whine in Peyton's head screeched to full volume. He poured a handful of beans into the coffee grinder and pressed the lid. The high, drill-like buzz filled the room, drowning out the whine. He held the button down on the grinder longer than was necessary.

Silence filled the room when he finished and lasted until he filled the coffeepot with water.

"Look," Malcolm whispered, "um, Bethany might, you know, say something to Dair."

"If she does, then I'll explain. But she might not."

"You shouldn't keep secrets from your wife."

"It's not a secret *from* her, really, because it has nothing to do with her. She doesn't need to know. Okay? It would only change how she feels about you, and—" He stopped abruptly as Dair came back into the kitchen, still in her robe. Peyton hadn't heard her on the stairs. She casually handed him a blue fleece pullover, and he wanted to kiss her. She poured herself some orange juice and offered some to Malcolm, who declined. Peyton gratefully pulled on the fleece.

"Those are beautiful," she said, tipping her head toward the flowers. "Those are for Marielle?"

Malcolm nodded. She hesitated, looking at him, then took a sharp breath and asked, "Have you talked to Gayle lately?"

Malcolm frowned and scratched at the stubble of a mustache and goatee stippled around his mouth. "Uh . . . no. I mean, I talked to her on the phone. I haven't seen her since she got back."

Dair pursed her lips and studied Malcolm. "You weren't over there Saturday? Or any time recently?"

Malcolm looked from Dair to Peyton and stammered, "N-no." Peyton knew Malcolm must have been thinking Peyton had betrayed his trust. Peyton shook his head slightly at Malcolm. Dair seemed uncertain, as if she wanted to ask more but didn't know what.

"The autopsy results are in this morning's paper," Malcolm said into the awkward silence. "They did a blood analysis. They found . . . heroin." He stumbled over the word, the way they all did over Craig's name. The feelings of loss were similar, Peyton knew all too well.

"The police told us that last night," Dair said. "But it can't be right."

Peyton nodded. "Craig wouldn't know heroin from Sweet'n Low, much less know what to do with it if he did. And I can't see him *wanting* to." Thinking about it provoked the whine in his brain. He pretended it was a violin and visualized the fragments of choreography he'd learned of a new piece titled *What Is Found, What Is*

Lost, What Is Remembered. The music written for it haunted him. He used it now to disguise the shrill sound of his craving.

"The paper said they searched his apartment," Malcolm said. "They didn't find anything—no drugs, no women's clothing, no suicide note."

Peyton sighed. It seemed too exhausting to try to explain the clothes and the window and the parrot to Malcolm. The police'd been very interested in the clothes and window—all this seemed to support their drug deal scenario—but hadn't taken the information about the parrot seriously at all. To their credit, they hadn't laughed or cut Peyton off, and the one detective had dutifully written down his account. He knew they'd probably had a good laugh at his expense when they'd left, though. Bunch of damn junkies, he imagined them saying, thinking we can take a statement from a goddamn parrot!

"Well," Dair said, "I've got to go get ready."

Malcolm watched her leave the room, his face anxious.

Peyton poured the water into the top of the coffeemaker and turned it on. Both he and Malcolm stood waiting for its gurgling to begin, like waiting onstage for a cue.

When it bubbled to life, Peyton said, "Just so *you* know, Dair knows you had a key to Gayle's house."

"Oh," Malcolm said, as if finally understanding Dair's questions. Then he frowned. "How'd she find that out?"

"Gayle told her."

"What the hell?"

"Yeah . . . I don't know, but Dair's really freaked out. You know she's been feeding Gayle's cat, bringing in her mail."

"Why would Gayle tell Dair that? What a fucking bitch. And I could've fed her damn cat, if she hadn't gone all weird on me."

"Hey, she tried to help you, which is more than I ever expected from her."

"But why is she blabbing all this—"

They heard footsteps on the stairs and looked toward the living room.

"Oh," Matt said, freezing in the kitchen doorway, staring at Malcolm, surprised. "Uh, hi."

"Matt, this is Malcolm Cole, a friend of ours."

Malcolm smiled. "Hi there."

Dark smudges circled Matt's eyes. The poor kid wasn't getting much sleep.

A fresh, yeasty aroma reached Peyton from the white bakery bag Malcolm had set on the table. His stomach growled, craving pastries and cinnamon rolls. He needed to eat. Malcolm's voice was already too similar to the whine. The last thing he needed was to get blasted with it in stereo. "You want some pancakes?" he asked Matt. It was the only thing he knew how to do for this boy.

Matt shook his head. "No. Mom says we'll go out to eat."

That made Peyton nervous. In a restaurant they might overhear other people discussing Craig and this bogus autopsy. If he were Marielle, he'd lock himself inside. But he wasn't. And it struck him that Marielle was moving through this pain fueled on nothing but her own authentic feelings. Okay, so she'd had a little too much to drink last night, but only a little. Nothing like the oblivion he'd embrace if he ever lost Dair.

Malcolm sat at the table, scooting the mail and some papers out of the way. Cassie's workshop brochure sat on top of the pile. She'd left Peyton one, just as she'd promised. Peyton reached into the purple cupboard for some coffee mugs.

The dogs barked at the back door, demanding their breakfast.

Marielle came into the kitchen, her eyes puffy, her skin sallow. "Malcolm?" she asked.

He stood and shuffled his boots. "I—um—just wanted . . . I knew Craig and . . ."

"Thank you," Marielle rescued him. "Craig said wonderful things about you. And so did Jimmy. I guess we both knew each other's . . . others."

At this Malcolm looked as if he might vomit. Instead he handed her the gifts. Marielle went through all the motions of friendliness and good manners—oohing over the flowers and the apple-filled croissants in the bag—but she reminded Peyton of someone just marking the steps in rehearsal.

Malcolm sat back down and fidgeted with the mail on the table, turning Cassie's brochure over and over again in his hands.

"Thanks for letting us stay," Marielle said to Peyton. She hesitated at the back door, and Peyton watched her body language shift from resolve to surrender. She turned back to him. "Um . . . could you come next door with me? Just to make sure everything is okay?"

Matt looked up at his mother with alarm.

Peyton nodded, swallowing, her fear like a knife in his gut. Last night, after the police left, he'd hammered two boards across the intruder's window in the basement.

Malcolm looked confused.

"I'll be right back," Peyton told him.

Peyton slipped out the back door with Marielle and Matt, into the dogs bouncing around them. Marielle was watchful and wary, looking over her shoulder as she unlocked the back door. Her fear sang shrilly in the air around her, pulling on Peyton's insides like a Celtic fiddle. "Matt, come on," she said sharply. She locked the door behind them.

Peyton made a complete tour of the house, checking closets and behind doors, just as he had last night. Matt watched with round, frightened eyes. Marielle stood tense, ready to bolt, it seemed, if Peyton found anything.

At the back door when he'd finished the inspection, he asked, "Will your mom or anybody be able to come for . . . for the funeral?"

She lifted her gaze for a second, then dropped it to her feet, blushing. "No. Um . . . it's hard for her to travel. She's . . . she's so far away." She looked up, but at the wall behind his head, avoiding his eyes. The fiddle music rose again, a raw, pulling sound. He didn't understand why she would lie about this.

"I—I just wish someone could be here for you," he said.

She stretched her lips into a thin smile. "We're okay. We've got you guys."

Peyton felt sorry for her. They were a pretty motley crew.

She hugged him, and he heard the locks click behind him as he left.

He squeezed back into his own kitchen door, almost letting the dogs in as he did. When the door shut on them once again, they whimpered. Peyton knew they were hungry and probably pissed about the delay in their breakfast.

Dair came into the kitchen before he could speak to Malcolm again, showered and fresh, so beautiful that he wanted to whisk her back upstairs to bed. Her wet hair was braided down her back, and she wore her khaki zoo uniform—safari shirt and the shorts that showed off her tanned, toned legs. She poured herself a cup of coffee. Malcolm had already gotten his own while Peyton was next door.

"Okay, you guys," Malcolm said in a bemused tone. "What is *this?*" He held Cassie's brochure in his hand.

Dair just smiled and sat at the table with her mug, looking as perky and robotic as someone on a commercial.

"This is yours, right, Peyton?" Malcolm asked. "This is something you would do. Don't tell me you believe in this?"

Peyton nodded. "Actually, I do. I want to find out more about it."

"So you think you were a dog in another life or something?" Malcolm joked. He always teased Peyton about his belief in reincarnation. Peyton regretted all he'd revealed to him recently—that he feared he would never finish paying for the lives he'd taken in the past until his own was taken by someone or something to balance it out. He hoped sharing that hadn't been a mistake. Malcolm chuckled to himself, and Peyton's stomach tightened. Peyton was only trying to help Malcolm after all. And lying to Dair to do it. No . . . that wasn't true. That wasn't really why he'd lied to Dair. But it was a more comfortable explanation to himself.

"I guess cats are all reincarnationists, right?" Malcolm asked. "With their nine lives?"

Peyton pictured an aikido move in his head, taking Malcolm's comment and diverting it, pushing it aside before it reached him and pissed him off. He got a little too much pleasure from the image of the question crashing into the wall and splintering, though, for the move to have been successful. He breathed deeply, walked to the counter, and opened a loaf of bread. He put two pieces in the toaster and asked Malcolm, "Want some toast?"

Malcolm grimaced and shook his head. He continued reading the brochure, and Dair watched him. And Peyton witnessed the strange phenomenon he'd seen before: Dair could deny her mother's abilities, but nobody else better do it. But Malcolm missed Dair's cold eyes as he continued reading the brochure. "Sixty dollars?" he asked in awe. "You'd spend sixty dollars for this?"

"Yeah," Peyton said. "You get some books about it and lunch, too." He opened a cupboard for the peanut butter. "You can take a pet and she'll do a reading of it."

Malcolm shook his head. "What kind of people sign up for this? Are they those radical vegan people who throw red paint on anyone in fur?"

Peyton laughed out loud, picturing Cassie doing anything so extreme. Dair snorted, but her spine stayed stiff.

"No," she said, "it's not like that at all. This workshop is run by my *mother.*"

Peyton had wondered if she was going to admit that. He wasn't going to if she didn't. That red stripe crossed Malcolm's face again, and Peyton watched him replay his comments in his head, wondering just how badly he'd offended her.

His toast popped up, and he tossed the bread onto a plate before it burned his fingers.

Dair went on. "It's just people who want to improve their relationships with their animals."

Malcolm raised his eyebrows, scratching at his new, stubbly goatee. "*Relationships?* So they think their relationships to animals are as real as their relationships to people?" He didn't laugh, but he was so totally clueless that he still offended Dair.

She set down her mug and folded her hands in front of her. Oh, man. Peyton spread peanut butter on his toast and hoped sparks didn't fly.

"I'm not sure I understand," Dair said. "How can a relationship with any living being be more or less 'real' than a relationship to any other being?"

Malcolm paused. He seemed finally aware that he needed to watch his step and began to fidget with the zipper of his leather jacket. "Well, come on. You can't really have a relationship with an *animal.* I mean, don't you think that only people who have trouble handling relationships with other people think that?"

"No. I believe that anyone who doesn't recognize the similarities probably doesn't have much success with their human relationships, either."

Peyton winced. That was harsh. He sat at the table with his toast and coffee and gave Dair an imploring glance. She caught it and softened.

"I mean, c'mon," she said. "Blizzard and Shodie live in our house.

Whenever we're home, we're with them. Our relationship with them is very real."

Malcolm looked skeptical and zipped his jacket up, then down.

Peyton sipped his coffee. If coffee were music, it would be swing, with a hi-hat and snare keeping its beat.

Dair stood and dumped her coffee in the sink. "I've got to go," she said.

Peyton knew the Children's Zoo didn't open until noon, but he didn't say anything.

She leaned over and kissed him, and he felt that rush of déjà vu at her kiss, like a ritual fix spreading through his veins. "Bye, love," he said.

"Bye. See ya, Malcolm." Peyton stood and opened the door for her and watched her speak to the dogs and scratch their backs before heading out the gate and to the zoo.

"Well, I screwed that up," Malcolm said. "You're right: Don't tell her about Saturday. Not now."

Peyton laughed and shook his head.

"She hates me, I think."

"She doesn't hate you, but hell, you just insulted her mother."

"No, but before that, even. Like when I first got here. Asking me about Gayle and then . . . she doesn't like me."

"She likes you," Peyton said, not having a clue if it was true or not. He thought this over. He remembered what Dair had said about maybe Malcolm being involved with Craig's death, but he didn't believe it and knew Malcolm didn't need that added worry, so he said nothing. Plus, he thought Dair had been odd with Malcolm, too. And not just with Malcolm, but in general. He'd felt it ever since he'd seen her in the airport, before they'd learned that Craig was the man who'd fallen and died. But it was that time of year, after all. "It's not you, Malcolm," Peyton said. "Her birthday's coming up."

Malcolm's face changed. "Oh, that's right."

"She always gets a little depressed, a little . . . strange."

Malcolm nodded. Everyone knew about Sylvan. Everyone expected Dair's gloominess around her birthday and gave her lots of room for it.

Peyton ate his toast in silence. Malcolm stopped fussing with his zipper and tapped the brochure on the table instead. "Peyton, you believe some seriously weird shit."

Peyton shrugged and kept chewing. If peanut butter were music, it would be a blues tune, thick with saxophone.

Malcolm zipped his jacket up and down again, troubled by something. "I've been thinking about what you told me about reincarnation," he said at last. "All that stuff about addiction maybe being left over from another life? I don't buy it."

"That's fine—"

"I don't buy it because of Craig."

Peyton stopped, his tongue glued from the peanut butter. He searched Malcolm's face. He'd break Malcolm's neck if he used Craig's death just to mock him.

"I mean, what? You really think Craig deserved this? That he did something bad and this is the payback?" Malcolm wasn't mocking. His eyes were pink and weepy. "It's totally fucked up to say he *chose* this. It's bullshit."

Peyton shook his head.

"But that's what you said," Malcolm protested. "You said we make choices, and the consequences register in other lives."

Peyton got his tongue to work. "But it doesn't mean Craig did anything *wrong*. Sometimes suffering is in preparation for something in our future."

"What?"

This anger, this bitterness, was a side of Malcolm he'd never seen. Offstage, Peyton had only seen the stuttering, shy Malcolm, the one who'd looked pathetic and miserable when he'd recognized Peyton at an NA meeting.

"Seriously," Peyton said. "Like, there's this story of a soul who lived three lives of suffering—once as a beggar, once as a peasant during a famine, and once as a diseased child who died young. All those lives were to prepare the soul for a life as a king with great compassion and understanding."

"That's a fucking fairy tale, Peyton."

Peyton took another bite of toast. There was no need to keep trying to explain, if Malcolm felt this way, but Malcolm wouldn't drop it.

"It's just stupid to think we *chose* to be addicts. For what? And Craig *chose* to dive off 75?"

Peyton sighed. "*We* don't choose—"

"You just said we chose."

"No. Listen: It's not *us* that choose. Not Malcolm and Peyton—two guys sitting in a kitchen, okay? Our *souls* choose. It's like . . . they have this course of study, right? And each life is a class. This class"—he touched his chest—"this body, didn't choose my present life. My present body didn't exist until after those choices were made."

Malcolm fell silent and began zipping and unzipping his jacket again. "So you think Craig's somewhere right now choosing where he goes next?"

"Something like that."

Malcolm stopped zipping and leaned forward in his chair. "And he'll be back?"

"Not as *Craig,* no. But Craig's soul isn't finished."

"So . . ." Malcolm paused, his weird little hands frozen on his zipper. "So, some little kid could be born and end up in one of our classes at the Playhouse . . . and really be Craig?"

"Maybe."

"Would he recognize us?"

"Probably not."

"What fucking good is it to have former lives if we don't remember them? How's he supposed to learn from experiences he can't even remember?"

Peyton didn't answer at first. Some people did remember. He remembered. Bits and pieces. "Malcolm, look. None of it makes sense if you only look at it in terms of *this* life. But this life is just part of a bigger whole. It goes way beyond this body. It's huge. It's . . ." Peyton had always pictured it as a symphony. A symphony of exquisite complexity and beauty. Themes were begun in one century and developed in the next and variations played on them in another. But he didn't want to tell Malcolm that. He tried to think of a way he could describe it. But he couldn't. Instead he said, "If Craig's *soul* came into our lives again, yeah, we might feel a connection to it. You know how there are people you immediately feel that with?"

Malcolm nodded. "You think it means you've known them before?"

"Yeah. Yeah, I do. I felt that way when I met Dair. Like we'd had years together already and were picking up where we left off."

Malcolm resumed zipping. It drove Peyton crazy. "So you and Dair have been married before, in other lives?"

"Maybe. Maybe not. Maybe we were related in some other way. Maybe she was the man, I was the woman."

Malcolm raised his eyebrows.

"Or maybe," Peyton said to those raised eyebrows, "we were just friends."

"Or could you have been members of a family?" Malcolm asked. "Like maybe Dair was your mom once or something?"

"Yeah," he said. "Or I could've been her sister or something."

Malcolm wrinkled his nose. "Isn't that creepy? Like . . . incestuous?"

"*You* said she was my mom!" Peyton teased.

"No, seriously," Malcolm said.

"No, it's not creepy or incestuous because it wasn't *us.* We are now in *these* bodies. This incarnation is the only one we need to worry about. That's our job."

Malcolm sighed. "It's weird. I just . . ." He looked across at Peyton, his eyes watery again. "Craig can't be gone, you know?"

"I know," Peyton whispered.

"I should get going," Malcolm said, zipping up his coat with an air of finality. "I just wanted to bring that stuff by for Marielle."

"Where you going now?"

He made a face. "To a meeting."

"Good."

"You wanna come?"

Peyton hesitated. He didn't really want to. But he really didn't want to be alone, without Dair, without the possibility that Craig would drop by. "Not this one," he said. He only went to NA meetings once a month. And he felt guilty regretting that attending an extra one out of the blue two months ago had led to this: Malcolm here in his kitchen on this Monday morning. Lying to his wife. Feeling somewhat responsible for a person he wasn't sure he even liked.

Peyton got up and walked Malcolm toward the door.

The phone rang behind them in the house. "I'll see ya later," Malcolm said.

They stood awkwardly, uncertain whether to shake hands or hug. They did that punch-the-shoulder move.

Peyton closed the door and made it to the kitchen phone before the machine picked up.

"Peyton? It's R.B." The kind, bass voice of Dair's dad was as familiar, as welcome, a sound as a childhood song. Eight years ago, Peyton had known who R.B. was the second he'd heard him speak, before Dair ever introduced them in that crowded living room at his debut Thanksgiving with her family.

"Hey, R.B."

A long silence followed, but a silence that felt full of information.

"Cassie told us. I'm sorry," Peyton said. "This feels really . . . wrong."

"Yeah, I think it is."

They paused. Peyton knew R.B. hated the phone as much as he did.

"You know what?" Peyton asked. "I was thinking of driving over today. Is that okay?"

R.B.'s voice brightened, as he said with surprise, "I think I'd like that."

"I would, too. I could leave here pretty soon. I've got the entire day free." Peyton didn't have to tell his father-in-law those were dangerous days for him. R.B. already knew.

"Meet me at the barn," R.B. said. "I've got a couple of afternoon appointments, but it shouldn't take long. Is Dair there?"

"No, you just missed her. She just left for the zoo."

A long pause followed. "Is she okay?"

"I think so. She was thrown. So was I, but she's okay."

"I should've called her . . . but I can't talk on the damn phone. I should've talked to her before, but I just . . . I was thrown, too."

Another pause.

"I'll see you soon," Peyton said.

"Thanks, son." R.B. hung up.

Son.

Peyton could tell that man things he could never tell his own father. He could confess anything to Cass that he'd never hint at to his own mother.

Cassie had told Peyton often that his totem was the wolf. And this totem was supposedly a reminder to listen to his own inner thoughts, his intuition. She'd even shown him a book that explained the different totems. He'd memorized one line: "Learning to trust your own insights and to secure your attachments accordingly is part of what wolf medicine teaches."

So he was trying to trust what his intuition told him about this divorce.

It didn't make sense. He'd heard Cassie's version of it, but he wanted to hear R.B.'s.

And he was trying to trust what his intuition told him about Sylvan.

That Dair's drinking problem was tied to Sylvan. That the anxiety Dair felt when Peyton asked her about her twin was too strong, too sharp, too raw, for a loss that was twenty-five years old.

And if Dair didn't talk about Sylvan, Cassie and R.B. probably didn't, either.

And maybe, just maybe, Sylvan had something to do with this divorce.

Maybe Peyton was the only person objective enough to see this. Maybe he could help them all. He hoped so.

He'd wanted to ask R.B. about Sylvan for years.

Today, he vowed, he finally would.

Chapter Eleven

Dair walked down Vine Street, calves burning, out of breath, the chill morning air smarting her throat. There was no need to hurry, except to escape her own confusion. Why was she so mad at Malcolm? She didn't care what he thought.

She slowed her pace at the Erkenbrecher Avenue pedestrian entrance to the zoo and waved at the girls at the gate. "You're early," one said.

"Yup." She had nearly half an hour before she had to be "on" at the Children's Zoo. "Beautiful morning." It was, truly, but one of those bright, misleading autumn days that promised more warmth than it delivered. She hadn't grabbed a sweatshirt or jacket when she'd left the house. She crossed her arms and rubbed them with her hands as she strolled the wide blacktop paths. The place was nearly empty since it was early on a Monday with school back in session. She loved this season at the zoo—the cooler temperatures made the animals more active, and the smaller crowds made them more relaxed.

She paused in a sunny spot at the Vanishing Giants exhibit, where Tibaba, the African elephant calf, romped in her landscaped playground. Leaning on the fence to watch her, Dair felt some of her irritation ease away. She should feel sorry for Malcolm, really. He missed out on something so rich. Her relationships with Blizzard and Shodan and Godot were healthy and nourishing. Invaluable to her. And her relationships with Peyton and with Marielle and Matt were the same way. And it used to be with Craig, too. She squeezed the railing under her hands. Craig. He *couldn't* be gone.

Tibaba drew designs in the dust with her trunk, occasionally tossing some of it onto her back. So, last night—in a conversation that now felt years ago—Dair's mother said Tibaba wanted a new home. This new Vanishing Giants complex was a fabulous habitat, huge and roomy, with giraffe and okapi in nearby enclosures to keep Tibaba and the other elephants company. Dair's chest tightened. Of course Tibaba wanted a different home. She wanted her *own* home. She'd been found beside her dead mother's body, her mother's face chain-sawed off for the tusks. Rangers in Tsavo National Park in Kenya figured this beautiful elephant had spent at least three whole days and nights weeping beside her murdered, mutilated mother. And yes— she pictured Malcolm's skeptical face—elephants *did* weep, and for reasons similar to human's own.

She pictured her father's skeptical face as well, but the image was murky. Although he'd never treated any elephants in his practice, surely he'd agree that they wept, felt emotion. Again Dair had the un-settling feeling that there was more to her parents' split than the idea of animal communication.

Tibaba sprinkled more dirt on her back, then playfully tossed some in Dair's direction, although it fell short of hitting her. Tibaba let her trunk hover over the geometric design she'd drawn, then pivoted on her back legs to a new stretch of sandy dirt, which she smoothed clear with her trunk, and began to sketch a new pattern.

Did people resist this idea of communication because it threat-ened to change too much in their world? Is that why Dair resisted it? Only a day ago Dair too would've been mortified by her mother's upcoming workshop. That's why it was ridiculous that she allowed Malcolm to piss her off so much; it was irrational. But being pissed at him felt safer than her other emotional options this morning.

Tibaba apparently didn't like the results of her latest artistic at-tempt and smudged it out with her trunk. She shuffled the dirt with her feet, then ambled into her drinking pool. Dair watched Tibaba fill her trunk with water, then curl the trunk to her mouth to drink.

After watching all that drawing in the dust, Dair imagined the drink's cool, soothing slide down Tibaba's throat and wanted one of her own.

This morning she'd taken the vodka bottle from the shoe box and returned it to the closet, figuring Peyton wouldn't check the same place twice. For the ten minutes it'd taken her to shower, she'd told herself she wouldn't have a drink. But by the time she'd braided her hair, she longed to feel the bottle in her hand, the burn of the vodka on her tongue, the slow heat spread in her chest. She stood at the bathroom sink and held her trembling hands in front of her, feeling queasy, weak in her joints. She told herself she'd have coffee and eat a muffin, but that thought made a wave of nausea pass through her, leaving her clammy with sweat, and she'd reached into the closet and burrowed for the bottle.

Her eyes stung as she pushed off from Tibaba's fence and walked on, wandering past the Reptile House and Monkey Island, where not a single monkey was currently visible. Peyton was right—this was a new step. Why was she hiding it? She really would dump out the vodka. She'd buy a new bottle today and put it back in the freezer, where Peyton could keep tabs on it. This thought comforted her.

She found herself at the Cat Grottoes, and from where she stood she counted only four other zoo visitors. These were the people who most intrigued her, not the throngs of visitors who flocked here on summer days. Dair liked to ask children what animal was their favorite. They always had a ready answer—there was a particular animal most of them wanted to see first, and observe the longest, when they came here, although most of them couldn't explain why. Her mother would claim that was their totem animal, an animal that provided guidance and wisdom in some area they lacked. Totems chose people—not the other way around, and she knew that a totem was rarely a person's own companion animal. Maybe hers was the chickadee, visiting her in dreams. She'd have to ask her mother what a chickadee stood for. She wondered what Matt's favorite animal was when he came here with Mr. Lively. She still hadn't told Marielle about it; they'd gotten distracted by the autopsy results.

That autopsy. She shivered. She wouldn't know how to use heroin even if she did have the inclination. She was certain Craig didn't, either. Somehow she knew this had been done *to* him, was tied to those grass- and bloodstained clothes. What had happened? Would they ever know?

Dair rubbed the goose bumps on her bare arms and walked briskly up the hill but stopped outside the Komodo dragon exhibit. She still had twenty minutes before her class of fifth-graders arrived at the Children's Zoo. She leaned with her back against a wall, absorbing warmth from the sun-soaked wood. Inside this building was a male dragon, nearly ten feet long and 275 pounds. One of the most dangerous reptiles in the world, but Dair would rather be locked inside his habitat than come face-to-face with a human intruder in her own home.

"Dair?"

She turned and there stood Andy Baker, his blond hair lifting in the breeze, just as it had the day they'd both watched Craig die.

Dair was unable to prevent her spontaneous smile, but it crashed quickly as they looked into each other's faces and thought of Craig.

He reached into his jacket and pulled a pack of cigarettes from his shirt pocket. He held one out to her, but she shook her head no. He lit one for himself, then they walked down the gently sloping blacktop toward the African veldt exhibit. She became acutely aware of the rich, horsy smell of straw and manure, the sun's warmth growing stronger, the continuous screeching racket of the birds in the nearby Wings of the World walk-through flight cage. She led Andy to the fence overlooking the Rhino Reserve.

"I still can't believe it," she said. "We were there when it happened."

Andy leaned his elbows on the fence and turned his head to her—fixing her with those sleepy eyes, the color of steel, with a hint of blue, like an overcast sky. He nodded.

"I keep thinking about it," Dair said. "That we were *right there* and didn't know it was him. We watched him die and had no clue what we were seeing."

The overcast sky in his eyes turned slightly pink. He stood up straight and turned around to lean on the railing, his back to the rhino kneeling in the mud. "I liked him," Andy said, taking a drag off his cigarette. "A good guy."

"God, I'm gonna miss him," Dair whispered. Tremors began in the corners of her mouth, and she hiccuped a small sob.

"Hey," Andy said. "Hey, it's okay." He put an arm around her shoulder. She breathed slowly, deliberately, and counted to twenty.

Andy kept his arm around her until she composed herself. When she shifted slightly and took a deep breath, he let his arm fall free. "Sorry," she said, wiping her eyes.

"Don't worry about it." They turned and looked at the rhino. A bird landed on its back, but the rhino only blinked.

"So . . . this dress," Andy said.

Her heart lurched.

"Was it—I mean, did you know he liked to—"

"He didn't," she said. "I mean, he never told me that. He would've told me. He would've known we wouldn't care. But, no. He never wore women's clothes."

What's the worst thing you've ever done? Craig had asked her. Surely that wasn't his answer to the question. Why would that be some terrible secret?

"Did you . . . did you see the paper this morning?" Andy asked. "They did an autopsy, and they said he was on heroin."

Would she have to have this conversation with *everyone?* She shook her head. "It can't be right. There's no way he took the heroin on purpose. He wouldn't. That is so unlike him. Don't you think?" She wondered if anyone would have thought it was like or unlike Peyton back in the days he used. This thought chilled her. Maybe Craig *did* use heroin. Maybe he *was* a cross-dresser. How could anyone know?

Andy shrugged. "I've only been here a few months."

"Oh, come on. You saw enough in a few months to know what he was like."

Andy nodded and took a drag off his cigarette. "But you knew him really well, right?"

"He was one of my best friends."

Dair watched the bird peck at something on the rhino's back.

Andy cleared his throat and asked, "And you were . . . *just* friends, right?"

She turned her head to face him. "What?" She honestly thought she hadn't heard him.

He glanced at her, patches of red blooming in his cheeks. "Look, this is none of my business, but, well . . . I heard that you might've been, you know, having a thing."

"No!"

Andy nodded. "I didn't think so," he said as if he'd won something.

"Who said that?" She felt another wave of nausea, like this morning when she'd stood in the bathroom and thought about eating without a drink.

"I knew it wasn't true. I told them that."

"Who?"

"It's nothing," he said, shrugging. "Just stupid talk."

"Andy!" Dair grabbed his sleeve, and he looked almost startled. "You can't start something like that and not finish it. Tell me who said it and what exactly they said." She let go of his sleeve. "One of my best friends is dead. The paper says he's a cross-dressing heroin addict, and now, on top of that, he's being accused of sleeping with a married woman? Not to mention what this little rumor suggests about *me*. Andy, come on, who told you this?"

He frowned and let the ash on his cigarette grow precariously long. "Well . . . I heard it from some of the tech guys, union guys. But they were talking about how they heard it from someone else. I don't know who started it, really. But the guys, they didn't believe it."

A surge of gratitude and affection for those union guys moved through her. She'd often found herself in conversation with them outside the stage door on breaks. Her "social" smoking had bridged the gap that often existed between the tech staff and actors. It was just like the union guys' tough brand of loyalty to defend her against rumors. "When was this?"

"Yesterday. When we were loading in that touring Broadway revue."

She leaned her head down on the railing, feeling weak. "He'd been dead one day, and they were talking trash about him?"

"Dair," Andy said, "I'm sorry. I shouldn't have said anything."

She lifted her head. "Oh, my God, I'm glad you did. I need to know that people are saying this. I just can't believe anyone would start this, I—"

Dair didn't tell this to Andy, but the weird thing was that she and Craig had joked about it themselves—how everyone but Peyton and Marielle probably thought they were having an affair. But it was a joke, nothing more. It felt tainted, wrong, for people to have thought this. One more thing to sully him now that he was gone.

She lowered her head again. "Craig was just my friend. And my husband's friend."

"I'm sorry," Andy said again. He put a hand on her shoulder. His hand reminded her that *Craig* had teasingly accused her of flirting with *Andy* when they'd first met him. In a flash she was back in Craig's car, driving home from a Queen City Shakespeare Company meeting in August, a summer thunderstorm—the last rain they'd seen—drumming against his windshield.

"Please," she'd said, laughing, when Craig said this.

"Well, you did," Craig had said, grinning but keeping his eyes on the slick road before him. He'd had a late evening shadow of a beard on his strong, sharp jawline.

"Are you jealous?" she'd teased him. "Am I supposed to flirt only with you?"

"Yes," Craig had said, pretending to pout.

"Andy knows I'm married," Dair had told Craig. "And *I* know I'm married. Quite happily, thank you very much. So don't worry."

And the image was gone, replaced by the landscaped hill below her, ending in the rhino's acre of African grasses and mud.

Andy took his hand off her shoulder, and she stood up straight. Was it true? Did they flirt, she and Andy? Maybe they did. Nothing major, but there was something so 1940s black-and-white-movie romantic about a guy lighting her cigarette, holding eye contact while he did it. But it was harmless, nothing different from the platonic flirtation she'd shared with Craig. She didn't want anyone but Peyton, couldn't entertain the thought of cheating on him.

"I love my husband," she said. "And Craig was crazy in love with someone else."

Andy nodded. "He was engaged to that sign interpreter, right?" He must have seen the surprise in her face, because he added, "Gayle told me that. She was at the Aronoff last night when we were loading in that touring show." Andy paused. "So how's she doing, Craig's fiancée? What's her name? Marilyn?"

"Marielle," Dair said. "She's pretty devastated." Dair pictured Marielle's dead, vacant eyes, her sleepwalker's movements. Dair and Andy didn't look at each other; they just kept watching the rhinoceros. "Do you know her?" she asked idly, wondering who on earth could have started such a rumor about her and Craig.

"I've seen her," he said. "She led a tour of the theater for St. Rita's School for the Deaf. Steve pointed her out, told me she was Craig's girlfriend. But I haven't really talked to her. Does she ever sign shows?"

"I wish. She did it once when the scheduled signer was in this horrible wreck, but only because it was an emergency. She's too shy—

she hates to be in the spotlight, in front of crowds. She did a great job, but I think it literally made her sick."

"I can relate," Andy said. "I'll stay on my side of the spotlight, thank you very much."

Dair smiled. "It's really hard for me, on those matinees that get signed. I have to tell myself, Don't look at them. I start watching them and pretty soon I'm mesmerized. I forget my lines, I forget I'm in a play, I just stare at them—it's so beautiful, it's almost like dance."

Andy chuckled and shook his head. "I usually get caught up in watching to see if what they sign is really what you all are saying. I've almost missed cues because of it."

"You can read sign?" she asked him.

"Yeah, my twin brother's deaf."

A spinning sensation began. "Really?" Her throat was suddenly parched.

"Yeah. You had a twin, right?"

She kept her mouth shut. She nodded, a small, barely discernible movement.

"Craig told me that," Andy said. "I'm sorry. I shouldn't have—"

"No it's okay," she said, surprised at her hoarse voice. "It was a long time ago."

"Identical?"

"Nope. You?"

"Nope." Andy put out his cigarette on the ground, then stooped to scoop it up and toss it in a trash can surrounded by lazily hovering bees. "Still, though," he said. "To lose him would kill me, I think."

Dair nodded. Why had Craig told Andy about Sylvan? And when? Before that night at Palomino's when she'd opened up the cage and let that bird out? God, it had felt so good.

"You just turned white as a ghost," Andy said, true concern on his face. "Are you cold? You want my jacket?"

He wore a hunter green fleece. "Really?" she asked. "I'm actually freezing."

"Here," he said, unzipping it and sliding it off, then handing it to her. He had a long-sleeved shirt on underneath. "I gotta head out of here soon anyway."

She slipped into the jacket, warm with his body's heat and that apple scent of his. "Thanks. This is great."

The rhino stood up and lumbered over to the pool of water. The bird on its back flew away. They watched in silence.

"So . . . ," she said, hoping to change the subject. "What are you doing here?"

He shrugged. "I haven't been able to sleep lately. You know, since . . . since Craig jumped. And I want to learn the city. Try to plan good places to bring Eric when he visits."

Andy had a son, but only for a few weeks in the summer and one week after Christmas. Divorced. Custody bullshit. But he talked about Eric all the time.

"We only have one week in December," Andy said. "So it's gotta be good."

"We have the Festival of Lights in December. It's pretty cool. There's even ice-skating over by the picnic grove. Does he like to ice-skate?"

Andy grinned. "We'll find out. But he loves animals. He loves the zoo."

"All kids do," Dair said.

Andy shrugged and grinned. "I grew up surrounded by animals. I miss 'em."

"Me, too. My dad's a vet."

"No way!" Andy said. "This is weird—my dad was a vet. Twins and both dads veterinarians. I wonder what else we have in common?"

Dair laughed, knowing the coincidence was only half what it seemed.

Andy grinned, reached for another cigarette in his pocket, but put it back. "All right, 'fess up: How many animals?" he asked.

"Back then? Oh, God. Three dogs, five cats, a rabbit, and a chickadee." She pictured the gray-and-white bird at her window.

He chuckled, leaning his elbows on the railing again. "Yep. Five dogs, countless cats, goats, and chickens."

"Chickens?"

"Oh, yeah. They were my 4-H project. Five white ones named Helen, and three red ones named Laura."

Dair laughed. It felt good. There hadn't been much reason the past two days. But she also felt, with a sharp pang, as if she'd been caught doing something wrong, as though it were somehow disloyal to Craig to feel anything but sorrow.

The rhino emerged from the pool and rolled in the dirt of the shore, caking himself in the greenish mud. He stood and shook his body, a look of satisfaction on his face.

A high-pitched train whistle made Dair check her watch. The children's voices were audible over the chugging engine. "I've gotta go," she said. "I'm introducing our walruses to a group of thirty fifth-graders. Wanna watch? They're pretty cool—the walruses, anyway. I don't know about the fifth-graders yet."

"Nah," he said. "I need to get going. Listen, it was great to run into you."

"Yeah." They hugged awkwardly. "Thanks for telling me about that rumor," Dair said. "There's a read-through tonight, and I'm glad I didn't walk into that unaware."

"Oh, I don't think you'll be walking into anything. It was just talk." She felt small and insecure. "I'll get this jacket back to you sometime soon."

"You could give it back to me tonight. I bet we won't be done loading in that revue before your read-through." The Aronoff Center for the Arts housed three different theaters.

"Okay." It was reassuring to think of Andy and the tech guys being in the same building as her rehearsal. "It'll be weird tonight," she said. "Craig was supposed to be in it."

"This is *Othello,* right?" Andy asked.

"Yeah. He was Iago. I wonder if there'll be a replacement Iago yet."

"There is," Andy said. "Gayle told me. It's Malcolm Cole."

Chapter Twelve

As soon as her zoo shift ended, Dair wanted nothing more than to be with Peyton. She nearly ran home, already imagining the secure cocoon of his embrace. Already drinking in his easy voice. Counting on him to untie the tangled cords of dread that had knotted themselves in her chest since she'd spoken with Andy about the rumor and the read-through. But when she reached the back gate she knew he wasn't home. She knew before she checked for his car on the street. Something was missing, felt empty, as it always did without him.

The dogs barked, greeting her from inside. Shodan pushed her face out of the cat door, the flap resting on her forehead, barking eagerly. Blizzard's deeper, rougher bark boomed behind her.

"Blizzard! Shodan!" Dair's own voice startled her from upstairs. Shodan stopped barking and tilted her head, craning to see Mr. Lively's back door. Captain Hook knew that those were the dogs' names. He never called them if they weren't visible or barking.

Dair unlocked the back door, and Blizzard stood and put his paws on her shoulders. She kissed his broad white snout, while Shodan wriggled with delight, toenails clicking on the kitchen tiles.

On the counter, Dair found a note written in Peyton's tidy but slanted left-handed writing, just like her own: "Hey, chickadee, I'm off to visit your dad. Good luck at the read-through. Knock 'em dead, my darling. Treats for you later."

The words made her feel as if she'd just come down with the flu. "Off to visit your dad"? Shit. She read the note again, a heavy ache settling into her elbows and knees, all of her joints.

Her dad. Her poor dad. Her parents, two people who were in so many ways perfect for each other—divorcing. If they couldn't stay together, who could? Maybe Peyton could get to the bottom of the problem.

But . . . what if Dad and Peyton talked of *other* things? Her dad wasn't much of a talker; surely he and Peyton wouldn't chat long.

While she read, the dogs pressed their damp noses against the bare skin of her legs, licking and snuffling. A horrible fishy smell clung to her from working with the walruses—since her demonstrations were aided by a bucket of raw herring treats—and the dogs seemed to find it a captivating, alluring perfume.

She gave each dog a biscuit, let them out into the yard, and called for Godot, who usually materialized five minutes or so after a summons.

She stood in the door fame, watching the dogs check the borders of the yard, and fought her impulse to call her father's vet clinic and make up some emergency so that Peyton had to come straight home.

If she called, what could be wrong? The dogs got loose and were missing? She saw someone trying to come through Marielle's window again? She was violently ill? Injured? She'd cut her hand on a broken glass and needed to go to the emergency room for stitches? From the door frame she looked over her shoulder into the kitchen and eyed a drinking glass sitting by the sink. She sighed . . . things were getting bad if she was seriously considering wounding herself to keep Peyton from knowing the truth.

That briny, fishy reek floated around her in a slight breeze, making her crinkle her nose and exhale sharply. She left the dogs outside and headed up to the shower.

Once she'd pinned her braid to the top of her head and got in the shower, Godot appeared. He stood on his hind feet outside the clear glass door and wailed. "I'm okay, sweetie," Dair called. He always seemed distressed, concerned for her safety, when she showered. Perhaps he expected her to feel as he did when he poked his head out of the cat door into the pouring rain. He'd pin his ears flat and scowl, flicking one paw and then the other.

Dair frowned, squinting through the water. She didn't know what he thought, really. She was just projecting something cute onto him, making stuff up. She had no idea what this little creature wanted.

When she shut off the shower and slid open the door, Godot immediately leapt inside, onto the wet floor, and sniffed her feet and calves. He stood on his hind legs again, reaching his front paws up her thighs, urgently mewling, *"Rrack. Mmrack."* Dair stared down at him, met his golden eyes.

This little creature. This was another species. Yet here he was, living in her home, touching her naked body, wanting to communicate something to her. What an odd, odd thing when she thought about it.

"Mmrack. Mrrff." His tone sounded as though he were using profanities. Was he scolding her for being so careless as to be caught in this downpour every day, sometimes twice? Was she a moron for not noticing that every time she stepped into this closet she got drenched?

Godot licked the beaded water from her left calf with his sandpaper tongue as she dried off. She bent down to stroke between his ears. He purred loudly. "C'mon," she said. In the bedroom she dropped the towel on the unmade bed. Godot jumped up onto the bed and began to knead the wet towel with his paws.

Dair pulled open a drawer and froze. Her stacks of underwear were neater than usual. She never folded them; she just threw them in the drawer straight from the dryer. Her first thought was of Marielle's intruder, and she wheeled around to face the room, wanting to pull the wet towel back around her as if someone might be watching her that very minute. She took a deep breath, and although she knew it was absurd, she couldn't help it—she looked under the bed.

Her sweater- and shoe boxes were lined up differently from usual, including the Capezio shoe box that had temporarily housed her bottle of Absolut. A slow dawning broke over her.

Peyton, you're a bad detective, she thought. Too obvious. Oh, love, so you were still searching, weren't you? You didn't believe me for a minute last night.

Goose bumps rippled her naked skin. She rushed to the closet and dug her hands in the stacks of sheets, but the bottle was still there, hiding in the back. Had he found it and wasn't going to tell her? Had he just left it there, planning to confront her later?

Surely he wouldn't go off to talk to her dad if he'd discovered the bottle. Or was he going to talk to her dad *about* the alcohol? That might be a relief, in a way.

Or would it? Would Peyton suggest that her drinking problem had to do with her sister's death?

Oh, God. She uncapped the bottle and tipped it back, but the burn of vodka in her throat also burned her with a realization: For eight years she'd been able to tell herself that the only lie she'd ever told Peyton was the lie about Sylvan. That wasn't true anymore. The burning spread to her eyes, her chest. She didn't want to lie to Peyton again. The one lie was bad enough. This new lie had not yet grown wild; it was still docile enough to be managed, handled. She walked straight into the bathroom and poured the vodka into the toilet. It took longer to empty than she expected, and she felt as if she were watching a movie version of herself as the clear liquid filled the bowl. She thought about leaving it there since it looked like water. Then she thought about dropping to her knees to lap from the bowl the way Blizzard sometimes did. When Godot brushed past her to sniff at the toilet, she quickly flushed it.

The bottle. What to do with the bottle. She yanked on jeans and a purple turtleneck sweater, then wrapped the bottle in newspaper and scampered barefoot through the sharp, dry grass to their trash cans. She buried the bottle deep in Marielle's can, then scurried back into the house with the dogs. There. She'd told the truth, in a backward sort of way.

And, of course, deep, gouging regret stabbed her almost at once. But she welcomed the pain; she felt like doing penance. Peyton deserved better. She'd lied to him and should suffer for it. She didn't have to drink. She didn't have a problem.

The purple of the turtleneck caught her eye in the mirror. It was the exact shade of purple as the dress both she and Craig had worn. She jerked it over her head and tossed it into the hamper, selecting a black cashmere V-neck instead. Her hair had dried in a braid this morning, so she brushed it out into voluminous waves and put on lipstick and earrings. Examining herself with the impassive eye of a person who regularly put herself in front of a paying audience, Dair decided that, on the outside, at least, she looked good.

Her hands trembled slightly, and she thought longingly of the alcohol she'd poured away. She shook out her hands in front of her, rolled her shoulders, her neck. She'd be okay.

She picked up her script and opened the door to leave.

"Wish me luck," she told the dogs and cat. The dogs wagged their tails and grinned, tongues tolling. The cat stared, expressionless.

Once Dair found a parking spot on Seventh Street, she delayed going inside the Aronoff Center. She felt she should do something to prepare, to steel herself, but she couldn't think of what that might be, except have a drink, so she finally got out of the car, making sure she had Andy's fleece jacket, and walked slowly to the stage door.

She entered the glass-enclosed lobby, signed in at the security guard's desk, and made her way to the main theater's lobby. Procter & Gamble Hall seated 2,700 and was where all the big touring shows performed, as well as where Peyton's dance company held its home shows. That was where Andy was loading in the Broadway revue.

Dair's shoes echoed on the gorgeous marble floor, patterned in rich green, pink, cream, and dark burgundy tiles. Tonight the building was quiet and churchlike as she walked past the box office to the smaller Jarson-Kaplan Theater, where *Othello* would rehearse and perform.

C. J. Slaughter, the man playing Othello, saw her first as he came up the stairs from the rest rooms. "Hello, Dair," he said, his voice intoxicatingly sweet and rich, like Chambord—raspberry liqueur. He hugged her, leaving a hint of his musky cologne on her sweater. "How are you doing?" he asked, holding her at arm's length and peering into her face.

She assumed he meant Craig. "Okay, I guess." She cursed the blood rushing to her face. "How 'bout you?"

"In shock," he said. "Still in shock."

She sometimes gawked when she looked at C.J. Tall and broad shouldered, he was, with a bald head and a neat, tidy mustache and goatee. His skin was dark, a velvet, almost blue black.

"Hey, look who's here," she heard a melodious voice purr behind her, and recognized Bethany Butler, their Desdemona. Dair turned to face Bethany's creamy whiteness, her pale blue eyes, her fine, flaxen hair. It was masterful casting. Bethany was petite to C.J.'s bulk. Almost luminous to his darkness. That full mane of hair to his shiny baldness. Everywhere she was fine and angular, he was broad and generous. The effect was breathtaking.

C.J. and Bethany embraced and kissed each other on the lips, then

Bethany put an arm around Dair's shoulder. Bethany smelled like vanilla. "How ya doin', hon?" she asked. She waited sincerely for Dair's answer; it wasn't just small talk. Everything about Bethany was sincere. It'd be easy to hate someone so gorgeous, so talented, who waltzed away with all the good roles in town, except that she was so damn nice—the sort who brought cookies to rehearsals and made everyone homemade cards for opening night.

The three of them walked into the theater, where three long tables were set up on the bare stage, already crowded with actors. Rosylyn, the director, sat with the stage manager, appearing to argue over something on the schedule spread out before them.

Dair adored this theater. It seated 437 and was modeled on an Elizabethan theater, with two narrow seating balconies stacked above each other. The rich teal velvet and cherry wood seats and the rust red walls were warm and welcoming.

Dair didn't know all the people at the tables, but there was much she could discern about them before anyone made introductions. The younger ones, most likely students from the Cincinnati Conservatory of Music, milled about in groups of their own. They wore CCM show T-shirts, which Dair knew to be from the latest productions they'd been cast in, all of them desperate to advertise their credentials. Beneath their cool, blasé facades, she could scent their childlike enthusiasm. For most of them, these small roles as the various officers and attendants represented their first professional work.

Some older gentlemen were seated with thermoses before them, crossword puzzles already open and begun. Cast as the senators and kinsmen to Brabantio—the father of Desdemona—these were the veterans, men who had spent their lives and made their livings in the theater.

Dair climbed the stairs to the stage and set her script at one end of the table, next to Bethany. Another script slapped down next to hers, and Kitten Silver hugged her and kissed her cheek. If Kitten Silver didn't sound like a porn star name, Dair couldn't think of a better one. But Kitten looked more like an elf, with her short, pixieish black hair highlighting her huge catlike eyes, her slight, gymnast's build. "We girls gotta stick together," Kitten said. "We're it."

Dair knew she meant they were the only three female roles in the entire play. Desdemona, the saint; Bianca, the whore; and Dair's own role, Emilia, somewhere in between.

Kitten dragged Dair by the arm out of the theater, back into the lobby, toward the dark concession counter. "So . . . what's the scoop? Everyone's afraid to ask."

"I don't know what you're talking about." Thank God Andy had warned her.

Kitten leaned in close, still holding Dair's arm. "I think you should know: Rumor has it that you and Craig were having an affair."

Dair both admired and despised Kitten's forthrightness, the way she made this blunt declaration. She jerked her arm from Kitten's grip. "The rumor's wrong."

Kitten crossed her arms and raised her eyebrows. "C'mon, you can tell me."

"Kitten—this isn't just some interesting gossip. Craig is dead. He's gone. And he deserves better than this bullshit. Who started this rumor?"

Kitten raised her huge eyes to the ceiling, thinking, but shook her head. "I don't remember." She dismissed the question with a wave of her hand. "Did you know he was on heroin?" Her gleaming eyes and half smile reminded Dair of someone asking about a crush. Dair wanted to slap her.

"He wasn't a user . . . it wasn't . . ." Dair wanted to lie down. She was too tired to stand up, much less try to explain this to anyone.

Kitten must have seen the exhaustion, the despair, on Dair's face, because she opened her arms and hugged her. She didn't let Dair go; she held her, long enough that Dair began to feel irritated. Looking over Kitten's shoulder toward the darkened concession counter, Dair heard whispers. She froze. Kitten noticed and released her. "What?" she asked.

Dair nodded toward the counter. "Is someone back there?"

Kitten looked, too, and they both held still, listening. It was unmistakable—there was a hissed, furious conversation going on in the dark. Dair heard, "That's ridiculous! He wouldn't," and recognized Gayle's voice.

Kitten walked to the counter and demanded, "Who's back there?"

A pause, then Gayle said cheerily, "It's Gayle. I'm making coffee."

"In the dark?" Dair loved Kitten's boldness when it wasn't directed at her.

"I can see fine from the lobby light, darling." But Gayle flipped on the light behind the counter, and Malcolm Cole stood there beside her. The hair on Dair's arms stood up.

Gayle busied herself making the coffee she hadn't been making before, but Malcolm stood still, blinking in the light as if disoriented. He blinked again, then focused on Dair. "Hi again," he said. Dair nodded at him and walked back into the theater.

Kitten followed her. "What's going on with them?" she asked.

Dair shrugged, went back onstage, and took her seat at the table.

The stage manager, a skinny guy with too many piercings in his face, scurried around taking attendance. Dair scanned the room and realized with a sharp pang that she was looking for Craig out of habit. Craig, strolling in at the last minute, but with that ready, mischievous laugh that made everyone forgive him. There would be no last minute entrance tonight or ever again. For one second she felt the sensation of falling.

"All right, everyone, let's get started," the stage manager said. "Can you all grab a seat at the table?" People stopped their milling and pulled out folding chairs at the long table.

"Can I squeeze in?" Malcolm asked, and shoved his folding chair between Dair and Kitten. Kitten rolled her eyes at Dair. So much for "the girls" sticking together. Those sharp bird-beak stabs of Dair's heartbeat began. Malcolm felt too close; his presence made her claustrophobic. And the scent of cigarette smoke and his cologne combined unpleasantly into something like charred spices.

"Hey, um, listen," Malcolm whispered in his usual halting speech. "I'm sorry about, you know, this morning. I didn't mean to offend you, you know, about the animal thing—"

"It's okay," Dair said, and turned away from him, angling her body toward Bethany on the other side of her.

"Welcome, everyone," Gayle said. "I'm Gayle Lyons, artistic director of the company." She introduced Rosylyn, the *Othello* director, a guest from Chicago, and the stage manager, then she said, "We have some sad news to discuss this evening as well."

There was a shift, a movement onstage, and about twenty heads turned almost imperceptibly in Dair's direction. She swallowed and wiped a line of sweat from her upper lip. She'd been a moron to dump out that vodka.

"We recently lost a dear friend when Craig MacPhearson died on Saturday. It feels wrong to meet without him. It feels wrong to go on with the show so soon after this loss, but Craig would understand. He would want us to move on."

Dair winced. That speech was so lame. Craig wouldn't want them to go on. He'd be pissed he wasn't in the show, slighted that he'd been replaced so quickly. It was the rest of them who didn't want to halt work on the production. They had contracts, they needed the checks, they wanted their Equity points, their names in the reviews.

"I want you all to know that there is a gathering at my home after his memorial service on Wednesday. You all are welcome to attend. It will be a celebration of a great life, a great friend . . ." Gayle faltered, her lip twitching, her voice jumping too high. It sparked the same reaction in Dair's own lip. Gayle took a moment, took a breath, and took just a few seconds too long to be believed, making her emotion seem overdone, melodramatic. "There is some mystery regarding the circumstances of his death," she said, and again there was that shift in glances in Dair's direction. She felt the searching, the wondering, in their collective gaze. God, why hadn't she braced herself with a drink? She tucked her trembling hands between her thighs. "And we should band together to remember what we know about Craig to be true, not . . . not these strange, disturbing reports the media would have us believe."

Gayle went on, but Malcolm touched Dair's knee, making her jump, and leaned in close to her ear. His voice was not accusing; it was strangely almost pleading as he whispered, "Why was Craig wearing your dress, Dair?"

She whipped her neck around to face him, causing Bethany to turn slightly at the movement. Dair stared into Malcolm's eyes. "It wasn't mine," she whispered.

"But the dress you wore to auditions . . ."

Bethany turned again and frowned, the way people did at first when someone was talking in a nearby seat at the movie theater, hoping they'd get the hint.

Malcolm snapped to attention when Gayle introduced him as the new Iago. He nodded briefly, humbly, and stammered his thanks as various people murmured their approval.

And a thought crossed Dair's mind with a chill: How did Malcolm know what the dress Craig had on even looked like? It was hard to breathe, that bird beak hammered so fast.

Gayle announced, "Well, there's coffee in the lobby behind the concession counter, real and decaf. Help yourselves now, if you like. Take a few minutes, get situated, and then let's get started on *Othello*."

A flurry of movement and scraping of chairs followed as several people stood up and headed out to the lobby and the concession counter. Rosylyn, the director, looked exasperated, perhaps sensing that this death, and Gayle's drama, had upstaged her.

Dair stood and walked with Malcolm toward the stage-left wing. "What makes you think it was my dress he died in? You didn't see it, did you?"

He frowned, confused. "Yeah, we read together at the auditions, you looked great, I—"

"No, I mean, you didn't see it *on Craig*, did you?"

He turned bright red. "No!" He lowered his voice, his eyes scanning the room, as if fearful.

"Well, that's interesting, because all the paper said was that it was a purple dress. There's a lot of purple dresses in the world. Why would you immediately assume it was the purple dress I wore *once* unless you'd seen it on Craig yourself?"

"I—but . . ." He looked lost. He gestured across the stage. "Well, Gayle told me it was your dress."

"What?"

He seemed startled at her reaction. He floundered, his mouth open.

"Oh, please, Malcolm. I find that pretty unlikely."

He nodded. "She told me people were saying that you—"

"It was *Gayle's* dress," Dair snapped. "I borrowed it from *her*. So you need to make up some better lie."

"I'm not lying." He looked across the room at Gayle and frowned.

Dair looked at his face, his fine, delicate features. Everyone was so shocked by the suggestion of Craig's "cross-dressing," but no one would be surprised if it had been Malcolm in a dress. She'd seen him do drag on numerous occasions. With the new goatee it was difficult to imagine him passing as a woman. Actually, there wasn't one feminine thing about him when he wasn't in drag, except maybe his hands. She found herself idly searching his face for a hint of that female persona she'd seen him inhabit.

"Hey, my man," C.J.'s voice boomed as he came up between them. "Welcome," he said to Malcolm, clasping his hand.

"Thanks," Malcolm said, his face anxious. "I'd give anything not to have this, you know."

C.J. nodded somberly.

"Big shoes to fill," Malcolm said.

"Amen," C.J. said. "But you'll rise to the occasion."

"I hope." Malcolm stared out at the darkened theater and scratched at his goatee stubble. "Hey, I'd better grab a cup of coffee, looks like Rosylyn wants to start." He abruptly hopped off the stage and headed for the lobby.

"That is one odd man," C.J. said, staring after him.

"All right, everyone," Rosylyn called. "Let's get started."

C.J. squeezed Dair's shoulder and guided her back to her seat. The rest of the cast took their chairs, and there was a dying down of the scuffling noises. Malcolm's chair remained empty, and when Dair looked for him, she saw him engaged in an intense, whispered conversation with Gayle just inside the theater doorway. Oh, shit. Did Gayle *really* tell Malcolm it was Dair's dress? Why?

"Could we please get started?" Rosylyn asked.

Gayle and Malcolm didn't seem to notice. Everyone watched them. Dair felt sick.

"Hey, Malcolm?" Rosylyn called. "We need you, okay?"

He nodded and ducked, as though she'd slapped his hand, and hurried back to his seat. Gayle walked more slowly, crossing the house and walking onstage on the other side of the table, her eyes on Dair, her face set and angry. Oh, shit.

"All right," Rosylyn said, ignoring Gayle as she settled into the seat beside her. Rosylyn began her spiel about what she was looking for in the read-through tonight, how she'd be stopping them to discuss certain issues and design concepts as they came up.

Malcolm leaned over and whispered, "She says you didn't borrow any dress." What the hell was his problem, scrambling around blabbing all this bullshit gossip?

She couldn't look at Gayle but felt Gayle still glaring at her. With her eyes glued to her script, Dair felt she was drowning. Dry heaves threatened to start any minute, heaves she knew would be calmed by just one soothing sip of alcohol. Sweat trickled under her arms, between her breasts. She picked up her hair to cool the back of her neck.

"All right, then," Rosylyn said. "Let's begin."

The stage manager began to read in his high, nasal voice. "Act one, scene one: Venice, a street. Enter Roderigo and Iago." And Malcolm and an actor from Indianapolis jumped into action with the opening scene.

Dair listened to Malcolm, hating him, thinking him as evil as Iago himself. But Malcolm was good and sucked her in. It amazed her that he could be so skittish, so inarticulate offstage, able to seem comfortable only as someone else. As Iago he was suddenly sinister and confident and gave Dair shivers as he read, "For when my outward action doth demonstrate the native act and figure of my heart in complement extern, 'tis not long after but I will wear my heart upon my sleeve for daws to peck at—I am not what I am."

Dair jumped when a hand touched her shoulder. Gayle stood beside her, lowering her lips to Dair's ear. "Can I talk to you a moment?"

Rosylyn glared at Gayle with barely concealed annoyance. Dair had several pages before her character, Emilia, appeared, but she wanted Rosylyn to protest, to tell Gayle that Dair had to stay. Rosylyn just pursed her lips and dropped her head over her script. Others looked curious, but Malcolm kept reading, and Dair stood and slunk out of the room after Gayle. Gayle led her out of the theater, all the way past the box offices, back to the Procter & Gamble Hall lobby before she spoke. Dair halfway wondered if she should have brought her jacket and purse. Was she being thrown out?

Finally Gayle stopped and crossed her arms. "You 'borrowed' clothes from me?"

Dair exhaled and leaned against the gray wall, engraved with donors' names. "Yes, I did, Gayle, and I'm sorry. It was tacky and unprofessional, and I'm sorry."

Gayle seemed surprised and somewhat let down at this confession, as if she'd expected Dair to offer excuses. Dair knew they were way past the point of her saying something lame like "Well, you did say that I could help myself to anything."

Gayle shook her head. "I'm very disappointed. I can hardly believe this, this betrayal of my trust."

Dair nodded. She took it. Gayle was right.

"When were you planning to tell me, Dair? When the police came to *me* wanting to know how Craig obtained a dress of mine to take his suicide leap in?"

"Gayle, please. I was going to talk to you. I'm very concerned. The dress is gone from your house—"

"Well, *hello*. Obviously, if this is the dress he died in, it's gone from my house. I think this is an important detail the police should know about, that the dress—"

"No, no, no, Gayle, please listen: I cleaned the dress and returned it to your closet. I took it back almost a week before this happened, before Craig . . . died. Someone took it from your house after I—"

"Look, I don't know what was going on with you and Craig, but you can't withhold—"

"*Nothing* was going on with me and Craig. Why is everyone saying that? I'm telling the truth: I returned the dress to your house, and after Craig died, when I came to feed Tuxedo, I checked and your dress was gone. But I know I returned it. Someone else took it from your closet—"

Gayle spread her arms in exasperation. "And just who would break into my home and steal a dress? Do you think Craig broke in and—"

"You told me Malcolm had a key to your house."

"You're trying to shift blame to Malcolm?"

Dair lifted her chin. "I'm not trying to 'shift' anything. I'm just trying to figure out what happened. Look, I did a wrong thing, a tasteless thing, there's no excusing that. But I took the dress back. I put it back in your closet. And Malcolm says *you* told him it was my dress. Why would you say that?"

Gayle opened her mouth, apparently to answer, but something shifted in her face. Dair saw it. She didn't know what Gayle had thought of or what changed her mind, but some startling emotion Dair couldn't identify flashed there, then settled into disgust.

"Why were you there at the time of Craig's death?" Gayle asked, nostrils flaring.

"I was on the way to the airport. But why would you tell Malcolm it was my—"

"Had you been in my house?"

"No. Well, yes, *earlier.* Much earlier. I fed Tuxedo before I went to the Playhouse."

"I don't feel comfortable with you having my key anymore."

Dair nodded, feeling strangely relieved. "Okay. I understand. But Gayle, Malcolm had a key, too. Has he given that back to you?" She thought of the fresh flowers in Gayle's bedroom. "Does anyone else have a key to your house?"

Gayle's eyes flashed. "That is none of your business."

"Gayle, please. I worry about you. I think something happened at your house while you were gone. We found out that someone's been entering Marielle's house when she's not home, and maybe someone is doing that to you as well."

"How did you find that out?" Gayle asked, her voice rising too high.

Dair thought of Slip Jig but said, "There was a window open in her basement." She had to give Gayle more than that. "And a man's footprint on her son's paintings on the table below the window." Dair wondered about her own wording. A *man's* footprint. Slip Jig had said it was a man—but what if it was a woman dressed like a man? Could her mother be mistaken about what she saw? Could cats differentiate human sexes by smell?

"Was anything stolen?" Gayle asked.

"No. Nothing that we can tell."

"Dair," Gayle said, shaking her head again, running her hands through her long chestnut hair, "people don't break into homes to steal nothing, any more than they break into homes to steal one dress."

"But I—"

"Darling, 'Methinks the lady doth protest too much.'"

Dair barely managed to keep the "Fuck you" from escaping her lips, but she was pretty sure Gayle picked up on it anyway. How was that for telepathic communication? The two women glared at each other.

"I want my key back," Gayle repeated.

Dair said coolly, "I'll bring it over as soon as rehearsal's done."

Gayle shook her head. "No. No, don't come tonight." She said it as if she already had some unpleasant task scheduled for later. Her nostrils flared again. And her lips nearly disappeared, they were pinched so tight. "Just bring it to rehearsal tomorrow night. I'll be here, in the box office, when you arrive."

Dair nodded.

Gayle cleared her throat. "The fact that Malcolm had a key to my home is not something I want spread around. Do you understand me?"

Dair lifted her chin again. "Yes, I think I *do* understand you, Gayle, and I don't like it. I think the police need to know that—"

"Oh, I'll talk to the police all right," Gayle snapped, her face red, her voice tight, as if fisted around her fury. "I'll talk to the police *tonight*. And *you'll* talk to them, too."

Gayle turned and walked back down the marble hall, leaving Dair there, smoldering. If Gayle called the police on Dair, then Dair had plenty to tell them besides her "borrowing" of the purple dress. Gayle handing out keys all over the place. Coming back into town early. She could've been home by the time of Craig's death, for all Dair knew.

Although Dair wanted nothing more than to leave, hit the liquor store, and go home with a new bottle of Absolut, she followed Gayle back to the read-through. The rest of the cast seemed to hold their breath until she sat at the table again and turned her script to the page Bethany was on. Dair felt her anger run into a drain around her feet.

Without the thick cloak of anger, Dair felt naked, raw, as they reached her first scene. Her voice shook as she read. And her hands trembled on the paper, so she left her script flat on the table and clutched Andy's fleece jacket in her lap for comfort.

Malcolm was a poisonous Iago, already reading his lines to her with a taunting sort of sneer, speaking of all women, "You are . . . players in your housewifery and housewives in your beds." She hated him, and her face flamed red at every mention in the script of infidelity.

And as Iago spoke of his plans to ruin Othello—"I'll pour this pestilence into his ear"—and of Desdemona—"So will I turn her virtue into pitch"—Dair thought this was exactly what had been done to Craig.

They read through act III, and the stage manager announced a fifteen-minute break. Dair leaned down to tie her shoe so she didn't have to make eye contact with anyone. When most of the chair scuffling had stopped, she stood up, trying to be cheerful, game. She found herself alone onstage with the stage manager, who stared woefully at his watch and twirled the ring in his left nostril.

She carried Andy's fleece jacket into the lobby. Malcolm was talking with C.J. and Bethany at the concession counter, gesturing occasionally in her direction. Near the rest room alcove, Kitten watched, enthralled, as Rosylyn and Gayle exchanged words. Dair looked toward the stairs where some younger guys, from CCM, turned their shoulders slightly when she looked at them. She was back in fifth grade—the freak no one would talk to. People might bark at her any second.

Dair retraced her steps back to the Procter & Gamble Hall lobby, went up the grand marble staircase, and slipped through the double doors into the theater. The houselights were on, the set assembly for the touring revue almost complete. Terry, one of the union guys she knew, drilled a flat into the stage floor. She walked down the aisle, ducking under a ladder set up to adjust lighting instruments, to the stage's edge. "Hey, Terry," she called.

He stopped drilling and smiled.

"Seen Andy?"

Terry sighed and gestured with his head. "Check outside."

Dair laughed and headed for the stage door where she'd signed in. And outside, thank God, Andy leaned against the building, smoking under the blue awning.

"Well, hello again," he said, grinning when he saw her.

"It's true, what you said." Dair handed him his jacket, which he tucked under his arm. "Everyone thinks I was sleeping with Craig."

Andy handed her a cigarette, which she took without a word. He lit it, keeping his eyes on hers, not the flame, clicking shut the lighter only when she stood and took a deep drag. "Not everyone believes it. The union guys don't. Don't worry."

Dair slumped against the building, feeling queasy. She looked at this familiar street—the parking garage right across from them; the photo shop; First Watch, where Dair liked to eat breakfast; the Orient, where she sometimes slipped into the bar and had a glass of wine or two by herself. "This is so . . . wrong," she said. "This can't be happening. Do you feel that way, too? That we couldn't possibly have seen what we thought we saw?"

Andy stared down at his shoes. "People keep asking me about it. They know we were there. And each time I tell it, it feels a little more real, a little more true. It's weird, but it actually helps to tell the story."

Dair nodded. She knew what he meant.

Andy paused thoughtfully. "Last night, when Gayle came by the theater, we talked about it. She was so weird. Drilling me on who was there, making me describe how it happened, what I'd seen, what you'd said, what the police did."

"Really?" This quickened Dair's pulse.

He nodded and smoked a moment, then his eyes lightened. "Oh, hey, you know what? I asked around, trying to figure out who started that rumor? And most of these guys say Malcolm told them, so maybe you should talk to—"

"Malcolm Cole? That *shit*."

"Yeah, and it gets better. The guys have some dirt on Malcolm, too."

Dair paused. She wanted to ask what it was, of course, but it troubled her that the same guys who claimed not to believe dirt on her were spreading it around on someone else. But curiosity—fueled by anger—won out. "What?" she asked.

Andy grinned. "You'll never guess who Malcolm's bumping uglies with."

Dair raised her eyebrows. "How charming," she said of the expression. Of all the dirt she expected on Malcolm, this wasn't it. His boyfriend had only been out of the picture for a month or two. Andy had only been in town that long, so he'd never seen Malcolm and Jimmy together. "You're right," she said. "I can't guess. Tell me."

Andy paused, with an expression that told Dair to brace herself, and said, "Gayle."

Dair would've laughed, but since Saturday anything felt possible. Before Saturday she would've laughed at the notion of Craig in drag or Craig on dope, but now . . . "W-why would you say that?" she asked.

"He's been seen leaving her place. Apparently he's even got a key."

Dair swallowed, thinking of Gayle's declaration that she didn't want this spread around. Why? Because Malcolm was gay? Or, at least, reputed to be? Dair nodded. "I heard that. About a key." She felt sick. Had everyone already known this but her?

She pulled another drag off the cigarette, and although it soothed her somewhat, it was a poor substitute for what she really wanted. "God, I need a drink." She stared across the street, wondering if she could get served at the Orient and be back in—she checked her watch—seven minutes.

"Ask and you shall receive," Andy said with a sly smile, pulling a thin flask from the inside pocket of his Aronoff jacket. He held it out to her.

"You are my hero," Dair said, meaning it. She took the flask, unscrewed the top, and sniffed. "Scotch?"

He nodded.

Dair wrinkled her nose but took a swig. She growled and stomped her foot as the Scotch smarted down her throat like cough medicine. "God, how can you drink this stuff?"

Andy laughed. Dair took another swallow, which made her convulse with shudders. She longed to take another—imagining the stuff might be close to likable over ice—hell, she'd like to polish off the entire flask, but she made herself hand the flask back, not wanting to appear as needy and desperate as she felt. "Thank you from the bottom of my heart."

Andy pocketed the flask and said gently, "Hang in there, Dair. It'll all be okay."

The soothing flush of his words and the alcohol rose to her brain, and without warning she felt she might cry.

"Thanks," she said, embarrassed, and reentered the Aronoff, nodding at Joe, the security guard. Back in the Jarson-Kaplan Theater, she took her seat, one of the first at the table. At least she could stay on Rosylyn's good side.

The last two acts went uneventfully, and the Scotch melted into Dair with a warming calm. She risked glances at Gayle on occasion, but Gayle stared down at her script, chewing a thumbnail. Dair counted five pages that Gayle failed to turn when the rest of the cast did.

When rehearsal ended, Malcolm leapt from his chair and fled the theater. Dair followed him through the bustle of cast members gathering their belongings. He stopped on the marble stair leading up to Procter & Gamble Hall, obviously waiting for someone. He seemed startled when he saw her approach.

"Sorry, Dair, I didn't mean to get Gayle pissed at you, I—"

"Look. I'm on to you," Dair said, climbing up two stairs to where he stood.

Malcolm blinked. "What?"

"I know you started those rumors, you little shit, and you better go right back and tell everyone it's nothing but a goddamn lie."

Malcolm backed up against the railing, clutching his leather bag protectively in front of him with his delicate little doll hands.

"Why'd you have a key to Gayle's house?"

Two little stripes of red appeared on his face. "I . . . well, that's—"

"Why didn't you give it back like you were supposed to?"

"I—I lost it. I couldn't find it at the audition. I kept thinking—"

"Please," Dair said. "You need to come up with better than that. Don't be trying to drag me into your mess if all you've got is a flimsy 'I lost it'—"

"I *did* lose it, and what the hell does that have to do with any—"

"And if Gayle's gonna have me talk to the police," Dair said, "because of what you told her, then you can be damn sure that they're gonna talk to you, too."

Malcolm's eyes and mouth went into round O's. "The police? W-why would I have to talk to the police?"

Dair moved close to him, in his face. "I don't know what's going on, or who has something to hide—you or Gayle or both. Tell me: Why'd you have a key to Gayle's house?"

Malcolm sniffed loudly. "Jesus, Dair, have you been drinking?"

She backed away from him, knowing she smelled like Scotch.

He started to speak, then stopped as Gayle rounded the corner of the staircase and almost plowed into them.

"What's going on?" Gayle asked in a high-pitched, anxious voice.

"Nothing," Malcolm and Dair answered in unison, then looked at each other, surprised.

"Dair? Malcolm? I thought we understood each other." Gayle's eyes were in that unblinking gaze again, reminding Dair of the bald eagles at the zoo.

"We were just talking about the show," Malcolm said, touching Dair's arm. Dair sensed, almost smelled, his fear, like a musky cologne. It confused Dair. Especially since Gayle was also exuding fear, nearly panic. Dair looked back and forth between the two of them and recognized that Gayle didn't want Dair and Malcolm talking to *each other.*

"See you guys tomorrow," Dair said with false cheer, and fled down the stairs and outside.

Dair drove home, too fast, furious and confused. She needed Peyton. She wanted Peyton home. Then she moaned. Peyton had gone to see her dad. Oh, God. Was this the night it would finally all come down? The night she'd been dreading for eight years?

He was home, but the house was dark, the only light spilling from the basement windows. Dair stepped out of her car and heard the clicking, like a distant swarm of locusts.

Peyton was dancing. Dancing at ten-thirty at night.

Chapter Thirteen

What Is Found, What Is Lost, What Is Remembered was the title of the new dance Peyton rehearsed.

He worked a piece of it in the basement, on the scuffed and gouged wooden dance floor.

Stomp, fl-ap, heel, stomp.

Toe-toe, heel-dig, stomp.

Turning to the right, he used a basement window to spot, while his feet flashed through: spank, stomp-shuffle, toe-shuffle, stomp-shuffle, toe-shuffle, stomp, toe-toe.

Shlurp, toe, pop, heel.

Chug, toe-toe-heel, slide . . . heel.

The slide was cool. Up on his toes—literally—skating about a yard on the metal lip of his shoes' ball taps, knees bent, like a skier *en pointe*. The gliding taps shaved the wooden floor with the satisfying ring of a sword being drawn. The slide ended with a clean smack of his heels.

What Is Found, What Is Lost, What Is Remembered. Felt like the story of his life.

What is found: He'd found Dair, thank God. Against all the odds, he'd found her, by accident, in the park, with a fluffy white puppy. And known that he'd known her before.

What is lost: Dair had to stop drinking. She had to get help. Peyton knew this, but for the very reasons he knew this, he was not the one to push her.

What is remembered: A life before. A connection. A time Dair had watched over him, mourned for him.

But he wasn't sure. He'd thought he had it all figured out. He'd thought he'd get the information he needed today, but he'd only grown more confused. What is lost.

Stomp, fl-ap, heel, stomp.

Toe-toe, heel-dig, stomp.

Peyton paused in the basement, panting. His shins ached from the roll up onto his toes for the slide.

Moving on. He started the next section, slowly, haltingly.

Crunch, hop, brush, step-chug.

Turning to the left: shuffle, pull-back, step toe, chug-chug-chug.

Press, cramp roll.

One of the things Peyton loved about dance was that every move, no matter how complicated, could be broken down. Dissected into parts, to be examined, practiced, until it could go back into the whole.

The goal was the whole, of course. To be able to think of whole combinations as one movement, without the division in his brain of individual steps. But sometimes the only way in was to isolate and break it apart. A cramp roll started as toe . . . toe . . . heel . . . heel . . . separated and deliberate, until it gathered speed and finesse and blurred into a drumroll.

That's what he'd wanted to do today, with Dair's family history, but the breaking apart was leading to only more confusion, not to any clarity.

Seeing R.B. had been great, but strange. Peyton loved that big bear of a man with his head of white hair, his sparkling, fiery eyes. R.B. and Peyton had gone in R.B.'s cluttered truck for a follow-up visit to a horse R.B.'d stitched yesterday, after the horse had caught his nostril flap on a nail and nearly sliced it off. R.B. told Peyton they had a twenty-minute drive, so Peyton figured he had time to approach the subject; but once Peyton had cleared himself a seat among the heartworm pill samples and boxed flea collars, he'd hesitated, sensing a looming point of no return—a feeling similar to one he'd had nine years ago, when he'd had to tell his artistic director about his drug history. Maggie had been ready to hire him, and although it was tempting to believe that once she knew him, once he'd proven himself as a member of the company, she couldn't possibly let him go when she learned the truth, he was too nervous to bank on that. He couldn't keep something like that secret without being sick with it. He didn't need that stress.

Plus, laying it out there felt like protection. Upped the stakes on himself. Placed another obstacle across the wrong path.

Peyton had the advantage, here, in the truck cab, since R.B. had to keep his eyes on the road. Peyton leaned against the passenger door and watched his father-in-law's stooped shoulders, his weary profile.

"I'm really sorry about the divorce," Peyton said.

"So, it's a divorce?" R.B. asked, looking more tired. "I thought we were just separating."

Peyton swallowed. "Cassie said you might divorce."

R.B. shook his head. "I tell you, son, make sure you and Dair talk about everything possible. Don't keep anything back, even if you think it'll hurt her. You gotta tell her everything. If you don't, this'll happen. Something from way back when will fester and ooze and drive you apart." His words were swollen with regret.

Peyton felt himself go still inside. He hadn't expected it to be this easy, for R.B. to reveal another key to the breakup so readily. "But . . . I thought this was about the animal communication?"

R.B. frowned as he slowed to take a turn onto another road. He shook his head. "She's the one who's not communicating, if she says that's the reason."

"So you do believe in it?"

"Does it matter?"

"I think it matters to her."

R.B. sighed. "I think it's possible."

Peyton waited for him to say more.

"The woman knows animals. She understands their behavior. She's open and patient and so can read them pretty well. But as for knowing their thoughts, I'm not sure. I'm not sure I want to believe we can know their thoughts. I think that's part of the beauty of living with other animals, that we can't know. But that's . . ." He sighed and draped his wrist over the top of the steering wheel. "It isn't the communication I have a problem with. It's what it does to her."

"What do you mean?"

R.B. sighed. "It . . . whatever you believe about what she does or how she does it, she has this . . . this . . . skill."

Peyton nodded. "It's a gift."

"It's a *curse*," R.B. snapped. "It takes its toll on her. I think it's dangerous." He made a growling noise. "But this is all beside the point. The point is that two people who *could* tell each other their thoughts *didn't,* and now something good is ruined."

"I thought . . . I mean . . . R.B., I saw her do her . . . her thing last night. She got information from the neighbor's cat that she couldn't possibly have known any other way. I mean, she . . . like she could describe this woman's bedroom, and she'd never been inside that house. But it didn't seem to affect Cassie badly. I mean, she seemed tired, but that's all."

R.B. said nothing. He kept his eyes on the road but contorted his face in an odd grimace, as if he were chewing the inside of his lip. Then he nodded, as if to himself. "If she told you that's why we're splitting up, then I don't care what kind of workshop she's having this Saturday—she's got a serious problem with human communication, because that's not the reason she gave me."

Peyton tried to picture R.B., with his familiar calm and ease. He wanted not to have brought R.B. to these emotions—this pain, this sorrow, that crossed his face in waves, washing up from some dark shore inside him, a shore Peyton had never seen in all the years he'd known this man. But . . . was it possible they were sitting on something as simple as a misunderstanding? This thought made him bold.

"What's the reason she gave you?" Peyton almost whispered it. It wasn't like him to ask personal questions. It wasn't like R.B. to reveal things. They talked sometimes, in coded, vague ways, about Peyton's former drug problems, but R.B. never pried for details, and Peyton rarely volunteered them. R.B. had once, in passing, mentioned to Peyton that he'd read a book about narcotic addiction and that he admired Peyton for what he'd managed to escape. That was it. The fact he'd found the book and read it said everything else Peyton needed to know. R.B. wanted to understand Peyton and was willing to do a bit of work to do so. Peyton's own parents had never made the slightest effort.

Peyton wanted there to be a book, now, for him to buy and read, to understand what was happening to R.B. and Cass. And to Dair. For what had happened to this family when Sylvan died.

R.B. didn't answer his question for so long, Peyton feared R.B. actually hadn't heard him, but eventually R.B. said, "Something . . . happened a long time ago. We were young. We didn't have a clue."

Peyton didn't ask what he meant. He waited. And R.B. eventually said more. "We'd never been through a crisis before. Talk about communication—we didn't have it yet to help each other. So we didn't. That's all. I didn't think I was more guilty than she was." He made a soft sound—a moan and a sigh combined. "The problem is that *she* thinks I think she's guilty, and I can never convince her otherwise." Barely audibly, he added, "Maybe I don't try. Maybe I do think so."

The rolling hills of the Ohio landscape seemed to tilt in Peyton's vision. He sensed they were about to step into forbidden territory, about to trek into wilderness he'd been aching to explore for eight years. "Are you talking about . . . Dair's sister?"

The truck lurched as R.B. braked. He looked as though Peyton had just plunged a knife into his gut. R.B.'s eyes reminded Peyton of Dair's last night when he'd asked her about the bottle. The truck slowed to about five miles an hour, but R.B. didn't seem aware. Fortunately the road was empty behind them. Dair had warned Peyton, pleaded with him not to talk about Sylvan. He might as well kick R.B. or stomp on his hands.

"Sister?" R.B. asked in a voice hollow with betrayal.

"I'm sorry," Peyton whispered. "Never mind. I shouldn't have—"

"Sister?" R.B. repeated in a tone that suggested Peyton had said "Dair's elephant." The muscles in his face twitched. "For Christ's sake, what did she say to you?" The truck crawled along in the center of the asphalt road, and Peyton wanted to ask R.B. to stop driving.

"Cassie? Cassie didn't tell me anything about Sylvan, she never has. It was Dair who—"

"Sylvan?" R.B. asked as if exasperated. "Now what the hell are you talking about?"

Jesus, it gave Peyton chills. But before he could answer, R.B said, "Shit," and braked, hard, making Peyton grab the dashboard. Some white tubes of horse wormer slid into Peyton's lap. He put them back.

"I passed the damn farm we were heading for," R.B. said. He pulled the truck over, though, stopping on a soft shoulder overlooking a field of pumpkins.

"She doesn't tell me anything," R.B. said, staring straight ahead as if he were still driving. "So what good does it do me if she can talk to animals? I can't. They can't tell me what she's thinking."

Peyton hated himself for bringing it up; it was stupid, selfish. He had no idea the pain they'd been through.

R.B. leaned his forehead on the steering wheel. Peyton reached out and patted his shoulder. "R.B. I'm sorry, man. I'm sorry."

"So am I," R.B. said without lifting his head, looking at the dashboard. "I don't know what to do. I don't know how to salvage this."

They sat, Peyton staring at the pumpkin patch, R.B. staring at the dashboard. Peyton let R.B. have his sorrow and his silence and didn't intrude on it. It rose from him like an oboe. Some hammered dulcimer as well, those plucking notes the sound of his strength being pecked at.

R.B. sat up. "Do *you* think Dair drinks too much?"

Although the change in topic surprised him, Peyton answered without hesitation. "Yes."

R.B. blinked. Then his mouth puckered and he said, "Christ." He put his head back down on the steering wheel. "Christ, Cass is right."

Peyton looked away, out at the pumpkins. "Yeah. She tried to talk to Dair about it."

"Did she? Good. But I meant Cass was right: I only see what I want to see."

Now Peyton blinked. "What do you mean?"

"You've got to stop her," R.B. said to the floor. "You've got to get her help."

"I know."

"Before it ruins everything."

"I know."

R.B. sat up and grabbed Peyton's shirt in his fist. Peyton fought the urge to resist, to react. "Peyton, you have to *do* something."

"I *know*." He tried to shrug off R.B.'s hand, but R.B. hung on. Without thinking, Peyton bent R.B.'s wrist in an aikido hold. R.B. gasped and let go, and Peyton immediately let go as well. "I'm sorry," Peyton said, and he meant it. He knew the flash of pain was fleeting, that it had lasted only as long as he'd kept hold of R.B.'s wrist, but even so, he was mortified by his instinctual action. "R.B. Don't forget who you're talking to. *I know*."

R.B. looked down at his wrist, flexed it, and massaged it with his other hand, but he didn't comment. Then he rubbed both hands over his face and sighed. "Talk to Dair," he said, putting the truck back in drive. "About everything."

Peyton did, didn't he? No . . . he hadn't told her about coming back early Saturday. About checking on her. About being Malcolm's sponsor. Maybe he should, although now she seemed determined to hate Malcolm. He didn't want to give her more reason.

What is found, what is lost, what is remembered.

Back home, in the basement, Peyton repeated the sequence from the top, arches throbbing, shins screaming, lungs aching, heart yearning for a rest.

The day hadn't gone as he'd planned. But trying to talk to R.B. had only been the first step, broken down. Peyton would master this combination. But it was clearly going to take more work than he'd originally expected.

Chapter Fourteen

Both dogs barked and wriggled as Dair entered through the back door, shutting it firmly to cue Peyton that she was back. She dropped her bag and script in the kitchen and waited, but Peyton kept dancing. Her heart tapped along with his speedy, staccato steps. She crouched with her arms around Blizzard—who tried to lick her ear—and listened. It wasn't hard stomping like yesterday. The sounds were fine, finessed, like castanets.

Shodan went back to the basement, toenails clicking on the wooden steps, and Dair followed with Blizzard. Dair went all the way to the bottom, and still Peyton danced. Oh, God. Was he so mad that he couldn't even speak to her? Look at her? He watched the floor, kept his eyes on his own flashing feet, his expression thoughtful, his tongue out between his teeth, its pink tip curled up and touching his upper lip. She saw he really didn't hear her; he was in his own world.

She sat on the steps and hugged herself, although the basement was warm, heat cranked high the way Peyton always had it when he danced. What did she expect him to do when he found out? If she had to direct that scene in a play, she wasn't sure how she'd coach it. Hundreds of versions of the scene existed in her head, but only one ending: Peyton left.

He kept working, embodying the dance and the music at once. He stopped, his back to her, and repeated one step several times, a combination that ended with his right foot up behind him, twinkling its silver tap at her under the lightbulb, reminding her of Bonnie the Clydesdale, how the mare's horseshoes flashed in the sun when she trotted across the field.

Peyton repeated the combination again, and Dair watched with her familiar sense of gratitude and amazement: this beautiful, talented man chose her, loved her. He stopped, hands on his slender hips, staring at the floor, breathing hard.

"Hey," Dair said.

He whipped around to face her, taps clattering on the floor. He laughed and clutched a hand to his heart.

His first reaction upon seeing her was laughter. She breathed a sigh, releasing a breath she hadn't realized she'd been holding.

But it didn't lighten her as much as she had hoped. Had she entered the house with more anticipation than dread? She'd almost looked forward to the disclosure, wanted to feel that sweet release like the night she'd told Craig about the lie. But the bird was still in there, rattling its cage.

Peyton picked up a sweatshirt from the floor and wiped his face, then left it around his neck and approached her. She stood up. "I stink," he warned her.

"So do I."

He cocked his head, curious. Dair made a face. "Scotch. I had a couple sips of Scotch." He seemed uncertain what to do in the face of this admission. "It was from Andy's flask. I had a smoking break with him."

"Oh, so cigarettes *and* Scotch?" Peyton teased. His face was open, kind.

She nodded. "A couple sips and that's . . ." She paused, thinking. "And that's all today." That wasn't true. There'd been a sip of vodka that morning. No, there wasn't. She'd dumped it down the toilet. But that was after the zoo. There'd been a sip before the zoo, right? God, she couldn't even remember anymore. Besides, that bottle was gone and according to her lie had been dumped yesterday, so she couldn't have drunk from it today.

Peyton took her hands, making her think of Gayle. "And how do you feel?"

"Honestly? Right now I'm pissed off. The read-through was horrible."

"Why?"

"Well, there's a lovely little rumor going around that Craig and I were having an affair."

Peyton raised his eyebrows. "People are kidding, right?"

"No, they're not kidding."

"We've joked about that for years. Me and Marielle."

"Really? Me and Craig joked about it, too."

"But it's not true," Peyton said. And Dair loved him for saying it the way he did. A statement. Not a question. Not a flicker of doubt.

"Everyone else thinks it is. And Malcolm Cole started it."

"Malcolm?" Peyton asked. He laughed and said, "No," as if she'd told him her mother had kicked a cat.

"Well, he did. He's stirred up all this crap, and remember, he's the one with a key to Gayle's—"

"Dair, that's . . . that's just—that can't be right."

That was the wrong answer, and it stung her. All she wanted was for him to side with her, to *consider* it, for God's sake. Couldn't he tell that's all she needed? "How do *you* know?" she snapped.

Peyton wiped his face again with his sweatshirt and didn't answer.

She sighed. She didn't want to argue with him; she wasn't mad at *him*. "It was awful," she said, trying to soften her tone, trying to convince him. "And Malcolm asked me if that was my dress that Craig died in, and when I told him I borrowed it from Gayle, he went and blabbed to her, and now she's all pissed at me and is going to tell the police."

"Why is Gayle pissed?" Peyton asked, tilting his head. "Because the dress is gone?"

"Right. I told her that I'd put it back, and that someone must've taken it after I returned it."

"But . . ." He looked baffled. "Did you tell her about Marielle's intruder? Why would she be mad? She ought to be scared. I mean, she knew you borrowed the dress, right?"

Dair considered her answer but was too tired to add another lie to the pile. She shook her head.

His eyes widened. "You just *took* it?"

She nodded.

"Dair." He sounded amazed.

She nodded again and said, as statement of fact, not in way of an excuse, "But I cleaned it and returned it, and then somebody *else* took it, and it's the dress Craig died in."

Peyton stared, processing this information. "Shit," he said. She saw him replaying the information in his head. "And you had a key to Gayle's house, and Craig died near that house, and . . ."

"Right. And Gayle and Malcolm are both acting really strange and mad at me. This is really screwed up. I'm scared."

"Chickadee, you have got to stop lying."

"I know." She felt that fluttering torture against her ribs just as she had that night at Palomino's with Craig. Those wings would torment her until she blurted it; she teetered on the edge, almost wanting to get it over with. "I know. It's out of control. I think I need help."

She sat on the steps again. She couldn't remain standing; her legs threatened to give out any minute. "I'm so tired of it all. I—I really can't do this anymore." It was too much effort to keep moving, much less keep lifting the weight of the lies.

He looked down at her. "It'll be okay," he said, offering his hand to hoist her up. "After a rough night, you deserve some treats."

She let him haul her to her feet and tried to be grateful, involved. "That's right, in your note you promised me treats." He grinned and turned her shoulders to face up the stairs, then put his hands on her butt, pushing her to get her moving.

Dair laughed and let him guide her to the top of the stairs, where he kissed her and very kindly said nothing about the Scotch or cigarettes.

"Is my treat in the bedroom, by any chance?" She wanted to lose herself in him. She wanted to do something that required no talking, no thinking, no keeping track.

He grinned, that little scar by his eye disappearing in his laugh crinkles. "Actually, if you'd rather . . . I had a different treat for us . . . but, maybe we could combine them."

"Ooh, now I'm really curious."

He opened the freezer and flourished a pint of Graeter's ice cream—black raspberry chip.

"Oh, my," Dair said.

"And wait, there's more." He pulled a jar of fudge out of the fridge, took off the lid, and popped it in the microwave.

"What prompted this treat?" she asked as he got out bowls and divided the container of ice cream into two servings.

"Honestly?" he asked.

She laughed at his question. Did he have different versions? "Yeah. Honestly."

He turned to face her. "You dumped your bottle of vodka."

She froze. How did he know that? Oh, that's right, she'd told him that *last* night, but she hadn't poured it out until today. The microwave chirped. She longed to lie down on the floor.

"And that," he said, taking out the warm, now syrupy fudge, "is worth celebrating." He dipped his finger in the hot fudge, spread it on her mouth like lipstick, then proceeded to kiss it from her. When he finished, and Dair stood there pleasantly intoxicated, he continued speaking as if he'd never stopped, "And because it's never healthy to give up all vices at once, giving up one means we should indulge some others." He dipped his finger in the fudge again, but this time as he brought his finger to her lips, she opened them and sucked off the chocolate. His voice grew huskier as he whispered, "Everything in moderation . . . *including* moderation."

She released his clean finger, and he opened a drawer and took out two spoons. He poured the hot fudge over the giant ice-cream piles and presented her bowl to her with a bow. Dair followed him into the living room, where they both sat on the couch, cross-legged.

"Did you have rehearsal today?"

He shook his head. "We start again tomorrow." He took a big bite of ice cream and said around the mouthful, "You know how everyone asks if we're like Riverdance?"

Dair tried not to grin.

Peyton took another bite of ice cream and tapped his spoon on his lip thoughtfully. "Maybe I could be as famous as Michael Flatley, Lord of the Dance."

"Oh, yeah, how?"

"Maybe I'm just not taking off enough clothes."

"Ooh. I'll help."

"Would you?"

"Sure, come over here."

They reached to put their ice-cream bowls on the trunk. "Oh, our ice cream will melt," Peyton said, pretending to be sad, as if weighing whether to eat his ice cream or have sex.

"Get over here," she said.

"No, we don't want to be wasteful," he teased. He fed her a spoon-ful and pulled her black V-neck over her head.

"Hey," she protested around the cold sweetness in her mouth, "I'm supposed to be taking off *your* clothes."

He shrugged. She fed him a spoonful and peeled off his sweaty, sleeveless T-shirt.

His fingers skillfully unclasped her bra and tossed it over the trunk to the floor.

She scooped another spoon into his mouth and tugged down on his sweatpants.

The next spoonful Peyton let fall, with a plop, onto her chest. She gasped at the coldness. "Ooops," he said, "sorry. Let me get that." With the spoon, he chased the bite of buttery cream around and around her right nipple. The cold raised the nipple sharp and hard, and goose bumps sprinkled all over her body. "I just can't seem to get it," he said, sliding the melting mound over to her left nipple. Although her breasts tightened with the cold, they sent direct signals between her legs, where the reaction was warm.

"M-maybe the spoon is n-no good," she said through chattering teeth.

He clinked the spoon back into the bowl and lowered his head, using his very warm mouth instead. She moaned as he lapped the ice cream from her. Some of the melted cream ran down between her breasts, pooled in her belly button, and continued.

"Uh-oh," Peyton said, working at the button of her fly. "Better get these off you before they get sticky."

"Too late," she whispered. She wriggled her hips, helping him slide off her jeans and panties. He scooped up a spoon of ice cream from her bowl and placed it between her legs.

She sat bolt upright. "Ah, ah, ah, too cold, too cold, too cold!" He scooped it up with his hand, dropped it in a bowl, and placed his warm mouth over the tingling flesh. "Oh, my," she said. "Oh, my." Then she said nothing more for quite some time as he worked to make up for his error. Their chests and bellies stuck together with the melted ice-cream residue and parted with little kissing sounds that made them smile.

"We're disgusting," she said later, laughing as they lay, panting, on the couch, their gooey bodies squishing like the floor of a movie theater.

She had her head on Peyton's chest, his heart drumming in her ear, his arms around her, his legs wrapped around her own. They found themselves in their tight little ball on the couch, two long bodies occupying a small space.

The read-through flashed through Dair's mind, and tension seeped back into her neck and shoulders. She wanted to focus on the present like Blizzard or Godot, but there she was, happy and safe and satisfied yet unable to savor it because of what had happened an hour ago or what might happen in the next.

"I'm sorry about the read-through," Peyton said into her hair. "The rumor. It'll pass."

"I don't know. Gayle's gonna have the police talk to me about the dress."

"Just tell them the truth," Peyton said as if that were the easiest thing in the world. "I mean, what else can you do?"

Was he joking? What else could she do? She could do what came more naturally than even loving him. She could lie. But it was so confusing now that she couldn't keep track of what was true and what was false.

"It's hard," she said, surprised by her own small voice.

"What is?"

"Telling the truth. I lie all the time, Peyton."

He chuckled. "Well, you're not gonna lie to the police."

He seemed so sure. God, what would he do? How would he react?

"What?" he asked, stroking her hair. "What is it?"

She opened her mouth and thought of a dozen ways to say it. Opening lines flew through her brain, as those wings in her chest struggled and beat against her ribs. She could say, "Peyton, I lie all the time, even to you." She could say, "Would you hate me if I lied a big lie?" She could say, "It's not 'reality enhancement,' Peyton, it *is* my reality. I've lied something almost into existence. It's real to you." But she just kept her face glued to his chest, his heartbeat thrumming in her ear. Across the room she saw Blizzard snuffling around the trunk, working up the courage to lick the ice-cream bowl.

Peyton's abdomen tightened beneath her, his muscles rippling as he gathered himself to sit up. She exhaled and tried to keep him on the couch. "Dair? What's wrong?"

"Nothing," she said. "Long day." She tried to change her energy and asked in a chipper, perky voice, "So, how was *your* day?"

He hesitated. "It was . . . odd."

Now she tightened. "Odd? How? Is my dad okay?" She sat up, peeling her belly from his with a sticky smack. She sat cross-legged and wrapped her arms around Peyton's bent knees, staring down at him on his back.

"He seems okay, he's just . . . He was really happy I came over. I could tell it meant a lot to him."

Dair squeezed his knees. "But what was odd?"

"Well, we had a strange conversation."

That chickadee started its *thunk thunk thunk* on her sternum again. "About what?"

"About your sister."

The *thunk thunk* stopped abruptly, but its absence was even more excruciating. Blizzard lifted his head toward her, ears up. Peyton wrinkled his forehead and reached for one of her hands. "Hon, it's okay. I worry about all of you. You can't pretend she didn't exist."

Dair opened her mouth to say, "She didn't," but the effort to speak was too much.

"It's not healthy," he continued. "Your dad got almost . . . I don't know how to describe it. I think you all need to talk about it. You need to do something, go to her grave or something. Go to counseling. It's time to do something, to let it go."

Breath came back into her throat like someone turning on a faucet. In a hissed rasp she said, "I have let it go, Peyton. *You* keep dredging it up."

"But how can you let it go when you don't ever talk about it? I got the impression from your dad that he and your mom have hardly ever even talked about it."

Of course they hadn't. How could they talk about something they didn't know about? "Don't bother them about it, Peyton, please. I thought you went to talk about the divorce."

"I did, but that's the thing—your dad started it. He says the communication thing isn't their real problem, or at least not the communication with animals. He says their problems started with not talking to each other, and how they didn't know how to get through a crisis together, and I asked, 'You mean Dair's sister?' and then he acted all . . . like I think he was *angry* that I even knew about her. He says the reasons Cassie told us she wants a divorce are not the reasons she told him—"

Dair's head spun. She wanted to lean down, shake his shoulders, shut him up. She wanted to drill him with questions: "You said 'Dair's sister'? You said those very words, and he didn't respond?" How did she get so lucky? Only it didn't feel like luck at all. It felt like a curse. How could that question not have turned into a disaster? She was weary of waiting for the wreck. The suspense was literally killing her.

"Don't bother them," she begged. "Please. I know you mean well, but—"

"But, don't you see, Dair? The animal communication is not the reason they're splitting up. They're splitting up, I think, *because* of Sylvan. So there's hope, right? We could get you all to talk about this, and maybe they'll stay together."

"No, Peyton."

"But—"

"They are *never* going to talk about Sylvan." She swallowed, her throat dry, aching. She longed for some cool white wine to soothe it. Her father. She felt that combination of love and hate toward him. He must be protecting her just like Mom did with the vodka bottle last night. She hated him for not getting it over with, for not saying to Peyton, "What the hell are you talking about?" But that wish was more cowardly than keeping the lie alive. Did she really want Peyton to find out from someone else? If there was a scrap of hope, any chance at all of changing the ending of the scene, the truth had to come from her.

She took a deep breath and opened the cage. "Peyton, it's all a lie."

Had she actually said it? Finally said it out loud? Would the bird fly?

He frowned, forehead crinkling. He opened his mouth to protest, but she kept talking. "I made up Sylvan. She never existed." There. She'd said it. But it didn't feel at all like when she'd told Craig. The bird wouldn't move. A rush of adrenaline flooded through her as she pictured herself yanking it from the cage, hurling it into free fall when it refused to fly. "My dad isn't in denial; he honestly had no idea what you were talking about. He's just trying to protect me because he knows what a liar I am. He shouldn't have done that. I've been waiting for this to happen. I thought when you finally asked him or my mom it would all come out, but somehow it didn't, unless, unless you know it's a lie and you're just testing me, playing with me. Are you? Is that what you're doing? Because I'd deserve it."

Peyton's face had settled into a stillness. "What are you talking about, Dair?"

She pulled away from his knees and put her own legs over the edge of the couch sitting sideways to him so she didn't have to look at him. She kept babbling, just as if she were drunk in a bar—still aware enough to know she was making an ass of herself, but too far sloshed to stop. "Sylvan never existed. I never had a twin. I told you how I used to lie in the park, remember? How I'd make up stories about where Blizzard came from?" Blizzard raised his head at the sound of his name. Dair risked a glance at Peyton, who still lay in the same position as if afraid to move. "Well, when I met you I just made up the idea that I'd lost a twin. You said something about your sister and you asked me if I had any brothers or sisters, and I just made it up, on the spot, the same way I'd make up lies about Blizzard."

Peyton lifted himself to sitting. "Dair?" he whispered. "What the hell are you doing?"

"I'm telling the truth. I was going to tell you, way back . . . at the . . . beginning. I wanted to tell you, but then you told me about rehab and you said you knew I'd understand because I'd lost part of myself, too." She'd always pictured herself crying during this scene. But now that she'd opened the cage, her chest felt empty. She felt nothing. Except maybe surprise. Surprise at her lack of emotion. Like a bad actress, she recited a monologue she'd memorized but hadn't otherwise prepared. The only thing that felt right was being naked. Somehow that awful vulnerability seemed appropriate.

The thought of hurting Peyton shredded something within her. She couldn't cry because she wasn't allowed to hurt, too. She didn't deserve it. It all belonged to him.

She turned her head to look at him, now sitting cross-legged at the end of the couch. He seemed concerned, befuddled, and his nudity was too dear, too painful, for her. She closed her eyes. "You're just denying it," he insisted. "Like your dad."

"No, Peyton."

"But, you told me about . . . I mean your mom said . . . and . . . and the sunflowers you two planted in your backyard. I've seen pictures of them."

Dair shook her head. "You've seen pictures of sunflowers I planted. There was no Sylvan in those pictures."

He inhaled sharply and said, "Because you tore up all her photos when you were sixteen. Six years after she died."

Dair closed her eyes. "It's not true, Peyton. I lied."

"But—wait, wait a minute: Your mother said her *name*. Right in that kitchen"—he pointed—"just the other night. Your mother has talked about Sylvan."

She couldn't look at him. "Sylvan was the name of my chickadee."

Silence. Blizzard tentatively licked the edge of an ice-cream bowl, keeping an anxious eye on them. Neither of them moved to stop him. He began to lap with more confidence.

"Jesus Christ!" Peyton said. He shook his head. "No way. No fucking way. You didn't lie to me for eight fucking years."

She nodded.

"Why?"

"I told you. You thought that was why we found each other."

He stared across the room and said, "It obviously wasn't why."

"That's what I was afraid of."

"No, you don't understand," he said, standing up, causing Blizzard to slink away from the bowl. Peyton reached for his sweatpants and yanked them on without his underwear. "There was another reason we found each other. Nobody made *that* up, that connection. Did they?" He turned to her, his eyes hard and flat.

"No," she whispered. "That's the truest thing I know."

"Is it?"

She nodded and felt an emotion finally begin to swell within her. Tears stung her eyes.

"Huh," he said, tying the drawstring at his waist with furious, quick motions. "That's funny, because all of a sudden it feels like the cheapest, flimsiest fucking lie that I know!"

He might as well have backhanded her. She almost wished he would. "Peyton, please don't—"

"You could've told me. You could've said way back then that it wasn't true, and it wouldn't have mattered. It would've been funny. But eight years? Jesus, Dair. How could you do that?"

She opened her mouth. She didn't know what to say.

Both dogs stood, wagging their tails low to the ground.

"I mean, literally, how did you do that? That took some fucking work, some fucking planning. Why would you keep that up? I fucking talked to your mom and dad about it. They probably both thought I was shooting up again or something. Oh, my God, when I think about—you have no idea what I've—" He stopped and raked his fingers through his hair as though he'd rip it from his scalp. "What else have you lied about?"

She knew there was no way to answer that question. He knew it, too. "No, don't even tell me. I don't want to know. It's all a lie, isn't it?"

"No, Peyton. I'm sorry."

He moved to the stairwell and paused at the bottom. "Who else knows this? Am I walking around like an idiot?"

If she was telling the truth, it would be all or nothing. "Craig knew."

She couldn't describe what happened to Peyton's face. Something . . . vanished, peeled away, revealing a new, raw layer of betrayal.

"You told *Craig?*"

She nodded.

"My best friend? Every time I was hanging out with him, he knew my wife lied to me? That I was this stupid moron believing in your stupid lie? Jesus!"

"No, Peyton. I only told him recently. You were on tour. You were never with him . . . after he knew."

Peyton moaned and held his hands over his face. "Oh, God. I've talked to him about this. I told him—" He dropped his hands, his eyes fevered as he stared at her. "What did he say when you told him?"

Tears burned down her cheeks. "He was . . . he cried. He told me I had to tell you."

Peyton shook his head.

"He said he'd tell you himself if I didn't tell you soon."

He looked at her a long moment, as if trying to see inside her. "Were you fucking him?"

She winced at the harshness, the ugliness, not just the accusation. "No, I wasn't. He was in love with Marielle, and I'm in love with you."

He snorted. "That's funny." He leaned on the stair banister. "I thought when you loved someone you told them everything; you confided in them. You shared your dreams, your hopes, your fears, your *mistakes.*"

"Peyton, please. You shared all that with me. You told me about rehab the very night I was going to tell you. I thought you were the bravest, most courageous man I'd ever met. After you shared all that, this seemed so . . . stupid, so cowardly."

"Not half as much as it does eight years later!" he yelled.

Shodan whimpered, but Blizzard growled.

"I'm sorry." God, what else was there to say?

Peyton turned and punched the wall behind him. Dair cringed at the swiftness of the movement, as well as its violence. He left a red swipe on the wall but didn't appear to register any pain. Blizzard's hackles raised, and he stepped between Dair and Peyton.

Peyton froze. "You didn't kill him, did you?" The question was sincere and hit her as hard as he'd hit the wall.

"No! Peyton. Oh, my God. No."

He stared at her. Blood dripped from his knuckles to the floor. "I thought I knew you." He sounded defeated.

"I'm a liar," she said.

He nodded. "And a drunk."

That word, *drunk,* socked her in the stomach. She couldn't catch her breath and almost dropped to her knees as he walked away from her, up the stairs. Tears blurred her vision as she fumbled for her clothes and redressed on top of the sticky, dried ice cream. Blizzard growled, trying to block her at the bottom of the staircase. "It's okay." Dair stepped over him on trembling legs. He followed close behind her.

"Oh, no," Dair said in the bedroom. "No, please don't." Peyton threw clothes into his duffel bag. She grabbed his arm, but he jerked it away. "Peyton, don't leave, we need to talk about this, we need to—"

"*I* need to get out of here and think," he said. "I don't think *we* need to do anything. And I don't give a flying fuck what *you* need at the moment."

"Peyton. Please listen to me just for a minute. Please?" He paused in the doorway. Blizzard never took his eyes from him. Dair sat on the bed and spoke slowly, carefully, knowing she had one fragile chance at keeping him here. "I am sorry. I know that doesn't mean shit to you at the moment, but please, please believe me. I know I've done a terrible thing. I told you in the basement tonight that I need help."

"I'm inclined to agree with you now."

She nodded. "Please know that I was scared of losing you, scared of hurting you, and as cowardly as that was, those are the reasons I didn't tell you. I wanted to delay this very moment." Her voice started to crack. "This very moment when you'd . . . leave."

He looked out into the hallway. When she stopped talking, he waited for a moment, then, without looking at her, asked, "You done?"

She sniffed. "Yeah."

And he walked away, out of the door frame and down the stairs. Blizzard followed him.

"I'm not a drunk," she whispered. She stayed on the bed, afraid to move, wanting to believe that if she froze, the rest of the scene would as well. Blizzard barked and kept barking. Above her head she heard Caption Hook shout in her voice, *"Blizzard! Shodie!"* and then a few minutes later: *"Those damn dogs."*

Blizzard kept barking, a lonesome, plaintive sound.

"Hush, Blizzard," Dair called, pushing herself off the bed. She recognized something in those barks, something she wanted to deny. She walked down the steps slowly, wanting to postpone knowing for sure.

Blizzard heard her coming and met her at the bottom, whining and anxious.

He wanted to know why he didn't get to go in the car with his sister.

Peyton had taken Shodan with him.

Chapter Fifteen

Dair heard knocking. Was it that damn chickadee again? Her brain felt swollen, sluggish, her neck cramped. She rolled her neck, turning her head, and her brain slid inside her skull a few seconds behind.

More knocking. And Blizzard barking. She opened her eyes onto a flock of birds. Where the hell was she? But then she saw the birds were only wooden, hung from her yellow ceiling. She was in the kitchen. On the floor.

She moved her head toward the knocking in the hall, but the view as well as her brain slid behind with a split-second delay. The walls spun, and she breathed deeply to keep from puking on herself.

In cautious slow motion, she sat up, her tongue thick inside her cotton mouth. For a moment the knocking stopped, although Blizzard kept growling and jumping on the front door. The echo of the knocking continued inside her reeling skull.

Gathering herself into a cross-legged position, Dair bumped an empty wine bottle with her knee and sent it spinning across the floor, as in a game of spin the bottle in junior high. She watched it careening, and when she tried to pull her eyes from it, the rest of the room mimicked its twirling motion.

She shut her eyes, but that made *her* spin, which was worse, and she popped her eyes back open just as the knocking on the door started again.

The phone rang.

She turned to the sound too quickly, making her brain slosh. The slosh in her head prompted a sloshing in her belly, and she hauled herself to the sink in time to vomit. She vomited twice, watching the red brown Cabernet Sauvignon slither down the drain.

She turned on the water and washed out the sink, then ducked her face under the faucet to rinse her mouth. Her brain threatened to split from the hammering of Blizzard's bark, the echo of the pounding, and the phone's piercing jangle. Why didn't Peyton answer it?

Peyton.

Oh.

Peyton was gone.

Oh, God. Maybe it was Peyton on the phone. Dair reached for the receiver on their kitchen counter, fumbled it, then brought it to her ear. "Hello?"

"Dair?! What are you doing?" It was Marielle.

Before Dair could answer, Marielle said, "The police are on your porch. Why aren't you answering the door? Are you okay?"

The police? Oh, God. Peyton had gone out angry. Something awful had happened, He'd wrecked his car. He'd thrown himself off the— No. Gayle had told Dair she was calling the police.

"I wasss . . . sssleeping." Dair had difficulty letting go of that "s."

Marielle paused. "Oh, sweetie, are you drunk?"

"Yes. But I'm okay. I'll answer the door right this second."

"Do you want me to come over?"

"No." Dair hung up. She leaned her cheek on the sink. Peyton was gone. And she was a liar and a drunk. She'd proven him right, hadn't she? One empty bottle on the floor. Another open, still half-full, standing by the cupboard. A corkscrew she didn't remember using lay beside it, a cork still embedded on its point. But it didn't matter anymore, did it?

Blizzard barreled down the hall, growling, setting the empty bottle spinning again as he rushed to the back door and started barking there. Dair didn't know which was worse, watching the bottle or listening to him bark. "Blizzard, hush," she croaked.

She jumped when the knocking began on the back door. She stood up and swayed, tottering, feeling as if she were falling into outer space, total surprise washing over her that she didn't remember this wide, yawning canyon existing in her kitchen ever before. Reaching out, flailing, for something, anything, she caught herself in the ribs on the table, crying out as she crumpled to the floor. Blizzard stopped barking and rushed to her side.

"Ow-ow," she panted, pressing a hand to her ribs. That sobered her up a bit.

"Ms. Canard?" a deep voice boomed through the back door. "Are you all right? It's the police, ma'am. Please open up."

"Coming," she called as chipperly as she could.

She dragged herself up, using both Blizzard and the table. Blizzard didn't resume barking, since Dair had spoken to the voice outside.

Once standing, Dair shuffled to the back door, trying to avoid any more yawning pits. She peered out the window and saw a uniformed officer. "Please open the door, ma'am," he said, then said something into the radio on his collar.

She tried to move deliberately, with concentration, but opened the door with too much force, slamming the doorknob into the wall behind them. "Oops," she said, waving her hand at it. Then she took that hand in her other as if trying to control herself.

"Are you okay, ma'am?" the officer asked, frowning. He looked fifteen, even had freckles. Daylight eked into the sky behind him. What time was it?

"I'm a little sick. I couldn't make it to the door, I was . . ." Dair waved her hand again, searching for a word, but the gesture made her lose her balance, and she leaned into the door frame for support. "Indisposed," she said.

"I see." He paused a moment. "Is that dog safe?"

"Oh, yeah."

"May I come in?"

"Sure." Clutching the door frame, she turned herself around in place and realized she could've tumbled down the basement steps a moment ago when she'd lost her balance. She kept hold of the wall until she'd passed the opening to those steps. The smell of vomit hovered in the kitchen. Dair turned on the water in the sink and poured too much dishwashing soap under the stream. "Sorry," she said, turning her head to the officer, listing a bit in his direction. He looked at the bottles. So did she. She could just leave them there now if she wanted. She didn't have to hide them. She didn't have to replace them. If Peyton was gone for good, maybe she'd just line the bottles up on the counters like in college.

"I'm going to let my partner in your front door, ma'am."

"Oh, okay." Dair shut off the water and dried her hands on her jeans. What did she look like? She patted the top of her head, felt her hair standing up in the back. How long had she been on the floor? What time was it?

But before she could focus on the clock, Blizzard started barking again. "Blizzard," she called, stumbling down the hallway. "It's okay. He can come in."

She bumped her shoulder into a wall as she made it to the living room. The two men stood in the front door, eyeing Blizzard. "'S okay," she said. "He won't bite you. C'mere, Blizzard." She fell onto the couch and wanted to rejoice. Sitting down felt like making it to an island after swimming in the open sea for days.

The cops came in but remained standing. The fifteen-year-old redhead who'd entered the back door took notes. The front-door officer looked older. He was tall, thin, and blond. And he wore khakis and a nice blue shirt and tie, not a uniform. "Had a bit to drink, ma'am?" Tall Blond asked her.

"Yup." She stopped herself from telling him she was, in actuality, skunk drunk. Being drunk wasn't a crime. She was in her own home, after all. They hadn't caught her speeding or killing pedestrians.

"You think you're okay to answer some questions for us?" Tall Blond asked.

"Sure." She pulled her legs up onto the couch and hugged herself, noting with horror that her bra was still on the floor and that she had ice cream on her chest and neck, probably visible in the V-neck sweater. Oh, God, what did she look like? "Sit down," she offered again, but they didn't.

Blizzard sat close to her, his head on her bare right foot that poked out from her cross-legged position.

They asked her about Gayle's dress. And Dair told the truth. Yes, she was aware that taking the dress without permission was, essentially, stealing Ms. Lyons's property. Yes, she knew the date she'd removed the dress. Yes, in fact, she could tell them the exact date she'd taken it back. But, yes, come to think of it, she did realize that the dry cleaner's receipt in no way proved she'd returned the dress to Ms. Lyons's home.

Their words sounded slow, as on a stretched, heat-damaged audiotape. Those slow voices expanded in her mind, and she found she had to pause and translate before responding.

Tall Blond asked the questions.

"Were you and Mr. MacPhearson involved in an affair?"

Pause. "No."

"Is your husband at home?"

Pause. "No, he left."

"For work?"

Pause. "No, he left. He left me. I don't know if he'll come back at all."

"Is this because of the affair?"

Pause. "I wasn't having an affair. I told you."

"That's right."

Dair narrowed her eyes at him. He was humoring her. Patronizing her.

"Our records show you were present at the time of Mr. Mac-Phearson's death quite near Ms. Lyons's home."

"That's right," she said, nodding. She wished she hadn't nodded. It made her tip forward, and she reached out a hand to the trunk to stop herself from falling off the couch.

"Did you recognize the dress he was wearing?"

Dair thought a moment. "I did. I recognized the dress right away. But I didn't recognize Craig. Mr. MacPhearson. I thought he was a woman."

"So you weren't with him right before he fell?"

"No." She was careful not to shake her head.

"Were you with"—Tall Blond flipped through his notebook—"Andy Baker right before Mr. MacPhearson fell?"

"No." Damn. Gayle seemed determined to suck them all into this mess. "No, I saw Andy there, after it . . . happened."

"Why were you in the area?"

"I was on the way to the airport to pick up my husband."

"Oh? And where was he coming back from?"

She tried to remember. "Atlanta? No . . . New Orleans, I think. He was at a lot of places. He was on tour. I don't remember the last city he was in."

The officer frowned. "What kind of tour?" he asked. Dair told him. It got complicated.

When the Redhead asked, "So is this company like Riverdance?" Dair giggled and almost couldn't stop. She struggled to regain her composure.

"Do you know what flight he was on?" Tall Blond asked.

She tried to think but snorted and giggled again, picturing Peyton's reaction when she told him of the Riverdance comment. But then . . . she remembered she couldn't tell Peyton because Peyton was gone.

"Ma'am?" Tall Blond asked. "Ma'am, are you all right?"

Tears pooled in her lashes, blurring her vision. "No," she whispered.

The two cops looked at each other. "Uh," Redhead said, looking around the room, "are you going to be sick?"

"No." She touched her lashes with her fingers, releasing the tears. "I can't remember what flight he was on. The itinerary is still on the fridge, I think." She pointed back down the hallway toward the kitchen.

Oh, God. Peyton was gone. It had finally happened.

"Ma'am?" Tall Blond waited for her to look at him before proceeding, which she thought was a very smart move with someone so intoxicated. The buzz wore thin, though. "Ma'am? When did your husband leave?"

"For the airport?"

"No. You said he left you. When did that happen?"

"Oh." She thought. "What time is it?"

He looked at her in surprise, then looked at his watch. "It's six-thirty."

"Six-thirty?" She frowned. Six-thirty on Tuesday morning. Did they often come to people's homes so early? Wasn't that a little rude? "I'm sorry," she said. "What did you ask me?"

"When did your husband leave?"

"Oh. Last night. Around eleven. Or maybe midnight. I think."

He looked at her a moment before writing that down. Dair hated the pity in his eyes. Redhead came back with the flight itinerary. "Checks out," he said. Why did they care? Did they think she was lying about the airport? What had Gayle suggested about her?

"Can we keep this?" Tall Blond asked.

"Okay," she said. "That tour is over, though, you know."

"Right." He was patronizing her again. She longed for them to leave. She was so tired.

And Peyton was gone.

They asked again if she'd ever had an affair with Mr. MacPhearson.

"No."

When was the last time she'd seen him?

She stared at them. "The last time I saw him, he climbed over my car in a dress and ended up dead on Clifton Avenue. Only . . . only I didn't know I *was* seeing him, so . . ."

Tall Blond cleared his throat. "How 'bout the last time before that?"

"Thursday night. I said hi to him over at Marielle's, next door."

Had she ever seen him in a dress before?

"No."

"Did you ever know him to take drugs?"

"Nope." She shook her head and leaned dangerously to her left, then straightened herself. Extraordinary thirst overcame her.

"Do you know anyone who is involved in drugs, particularly narcotics, like those found in Mr. MacPhearson's autopsy?"

She thought about that answer. "No," she said, certain she wasn't lying. Peyton wasn't using. Would he now? Had she driven him to it? Where had he gone? What would he do? Her eyes burned again.

"Did you ever meet Mr. MacPhearson at Gayle Lyons's home?"

"Well . . ." She felt she was on the stand. Did she need a lawyer? Was she blabbing bad things? Should she just shut up? She was really, really plastered. She was a drunk, just like Peyton said. A sloppy, nasty lush. "We've been to parties there."

"But did you ever meet him there while she was gone, while you were looking after her cat and her mail?"

"Oh." They were on that again. "No."

"Did you ever meet Andy Baker at Gayle Lyons's home?"

"What? No!" God, how bad was this going to get?

"But you did have a key to her house, is that right?"

"Yes. But I'm not the only one with a key."

The cops looked at each other.

"There's a guy named Mal-colm Cole," she said, overpronouncing the name. "Gayle told me he had a key, but he was supposed to return it, only he says he lost it. *And,* he does happen to wear dresses sometimes for drag acts."

Tall Blond frowned and studied his notepad. He hadn't written anything while Dair talked, so she wondered what was there for him to look at. "Ms. Lyons didn't mention Malcolm Cole to us."

"And Ms. Lyons," Dair said, knowing she shouldn't, "asked me, just this evening, not to tell anyone that Mr. Cole had a key to her house."

Redhead raised his eyebrows. "Is that so?"

"*And,*" she added, "Ms. Lyons is rumored to be having an affair with this same Mr. Cole." She feared that any minute she'd slip into an English accent with all these "Misters" and "Mizzes" flying around the room.

Tall Blond cleared his throat and looked skeptical.

"Look," Dair said, "I know I'm drunk, okay? My husband and I just had a horrible argument, and he left, and I drank *way* too much. But I'm not making this up. I think someone was in Gayle's house besides me. Things were . . . weird there, when I watched it. And I don't understand why she doesn't want anyone to know Malcolm had a key to her house."

"What was weird in her house?" Tall Blond asked, finally sitting down. Redhead did, too, as if he'd been waiting to do it.

Dair told them. About the stripped bed. Gayle coming home early. The flowers in her bedroom. The closet where the dress had hung. The dry cleaner bag ripped in half.

"MacPhearson's clothes were here," Redhead said, pointing at the wall, indicating Marielle's half of the house. He was talking to Tall Blond, not to Dair. "What if he was left someplace without any clothes?"

Tall Blond nodded.

"Those cops last night wouldn't talk to us," Dair said. "They thought it was a drug deal."

Tall Blond didn't answer, didn't deny it or assure her that he didn't think it was a drug deal. He made a sucking noise through his teeth as he flipped through several pages of his notebook. Then he snapped it shut. "You wouldn't happen to know how we could get in touch with this Malcolm Cole, do you?"

"As a matter of fact, I do," she said. She rose from her sitting position, and both cops rushed to steady her as she teetered and almost fell over the trunk. She stood a moment, willing her brain to work, to remember where she'd left her *Othello* script. She walked down the hall to the kitchen. Her script still sat on the counter, where she'd dropped it as she'd come in last night. When Peyton danced in the basement. Before she'd ruined everything. She leafed through the script for the folded-up contact sheet. She turned to take it to the cops in the living room, but they'd followed her, and she almost walked into them. "Shit," she said. "Sorry." She unfolded the list but said, "Shit," again. "He's not on it. Craig is. You know—Mr. MacPhearson. He was supposed to play Iago."

Tall Blond looked at the contact sheet. "Hey. You were in *Taming of the Shrew,* right? Last spring?"

"Yeah," Dair said. "I was the shrew. Mr. MacPhearson was Petruchio." She'd grown hooked on saying "Mr. MacPhearson." She liked the way the M's rolled in her mouth.

"The deceased? He was the tall guy in the play? The one who married you?"

She nodded and grabbed the kitchen counter for balance. She shut her eyes and saw Craig as Petruchio, both of them crawling and wrestling their way across the stage, hurling insults at each other. They'd had such fun. She heard the applause, felt his hand on hers at curtain call, saw him grinning at her.

"My girlfriend made me go to that," Tall Blond said. Dair opened her eyes, and the applause stopped. "You were really good. I thought you looked familiar, but I didn't . . . you know . . ."

"Yeah," she said, patting her hair. How hideous did she look? "I need a drink."

"Oh, I think you've had plenty."

"No. Water," she said. "I'm thirsty."

Dair opened a cupboard and fumbled for a glass. "Uh, here," Tall Blond said. "Let us get that." He guided her to a chair, where she sat with a plop. Redhead filled a glass with water at the sink. Blizzard hovered at Dair's side. She wondered vaguely where Godot was.

She took the glass with gratitude. "Go easy," Tall Blond said, taking it away from her when she tried to guzzle it all. "A little at a time. Got any crackers?"

Crackers? God, what a *great* idea. She pointed to another cupboard, and Redhead handed her the box.

"So," Tall Blond said, looking up at chickadees hanging from the ceiling, "this Malcolm Cole is in the play now? Playing Mr. MacPhearson's part?"

"Yup."

"But you don't have a number?"

"Nope." She shoved a cracker into her mouth. Blizzard nudged her hand, and she gave him a cracker, too.

"He just moved, I think. I don't know where he lives now. He used to live on Dana Street."

Redhead looked at her. "That would be a starting place. Got a phone book?" She pointed to a drawer. He opened it and pulled out the White Pages. "Coal, like charcoal?"

"No. C-o-l-e."

He flipped through the pages. She ate another cracker, fed another to the dog.

"Bingo," Redhead said. "Cole on Dana. Phone?"

She pointed again. " 'S pretty early, doncha think?" she asked as he dialed.

He shrugged. "Police business." He listened a moment, then frowned. " 'No longer in service.' "

"Got the address?" Tall Blond asked.

"Yup." Redhead jotted it down in his notepad.

"We're going to see if we can locate Mr. Cole," Tall Blond said. "I think you should take some aspirin and go to bed."

"Okay."

"Here's my card." He handed it to her, and Tall Blond became Detective Darrel Monty. Attached to the card was an orange sticker containing tips for a safe and happy Halloween. "You call me if you think of anything else. We'll probably be talking to you again, okay? I might like to talk to you later, when you've had a chance to sleep this off."

Her cheeks burned.

They busied themselves, locking the back door and making her follow them to the front to lock it behind them.

Blizzard slipped past her onto the front porch. She stepped out, too, and called, "Blizzard! Come!" He paused on the porch steps and looked over his shoulder at her. "Stay," she said. He sat down on the top step, looking out into the early morning light. The chilly air and frost on the ground thinned her buzz even further. Her brain and vision didn't slog as much when she moved her head.

Officer Monty said, "Okay, then, well, we'll get going. We're—"

Blizzard let loose a deep bass barrage of barking and lumbered down the steps toward Marielle's side of the yard. "Blizzard!" Dair called.

"Blizzard!" Her voice echoed from upstairs. *"C'mere!"*

Both men stared at her, dumbfounded. "Holy shit," Redhead said, looking up. "Who was that? That sounded just like you."

"That is an African gray parrot named Captain Hook. We tried to tell the police about him last night."

The cops looked at each other.

"You made fun of us, didn't you?" she asked, her hands on her hips.

"Blizzard! C'mere, you silly!" Captain Hook called in Dair's voice.

"Holy shit," Redhead said again.

Blizzard bounded up the steps to Dair's side. She murmured, "Good boy," and grabbed his collar.

"We—we didn't know that it—," Detective Monty stammered. "That's a *bird?*"

She nodded, the crisp cold air clearing her brain. She breathed deep lungfuls of it.

Officer Monty took a deep breath, too. "All right, Ms. Canard, thank you," he said. "This is all very helpful. You lock up now, and take some aspirin, okay?"

"Thank you," she said. She pulled Blizzard inside and locked the door. She weaved her way through the living room as if her head were clear but her legs still drunk. Her bed called to her, but ravenous thirst made her will herself back to the kitchen, fumbling along the wall for support. In her clumsiness she stepped on Blizzard's front right paw, felt it grind under her fortunately bare foot. He yelped—a surprised sound that stabbed her in the heart. He'd only been lurking close to protect her, to guide her, and she'd hurt him. "Oh, sweetie," she crooned, kneeling down, losing her balance, and sitting beside him. "I'm so sorry. I didn't mean to hurt you." Blizzard licked her face, lapped the tears from her cheeks and her eyelids. He knew it was a mistake. Dair's mother spoke of "intentions." Blizzard knew it was not Dair's intention to hurt him, so even though she'd caused him physical pain, he forgave her. Would Peyton ever? Would he understand that it had not been her intention to deceive him, to hurt him? He'd been so determined that she'd had a twin and that her loss somehow connected them. Her intention had only been to be with him, to have him stay in her life.

The phone rang. *Oh, God, please be Peyton, please be Peyton.* She crawled down the hall and clambered to the phone, picking it up with a breathless, "Hello?"

"Is, um, is Peyton there?" the familiar voice asked.

"Malcolm?" The crackers in her stomach cartwheeled.

"Yeah. I'm sorry." His voice was small and pleading. "I know it's early, but it's really important. Can I—could I talk to Peyton? Please?"

"No. You can't. And the police are on their way to talk to *you.*" She hung up. She'd never hung up on anyone in her life.

The phone rang again under her hand. She snatched it up. "What the hell is your problem?" she yelled. "Leave me alone!"

"Dair?!" It was Marielle. "What is going on?"

"Oh. Sorry. I thought you were someone else."

"Are you okay? What did the police want?"

Dair filled her in as best she could, not telling her the rumor of the affair. She couldn't stand for Marielle to wonder, for her to doubt that Craig loved only her. Marielle didn't ask anything about Peyton, and Dair didn't tell her. Marielle would find out eventually, but right now Dair was just too tired. When she hung up, she sat on the kitchen floor with Blizzard's giant head in her lap, his big brown eyes watching her with concern. It reminded her of sitting in the park with Marielle. That ability to simply be with someone in pain was so rare among humans. Godot *ca-clunk*ed through the cat door and came to them, touching noses with Blizzard, rubbing his head on Dair. He, too, looked into her eyes. She stared back, ashamed of her drunkenness. How could they stand her? She was disgusting, pathetic. She leaned her head back against a cupboard and wept.

After several moments Godot yowled and Blizzard stood, both of them in apparent agreement that it was time she went to bed. She stood and did what they wanted.

Dair woke, in her clothes, with a hammering headache. Blizzard licked her ear. Godot kneaded her belly. Dair closed her eyes again. She didn't want to wake up. She didn't want to remember what had happened. She didn't want to move through a day without Peyton, even though most of Tuesday was nearly gone.

She considered just staying in bed and never getting up again. She could stay all sticky and dirty and reeking of the wine she must've spilled on herself, but Blizzard whimpered to be let out, and both he and Godot needed to be fed.

Once she'd done that for them, she didn't know what else to do, so she showered and shampooed her hair. She examined the mottled bruises on her rib cage, hipbone, and legs with horror and disgust. She dressed. She ate more crackers, took more aspirin, and made a pot of coffee. She drank three big cups with healthy shots of Kahlúa.

Contemplating the bottles on the kitchen floor nauseated her. Peyton was right to leave her. The sour smell of vomit still lingered in the air. She was repulsive. She snatched up the half-empty bottle and poured it down the sink. Fueled by her loathing and shame, she dumped the rest of the bottles, too, and threw them, with a splintering crash, into her own trash can.

The Kahlúa stayed. Just in case. She turned that bottle around and around on the counter, wanting to smash it open and rake the broken glass over her flesh. Instead she uncapped it and drank a long slug before shoving it into a cupboard and slamming the door so hard that the chickadees swung from the draft.

"Peyton," she said aloud. She *had* to talk to him. She had to hear his voice even if he cursed at her. Where would he go? She knew he wouldn't go to his own parents, and she doubted he'd go to hers now. His best friend was Craig . . . but Craig was dead.

She dialed his cell number but only got his voice mail. "I'm sorry," she whispered. "I love you. Call me. Please?"

When she hung up, Blizzard whined, wanting in the back door. She let him in. He seemed anxious, and she knew he missed Shodan. Godot stuck close to the house and was underfoot every time she moved.

She didn't know what to do with herself. Without Peyton she felt she was suffocating, as if some air supply had been severed. She wandered down to the basement and lay on the dance floor, running her fingers in the deep grooves and scars in the smooth wood. She closed her eyes and pictured Peyton dancing—how serene he'd looked before she'd spoken last night.

Calling in sick for her own rehearsal occurred to her, but she changed her mind. She wanted to return Gayle's key. And she wanted to be busy. What would she do if she canceled besides pace the house and wait for the phone to ring? She'd just guzzle the Kahlúa. As it was, she'd probably polish it off *after* rehearsal.

The phone still didn't ring. No amount of aspirin put a dent in the headache drilling in her brain.

She studied her script. She checked to make sure the phone had a dial tone. It did.

And somehow, miraculously, the time came to go to rehearsal. A purpose. That's all she wanted. Something to do. She picked up her script, made sure she had Gayle's key, and drove to the Aronoff.

She parked and walked inside to the theater, twenty minutes early. The long tables had been moved out, and some wooden rehearsal blocks sat in the middle of the empty stage, to act as any furniture they needed. The stage manager knelt on the floor, taping out the dimensions of the set in various colors of spike tape. The folding chairs from last night lined the back wall. The older actor playing Brabantio sat leafing through his script. Both he and the stage manager nodded and greeted Dair warmly enough. "Seen Gayle this evening?" she asked, setting her stuff on a chair.

"No," the stage manager said, cutting a piece of green tape. "And I need her key to get into the box office to use the copier."

"Hmm. She's supposed to be here."

"Tell me about it," the stage manager said.

Dair wandered out into the lobby toward the box office, even though he'd just told her Gayle wasn't there. Sure enough, no one answered her knock, and the door was locked. She could wrap the key in a piece of paper with Gayle's name on it, slide it under the door, and be done with it. Turning to head back into the theater to grab paper out of her notebook, she almost bumped into Malcolm Cole.

She faltered a little when she saw him, and he seemed to, too. Had he been surprised by his police visit, or had he been ready for them? She'd halfway expected him to have been taken into custody. And she vaguely recalled screaming at him on the phone this morning.

They stood, a few feet apart. He held a carry-out coffee in one hand and a fistful of sugar packets in the other. Enough sugar to fill the cup. He looked cadaverous—his skin the milky gray of a sky before snow, except for his raw, pink nose.

Dair found herself half-afraid, half-embarrassed. "Um . . . seen Gayle?" she asked.

"No." He sniffed, wiping at his nose with his leather jacket sleeve. "She's not in the box office?" He looked past her, toward the dark door.

"No."

"Then I can't help you. Sorry." He walked around her and went into the theater, as if he didn't care about her, as if they'd never spoken, as if both of them hadn't been questioned by the police this morning. It felt so anticlimactic.

Other cast members arrived, and Malcolm picked a seat far across the stage from Dair, setting his coffee and sugars on a rehearsal block. He took a tissue from his pocket and blew his nose. Then he poured ten sugar packets into his coffee. Two other packs he emptied straight into his mouth, chewing the sugar dry. No wonder he never stopped moving—his legs bouncing as he sat, a frenetic sort of twitchiness running through him.

When Dair had to stand near him onstage, she saw that he'd gnawed many of his fingernails down to the raw, bloody nail beds. He pulled on his goatee, scratching it as if he wanted to rip it off his face. And his nose ran relentlessly, the soft honk of him blowing it punctuating rehearsal throughout the evening.

They were blocking the play out of sequence, Rosylyn wanting to work the scenes with the groups of military officers first, since those parts were played by CCM students who would be in a CCM show this weekend and unable to attend *Othello* rehearsal again until Monday.

So on the second night of rehearsal, Dair found herself already in the last scene of the play, facing Malcolm and challenging him, "You told a lie, an odious, damnéd lie; upon my soul, a lie, a wicked lie!" Her face burned, and tears threatened under the surface of her words. The lines shamed her—she spoke them to herself more than to Malcolm.

"Wonderful," Rosylyn gushed when they stopped. She looked at Dair and nodded. "Beautiful stuff. Let's see how far we can go with that."

How far? God, Rosylyn didn't want to know. Dair felt naked.

The look on Malcolm's face as he rushed in to stab her as Iago chilled her blood. He didn't even have a prop knife yet, just his clenched fist holding a mimed weapon, but her heart raced at the hatred in his eyes.

At last Rosylyn called a break. Dair booked out of the theater as fast as she could, checked the box office—still no Gayle—and ducked inside Procter & Gamble Hall. The houselights were on, and a woman onstage yelled at someone up in the booth, "I'm getting nothing, okay?" The woman gestured to her headset. "Nothing. Static, man. I can't understand one word you're saying!"

"For Christ's sake!" someone yelled from the balcony. "We just put new batteries in them. Shit. Hang on, I'm coming down."

Was Andy even there? They didn't appear to be working with lights at all. Dair wandered down the aisle to where a couple of tech guys she recognized sat on the edge of the stage. "Hey, Dair," they said.

"Hey, you guys. Listen, I understand I owe you some thanks, defending me from rumors."

Terry cocked his head, grinning. "What rumors?"

"You're too good to me. Is Andy around?"

In unison they said, "Check outside."

She laughed, which felt false and fake. If she offered that laugh onstage, no one would believe it. "Does he ever work?" she joked.

"Hardly ever," Terry said, and Dair wasn't sure he was kidding.

"Thanks."

She went back out and pushed open the stage door. For the split second before he saw her, a look of loathing sneered across Andy's face as he gazed up the street, but the smirk blossomed into a smile when he turned to her. Curious, Dair stepped outside and looked to see what Andy had been scowling at. Malcolm walked down the street toward them. He stopped when he saw her. Dair's breath stopped when she saw him.

"Hey, Dair," Andy said, beaming. "Smoky treat?"

"Please." She looked at Malcolm, who still stood frozen a few yards away.

"You gonna join us, Malcolm?" Andy asked, something taunting in his tone.

Malcolm closed the distance between them and pulled a pack of cigarettes from his pocket, lighting one with trembling hands. He saw

Dair notice and tucked one hand into his jacket pocket, but the one holding his cigarette still shook.

Andy lit a cigarette for Dair, and they stood in awkward silence. This was so strange. She'd never seen Malcolm smoke out here before. She wanted Malcolm to go away. She wanted to tell Andy about Peyton leaving, wanted his comfort, his apple-smelling arm around her shoulder. But she didn't want Malcolm to know anything about it, especially that she was home by herself.

Malcolm cleared his throat. "So . . . are you guys going to the funeral tomorrow?"

Dair stared at him. "Of course."

"Yeah, man," Andy said. "Everyone's going, paying their respects."

Malcolm opened his mouth, as if to ask Dair something, but looked at Andy and ducked his head. She was glad to have Andy as protection if Malcolm was going to confront her about his police visit.

"Hey, is Gayle up there yet?" Andy asked.

"Gayle? Artistic Director Gayle?" Malcolm asked.

Andy snorted. "Which *other* Gayle did you think I meant?"

Malcolm swallowed, and color seemed to drain from the rest of his face, leaving only an odd swatch of red across his upper cheeks. He sniffed, wiped his nose, and looked down at his leather boots.

"Seriously," Andy said. "I've been looking for her all day, trying to get details on this gathering tomorrow."

"She's not here," Dair said. "And she told me she would be."

Andy stared at Malcolm. That red swatch deepened again. "I don't know," Malcolm protested. "Why would I know where she is? I'm not her secretary."

Andy laughed. "Come on, man. You *live* with her."

The color disappeared from Malcolm's face this time, leaving not a trace of the swatch. "I do not."

"Whatever," Andy said. "Well, then, you *did*."

Malcolm turned cold, hateful eyes on Dair. Oh, shit. She realized that he thought she'd revealed this information. But she hadn't. She hadn't even told Andy that Malcolm had a key; he'd already known. Andy had jumped to this conclusion, but it sure seemed the right one, judging from Malcolm's reaction. Malcolm's hands stopped shaking, and he muttered something under his breath.

"What's that?" Andy asked.

"Bitch," Malcolm said.

"Hey!" Andy stepped toward him, fists clenched.

Malcolm's eyes popped open wide and startled. "Whoa. Hey, not *Dair*." He held up his hands. Andy stopped. "Jesus," Malcolm said, "what the hell is wrong with you?"

Dair stepped closer to Andy. She appreciated Andy defending her, but the last thing she needed was some stupid, testosterone-splattered confrontation on the goddamn sidewalk.

"So Gayle's the bitch?" Andy asked.

"Yeah," Malcolm said, not backing down. "As a matter of fact, she is."

"You guys, stop it," Dair said. "For God's sake. This isn't fifth grade."

They both looked at her, then only at their cigarettes. They smoked in silence.

"The gathering is at her house after the funeral tomorrow, right?" Andy finally asked.

"Yeah," Malcolm and Dair both said.

"How's Marielle doing?" Malcolm asked her.

Dair shrugged. "How do you expect her to be doing? She's devastated."

He nodded.

"Will she be there tomorrow?" Malcolm asked.

"At the funeral? Of course," Dair said.

"No, I mean, at Gayle's thing."

"Oh. I don't know. I assume so. But I'm not sure."

"She should be there," Malcolm said.

His comment irritated her for some reason. His hand on the cigarette trembled again. She kept catching him looking at Andy, as though he were trying to communicate something with his eyes. He reminded her of the chickadee. She swallowed.

Would Peyton be at the funeral?

He needed to be. He needed to mourn his friend. She hoped he wouldn't stay away because of her. She'd hate to deprive him of that. Surely he'd come. She wanted him there.

Her throat closed up, and the cigarette tasted nasty, bitter. She tossed it in the bucket of sand. "I'm going in," she said. "I'll see you." She touched Andy's arm. "I'll talk to you later."

Dair slipped inside the door, past the security guard, and back down the hall toward the Jarson-Kaplan Theater. Before she'd made it past the box office, though, she heard her name called.

She turned, and Malcolm clomped across the marble-tiled floor toward her. She knew it—he'd been looking for her outside. Wanting to confront her about the police. She steeled herself.

"Hey," he said. "Can I ask you a favor?"

She blinked, startled by his gentle tone. "Depends on what it is."

He didn't seem to notice. He ducked his head apologetically, as if he deserved her aloofness. "It has to do with Peyton."

The marble tile tilted under her feet. "What?" Did he know something?

"Um . . . did you—did you ever tell him I called this morning?"

"No. I'm sorry. Look, it was a bad time—"

"No, no. That's okay. That's *good*. This is gonna sound weird, but don't tell him, okay? It's important."

Dair blinked again. "Why? What did you want?"

"Just . . . just don't say anything. Please?"

What the hell was he talking about? She and Peyton never talked about Malcolm. Did Malcolm think he was the goddamn center of the universe? "Fine. Whatever. I won't say anything." She fought back her tears, not wanting Malcolm to see them.

Malcolm apparently had no idea how easy that promise might be for her to keep. But he could rest assured that if she ever spoke to Peyton again, her first topic of conversation would surely not be him.

Chapter Sixteen

Peyton almost whimpered along with Shodan as they watched Dair leave the Aronoff. Five Dobermans might as well be stacked on his chest. "Shh," he said, stroking Shodan's head.

When Dair reached her car, Peyton started to get out of his own, but Dair didn't drive away for a long time. It was too dark to see her; she was nearly a block away, but she appeared just to sit there. Finally the car started and pulled away from the curb.

Peyton got out, with Shodan on a leash beside him. Poor Shodie didn't know what the hell was going on. They'd wandered all night last night. Walking everywhere. This morning he'd bought her food and a bowl and fed her in the car. Then he'd gone to two NA meetings back to back—meetings in a different part of town from the ones he usually attended. Shodan had sat in the smoky church basement beside him, a perplexed expression on her noble face. Peyton didn't speak at either of the meetings. He didn't recognize a single other person there.

He'd showered at the studio this afternoon, both before and after rehearsal. Shodan had watched rehearsal, head on her front paws, her velvety brow wrinkled, her ears pinned tight against her skull. She loved the attention, everyone fawning over her, but she never lost that sense of anxiety all day. She still hadn't. Peyton hadn't, either.

He breathed in the chilly night air. Every vein in his body called out for a distraction, a release. He tried to ignore it, but it was hard to concentrate with the whine blasting in his head. He was surprised other people didn't comment and ask him to turn it down.

Shodan trotted beside him as they crossed the street to the Aronoff. He entered the stage door he'd seen Dair come out of and said, "Hey," to Joe, the security guard, who knew him and who made a face and shook his head at the dog. "Just a sec," Peyton promised. "I just gotta find someone." He hoped he wasn't too late. Malcolm might have already left.

Shodan walked gingerly on the marble tiles. Outside Procter & Gamble Hall, Peyton saw Malcolm talking to someone he didn't recognize. "Hey, Malcolm," he called up the stairs.

Malcolm broke away from the other man, some blond guy, who slipped back into the theater. "Hey, I don't wanna interrupt," Peyton said.

"No, that's cool." Malcolm eyed Shodan and fidgeted with the zipper of his leather jacket as he came down the stairs. "Uh, so, did you just talk to Dair?"

"No." Peyton didn't elaborate.

Malcolm looked surprised and then relieved. Did he know they'd split up already? "She just left, like five minutes ago."

"Oh," Peyton said. Again Malcolm seemed surprised that Peyton didn't rush back out after her. "Actually I came to talk to you."

"Oh. Look, I'm okay, man. I told you I'd call you if—"

"I left Dair last night. I need a place to crash."

Malcolm's hands went to his jacket zipper, the sound like sandpaper on Peyton's nerves. Shodan strained away from Peyton, sniffing at something on the floor. "Whoa. So . . . is it true? Was it true about her . . . and Craig?"

Something broke inside Peyton. He wasn't sure he'd be able to walk himself out of the building, he was suddenly so tired. His bones felt heavy. "I don't know. I have no idea."

"But . . . is that why you left?"

Peyton shook his head and sat on the stairs. Shodan stopped sniffing and returned to his side, licking his hand.

"Why, then?" Malcolm asked.

"She lied to me."

Malcolm zipped his jacket up and down.

"It was a big lie. Look, it's a long story."

"Yeah, yeah, I'm sorry, I— Of course you can crash at my place.

No problem. It's nothing fancy, you know, I was pretty broke after rehab."

"I don't care," Peyton said, and he really didn't. He found it hard to care about anything. Except maybe quieting that goddamn whine inside his skull. Would it stop if he slammed his head into these marble stairs? He pictured himself doing that. Shodan looked up and whimpered.

Peyton thought about all Cassie had explained. He could go to that workshop on Saturday. But it was only Tuesday. Saturday seemed five hundred years away, instead of five days. Or could he say four? Today was pretty much over. No. He knew better. There was still plenty of time to screw up in this day. He was back to "one day at a time."

Only this time he had Dair withdrawal.

"Oh, man, Peyton. I'm sorry. Let me grab my stuff. I'll be right back."

Peyton didn't move as Malcolm rushed away back down the hall. He leaned back against the stair, his hand on Shodan's head, wanting to be anywhere but there. Wanting Craig alive. Wanting Dair to be who he thought she was. Wanting all his pieces back together. He never thought he'd feel this way again. Humpty fucking Dumpty.

The lobby doors opened behind him, and the guy Malcolm had been talking to came out again and walked down the stairs. A tall blond guy, he looked vaguely familiar. Peyton nodded, and the guy nodded back, then disappeared into a rest room.

Come on, Malcolm, he willed. He wanted to feel grateful for Malcolm's willingness to house him at short notice, but the truth was he wanted Malcolm to get his ass out here and take Peyton someplace where he could sleep.

Malcolm returned, followed by C. J. Slaughter, who waved and clapped Peyton on the back. "Hey, Peyton, my man," he said in that bass voice of his. Shodan wagged her tail at him, but he didn't look twice at her, as if Peyton always went everywhere escorted by a Doberman. "How's it going?"

"I've been better," Peyton said.

C.J.'s face grew somber. "I'll see you at the funeral tomorrow. Hang in there."

Oh. The funeral. He thought Peyton meant the funeral. Well, that was true, too.

"Hope you feel better," C.J. said to Malcolm. C.J. walked away from them, out the stage door.

"Feel better?" Peyton asked.

Malcolm shrugged, blowing his nose. "Working on a kick-ass cold, that's all. Sorry it took me so long; the director wanted to talk to me. I can go now."

Peyton sighed and rubbed his face with one hand. "Actually, Dair told me you started those rumors about her and Craig."

"What?" He looked stunned. "So that's what she meant. Well, hell, I'm the last to know everything around here. I'm not hip enough to start rumors."

Shodan lay down. Peyton wanted to, too.

"Look, I'm on Rice Street," Malcolm said. "Over-the-Rhine."

Peyton knew he didn't mean the nice part of the Over-the-Rhine district. There was no way Malcolm was living in the old, Italianate buildings on the *National Register of Historic Places*. Malcolm must be in the low-income housing, some of the worst neighborhoods in the city.

Malcolm made a face. "Just follow me, okay?"

"Okay." And thank God they were on their way to his place. Peyton found a spot to park on Malcolm's narrow street and carried the dog food bag and bowl in with him, duffel bag on his shoulder, leash in his hand. The litter-strewn street was full of old, identical brick apartment buildings.

Groups of men, and a few women, huddled on most corners, someone occasionally ducking into a building, then coming out again, slipping unseen bags from hand to hand. Nice, he thought wryly. Just the place for a recovering junkie to make a fresh start.

Malcolm stood on the steps of his building, waving Peyton over against the wall, as Shodie peed. "I'm not supposed to have pets," he whispered. "I *really* can't get caught."

Peyton felt bad. He knew Malcolm was risking a lot, having been evicted from his last place, trying to rebuild something of a reputation.

They snuck up the stairs to his apartment.

The entire long, narrow apartment was the size of Peyton and Dair's kitchen. The door opened into a living room that led to a galley kitchen, one bedroom, and a bathroom. That was it. He had a

couch for Peyton to sleep on—a bad orange-and-brown-plaid couch
still wearing a Salvation Army tag. But that was all Peyton wanted. A
place where he could shut his eyes and not worry. A place where
he didn't have to explain too much to anyone. And a place where
he didn't have to be alone, which was what prevented him from
finding a hotel. He feared it might be too easy just to disappear.

One of Craig's résumé shots lay faceup on the blue shag carpet.
Seeing it made a deep pulse, as if from a bass, course through Peyton. He pulled his eyes from it.

Malcolm dumped his bag and began rushing around, tidying, and
Peyton watched Shodan sniff around the barren living room. Other
than two framed Mapplethorpe photos still leaning against one wall,
not yet hung, the place was sparse and gave no clue to who Malcolm was the way most homes did. He and Jimmy had lost it all.
When Jimmy had hit bottom, he'd pulled a "geographic," entering a
rehab out of state, but Malcolm had been stuck here, sending every
last dime up his nose and into his lungs. He didn't shoot up, Peyton
had discovered at the meetings he'd attended with Malcolm, but had
smoked his heroin, fearing the risk of HIV from needles.

Peyton couldn't imagine smoking it. He'd loved the ritual of injecting it, tending to the veins, feeling it move through him, reaching his brain in seconds. He even used to count the seconds,
thirteen . . . fourteen . . . fifteen, and there it was—the rush, the embrace, the warm flush through his limbs.

Peyton shoved the feeling aside and followed Malcolm into his
kitchen and focused in on what Malcolm was doing. An empty sugar
bowl sat on the counter with a spoon in it. A plastic jar of honey
stood upside down beside it, drained dry. About twenty little restaurant sugar packs were scattered across his counter, and he swept
them in a wad, not making eye contact with Peyton. "You mother-
fucker," Peyton said.

Malcolm stopped, back to him, shoulders slumped. He didn't ask
Peyton what he meant. He knew.

"You don't have a goddamn cold. You're dope-sick, you shit."

Malcolm turned around to face him, and Peyton recognized what
he'd been too preoccupied to notice before. The clammy skin, the
runny nose, the miserable, twitching calves. Malcolm had used drugs
recently enough to be in withdrawal.

Peyton grabbed Malcolm by his leather jacket and slammed him into a wall. Malcolm's head hit with a thud, but he didn't protest. Shodan whimpered. "You're still *using?*"

"Just today," he whispered. "I picked up today."

Peyton wanted to slam Malcolm's head into the wall again and again. He wanted to punch him in the stomach. Bash Malcolm's face into his knee. And he wanted not to have thought of Craig the second he realized Malcolm had been using. Heroin in Craig's autopsy. But Peyton had been *with* Malcolm on Saturday . . . but only until one or so. Not at four-thirty, when Dair saw Craig die. "Why didn't you call me?"

"I tried."

Peyton pulled him off the wall and slammed him back. "Don't fucking lie to me."

"I tried! I called this morning."

Oh. Peyton let him go. Malcolm slumped to the floor, head in his hands. Shodan skittered in a nervous dance, haunches low to the ground.

"I wasn't there," Peyton said.

"No shit." Malcolm rubbed the back of his head.

"Did you talk to Dair?"

"If you can call it that. I think she was drunk."

"Shit." Peyton looked around the kitchen. Drunk? That hadn't taken long, had it? Was she okay? Stop it. He didn't care about Dair. He *wouldn't* care about Dair.

"It was only one bag," Malcolm said from the floor.

One bag, Peyton thought. One glassine bag, the size of one of those sugar packs Malcolm had tried to hide. "And now you're back to square fucking one," Peyton said.

Malcolm leaned his head against the wall with a wince and closed his eyes.

"Where'd you get it?"

Malcolm didn't answer. Peyton prodded him with a foot, and Malcolm opened his eyes and lifted one shoulder.

"Do you have any here?"

Malcolm shook his head. Peyton believed him. He knew that if he tore through Malcolm's entire apartment, he wouldn't find a dusting of the white powder, not even a plastic bag to lick. Because if Malcolm had any left, he would have taken it long before he felt this shitty and sick.

With horror, Peyton recognized that he was disappointed. That if there were dope here in this apartment, he'd partake without a second's hesitation.

And he *hated* Dair for that feeling. For one second he hated her intensely, but then, just as quickly, he didn't, and hated only himself. This wasn't Dair's fault.

Malcolm got back up and walked into the living room.

"Why today?" Peyton asked, following him out of the kitchen.

Malcolm turned, his eyes running tears to match his snotty, little-kid's nose. "I missed Craig, okay?"

Peyton sighed and looked away from him, back to the résumé head shot of Craig. Peyton crouched and picked it up off the blue carpet, but it was just one of a pile of photos—all of Craig. Craig backstage, clowning around with props. Craig eating carry-out in the greenroom. Craig at a cast party, Dair sitting beside him, head tipped back, laughing, a beer in her hand.

"Malcolm?" Peyton asked, that deep bass pulse throbbing again.

"Gayle asked for pictures of him," Malcolm said. "She's doing some display for the memorial." He shrugged and looked away.

"So, what the hell happened? I thought Gayle was gonna let you stay with her longer, until you saved up more money?"

Malcolm shuffled from foot to foot. "It didn't work out. She . . . I don't know, this is gonna sound bitchy of me, but she got herself a boyfriend, and then all her good, generous intentions for me sort of went out the window. Gayle's not the deepest pool around, you know?"

Peyton nodded. He found Gayle about as interesting and authentic as elevator Muzak, but she'd agreed to house Malcolm when he first got out of rehab, and since Dair didn't seem to know anything about Malcolm's "troubles," he assumed Gayle had actually been a bit discreet about it. But Peyton had been shocked when Dair told him she was watching Gayle's house—he figured Gayle would just have Malcolm bring in the mail and feed the cat. "Gayle has a boyfriend?" Peyton asked.

"Yeah." Malcolm scratched his goatee as if it drove him crazy. "Can you believe that? That bitch has a boyfriend and I don't?"

Peyton wondered how any boyfriend would feel about this collection of Craig photos.

Shodan's toenails clicked in the next room, on the linoleum kitchen floor. Peyton tried to picture someone with Gayle, in bed. He shivered. "Who? Who's her boyfriend?"

Malcolm shook his head. He looked down at his jacket zipper and ran it up and down as he talked. "I don't know. But I came in once and she was screwing someone in the living room. They scampered and I didn't really see anything. I just fled to my room in the basement, but she was mortified. She acted all different around me. Before, she'd been really supportive, you know? Like for real, concerned for me, and wanting me to do well, but then . . . once that happened, she got weird about my schedule and where I could be in the house." He stopped zipping and looked at Peyton. "I think whoever her boyfriend was wanted me out." Malcolm narrowed his eyes. "I could see where it was headed. I didn't want to be where I wasn't wanted. And the bitch has been *telling* people. There are people who know I was living with her, which pisses me off. I'm through with her. I mean, I confided in her. I was grateful. But, this sucks." He sighed and looked anxiously toward the kitchen, toward the tapping of Shodan's toenails as she explored. "And I guess she really let Dair have it, too. I didn't mean to get her in trouble. But . . . shit, now Dair *really* hates me. She's been acting different around me, too. I mean, we've never been *friends,* you know, but we got along. I think she's a great actress and all, but lately, man, she's, I don't know . . . but I guess, if you guys were having trouble, maybe that's all it was." He looked around the room and shrugged. "That, I guess, and what you told me about her birthday."

Peyton snorted. Malcolm looked over at him. "Sorry," Peyton said, not knowing exactly what he apologized for. "Thanks again, for letting me stay here."

"Sure. God, I know it's not much." The distaste on his face was clear as he surveyed the room. "It's just for now. Till I get back on my feet. I blew a lot of money, man. A lot."

"So, where'd you get the dope, Malcolm?"

He looked startled at the return to this topic. He shook his head.

"Malcolm, don't be an asshole. Do you need to go somewhere? Do you want to go back to rehab?"

"No. Don't mess with this, Peyton. I'm in a show, I'm—"

"You *asked* me to mess with this! You asked me to be your fucking sponsor. Come on. Where'd you get it?"

Malcolm stared back at him. "You're not a very good sponsor."

"Well, if I recall correctly, I said *no*, and you wouldn't—"

"Look, I tried to call you. If you have too much other shit going on in your life, then—"

"Where'd you get it, Malcolm?"

He zipped his jacket up and down three times, then said, "I copped it on the street." But he looked off to the side when he said it. Peyton didn't believe him, even though he knew Malcolm could score down there in less than five minutes.

"Who were you talking to when I got there tonight?"

Malcolm looked up, startled.

"Who was that guy? He looked familiar. Is he your dealer?"

Malcolm laughed. It was a real laugh. "Andy? Please. He's not a dealer."

"That was Andy? The lighting guy?" Malcolm nodded. Dair had talked about Andy. Craig had, too. They liked him. Peyton thought a moment, then said, "I've never met him, I don't think, but he looked really familiar."

"Maybe you met him in another life."

"Fuck you." Peyton wanted to hurl Malcolm into the wall.

Malcolm backed away, perhaps sensing Peyton's anger. "I'm sorry." He looked sincerely ashamed. Malcolm sat on the floor, cross-legged. Shodan snuffled back into the room. Peyton sat on the ugly couch and knew he wasn't getting up again until he'd slept a long time. "I'm really sorry, man," Malcolm said. "About Dair. It must've been bad."

Peyton rubbed his eyes. "It was."

"Can you fix it?"

Peyton sighed. "I don't know. I really don't."

Malcolm tugged on his goatee again and burrowed a finger into the blue shag carpet. "I like Dair," he said.

And without warning, Peyton's chest collapsed. Tears came. He put his hands over his face, the heels of his hands on his mouth, trying to be quiet. He couldn't stop. He melted into Malcolm's dirty couch, and he cried. Malcolm liked Dair? Peyton *loved* Dair. At least he thought he had. But he didn't know who she was. He didn't know what to do. How to go on. How to survive without her.

Shodan nuzzled his thigh, then left one paw there, as he shook with sobs.

Malcolm patted Peyton's shoulder, and Peyton heard him leave the room. As he cried, he was aware of quiet shuffling and puttering in the kitchen. The beeping of a microwave. And eventually Malcolm whispered in his ear, "Here, man. Hang in there."

He touched Peyton's head, stroked his hair once, then walked away. Peyton heard Malcolm's bedroom door close. When he removed his hands from his face, it was to a room lit only by a lamp on the floor. The pile of photos was gone. A blue sleeping bag sat beside him. On the milk crate that acted as a makeshift coffee table sat a cup of steaming liquid and a bottle of Tylenol PM. Shodan looked up at Peyton, her head and paw still on his thigh.

He stroked her face, and she licked the tears from his hands. He felt beat up, run over. "I'm sorry," he whispered. He leaned forward and picked up the cup. It was tea, smelled like chamomile. He sipped it. Soothing. He set it down and picked up the bottle.

The shiny blue-and-white pills promised a "sleep aid." One junkie knew how to comfort another.

If they couldn't make it go away, whatever hurt, they knew how to make themselves go away instead. Peyton swallowed two pills, which was what the bottle recommended, then took two more for good measure.

The next day, Wednesday, Peyton went to Craig's funeral, but it felt more like his own.

He tried to focus on his friend, on paying him the respect he deserved, on comforting Marielle, but his own loss felt heavier, more mournful, to him. He wanted a funeral for his marriage, for the last eight years of his life.

Before the funeral he waited on his own street, until he saw Dair finally leave with Marielle and Matt. He'd assumed Marielle had already left, since her car was gone, but then she'd pulled up in front of the house. Peyton wondered where they'd been. While Matt knocked on Dair's door, Marielle scanned the street as if looking for someone. When she noticed Peyton sitting in the car, she froze, then seemed to relax as she recognized him. She shook her head, her blond hair blowing in the breeze, and lifted her hand in a small wave. Peyton could tell she already knew he'd left. He wondered what version of the truth Dair had concocted for her.

When Dair came out of the house, Marielle didn't reveal Peyton's presence to her. They all got in Marielle's car, with Dair driving.

Once they were gone, Peyton took Shodan in to be with Blizzard. The two dogs danced with utter happiness and relief, licking each other's faces, grooming each other. Godot tore down the stairs, yowling, and Shodan touched noses with him. Godot stood under her as she resumed her grooming of Blizzard, and the cat looped his tail over her muzzle and rubbed himself against her chest.

Peyton's eyes stung as he watched them. He went upstairs to get the clothes he needed, but the bedroom almost brought him to his knees. He might as well be at a visitation. He stood before the furniture and objects he and Dair had selected and lived with together, wanting to kiss each one, find a way to say good-bye to it.

He decided to let Shodan stay there while he went to the funeral. He changed his clothes and left.

The parking lot and streets surrounding the funeral home overflowed with cars. Peyton wondered how many of them actually knew Craig and how many of these people were gawkers because of the news.

The funeral home was packed. Peyton almost left, almost ran away, but he forced himself to stand in the lobby doorway, looking into the crowded room.

Lots of people looked at him, then ducked their eyes away, and he knew the fact that Dair was there already only fanned the flame of the rumor. Didn't people find it odd that Marielle was letting her sit in the front row, holding her son's hand? Or did they think Marielle didn't know about the rumor? And *was* it a rumor? Who knew? It would be an easier explanation of why they'd split up. Peyton almost longed for it to be true. It would be easier to hate her, after all.

Peyton surveyed the rest of the milling crowd and noted with horror the open casket in the front of the room. He hated open caskets, found them ghoulish and bizarre.

Someone behind Peyton whispered, "Are you going to Gayle's afterward?" and another voice murmured, "Yes." That's right. Gayle was having a gathering, a sort of memorial for Craig. He didn't see Gayle in the crowd, but there were rows of chairs he couldn't see from where he stood.

Matt turned around in his seat, scanned the crowd, and jumped up and ran to Peyton. Marielle stood and called, "Matthew!" as if she feared he'd run away. Her panicked voice stopped every conversation in the room, turned every person around in their chairs to look at Peyton. It took every ounce of Peyton's control not to bolt. He kept his eyes on Matt and let the boy hug him. He moved inside the door, to let others in behind him, and crouched to talk to Matt. Marielle walked from the front of the room to join them, one hand on her heart.

"Why aren't you up front with us?" Matt asked. "We saved a seat for you."

Marielle reached them and took Matt's hand, looking anxiously around the room. "Come sit with us," she said.

Peyton thought about being up there with all those eyes on the back of his head. He didn't think he could be near Dair.

"Please?" Marielle asked. Matt took Peyton's hand, and Peyton let himself be led. As they walked forward, he saw Malcolm, who nodded at him with red, weepy eyes, crying already. C.J. sat near him. Bethany and her husband. Kitten Silver. Countless people he recognized. They reached the front row, and Dair looked up at him, her face full of anguish, expectation. He couldn't be cruel to her in front of all these people. He touched her shoulder, then stepped away from her to let Marielle return to her seat.

Peyton turned toward the coffin. Craig's combed, shiny hair framed a repaired, faintly bluish face, some of the bruises impossible to mask. The face looked like a hideous wax figure of Craig. Peyton wheeled away so quickly that he stumbled, and Dair reached out to steady him. He let her take his hand and pull him to a wooden folding chair beside her.

They sat, facing forward, legs and shoulders touching, in the cramped row. Close enough to smell her freshly shampooed hair, yet with miles yawning between them. Peyton looked down at her feet on the mauve carpet. Her ankles in their black tights before her black skirt covered them. He'd kissed those ankles. He'd kissed nearly every inch of this body next to his. Knew every delicious crevice of it.

Every mark, every scar, every dimple. Knew about the fine, spidery veins behind her knees, the rough, ragged skin on her heels, the mole next to her left nipple.

He knew she murmured in her sleep, he knew she cried sometimes for no reason, he knew she grew visibly nervous and pale whenever she saw twins.

From the day he'd met Dair, and she'd told him about her twin dying, he'd believed he'd understood a key to her personality. He'd thought that loss colored everything about her, the way his drug addiction colored his own.

And she'd fed that belief. And not one bit of it was true.

So when she cried sometimes, and it *wasn't* because of Sylvan—because there was no goddamn Sylvan—why did she cry? When she grew depressed around her birthday, was it all an act? The nightmares? She didn't fake the nightmares, did she?

Dair began to cry, little gasping sounds escaping from her. Her sorrow spread onto Peyton, like something spilled seeping into fabric. He tried to think of Craig and keep his sorrow for him.

Peyton looked at the coffin, catching a glimpse of Dair's profile, her burgundy sweater. She turned toward him, and he ducked his head again. She touched his leg, and he flinched. She drew her hand back as if from a striking snake.

The service began with the Lord's Prayer. Peyton kept his head bowed but his eyes open. He didn't say the words. Those words, this belief, were not his.

The room was too hot; there were too many bodies. His sweat felt wrong, thick and sickly. And in spite of the heat, he shivered. It was like detox, sitting there, those awful days when the need wasn't just in his brain. Those days of dry heaving and shaking, the goose-pimpled "cold turkey" skin, the insomnia, the runny nose, the unbearable longing for sugar. He closed his eyes, imagined sugar grating between his teeth like sand.

The pastor now read from Ecclesiastes: "To everything there is a season, and a time to every purpose under heaven." Those words Peyton could believe in, even though he was sure his view of heaven differed from that of the pastor's. This wasn't the end for Craig. The full life cycle of a human spirit ran not from birth to death, but from birth to birth. Craig's soul was simply at a transient midpoint.

What traces of this life would Craig carry into his next? Would the call of a wolf, perhaps, mysteriously haunt him? The flurried motions of American Sign Language? The sound of tap shoes? Would he have a fear of falling?

Peyton couldn't breathe. Thought he might pass out in his chair and almost wanted to. Was only aware of the cloying, suffocating ether of too many flowers in a small space. Was only aware of Dair beside him, and their nearly audible need to speak to each other.

When the service ended, Peyton felt trapped as a man led people out of their rows like some sick, twisted receiving line past the coffin and Marielle and Matt. Peyton stood and ducked out a side door into a narrow hallway, stumbling along, looking for a bathroom. He found one and went inside, splashing his face with cold water.

When he came out, Malcolm stood in the hallway. "You okay?" he asked, touching Peyton's shoulder.

Peyton shrugged.

"Did you talk to Dair?"

"Malcolm, we're at a funeral." He leaned his head against the wall. "I don't want to fight."

Malcolm leaned beside him. "You gotta talk. You gotta talk to her." He reminded Peyton of R.B. telling him that he had to talk to Dair about everything. Too bad R.B. never gave his daughter that advice.

Peyton thought about their conversation. How R.B.'d looked confused when he'd asked about Sylvan. The tone of R.B.'s voice as he'd asked of Cassie, "What did she *say* to you?" Peyton winced. R.B. must think he was still using, or he was stupid or babbling nonsense. Peyton didn't want that man thinking ill of him or wondering. Too many people wondered already. It had felt good to know there was someone who never questioned him.

But that was just one more thing he'd lost.

Chapter Seventeen

Sitting next to Peyton at the funeral home, sensing his pain, sensing him hate her, felt like hell. But it also felt right. Dair deserved it. She wanted to hurt.

And she loved him so much that she almost cried out when he touched her shoulder and sat beside her. He was so kind, too gentle to be hateful to her in front of everyone. Or maybe he was only keeping up appearances for Marielle. Who knew anymore?

Marielle already knew the truth. Last night, after rehearsal, Dair had pulled onto the street just as Marielle and Matt were leaving for a hotel. Apparently they'd spent Monday night at a hotel, too, returning to find the police on the porch at the crack of dawn, knocking on Dair's door. That was why Marielle didn't know Peyton had left. But she'd noticed that Shodan wasn't with poor mournful Blizzard in the backyard, so when she saw Dair pull up Tuesday night, she and Matt stopped and got out. She'd made Dair go next door with her, locking them in while they talked.

Matt had sulked upstairs to his room—complaining that he was tired of stupid hotels—and Dair told Marielle the whole story. Marielle's green eyes grew dark and dull as she listened. She signed something unconsciously while Dair talked, and at one point even put her hands over her ears, as if wishing she truly were deaf. "Oh, my God, Dair, *why?*"

And Dair found she couldn't explain that anymore.

"He wanted to believe it," she whispered. "And he had no reason to doubt me. I mean, what possible motivation would I have for making something like that up?"

Marielle nodded.

"He said he knew that's why we found each other. He said—" But Dair stopped. None of it made sense anymore. "I lied about it for so long, I started to believe it myself."

"Oh," Marielle said, her eyes glistening for a moment with something almost like admiration. "God. You must've felt so sick, carrying that around." Marielle's understanding was so welcome, so comforting, but Dair guiltily felt she didn't deserve it. She didn't feel half as sick as Peyton looked when he'd found out. "Oh, Dair, didn't you want to give it up? Didn't it make you so . . . weary?"

Marielle slumped over, elbow on the table, head held up on one hand, as if she were the one carrying something heavy. Her eyes were full of an insight, a shared pain, that chilled Dair. She wondered about Marielle, her reluctance to talk to the police, her strange behavior the night they'd found the clothes. What might Marielle be carrying herself?

"Weren't you tired?" Marielle asked.

"I was exhausted," Dair whispered. She didn't tell Marielle that giving it up did not provide the relief she'd wanted. The truth *did* hurt.

Marielle reached across her kitchen table and took Dair's hand, just as Craig had at Palomino's the night Dair had burdened him with this.

But Marielle understood in a way Craig had not. She didn't judge Dair, she didn't ask the question Peyton and Craig both had: *How?* She seemed to know. She took it for granted that it could be done. An odd sort of sisterhood enveloped them at the table.

"You're tired, too, aren't you?" Dair asked.

Marielle looked at her with those ancient green eyes.

"Tell me, Marielle."

Marielle *didn't* ask, "What do you mean?"

For a moment Dair thought Marielle might let it go, her own bird. She saw her consider it. But Marielle shook her head, looked at her watch, and said, "We need to go or they might release our room."

Dair had the sense she was talking to a stranger.

Was that what Peyton felt when Dair had told him the truth?

Was that what he felt right now, sitting so close to her in this funeral home that they couldn't help but touch? She wondered where he'd been, where'd he'd slept, where sweet Shodan was this very minute. Peyton didn't smell like himself; he smelled of cigarette smoke and a shampoo that wasn't his own.

She wished she could discern from those odors where he'd been, like Blizzard, gleaning information from scent alone.

Dair tried to concentrate on this moment. The coffin. The pastor. Marielle shaking with her sorrow. Peyton like a stone, hard and cold, but not unfeeling. Sitting so close to him, her body absorbed his pain, the way it used to absorb his warmth in bed. Her chest ached as though her ribs would crack.

As soon as the service ended, Peyton bolted. The way he leapt up and took off felt as though he'd spat on her.

As people filed past Marielle and Matt, and some of Craig's cousins, Dair longed for a drink. She hadn't had one that morning, as punishment, to prepare herself to see Peyton. All that was left in the house was the Kahlúa. She'd drunk her coffee without it, but she still had the bottle in the cupboard. It was good to have a little security on hand. And if Peyton couldn't bear even to sit next to her and was never coming back, who really gave a shit what she drank and what she didn't?

The line went on forever. Every theater person in town was here, it seemed.

Bethany and her husband hugged and kissed Marielle, and Bethany hugged Dair as well. She squeezed Dair's hands. "I'm sorry," she whispered. Dair had no idea anymore what people meant when they said that to her. Just a general statement on her being? It felt like it.

C.J. came through the line, and Marielle stood up to hug him. They held each other a long time. Malcolm Cole was behind C.J. in line. Dair watched Malcolm, saw him scanning the crowd, which he could do now that he stood up front. Whom was he looking for?

Marielle received Malcolm warmly. He took her hands in his, reminding Dair of Gayle, then lifted Marielle's hands to his mouth and kissed them. Oh, please.

He saw Dair watching him, and his face shifted. He nodded at her, stepping to her side, but she remained seated and offered no invitation for any kind of connection. He touched her shoulder and leaned toward her, his long hair falling forward. For a horrible moment she thought he was about to kiss her. He whispered, "I'm really sorry about you and Peyton. I hope you work things out. You guys are great together." He squeezed her shoulder and moved on, missing her dumbfounded expression, missing the fact that he'd left her paralyzed.

How did he know that? How could he possibly know that?

Dair snapped back to life when she heard Matt say, "Mr. Lively!"

Their neighbor stood before Marielle. He walked with a cane and wore an old brown suit that looked as if it had been folded, and not very neatly, for years. Creases ran through the jacket and pants at odd, diagonal angles. Marielle burst into tears. She started to stand again, but he wouldn't let her. He patted her head, then Matthew's. Dair had never told Marielle about Matt and Mr. Lively going to the zoo Saturday morning. If Dair told her, would Marielle always wonder what would've happened if Matt'd been home when Craig came over? And maybe Marielle *did* know; it seemed she was keeping a secret, too, but Dair couldn't fathom what it could be.

Mr. Lively came to Dair's chair. He squeezed her outstretched hand in his dry, papery own, but with a furrowed brow and pursed lips. "Thank you for being here," Dair whispered.

"Well, of course," he said in a stern voice, as if about to offer some perfectly sensible, logical reason why he should be. He looked back at Marielle, and his eyes watered a bit. "Oh, well, I wanted to come. . . . "

Mr. Lively started to walk on but stumbled on the edge of carpet and nearly tripped. Dair stood, steadied him, and said, "Let me help you outside."

He shrugged her off. "I can walk."

But she stayed by his side, escorting him into the hallway. Her good deed brought her face-to-face with Peyton, who talked to Malcolm. Had Peyton told Malcolm? Was he telling everyone? Did people know she'd lied?

"Excuse us. Can we get through?" Dair asked, hating her weak, wavery voice. Peyton moved, turned his back, as if he didn't know her. It wasn't an unkind or cruel movement, but its indifference nearly crippled her. She was grateful she had Mr. Lively to hold her up, keep her from crumpling to the floor.

Malcolm moved, too, to make room, but his face was soft, his eyes kind. Dair and Mr. Lively passed them and headed down the hallway in the opposite direction.

Andy stood at the door where Peyton had first entered. He hovered in the door frame, watching the endless line snake up toward the coffin. His eyes were red and swollen. "Hey, Andy," Dair said.

He nodded and sniffed, wiping his eyes roughly. Dair turned away to give him a moment. "Are you going to the cemetery?" she asked Mr. Lively.

"Oh, good Lord, no. I need to get home." He always sounded as if he had so much to do there. She pictured Captain Hook calling for his "Papa."

Mr. Lively went outside, and Dair watched him make his cautious way down the stairs. When he was safely on level ground, she turned back to face Andy.

"Is that Craig's grandfather?" Andy asked.

Dair smiled. "No, that's our neighbor. He lives upstairs."

Andy nodded but kept his eyes on the front of the line.

"You going in?" Dair asked.

He shook his head. "No. Oh, no. I . . . can't. I don't do that open casket stuff very well. I . . ." He fidgeted with a button on his shirt. "I don't do any of this very well. Funerals." He shrugged and looked sheepish.

"So, you going over to Gayle's?"

He shrugged. "I dunno. Where is Gayle, anyway?"

Dair rolled her eyes. "Please. This little 'gathering' will probably have an ice sculpture and a string quartet."

Andy snorted. "Why didn't Craig's fiancée have the memorial? Gayle didn't take it from her, did she?"

"Oh . . . no. Marielle didn't want to. She can't be with that many people right now. She's exhausted. She and Matt are doing something with Craig's cousins, I think. She said she might come by later, but the way she said it, I know she won't."

He shivered and shook his head. "I can't imagine."

Dair watched him as he looked off toward the front of the room again. "Nope," he said finally. "I think I'll go walk by the river or something. I'll find my own way to say good-bye to Craig." He fidgeted some more with his buttons, which were fine, then said, "Where'd Malcolm go? He still here?"

Dair remembered their heated exchange on the sidewalk. "Probably." She looked back down the narrow hallway, but Peyton and Malcolm were gone.

"Who was that guy Malcolm was talking to?"

She swallowed. "Peyton? That's my . . . husband."

Andy raised his eyebrows. "Your husband? The black belt in aikido?" Dair turned to him, startled.

"Remember?" Andy asked. "You told me that at, you know, on Clifton Avenue. . . ."

Remembering that day made Dair's legs go weak, her knees threatening to buckle. She looked away again, to where Peyton and Malcolm had stood. She knew Peyton well enough to know that he was hurting bad, longing for a fix, hearing what he told her was the whine of wanting it in his head.

"What, Dair?" Andy asked, moving close to her. She smelled that apple scent of his.

She realized she stared down the hallway at nothing but was unable to pull her eyes away, to focus on anything else. "Peyton and I are having some trouble. He left. I don't know where he's staying."

"Oh, my God," Andy said. "I'm sorry." He squeezed her shoulder. Checking that there was no one near them, he lowered his voice and asked, "Because of what people are saying about you and Craig?"

Dair winced. "I wish," she said. "But it's lots more complicated than that." She knew what she'd done was a greater infidelity than having sex with another man. A deeper betrayal. She thought Peyton would have an easier time forgiving her if she had slept with Craig than for what she'd done.

"I'm sorry," Andy said again. "I've been there." Dair remembered what he'd said about being divorced, seeing his kid only a few weeks a year.

"The line's thinning, finally," she said. "I better get back to Marielle."

Andy squeezed her arm and headed out the door, the way Mr. Lively had gone. So many people had squeezed her arm today, or her shoulder, or her hand. Such an odd gesture. It communicated so many different things. Like a line in a script, it could be interpreted in a thousand different ways—it all depended on the delivery.

The cemetery was harder than Dair imagined. Only about half of the people who'd gone to the funeral home followed the line of cars out there. The route was odd, and Dair realized as she followed the procession on some strange side roads that it was intentionally planned to avoid both Clifton Avenue and where 75 crossed over it. Her chest ached.

Marielle and Matt rode with Craig's cousins ahead of her. Dair found it comforting to simply follow cars, to not have to make any decisions, to be led.

But the hearse led her to a hard place, where she saw her friend lowered into the dry, dusty ground. She had to stand there on the sun-bleached grass, with the leaves scattering all around them, reminding her of the day of his death, his hideous, obscene death, utterly alone.

Peyton also stood alone, fists balled in his pants pockets, tears streaming down his face. When Dair first arrived, she approached him slowly, but he lifted his head and shook it. She stopped and stayed where she was.

She felt she was being buried, too.

Dair almost didn't go to Gayle's, but she felt obligated. If she went home, she'd just drink the bottle of Kahlúa, then go buy more. And she wanted to give Gayle her key.

She blinked as she approached Gayle's house. A crowd stood in the yard. A big crowd; it wasn't just a few people smoking outside. Dair parked a block away in the first spot she found and walked down the sidewalk toward the house.

Bethany stepped from the crowd and met Dair on the sidewalk. "Wasn't the gathering supposed to be right after the funeral home?"

"Yeah," Dair said, eyeing the catering vans in Gayle's driveway. "Isn't that what she said at rehearsal?"

"Well, no one's home," Bethany said. "The caterers can't get inside. They assumed she was at the funeral, but I didn't see her."

C.J. came up to them. "Was she at the cemetery?"

Dair shook her head. Flutters of anxiety tickled against her ribs. Was Gayle gone? Had she left town?

Malcolm talked to one of the caterers in a van. "Hey, Dair, you've still got a key, right?" he called.

Bethany's face lit up. "Oh, that's right, you feed Gayle's cat."

"Yeah," Dair said slowly, feeling the key in her skirt pocket as if it were heated or radioactive, "but I don't think I should use it now . . . it doesn't seem . . ."

Malcolm walked over and joined them. "Where would she be? I think she planned to go to the funeral. This is really weird. We should go in and make sure she's not dead or something."

Bethany gasped at Malcolm. Even if the thought had crossed Dair's mind, it seemed tactless to say it out loud.

"Well . . ." If Gayle was fine, and she really was simply detained somewhere, she'd probably be pissed as hell that Dair used the key, but . . . Dair looked at the crowd in the yard, trampling the dry grass, a few people already heading for their cars to leave. Peyton walked up the sidewalk from the opposite direction. This was for Craig, right? "Okay."

Dair unlocked the front door and told Bethany, "Hold everyone outside for another minute, okay? Until we check things out."

Then she stepped inside and called, "Gayle?"

Dair headed down the hall to the kitchen. In true, organized Gayle fashion, everything was set up perfectly, with note cards on the kitchen island labeling where things should go—cards that read "Salmon," "Crackers," "Vegetable tray," "Fruit." One card read "Lilies," but there were no flowers to be seen. Was that where she was? Picking up floral arrangements?

But Gayle would never let something so important go until the last minute.

Tuxedo rubbed against Dair's shin. "Hmm?" he asked, as if wondering, along with Dair, what was going on. Dair looked at his food and water bowl, both empty and bone dry, and noticed the dirty kitchen floor. Gayle hadn't cleaned or gotten anyone else to. Those flutters of anxiety kicked in stronger, no longer tickling but scratching. Gayle was gone.

Dair left the kitchen and went upstairs, and Tuxedo followed her, repeating "hmm?" several times, like a small child tugging on her skirt. Everything was neat and tidy. No sign of Gayle or clue as to where she was. Had she left town? Fled? Had anyone seen her since Monday night?

Back downstairs, Dair moved through the living room. Tuxedo bumped into her shin, insistently "hmm?"-ing at her.

Dair turned to see Peyton in the dining room, looking at the table.

Malcolm stood next to him. Dair followed, as if pulled by a magnet, needing to be near Peyton even if he cut her again with his aloofness.

When she saw what the men looked at, her throat closed up. Gayle had made a display of Craig's photos. His résumé head shot, performance photos, candid rehearsal shots. Peyton held one of Dair hugging Craig, their faces cheek to cheek, hammy grins for the camera. Dair had one foot up behind her, in a silly pose. She saw Peyton wondering. Something worse than that bird beak sliced into her heart.

Tuxedo butted his head into her shin like a goat. "Hey, Tux, it's okay," she murmured.

Malcolm sifted through some other photos. Gayle had obviously not finished her display, but it had been a touching thought, a lovely gesture.

Tuxedo cried, a low, guttural cry unlike his usual questioning mew. She crouched to stroke him and noticed a frame on the floor, under the table, facedown. When she picked it up, broken glass rattled and fell from it. Under the cracked glass, the photo was of Craig and Marielle, outside the front door of the Ensemble Theater of Cincinnati, in warm weather. Marielle wore a sleeveless dress, and her hair lifted on the wind. Craig was in a polo shirt and jeans, tan, and grinning. They held hands, both of them turning toward the camera as if someone had called their names.

Tuxedo nipped her wrist as she held the frame. "Hey," she said, standing and setting the photo on the table. Small pebbles of glass fell to the carpet as she moved it.

Peyton frowned.

"Whoa," Malcolm said, but he wasn't looking at the smashed glass. He looked down at a stack of photos in his hands, his face pale.

"What?" Dair asked. Tuxedo cried that awful sound again and swiped her shin with one paw, snagging her black tights. "Tuxedo," she scolded, bending down to push him away. He batted at her when she shoved him, catching the back of her hand with his claws. "Ow." She snatched her hand away, shaking off the sting.

"Holy shit," Peyton whispered, and Dair turned her attention from the cat to the photos he and Malcolm looked at. She moved to see around Peyton's shoulder. They were photos of Craig and Marielle, and in each one Marielle's eyes were scribbled out, or an X was marked over her face.

The hairs on the back of Dair's neck rose as she remembered Gayle's reaction to Craig's engagement.

Tuxedo bit her ankle.

"Ow!" He really bit it, teeth sinking deep into skin, sharp, sudden pain like a wasp's sting. Blood welled from the punctures above her ankle. Dair clamped a hand over the wound to stop the burn. Tuxedo glared at her with his pale green eyes, panting as if he'd been working hard. He cried again, deep and growling, hardly sounding like a cat.

"What's wrong with him?" Malcolm asked. "Did he *bite* you?"

Dair nodded, not taking her eyes from the cat's.

Tuxedo turned his body and walked toward the kitchen but kept his eyes on Dair. He stopped where the white carpet met up with the black-and-white tile, and cried again.

This time Dair followed him, her ankle hot, her heart hammering. He walked to the door of the attached garage, where Gayle had come in on Sunday, scaring her. He stood up on his back legs and reached for the doorknob with his front paws. He wailed again.

Dair swallowed. She looked back at Peyton and Malcolm, who watched, perplexed.

She turned the knob. Tuxedo slipped out into the garage the second it opened a few inches.

Dair's chest felt constricted, the way it did when she'd had to wear corsets onstage. Deep breath was a struggle. But she didn't smell anything. She expected a car to be running, Gayle slumped behind the wheel. Or she expected Gayle to be hanging from the ceiling. When Dair opened the door all the way and flipped on the overhead light, though, nothing looked unusual. Gayle's car sat there, a silver Acura, along with a lawn mower, a snowblower, some gardening tools.

Dair stepped down the one concrete stair, past a case of Diet Coke, and a green recycling bin. She walked in the narrow space between the wall and the car.

Her foot kicked something that jingled and skidded ahead of her. She knelt and picked up Gayle's car keys, the key chain a long metal replica of a ticket to the Queen City Shakespeare Company. She clutched the keys in her hand.

"Dair?" Peyton asked from the door frame. She stood, thankful he even spoke to her.

Before she could answer, Tuxedo wailed, from the rear of the car, which echoed eerily in the garage. As Dair reached the back of the Acura, she saw a shoe on the floor. A stylish black-and-white, faux pony-skin shoe. Again Dair fought to breathe deep against her corseted rib cage and diaphragm, faintness blurring the edges of her vision.

Tuxedo sniffed the shoe and wailed.

She didn't take her eyes from Tuxedo nosing the shoe, the one lonely shoe, the sort of shoe no one would ever just leave somewhere.

"What is it?" Peyton stood behind her, hands on her shoulders. "Jesus," he said. Even in this horrible moment Dair drank in his touch, was grateful for it.

She opened her hand and showed him. "Her car keys were on the floor."

Tuxedo lay down hugging the shoe with his front paws, the way a child might clutch a teddy bear.

"Open the trunk," Peyton whispered.

Dair had to turn around to look at him; his voice, the way he said that, disturbed her so. But she held the keys, and that faintness, her inability to breathe, made her unable to talk or work her hands. Peyton took the keys from her, unlocked Gayle's trunk, and lifted the lid.

Empty. Empty, at least, of what they had feared. Empty except for two grocery bags—at least one of them containing coffee, judging from the aroma floating out of the trunk—and three boxes of brand-new matching wineglasses.

"I'm letting people in, okay?" Bethany called from the doorway.

Dair looked at her, and she must've recognized something in Dair's face. "Oh, my God," Bethany said. "What?"

"Could you call the police?" Peyton asked. He kept his eyes on Dair. She wasn't sure what she read there.

"Why?" Bethany asked, stepping into the garage. "What did you—"

"Just call the police," Peyton said in a tone that made Bethany blanch.

She nodded and retreated, but Malcolm filled the doorway after she disappeared.

For a moment, Dair thought she'd known what had happened. She thought Gayle had killed Craig and then herself, knowing she was about to be caught.

But she looked from the shoe to Peyton's face and didn't know much of anything anymore.

Chapter Eighteen

Dair sat on Gayle's back patio in a wicker chair, hugging herself. The Redhead and the tall blond Detective Monty from yesterday were there, along with a huge cast of other cops. It was now eleven P.M. Craig's memorial gathering had ended abruptly with the discovery of Gayle's keys and shoe and the arrival of the police.

Dair was one of the last people known to have had a long conversation with Gayle, and the entire *Othello* cast had witnessed it. But Dair had left Gayle on the stairs with Malcolm. No one had witnessed that, though, except for Malcolm himself.

Inside Gayle's house, through the sliding glass doors, Tuxedo paced like the leopard at the zoo. Dair rubbed her ankle, sliding her finger through the hole in her tights to touch the soft new scab with her fingertips.

Had Tuxedo tried to communicate more than the garage to Dair? Did the cat know what had happened to Gayle? Dair tried to concentrate, to focus on the cat, but she didn't know how to ask him a question. Should she picture Gayle in the garage, someone whacking her on the head, perhaps? But that was Dair's image, not Tuxedo's. How did she know what, if anything, was actually coming from the cat?

Monty talked to some other officers. Dair shivered in her sweater, relieved that she felt anything at all. She welcomed the cold. It was proof she wasn't dead.

Peyton had left after being questioned and had not said good-bye to her.

She massaged her throbbing temples with her fingers. The caterers had left a box of wine on the kitchen counter, visible through the patio door. They glittered, jewel-like, and Dair yearned for some.

She thought of Gayle's car keys on the floor. Had Gayle been arriving home from the grocery store and taken by surprise? Or had she been leaving, trying to flee?

Had she been running from someone, too? The way Craig had been? Who?

Maybe Malcolm still had his key. Andy'd said Malcolm used to live here with Gayle, and Malcolm hadn't denied it. But why would he live here?

Tuxedo continued his pacing, his plaintive wail audible even through the glass doors.

If only she knew what the cat knew, could see what he'd seen.

She closed her eyes and thought of her childhood cat, Snowflake. How she'd walk on Dair's chest and sit, her purr rumbling through Dair's body. Dair would look into those glacier pool eyes and—it was like a flash, like a brief clip of video.

It was like . . . Dair opened her eyes and looked at Tuxedo again. It was like Sunday, when she'd come over and checked on the dress. It was like *that*, like visions, split-second hallucinations in her mind. Those images of Craig—his bare feet on Gayle's basement carpet, his head on the guest room pillows. Had those come from *Tuxedo?*

That corseted sensation returned in her chest. Had Craig been here? Was he having an affair with Gayle? Was that what he'd wanted to confess that night at Palomino's?

Did Craig buy both Gayle and Marielle flowers on the same morning?

What were the other images she'd seen? Craig fumbling with Gayle's front door.

Could Dair trust herself? Was she just projecting? But she hadn't even been trying to communicate with Tuxedo that day; it just came to her. She'd been open for some reason.

Those beautiful wine bottles caught her eye. She hadn't drunk on Sunday. Dair couldn't get to the freezer. Maybe her mother was right about the static.

Dair stood, and the cops stopped their conversation. "Excuse me," she said. "Do you mind if I go in and feed the cat?"

They looked through the patio door at the black-and-white cat, his head back, ears flat, nearly howling at the ceiling.

"Sure," Monty said.

She felt them watch her as she slid open the door and stepped inside. What did they say about her once she was out of earshot?

The warmth of the house embraced her. Tuxedo trotted over, his big belly swinging side to side. She knelt and stroked him. "You poor thing," she said. She stared into his eyes, tried to be open but received nothing. She had no idea how to proceed. Was she trying too hard? Forcing it?

A picture of Gayle entered her mind. Gayle angry, arguing with someone.

Did that come from Tuxedo?

How was she supposed to tell? Feeling like an idiot, she busied herself opening the cupboard and then spooning a can of salmon-flavored cat food into Tuxedo's bowl. He inspected the food but sighed and didn't eat. She leaned one elbow on the kitchen island and reached down with the other arm to pet him.

He lifted his head, his green eyes meeting hers. A flash of Gayle shouting appeared again. These pictures were as fleeting as thoughts—they appeared and then . . . left. Dair tried to hang on to the image, for details, for more information, but it was as elusive as trying to stay in a dream.

She saw the black-and-white shoe. Was that the cat's thought or hers? She didn't know how to guide these images or if she was even receiving them.

How had it happened Sunday? In the guest room, the dry cleaner bag and the stripped bed had held the cat's attention. Dair needed a prompt, something to cue him.

Dair went down the basement stairs, and just as he had Sunday, Tuxedo followed her. The stripped bed was now made. Dair sat on it and patted the mattress beside her, inviting Tuxedo to come up; but the cat sat twitching his tail, looking at her like *Now what?*

Dair picked up a pillow and tossed it on the floor. Tuxedo approached it and sniffed, and when he lifted his gaze to hers, she saw Malcolm Cole. Malcolm's head on the pillow, reaching for the alarm on the nightstand.

The tap-tap-tap of the bird beak in her chest started. If Malcolm had lived there, of course he'd stayed in the guest room . . . right? That only made sense. But Dair had also seen images of Craig's head on these pillows on Sunday. Why did she keep seeing these young, attractive men in Gayle's guest bed? And had they been there together?

Was it Craig and Malcolm who had had the affair?

What's the worst thing you've ever done? The thing you think no one will forgive you for?

Tuxedo kneaded the pillow a moment, then lay on it, his front paws tucked under his chest. An image of Tuxedo in Malcolm's lap flashed through her mind. Malcolm on this bed, reading something, with Tuxedo purring in his lap, facing him.

She stood up. Tuxedo did, too, startled by her movement.

She opened the closet where she'd returned the dress and pulled out the dry cleaning bag. Tuxedo sniffed it, and Dair saw Craig, naked, with dried blood under his nose, panting, standing here at the closet, looking over his shoulder toward the stairs, holding the dress, tearing the plastic.

What did that image mean? Had someone attacked Craig at Marielle's and then brought him here? Craig's clothes under Marielle's bed—had the attacker stripped Craig? Here? Or there, at Marielle's? God, who could drag a naked man through the street and not be noticed? Or maybe . . . Slip Jig had pooped in Marielle's basement Sunday morning . . . had the attacker taken Craig's clothes off, here, at Gayle's, then returned the clothes to Marielle's after Craig died? Why? Why under Marielle's bed, unless to point to her?

"Hmm?" Tuxedo asked.

Dair tried to entice the cat to sniff the bag again but he crept away from it, acting uneasy about the way it expanded from its wadded tight ball. He stopped in the doorway to the basement bathroom, watching the plastic bag with his ears flat. Dair walked over and flipped on the bathroom light. The half-bath was stark, bare. She opened the cupboard behind the mirror. A razor, some shaving cream, and a tube of toothpaste sat on the shelves.

The razor was heavy and gray; this was not a woman's razor. Dair picked it up. Stubble stuck to the razor's edge. She lowered the razor to Tuxedo, who sniffed it.

Malcolm flashed into her head again—without a goatee and mustache, shaving his chin and jawline. Only Dair saw the doorway where she now stood. The view, the camera angle, was from the top of the toilet. When she closed the lid on the toilet, Tuxedo jumped atop it. She held the tube of toothpaste out to him but got nothing. She took off the cap and held the open end toward him. He sniffed, then drew his lips back in a grimace and recoiled.

When Dair held out the shaving cream, Tuxedo hopped off the toilet with a mutter, as if irritated. He trotted up the basement steps, leaving her at the bottom.

If she could believe herself and her ability, then Malcolm had definitely been here, in this bed, this bathroom. And so had Craig, naked and bleeding.

"Ms. Canard?" She jumped and recognized the voice of blond Detective Monty.

"Yes," she said, wondering how she would explain why she'd been in the basement.

But he didn't ask. When she climbed the stairs into the kitchen, he simply said, "You can go home now."

"Oh. Okay. Do you know . . . what happened?"

"Not yet."

Dair leaned against the kitchen island. "Okay, listen. I know this is weird, but I just have this . . . this *feeling*. Something really odd is going on with Malcolm Cole, and—"

Monty coughed, and Dair stopped. "Mr. Cole is not considered a suspect at this time."

"But he did have a key to this house, and—"

"According to your own statement, Ms. Canard, we have an approximate time for the initial attack on Mr. MacPhearson, as well as a probable time of abduction for Ms. Lyons. Mr. Cole has an alibi and a witness for both occurrences."

Dair frowned. "But . . . I mean, who? Who's his witness, because—"

"For both of the times we're considering, he was in the company of Peyton Leahy."

Dair stared at Monty's mouth and felt the floor sliding away beneath her. "Whoa, wait a minute, no. No, Peyton couldn't have been with Malcolm when Craig was attacked because he wasn't even in Cincinnati. I showed you the itinerary! You took it with you, so—"

"Your husband was not on the flight you thought he was. He

showed us valid proof that he was on an earlier flight and was in Cincinnati by nine A.M. Saturday morning."

A sensation of falling made her clutch the kitchen island. "What?"

He looked apologetic. "I'm sorry. I understand that you're having some . . . um, marital difficulty. I'm sorry to tell you that your husband has not been honest with you, but that is not a police concern. Our only concern is that your husband can vouch for Malcolm Cole for most of Saturday."

"Wh-w-wait. What? Why? I mean, what were they *doing?* Did Malcolm tell you this, because I know Peyton would never—"

"Your husband verified this. And there were other witnesses."

Dair blinked. "Where were they?"

Monty looked down and tapped his pen on his notepad. "I think . . . I think you should talk to your husband. I'm really not at liberty to tell you any more. I'm sorry."

She wheeled around and left through Gayle's front door. She wanted to ask him more but had too much pride and not enough courage. *Your husband has not been honest with you.* Words she should welcome, really, to even out the score, to level the playing field. But the words seared into her like a brand. Peyton had lied to her.

And that feeling was worse than she'd ever imagined it would be.

Although it was nearly midnight when Dair got home, she was relieved to see Marielle's lights still on, all over her half of the house. As Dair came in the back gate, Blizzard barked at the kitchen door. "Shh," she whispered, fumbling in her bag for her key.

When she opened the door, Blizzard leapt up and put his paws on her shoulders. She hugged him back and buried her face in his sweet-smelling fur. He hopped down, and Dair let him move past her into the backyard.

With her bag still hanging from her shoulder, Dair opened the cupboard for the bottle of Kahlúa and uncapped it. The heavenly coffee aroma filled her nose and mouth with flavor. Her hands tipped the bottle, and a mouthful of the liqueur slid onto her tongue.

Running footsteps on the stairs next door, in Marielle's half of the house, startled her. A door slammed, making her cringe. *"Who's outside?"* she heard faintly from above.

Dair capped the bottle, shoved it in the cupboard, and went out the back door. Through her back door window, she saw Marielle standing in the hall to the living room. She tapped on the glass. Marielle jumped and clapped a hand over her mouth, then hid herself, peering around the door frame.

"It's just me," Dair said, trying not to be too loud.

"Who's outside?" she heard again. In her head she said, Sorry, Mr. Lively.

Marielle moved cautiously into the kitchen, toward the door.

"It's me. It's Dair," and Marielle's shoulders slumped with relief.

Marielle unlocked the door and let Dair in, hugging her, her face red and splotchy with recent tears. "Oh, my God, Dair. Oh, my God. What is going on?" She locked the door again.

"Do you know about Gayle already?"

She nodded. "Peyton was here. He was waiting for me. We just got home an hour ago from being with Craig's cousins. He told me."

Peyton had just been there. And he'd left. As irrational as it was, Dair wanted to run outside, after him, as if she could catch up. As if she knew where he'd gone. As if she'd have anything to say to him if she did find him.

Marielle wiped her eyes. "He knows I know . . . about the . . . twin." It was as if she didn't know what to call it.

"How is he?" Dair asked.

Marielle's eyes welled with tears again. "I don't know, honestly. Not good, but . . ." She looked at Dair's face and seemed to sense what Dair wanted to know. "I don't think he's using, Dair. I don't think he would."

Dair didn't know if that was true. She couldn't imagine why else Peyton might lie about when he'd returned. And Malcolm—was he a junkie? Some kind of dealer? Had he sucked Peyton back into that life?

"Everything is falling apart," Marielle said. "Gayle's missing . . . oh, my God." She covered her mouth with her hand. "And they're questioning everyone and—"

"Did the police come here? To talk to you?"

Marielle nodded. "That's why Peyton came over. He figured they would." She sighed. "Matt and I were fighting . . . again." Her mouth crumpled up, and she waved a hand in front of her face, as if angry at herself. "Everything is falling apart," she repeated.

Dair knew that feeling, of her life dismantling. Was it bad enough yet for Marielle that she'd unload the burden she carried? The secret Dair knew struggled somewhere within her?

Marielle walked into the living room and slumped on the couch.

"I thought I heard a door slam," Dair said, sitting beside her. "Was that part of the fight?"

Marielle rubbed her face. Her full cheeks had grown gaunt in a matter of days, her honey blond hair lackluster. "Slamming doors, throwing things, screaming . . . he gets more like his father every day; it scares me."

Dair cocked her head. She'd never heard Marielle say much about Matt's father. And what she had heard had been only good. The urge to ask, "What do you mean?" pushed inside Dair's throat, but she swallowed it.

A high-pitched meow made Dair turn to see Slip Jig at the bottom of the stairs. It struck Dair that for all their language, humans sure sucked at communicating with each other.

"Peyton told me about the pictures," Marielle whispered. "My face."

Dair shivered, remembering. "Do you think Gayle had a . . . thing for Craig?"

Marielle made a sound, like a thoughtful hum. "No. Gayle had a boyfriend. Craig told me she was seeing someone."

"What? *Who?*"

She shrugged. "I don't remember. It wasn't anyone I knew."

This troubled Dair; it sounded doubtful. Was Craig covering up his own involvement in something at Gayle's? "Well, then who do you think marked out your—"

A door flung open upstairs and hit the wall with a reverberating boom. Both women jumped. "Mom?" Matt yelled.

"What, Matt?" Marielle's voice was quiet, almost begging.

He pounded down the stairs, making Slip Jig skitter from his path. "Where is it?" he demanded. His face was the picture of fury, his gray eyes dark and steel-like.

Marielle sighed. "I don't read minds, baby. And I certainly don't answer anyone who talks to me in that tone of voice."

He put his hands on his hips, and his voice changed from demanding to desperate. "My picture's gone. I'm sorry. I know I was rude, but don't take that. Please give it back!"

"What are you talking about, Matthew?" She sat up now, pulled away from Dair.

Matt's voice rose higher. "My picture of you and Dad. Did you take it?"

"No, sweetie, I didn't take it, are you sure it's g—"

"Yes, I'm sure!"

Marielle stood and went to him, but he jerked away from her. "Give it back!"

"Hon, hon, shhh, listen to me," she pleaded, trying to calm him, but he stormed back up the stairs. Dair followed her after him, still lugging her bag, feeling as if she'd never stop and relax anywhere again. In his room, Matt pointed to his dresser under the poster of the wolf pack. "It was here. It was right here! Where is it?" He began opening drawers and slamming them shut as he looked for it.

Dair looked where he had pointed and frowned. "What picture?"

"My picture of my dad! I just put it out Sunday and it's gone!"

Dair had never seen a picture of Matt's dad.

"Matt, sweetie," Marielle said, "maybe you put it away and forgot where."

"I did *not!*" he yelled, then froze, his smoky eyes wide. "Maybe he did take something!"

"Who?" Dair asked.

"The intruder."

Something crackled in the air around Marielle. Dair and Matt looked at her, alarmed. Slip Jig's fur puffed out, and she arched her back. Dair's own hair felt as if it stood on end. "You put it out Sunday?" Marielle asked, her voice strained, hoarse.

Matt nodded.

"Before or after Slip Jig pooped in the basement?"

"Before."

Marielle swallowed and looked around the room, as if she half expected someone to be there now. "Oh, shit," she whispered.

"Why would anyone take that?" Matt asked. "Who would want it but me?"

Marielle pressed a hand over her mouth. Dair could almost see her heart fluttering through her black silk blouse. "Oh, God. Matty, you need to put your PJs in your duffel, and some clothes for tomorrow—"

"Marielle!" Dair protested.

"We're going to a hotel," she said. "We're not staying here."

"Mom, I don't wanna go to another hotel."

"Pack, Matt," she ordered, "we're going."

Dair was dumbfounded. "But . . . Marielle, why don't you guys just sleep next door? Or I'll sleep over here. We don't have to leave. We can keep Blizzard with us and—"

"I don't want to be in this house," she said, moving past Dair, going into her bedroom. "It's not safe, especially with Peyton gone." Dair followed her and watched her snatch clothes from various drawers and throw them into a suitcase. She looked as though she were packing for more than overnight.

"Where are you going?" Dair begged, panic building within her. "Marielle, please. You're scaring me."

"I'm scaring you? You don't know what scared is, Dair." Her expression was one beyond terror. "No one's been coming into your home."

Those photos at Gayle's. The car keys. The abandoned shoe. These things made Dair bold. "Marielle, you have to tell me: What is going on?"

Marielle didn't answer; she kept packing.

"You know something," Dair said, her voice low so Matt, in his bedroom, wouldn't overhear. "I know you know something. "When Marielle didn't respond, Dair grabbed her arm, whipped her around to face her. "Do you know who killed Craig?"

Marielle's green eyes were dead. "No."

"You're lying."

Those eyes flashed to life, and she jerked her arm free of Dair's grip with such speed and violence that Dair thought Marielle would strike her. "Maybe I have a better reason than you did," Marielle hissed.

Dair backed away, the words the blow Marielle's hands hadn't delivered.

Marielle moaned and raked her hands through her own hair. "I'm sorry," she said, crying. "I'm so sorry, Dair. But . . . you don't know. Okay? You don't know."

Dair did know that she didn't want to sleep alone in her house, with no one next door, even with a giant dog. She knew the only way she'd sleep was to get drunk. And getting drunk suddenly seemed so dangerous.

Dair took her cell phone out of her purse and hit the power button.

Marielle looked fearful. "Who are you calling?"

"Afraid I'm calling the police?" Dair asked, wondering if maybe she should. Marielle froze. "I'm not," Dair said. "But if you're leaving, then I'm leaving, too. I want to go home."

And if she couldn't feel safe in her own house, she wanted to be in the only other house that felt safe. She dialed the number.

Marielle's digital clock showed one A.M. But there were some people you were allowed to call whenever you needed to.

Her mother answered on the second ring, breathless. Calls at this hour always meant death or tragedy of some kind.

"Mom?"

"Dair, what is it? What's wrong?"

"Can I come home?"

"Of course." Not one second of hesitation. "What's wrong?"

Dair took a deep breath. "Peyton and I had a fight. He left, and I don't want to be alone."

"Oh, sweetie," she said with a sigh. "Are you all right to drive this far? You haven't been drinking?"

"No." Dair didn't have the energy to feel angry. "I'll leave right now. I'm bringing Blizzard, okay?"

"Shodan's with Peyton?"

"Yes, only I don't know where."

"Oh, hon," she said. "Be careful. Please, *please* drive carefully."

"I will, Mom. I promise. I'll see you soon." Dair hung up and wrote the phone number on a piece of paper on Marielle's nightstand. She handed it to her. "Here. This is where I'll be. Please call me and tell me what hotel you're staying in, okay?"

Marielle paused a moment, then said, "Okay," but Dair didn't believe her. Marielle wasn't going to tell Dair where she was. Dair had this feeling, looking at her, that she might never see Marielle again. She might never see anyone she loved here again.

And after she'd packed some things, and loaded Blizzard into the car, and Godot, too, feeling too guilty and anxious to leave him behind, Dair drove off into the darkness feeling as if she were driving into a wilderness.

Chapter Nineteen

The tension of the long drive, her jangled nerves, her paranoid fear that every car behind them on country roads was someone following them, had nearly disabled Dair, and she didn't relax or breathe deeply until she felt her mother's arms around her, and then she was too exhausted to talk. She let Mom herd her into her childhood bedroom—with its mint green walls and pink-dotted white curtains—take off her shoes, and tuck her into her old twin bed under a pink-and-green comforter. She was aware of Mom stroking her hair for a moment and vaguely aware of her shutting off the lamp and leaving the room.

Blizzard crawled up and lay alongside Dair, his head on her chest. Godot sulked in the back of his cat carrier, refusing to come out the open door and explore her mother's house. Dair sank into oblivion.

And she dreamed her recurring dream. There was the chickadee at the window, the fluttering of the wings, those fine, thin bones battering at the glass, the sharp, black beak tap-tap-tapping. In the dream Dair leapt up and struggled to open the window, but the latch wouldn't budge. "Wait, oh, wait," she called, but the bird flew away. Dair pressed her face against the glass, crying, "Noooo," but the little dark-haired girl popped up before her, outside the window, grinning. She was back. Where had she been? And Dair forgot the chickadee and smiled at the girl. They lined up their hands on opposite sides of the glass and pressed their lips together to kiss. When they parted from the kiss, the little girl changed into Peyton. And Dair thought, I've been trying to find you, I've been trying to talk to you, and she fumbled with the latch again, but Peyton shook his head and backed away. No, no, *wait!* Dair pounded on the glass to get his attention, but he turned his back to her and kept walking. She stopped pounding but still heard the sound. It was the bird's beak, sharper, higher pitched than her knuckles. But where was it? Dair winced and realized it was inside her, trying to get out. She pressed her hands against her breastbone to stop the splintering pain. The little bird hammered, chipped away at her sternum, drilling its way out. Its beak broke through and sliced into her hands like tacks. It burst forth out of Dair's chest, blood spattering the window, bone chips hitting with sharp pings before the blood-soaked chickadee herself broke through the glass and flew away.

Dair woke herself with a violent kick of her legs and found her hands pressed to her chest. She sucked in a great gasp of air and sat up, then froze. She stared straight ahead at her childhood window, disoriented, believing for a moment that the dream continued.

Then Blizzard leapt atop the bed at her feet and woofed, and she remembered. Air filled her lungs again, but the throbbing pain in her sternum remained.

Blizzard walked up the bed beside her and laid his head in her lap. She stroked him and wondered where Godot had gone—the carrier was now empty. Nausea rolled through her, and her hands trembled. Her stomach flattened itself against the small of her back, and a series of mild dry heaves made her look around her room for a trash can to vomit in. The feeling passed, leaving her clammy with sticky sweat.

She swung her legs out of bed and stood, unsteady, wobbly. She lurched her way into the kitchen, Blizzard following her, and found her mother scrambling eggs, Godot stretched at her feet on the old blue linoleum floor.

The smell of the eggs made her stomach flop, and she eyed the sink.

"Oh, sweetie," Mom said, looking over her shoulder, "you look ill."

Dair was too desperate even to mutter a "Thanks a lot." She didn't care how she looked or that she was about to prove her mother right. "Mom? Do you have anything to drink?"

Mom held still, her spatula poised over the skillet of eggs. "I've got milk, and orange juice, and—"

"Mom. You know what I mean. Do you?"

"No, I don't."

"Not a beer? Not anything?"

She shook her head.

Dair's eyes filled with tears, and she folded up her legs and sat on the floor. Mom turned off the stove, moved the skillet, and sat right beside her. Godot lifted his head and looked at them. Blizzard again put his giant head in Dair's lap. Dair petted the long hair of his ears with her shaking fingers. "Mom, you're right. I'm in trouble. I need help."

Mom took one of her hands, her touch almost diagnostic. "How long, sweetie?" she asked as she massaged Dair's hand in both of her own, soothing the shakiness. "How long since you had a drink?"

The question surprised Dair. She thought about it. "Not quite two days." Was that all? It felt like two years. "But I—I had one swallow of Kahlúa last night. J-just one."

"And you're feeling it, aren't you?"

Dair nodded, breathing her careful, shallow breaths.

Mom released her hand and stroked Dair's hair. "Did Peyton's leaving have anything to do with you drinking?"

Tears ran hot down Dair's cheeks. Godot stood, stretched, and padded over to them. Dair reached out to caress his face as she said, "No . . . I don't think so, but I don't know anymore. . . . I made a huge mess, Mom . . . I told a lie. It wasn't about drinking. But I lied to him about that, too. But the other lie, it was bad. It was an awful thing. I—I don't know if he'll come back."

Mom's own eyes watered at that. "That would be such a shame. What was it, hon? What did you lie about?"

Dair opened her mouth but shook her head. "I'm too tired. I can't tell you right now." It shamed her too much to tell it. She was relieved Mom didn't know already; she'd half expected to find Peyton there. And Dair liked sitting here with Mom stroking her hair. If she told the truth, Mom might not do that.

Mom nodded and kept combing her fingers through Dair's curls, tucking them behind Dair's ears. Dair leaned her head back against the wall.

"If you've made it a couple days, hon, it'll only get easier."

Dair closed her eyes. "Is that true?"

Mom didn't answer for a moment, her hand resting on Dair's forehead. "Partly true," she said. "You won't feel sick. You won't shake. But it never really gets easier."

Dair looked into her mother's blue eyes, her face so open, so honest. "How do you know that?"

Mom smiled sadly. "How do you think?"

Dair stared.

"How did you think I knew you had a drinking problem?"

"But—but, I've never seen you drink."

She nodded, that sad yet serene smile remaining. "There's a reason for that."

"But . . ." Dair couldn't remember her mother ever drinking. Not even a glass of wine with Thanksgiving dinner. Dad had occasional beers, but Mom had never had one.

The women looked at each other. "When?" Dair asked her. Mom knew what she meant.

"Before you were born. Since I was a teenager."

Dair looked at her mother as if she'd never seen her in daylight before. She felt closer to her in that moment than ever before in her life. "Why?"

Mom sighed and wiped her eyes. "I . . . I had this gift, and I didn't know how to handle it. I . . . sometimes it was too much. It overwhelmed me. I needed to quiet it down." Mom nodded but looked down. A flush crept into her cheeks.

"Mom, I believe you." Dair took her hand. "About the animals. I remember it. Being able to do it."

Mom's eyes darkened with gratitude, and she left her hand in Dair's. "I've worried about you. I wanted to help you with it, to protect you, but you seemed so against what I could do. So embarrassed by it."

A bruised feeling ached in Dair's chest. "But you communicate now. The other night—you were amazing. You found a way to handle it?"

Mom nodded. "For years now. I learned to 'turn it down,' so to speak. I used to . . . it was awful. I—I'd feel their pain. If I went to a horse show, I might look at a horse and my back would spasm. Or sharp pains would go through my shoulders. My neck would cramp. Or my mouth would feel bruised and swollen. Depending on the riders, of course. The horses weren't *all* in pain. But if one was, I'd feel it. And I'd carry it around. And that was only the physical pain. Their other pain—their fear, their confusion—would stay with me, too. It was horrible. And alcohol was the only way I found to shut it off, to dull it. Back then. But . . . I figured out how to manage, how to protect myself without drinking. I had to."

"What do you mean?"

Godot rolled on his back and batted Mom's knee. She smiled and rubbed his belly while she spoke. "When I wanted to get pregnant. When I was expecting you, I had to quit. And it was hard, but in a way, easy, because of you."

"And you haven't drunk since then?"

Her smile faltered. "Oh . . . yes, I have. I quit, then, but I've quit *since* then, too. For a while, after I first quit drinking, I quit communicating with animals. I just ignored it. But being pregnant kicked in all that telepathic communication again. Stronger than before."

"Really? How?"

"Ohh, Dair," she said, resuming her stroking of Dair's hair. "You and I communicated before you were born. All mothers and their babies do. We *knew* each other before the first actual face-to-face meeting. So many nights after you were born I'd wake up, jolted out of sleep. The house would still be silent, but I'd *know* you were upset, you needed something. Before you actually cried, I'd know. You would have already told me. And I've heard lots of mothers describe this. Even mothers who laugh at the idea of telepathic communication."

Dair reached up and took her mother's hand from her hair, holding it. "So when did you really quit? How long since you've had a drink?"

Her eyes watered again. "A long time." She paused.

"How long?" Dair prodded.

"Thirty-three years."

Nearly as long as Dair had been alive. She couldn't imagine surviving without a drink that long. "So I was two?"

Mom nodded.

"What happened? What made you finally stop?"

Mom continued to pet Godot with her free hand for several minutes without speaking. Dair stroked Blizzard's head with her own free hand and kept hold of her mother's with the other.

"It was . . . worse when I started again," she said. "Before you were born, I drank like you do."

Dair winced.

"I was discreet. I was always drinking, but never drunk. But after you were born, and I wanted to drink, it'd changed. I couldn't do it like I did before. I was drunk a lot."

"What did Dad do?"

Mom exhaled and slumped her shoulders. "He'd look the other way, until he couldn't anymore. Then he'd clean me up and dry me out and pretend it never happened."

"Oh, my God," Dair said. "I—I don't remember this."

Mom squeezed Dair's hand. "Sweetie, you were just a baby."

Mom stopped talking, stopped moving. Godot butted his head under her hand, but she didn't react.

"Mom?"

She shook herself. "I had a wreck," she said flatly.

"You wrecked the car?"

She nodded.

"Were you drunk?"

She nodded again. "Plastered. One of Bob Henderson's foals caught its halter on a fence and choked to death. I'd spent a day feeling like I had asthma. I couldn't breathe. I couldn't swallow my food. I was suffocating. And when I found out about the foal, I knew that was why I was feeling that, and I drank everything I could."

She stopped. Dair waited.

"I drove off the road, into a tree. I didn't hit anyone else, thank God. But I totaled the car."

"Were you hurt?"

She sighed. She pulled her hand from Dair's, lifted the other from Godot, and rubbed her face, as if weary. "Yes. Not terribly. Some cuts. A concussion. Busted ribs. Nothing lasting, but I banged myself up pretty good."

She didn't remove her hands from her face.

"Mom?"

"I was pregnant," she whispered.

Dair frowned. "But I thought you said I was two—" And then it hit her. The hair rose on the back of her neck. She struggled to make her mouth work. "You were pregnant . . . again?" A strange feeling of hope rose within her. She didn't understand it; it didn't make sense, but this news kindled a yearning she couldn't articulate.

Mom finally lowered her hands and spoke to the wall across from them. "But we didn't know it. I didn't know I was pregnant. A doctor told us I wasn't just hemorrhaging, but had miscarried."

"You—you lost a baby?"

She nodded.

"Was it a boy or a girl?"

Mom blinked as if startled. "We didn't know. It was way too early. But . . . we were devastated."

"Mom, I— Why did you never tell me?"

She snorted. "What were we supposed to say? Point to the intersection and say, 'You might've had a little sister if your mom hadn't gotten plowed and trashed the car'?"

Dair put her arms around her mother and kissed her cheek. "No. No, of course not, but . . . this is a huge thing, Mom. This had to have such an effect on you guys."

Mom shook her head. "You wanted a sister so badly. You were convinced you were supposed to have a sister. You'd make up little stories about her all the time."

Again Dair's hairs rose, this time on her arms and legs, all over her body. Maybe Peyton was right. Maybe the little girl in her dream did mean something. Could she have sensed Mom and Dad's sorrow?

Godot wandered away, bored, perhaps. Blizzard stayed, lying at attention, watching them. "And I never drank after that," Mom said. "Not once. But I'd like to. I mean, I'd like not to want to, but I do. Does that make sense?"

Dair nodded. Perfect sense. What didn't make sense was her disappointment. That initial hope, that thrill, had faded. She'd been looking for release, perhaps. Wanting to understand the sense of loss that had haunted her all her life. She'd felt on the verge of a key, but . . . she looked into her mother's face and knew that loss wasn't from missing a sibling she'd never known.

She wished, selfishly, for her lie to have been more real, for this truth to be closer to the story she'd concocted. She wanted to be able to go to Peyton and say, "I *did* have a sister. I *did* know her." But it wasn't enough, this dead baby she'd never heard of until today.

"But seriously, Mom. How did you guys deal with it?" Dair wanted some clue, some guidance, some way to repair her own relationship with Peyton.

"We *didn't* deal with it."

"I mean, c'mon," Dair said. "You had to talk about it."

Mom pursed her lips. Lines appeared on her forehead. "I would like to." She stopped, her silence implying everything else.

What had Peyton said about his conversation with her father? "Does he even *know* you want to talk about it?"

When Dair didn't speak, Mom said, "Of course he does. How could he not know?"

"Are you saying you just think he *should* know?"

Mom scowled at Dair and let go of her hand. They'd suddenly reversed roles. Freeze and replace: They were into a new scene.

Mom stood up and returned to the skillet of eggs. Dair asked, "You're not splitting up with Dad because of something that happened over thirty years ago, are you?"

Mom turned the burner back on under the skillet and said, "Of course not."

Dair sighed. "You're right. You're not breaking up because of what happened thirty years ago; you're breaking up because of what *hasn't* happened in the thirty years since."

"Don't be ridiculous," Mom snapped.

"Mom, you have to talk to him."

Mom picked up the spatula and didn't answer.

"Why didn't you tell us the truth? Why did you tell us it was because of the animal communication?"

"It is. He doesn't believe me." Mom poked at the eggs and said, "He's always thought I was crazy, or that I'd been drinking. He acts like I'm going to go to pieces every time I work on an animal. To this day—just last Thanksgiving, I was talking about something I'd learned from an animal, and he asked me if I'd been drinking. Not in front of you and Peyton, of course. He pulled me out of the room and asked. I wanted to punch him."

Dair cringed, thinking of her inspection of Peyton's arms on Sunday night.

"Your father says I use the animals to avoid talking to him."

Dair didn't speak for a moment while Mom shoved the eggs around with the spatula. "Do you?" she finally asked.

"Of course not."

How could Mom not see that this was true? How could she not understand what had happened between them? Dair didn't know what to say, what to ask, although a million questions swirled around in her brain. "Mom, I love you."

Her mother turned, surprised, it seemed, and relieved. "I love you, Dair. And I'm sorry. I'm so sorry. I should have told you years ago." She moved the skillet off the burner and got out a loaf of bread. "How many pieces do you want?"

"Oh, God, I can't eat, I'll throw—"

"You need to eat. You'll feel better. Believe me."

Dair stared at her, skeptical.

"Skip the eggs," Mom said. "But eat some toast."

Dair nodded. Mom put bread in the toaster. Dair leaned against the counter and watched her. Blizzard stood at Dair's side and nuzzled her hand with his snout. "What did you like to drink?" she asked her mother.

"White wine," Mom said with no hesitation. "By the gallons."

"So, I inherited this from you." It was not an accusation, but motivated by curiosity.

"The inclination to drink? To drink too much? Yes, I'm afraid you did."

Mom scooped eggs onto a plate for herself. "Will it make you sick if I eat these? Because I don't have to."

Dair wrinkled her nose. "I just won't look."

"Want some ginger ale?"

Ginger ale and toast. An odd combo, but it sounded perfect. Dair nodded. And as Mom moved about the kitchen, fixing her toast, pouring her a drink, just as if she were home sick from school back in fifth grade, Dair wondered at how odd it was that she and Peyton, both people with obvious genetic tendencies toward addiction, had found each other. Was that the real connection, not the fictional tragedy that he'd believed? Who had passed the torch along in his family? Dair wondered. Or did someone have to start it, after all? Be the first?

Dair hoped she'd get the chance to ask him what he thought.

Chapter Twenty

Peyton sat on Malcolm's Salvation Army couch watching an overcast, dirgelike day dawning, muting all the colors in the trees. Maybe it would finally rain. The hard-packed earth, the papery leaves, even the arid breeze, rattled with craving.

He concentrated on the rattle, tried to make the sound maracas to get a little mambo step going in his head. Anything but that goddamn whine.

Shodan lay on the floor under Malcolm's window. She opened her eyes but didn't lift her head.

He felt the pull, the longing in his soul, to do harm to whoever had killed Craig. That craving was easier to focus on than the other. And that craving didn't make so much noise.

He pressed the heels of his hands hard against his temples, trying to squeeze the throb out of his head. Shodan whimpered. Peyton let go of his head, and the release felt good, but it was only temporary.

He scratched the scar by his eye. He should've gotten stitches for it way back then. He should've gone to the emergency room, but he hadn't.

There was enough sense in him that night, all those years ago, a tiny part of him still in control somewhere that knew if he went to a hospital, he'd likely end up in jail. He was so far gone, so strung out, so high.

He should've gone to the emergency room, not just for himself, but for the man he'd left in the subway stairs. That man. What had happened? Peyton didn't know. He'd lost time. Didn't know how he'd gotten to that green park bench where he'd come to, weak and shaking.

Didn't know why a sticky puddle of blood beneath him buzzed with flies. Couldn't remember which subway station or what time. Only vague snippets of sound and scent and sensation that he couldn't string together to make any sense. The sharp reek of the man's unwashed body and clothes in the hot, ovenlike stairs. That odor alerting him, turning Peyton around to catch only the end of the looped bicycle chain in his temple. The man's blistered lips from his crack pipe. Desperation in his eyes. The dull, wet thump of his skull on brick wall, the crack of ribs, the feel of bone giving under Peyton's knuckles. Stumbling away, up into the cool night air.

He might have killed someone and didn't even know for sure.

The man had tried to mug him, so it was self-defense, right? But the flash of the man's face was like looking in a mirror. That's where Peyton was headed; that's how he'd end up.

That was hitting bottom—wandering from station to station that next morning, clutching paper towels to his head, looking for blood on subway stairs, a body, a chalk outline, any sign of what had happened. That's what led him to rehab.

He rose from Malcolm's couch, moving stiffly. He'd been excused from rehearsal yesterday, for Craig's funeral, and he felt it. He sat on the dirty shag carpet and stroked Shodan's sleek sides. Her tail stump wagged almost imperceptibly. Shodan had saved his life after rehab. And she'd led him to Dair.

She lifted her head now and put her chin on his knee. Her dark brown eyes studied his face. He bent his spine and kissed her forehead. She licked his cheek.

"Wanna visit Blizzard?" he whispered.

She scrambled to her feet, eyes bright, pink tongue showing in her open mouth.

But when they got to their house, it was empty and quiet. No cars sat on the street. No lights or signs of life. Shodan bounded up the steps and around to the back gate and didn't even bother sniffing the yard but went straight into the house with Peyton, looking for Blizzard.

It was with a certain amount of shameful pleasure that Peyton recognized how Dair would feel when she found out he'd lied about his return on Saturday. He wondered if the police had told her.

He wandered through the house, calling for Godot. He checked the messages, but there were only three, one the nasal-voiced stage manager telling Dair there was still no news of Gayle and that there would be no rehearsal Thursday or Friday, and the other two hangups.

Dair must've gotten up early and taken Blizzard on a walk. Peyton slipped out the back, Shodan at his side, and knocked on Marielle's door, but no one answered. He knocked louder, longer, prompting Captain Hook upstairs to shout, *"Who's outside?"*

Mr. Lively's door opened. "Peyton?" he called.

Something shifted inside. He'd never known the man knew his name.

"What the hell is going on around here?" Mr. Lively asked as if Peyton were some sort of director of the household. The alpha male. The leader of the pack. "All that carrying on, late into the night, everyone leaving."

"Leaving? When?"

"It was one in the morning, and they were going to their cars, driving away, all of them, Marielle, the boy, your wife."

Your wife. The way the old man said that slapped Peyton. Implied a responsibility he'd shirked.

"Where did they go?" Mr. Lively asked.

Peyton shrugged. "I have no idea. I'm sorry. She didn't leave me a note." But he felt good knowing that Dair was with Marielle.

"Papa?" Captain Hook called. *"Papa, where are you?"*

"I'm here," he answered. "Hold your horses." He looked down at Peyton, then seemed to realize he had nothing else to say and started to shut his door.

"You okay?" Peyton asked him. "You need anything? While I'm here?"

"I need everybody back here and behaving like reasonable human beings."

Peyton watched the old man glare at him a moment and didn't know what to say. He was relieved when Shodan barked at the back door for him to let her back in. *"Shodie!"* Dair's voice called from upstairs.

Her voice sent a zip of adrenaline through Peyton, like a speedball of happiness and fear. He couldn't tell if he was disappointed or relieved that it was only the bird.

Mr. Lively closed his door.

Peyton went back in the house with Shodan. Where had they all gone in the middle of the night? Upstairs in the bathroom, all Dair's toiletries were gone. She'd packed to stay overnight somewhere, taking her shampoo, her moisturizer, her makeup.

Their bed was unmade, which didn't surprise him; Dair was such a slob. But something about her shape there in the mattress, the dent of her head on her pillow, her mint green bra on the floor, pulled on some cord within him. He climbed into the bed and hugged her pillow. Shodan looked over the bed at him and whined. "C'mon," he said. "It's okay." She crawled up and walked in circles on the bed before lying down beside him. He petted her and cried again, as he had at Malcolm's. Shodan licked his face. "What am I going to do?" he asked her. "What am I going to do?"

Friday morning there was still no sign of Dair or Marielle, and Mr. Lively reported that no one had come or gone from the house all day or night.

Their answering machine held a message from the nasal stage manager informing Dair that there would indeed be rehearsal Saturday night.

There were several other calls, all for Dair—Bethany and C.J. and that Andy guy she and Craig had talked about—all of them worried about Gayle and wanting to know if anyone had heard anything.

But the message from Marielle made Peyton go still, senses on alert, like a wolf hearing a twig snap somewhere behind it: "Dair, I don't want to tell where we are, I'm sorry. I know I promised, but I can't. I'll be in touch later. I lost the number you gave me. So I'm just hoping you'll check messages. We're okay. I hope you are, too. I love you, sweetie."

What the hell was going on? Dair wasn't *with* Marielle somewhere?

That was it. He had to call R.B. or Cass, which he'd been too freaked to do before.

Cassie answered on the third ring.

"Hi. It's Peyton."

"Hello, Peyton." Her voice soothed him, quieted the whine instantly. "Are you all right? I've wanted to call you, but I didn't know where to reach you."

He warmed all over. He loved this woman. "I'm worried about Dair."

"She's here," Cassie said.

Relief flooded through him, his eyes and nose burning. "Is—is she okay?"

He heard her inhale and hold her breath, as if deciding how to answer. He cursed the damn phone. He wanted to see her. "She's . . . fine," Cassie said. "I wouldn't say she's 'okay,' but she will be. Are you?"

He paused and said, "I'm 'fine,' too."

"Good. Now, how are the *two of you?* I hope you'll try to salvage this, whatever happened."

"You don't know?" He was almost sorry. He didn't want to have to explain it himself.

"No," she said. "And I don't want you to tell me. Not yet. Dair will tell me when she's ready. I think she needs to be the one to tell me herself."

Peyton nodded and wiped his nose and eyes with the back of his hand. "Is she . . . I mean, since we talked, is she—has she had a—"

"She's not drinking. She hasn't had a drink since she got here."

A cautious feeling of hope welled within him. "God. That's great. How's she doing?"

Cassie laughed lightly. "She's bitchy and moody and on my last nerve, and . . ." She inhaled again, her breath ragged. Her voice quavered as she said, "And I'm so, so happy."

That was it for both of them. They stood on the phone, sniffling and gasping into each other's ears, two hours of travel time separating them from hugging each other but wanting the connection anyway.

"I'll see you tomorrow," he said finally.

"Good," she said. "I love you, Peyton."

"I love you, too, Cass."

Saturday morning, Peyton pulled into Cassie and R.B.'s driveway, astounded by the number of cars there. Shodan stood on the seat beside him, wriggling her body, whimpering with happiness. Did she know Dair was there? And Blizzard? Or was it just the other animals? He saw people getting out of cars, lugging plastic carriers, or walking dogs toward the barn. A Rottweiler, a small poodle, some kind of beagle mix. This was going to be a zoo.

"C'mon," he said to Shodan, ruffling her ears. "Let's go check this out."

The moment they stepped out of the car, of course, Dair came out the back door of the house. Peyton wasn't prepared for his reaction to her—that he'd feel warmth, relief, the desire to take her in his arms. He hardened against it. Had an image of hurling those feelings away, diverting them into a roll fall.

In the few seconds before she saw him, he noted her gaunt cheeks, her empty eyes, how thin and frail she looked. She also looked so young, but maybe that was just seeing her here at her childhood home. Against this setting, Peyton couldn't help but see the childhood Dair superimposed on the present one, the childhood Dair he'd seen in all the photos, on the walls of the house, and in the scrapbooks. He'd believed her story, that she'd shoved all the photos of Sylvan down the garbage disposal. Anger flared again in the pit of his stomach.

She saw him in the second the dogs spied each other, and a flicker of fear crossed her face before she turned to the dogs' greeting, straining at the ends of their leashes. They had to walk toward each other to allow the dogs to touch, to greet, to reconnect.

The dogs stood on back legs, as if trying to hug each other, then dropped to all fours and sniffed each other's mouths and chests and rear ends. Then they licked each other's faces, all the while wagging their tails, joyful at this reunion.

Peyton and Dair stood, still and pained, the length of the leashes and the flurry of the dogs between them. Their eyes met, and she asked, "Why were you with Malcolm Saturday morning?"

So she did know. Peyton shrugged and said, "For a good reason. It had nothing to do with you; there was no reason, there *is* no reason why you had to know."

Dair watched the dogs, apparently accepting this. What else could she do? She was smart. She knew she didn't have a leg to stand on when it came to talking about betrayal of trust or withholding information. No matter what happened to them, Peyton realized she *never would* have that leg to stand on again.

And he had to acknowledge that glimmer: no matter what hap-

pened. There was still some open possibility about what that scenario might be.

"I'm sorry," she said. And he believed her. Even though he knew
he shouldn't; he'd believed every word she'd said about Sylvan, after
all.

"Do you . . . ," she asked. "Has anyone heard anything about Gayle?"

Peyton shook his head, and they led their dogs toward the pale
blue barn door. Inside, Cassie had tables set up, with coffee, juice,
fruit, and muffins. She arranged people into a circle. They sat in lawn
chairs, their dogs and cats in their laps or at their sides. Peyton
breathed in the sweet, elementary school smell of the wood shavings.

Cassie, in her usual overalls and T-shirt, beamed at them. "Hello.
Welcome. Find a seat." She didn't draw any special attention to the
fact that she already knew Dair and Peyton. She directed them to the
remaining empty chairs, which, thankfully, were not next to each
other. Dair sat across the circle from Peyton, though, and it was difficult for him not to look at her. Something about the way she sat,
her knees in her faded jeans together, shins apart, feet in her black
ankle boots turned in toe to toe, looked so vulnerable, so open to
hurt. She slouched back in her chair, as if already exhausted. He heard
her craving from all the way across the circle, felt her wanting a
drink.

Cassie wasn't a flashy workshop leader or even especially charis-
matic. She spoke quietly, so that they all held still and leaned forward
to hear her. She started, without any small talk, to go over the ba-
sics, how the communication worked, the information she'd explained
to Peyton last Sunday at dinner. Just last Sunday. It felt like years ago.
His whole life had changed in one week, really. This time last week
he was with Malcolm at an NA meeting, agreeing to be his sponsor.
Craig was still alive, although who knew what he was doing or where
he'd been—he'd still been alive. And wherever he was, alive, he'd possessed the knowledge inside him that Dair had lied to Peyton about
her entire history.

Peyton swallowed. He wanted to talk to Craig. He wanted to ask
him a million questions: How did you get her to tell you? What, after
eight years of silence, made her tell *you?* Did she explain why? Did
she seem sorry? Did you believe her?

But that was impossible. He'd never get to ask, to know. He tried to bring himself back to this moment.

Cassie asked the people in the circle to introduce themselves and their animals.

Among the members of the workshop were two cops with German shepherds who worked in a narcotics canine unit—they made Peyton nervous, even today.

Peyton's mouth felt dry, and he wiped his hands on his jeans, as if someone had asked him to give a speech. He was glad Dair's turn came before his. Would she say anything about him? And how would he feel if she did?

But she didn't look at Peyton when she introduced herself. She didn't mention that they were married.

She didn't even mention that they knew each other.

And maybe they didn't.

Chapter Twenty-one

Dair sat miserably in the circle and wondered what she was doing there. She was living the actor's nightmare—the dream of being onstage in a play she hadn't rehearsed. If her life was a stage play, it had turned into a fiasco. The set was going to fall down any second.

She wanted to learn more about the communication, but she wished all these other people weren't here. She wanted her mother all to herself. She finally wanted to learn what she'd bristled at Mom trying to teach her all her life.

They'd had great talks these two days. Dair felt as though she were in some kind of detox center, some bizarre farm retreat, with hours a day spent in therapy sessions, walking the fields with her mother and Blizzard, drinking tea, taking naps, lying in the dry empty creek bed. Dad was gone, the on-grounds veterinarian at some horse show in Columbus. Dair missed him, wanted to ask him a million questions, too.

Dair was a mess. She was scared, twitchy, nauseated, and stricken with insomnia that left her like a zombie during daylight hours. And wanting to drink consumed her.

She tried to soak up the childhood stories, the lessons, everything Mom said, tried to be the apprentice as if her very life depended on it. But she knew she was too desperate, too greedy.

Years spent tuning it out, training herself not to hear, not to listen, cluttered and obscured her new path, made her stumble every time she thought she'd found her footing. Flashes flew at her from the animals, but she didn't know how to control them, how to ask for them. Sitting in this barn, she found herself bombarded with noise and pictures. She remembered sixth grade, how the classroom gerbil had called out to her relentlessly.

It was as if that humiliation had been the excuse she'd been looking for. She'd embraced a reason to shut the communication off.

She tried not to look at Peyton across the circle. She felt his sorrow, his confusion. Imagined that she heard the whine he'd described to her. Blizzard licked Dair's hand.

"Before we do any of the exercises," Mom was saying, "you have to understand that your attitude toward animals will determine how open you are to their communication. You have to respect them as fellow beings. You may actually find that this practice improves your relationship with human animals as well. You'll notice a difference in how you interpret others' actions and words—you'll be less likely to project your own agendas, and you'll open yourself to simply receive communication."

Mom looked around the circle, apparently gauging the group's tolerance thus far, but her casual, open attitude seemed to make everyone eager, interested.

Every time Dair glanced at Peyton, he was looking at Mom as if enthralled. Shodan sat primly upright, her shoulder touching his knee.

Blizzard rolled on his side, wood shavings clinging to his long white fur.

The group laughed, and Dair shook herself back to attention. She had no idea what Mom had said that was funny, but Mom continued, "Don't *analyze* it. That's a big human hang-up. We want to process and analyze and judge every bit of information we get—" She stopped and looked over Dair's head at something behind her. "R.B.? Do you want sit down with us?" she asked. Her voice was inviting, totally unreadable in any other way.

Dair turned, as did everyone else, to see her father standing, leaning against his clinic door, arms crossed, his face now red. "Um . . . sure . . . is that okay?"

Mom nodded, and everyone shifted and scooted, making room for him. He picked up a bucket near the faucet outside his door and carried it to the circle. He turned it upside down and sat beside Dair. She smiled at him and felt instantly better.

"Do you want to tell us why you're here?" Mom asked him, and Dair wasn't sure she simply imagined the edge in Mom's voice.

Dad remained deep red. "I just, uh, want to find out more about this."

Mom waited, as if expecting more, then nodded and returned her attention to the group. "We'll start with visualization exercises—which will help in sending mental pictures to an animal. Most people find visualization gets incredible results: You can picture what you want to accomplish with your horse before a ride, or picture where you're taking the dog when you get in the car. Many people never master *getting* communication from other animals, but most animals are quite adept at receiving it from us if we bother to take the time."

Dad was bothering, she thought. He was here. Peyton was here, too.

Although Mom led them in a different exercise, Dair had her own mental picture she wanted to visualize.

Peyton followed Cassie's instructions and leaned back in his chair. Put his hands on his thighs. Opened his mouth. Closed his eyes. Breathed deep. Relaxed and listened. In her soothing, quiet voice, Cassie described a scene through a dog's eyes—a small dog. A Boston terrier puppy named Daisy, to be exact. Cassie was good, her instructions and guidance clear, but Peyton couldn't concentrate. His mind drifted. He caught himself off track, thinking of Craig and Gayle and Dair. Always Dair, many times.

He snuck peeks on occasion, and everyone seemed so into it that he felt like a loser. Even Dair seemed able to concentrate, although her knuckles showed white on the arms of her lawn chair. Maybe she was only concentrating on not being sick.

Eventually, Cassie ended the exercise. "It's okay if you got 'lost' or if you had trouble concentrating. Don't get discouraged. It can take a lot of practice. If your mind is busy, or preoccupied with something else, you can't listen and receive, or focus and send. It could take several practice sessions to work past that. And it might take big changes in your life—you might need to slow down, sleep more, spend more time outside, or you might need to give up substances that cloud or fluster the mind, like alcohol or too much sugar."

Peyton made fleeting eye contact with Dair across the circle, and they both blushed. That was their connection, really, not the twin. Their roots were tangled with their shared history with chemicals.

"We learn not to pay attention to ourselves in this society," Cassie said. "We don't listen to each other or to other animals. It all starts with listening to *yourself* and your feelings." She smiled. "You're going to get sick of hearing me say this," she said, rolling her eyes, "but it really does take practice."

It was like dance, practicing until the individual steps didn't exist and ran together into music. It was like aikido, practicing the walks, over and over again, until they became second nature. Until someone could jump you in a subway and you wouldn't think twice about it, you could avoid the attack without hurting them.

It was like life. It took practice. It took attention and time to get it right.

Dair grew more involved when Mom moved on and began to work with each animal and its person. And again, and again, just as in their kitchen with the messages she received from Blizzard and Slip Jig, Mom amazed people. No one seemed horrified by what they found out, as Marielle had been. No one had friends dead or intruders trespassing in their homes or mysterious articles of clothing appearing under beds.

But it was overwhelming. Dair felt naked and raw. She got some pictures, but some communication came to her in sounds, smells, some even in tastes. The images or sensations flashed to her instantaneously, almost before she had finished asking the question. Many times she assumed she couldn't be right because the image had come to her so fast, and she discarded the answer and asked for another.

"One of the biggest barriers to communication," Mom had told her as they'd worked with Godot, "is invalidating what you perceive. Don't doubt yourself. You have to listen to yourself."

Mom now worked with a white standard poodle puppy named Jazz. Dair tried to focus, tried to receive the communication, but Dad leaned over and touched her knee. She turned to him. "Your stuff is in the house," he whispered.

Dair nodded.

"You slept here?"

She nodded again.

"Without Peyton?" He tipped his head at Peyton far across the circle. Peyton, who avoided looking at them in an almost too deliberate manner. Dair could see the effort. "What's going on? I just now noticed he was here."

She sighed. "We had a fight. A really big fight. It was my fault."

Dad frowned and started to ask more, but Mom began to work with a paramedic and her Afghan hound sitting on the other side of Dad, and they couldn't keep whispering with her attention so close to them.

Each animal's style and personality came out clearly in Mom's messages. The Afghan hound was shy and revealed only snippets to Mom, snippets Dair wasn't able to pick up herself, but Daisy, the Boston terrier puppy, unleashed a torrent of images that nearly bowled Dair over.

As her mother worked her way around the circle, helping to connect the humans with their animals, Dair saw Peyton look at her from across the circle.

If she could get this part of her life back with practice, could she get Peyton back, too? What would she practice? Telling the truth? But there was no going back. If you flubbed your lines onstage, if you lost your place, the worst thing was to go back and repeat what you'd already said. You had to move forward. How many times had she coached kids in her improv classes, "Make something happen"? That was the key. And she thought of some of those horrible, deadly improvs, where the kids just got bogged down and the scene went nowhere, growing stagnant, rotten. "Make something happen," Dair would say. Sometimes she'd want to pull her hair out and begged, "Anything."

Peyton was relieved when Cassie called for a break, letting the animals move around, letting everyone hit the bathroom. He grabbed a muffin and R.B. came over to him, putting a large, calloused hand on his shoulder. "What's going on with you and Dair?"

"We're having a communication problem," Peyton said dryly.

R.B. looked concerned. "You gonna be able to patch this up, the two of you?"

Peyton chewed the muffin but didn't taste it. Everyone asked that. It was a given, wasn't it? No relationship was doomed. There was al-

ways the *ability* to patch things up. The question was, did you want
to? "I don't know," he said, answering R.B.'s question and his own.
"I'm not sure yet. I think so. I miss her."

Just saying those words seemed to make it more true. Peyton
looked around the barn for her and saw her standing, hugging herself, talking to one of the horse show girls. Blizzard strained at his
leash toward Shodan, across the barn, and when Dair looked to see
what he wanted, she saw Peyton watching her, and he thought she
was going to burst into tears on the spot.

Cassie called, "All right, let's come back and do some more practice."

He returned to his seat. Dair returned to hers. The dogs lay as close
to the center of the circle as they could, facing each other.

"These dogs know each other, don't they?" the paramedic asked.

Peyton glanced at Dair, and they both nodded. He felt the processing of this information going on in the barn. Two people, sitting
on opposite sides of the circle, their dogs straining to be close. Two
people who hadn't spoken to each other or acknowledged a connection between them during introductions. There they were in a
room full of people practicing being open and receptive. Peyton saw
the understanding in all their eyes.

"They seem really sad," the paramedic said.

"Well," Cassie said, "since we've brought this up, why don't we talk
to Blizzard and Shodan next? Some of you have picked things up
from them already."

Peyton heard Dair's heartbeat click into rapid fire again, like a
cramp roll.

"I get a sense that they both feel they did something wrong," Cassie
said. "But they're very confused and can't figure out what it was."

She looked at Peyton, then at Dair, and kept her tone open and
nonjudgmental. "So, are the dogs behaving differently? Now that
they're not together?"

He nodded.

"Now, I'm going to ask a question, and it's not meant to make you
feel bad," Cassie said gently. "I want everyone in the circle to think
about things in your own homes that have upset your animal friends,
whether it's moving, going away on vacation and leaving them ken-

neled, or taking them to the vet. Did anyone explain the situation to Blizzard or Shodan?"

Peyton shook his head, not looking at Dair. He assumed she shook hers, too.

"This is important," Cassie said. "We often forget that our animal companions, if they live with us, really are members of the household. Change affects them. It's easy to forget that they'd be upset by, let's say, a breakup, or we forget that they need to know why. So they may feel responsible for the situation."

There was a moment of silence, then R.B. cleared his throat and said, "People do the same with children."

A tension squeaked between him and Cassie. His words were not a question, were not really even a contribution—they were a statement, tinged with the slightest challenge.

"Don't you think?" he asked, voluntarily taking the edge off the challenge. "People often assume children wouldn't understand, anyway, so we don't make it clear to them what's really going on in events that concern them. We think we're protecting them, and we're really just adding to their confusion?"

Lots of people murmured in agreement, but Cassie stared at R.B. as if lost, her lips slightly open. She'd gone somewhere else, far away.

Dair spoke in a tentative voice, not at all like her rich, trained voice for the stage. "That's true in all communication," she said, looking at her dad. "Not just with children." She looked at her mother. Peyton wondered if anyone in the circle knew these were her parents. "If you don't make clear what's going on, if you assume they understand, or assume it doesn't affect them, you're not communicating. The other person, or animal, will feel responsible . . . or blame the other. But those are assumptions, not true communication."

The tension in that triangle held tight, R.B. looking at Cassie, Cassie looking at him, Dair glancing back and forth between them.

Daisy, the Boston terrier, yelped as if she heard that tension, as if it were too high-pitched for her sensitive puppy ears.

"So," the paramedic asked, "how should they explain it to Blizzard and Shodan? That seems very complicated, sitting down and explaining to them."

Cassie snapped herself back to the present, and Peyton saw her hearing the paramedic's question in a delayed fashion. "That may seem tough, but the important thing to remember is that our language requires feelings and thoughts to be complete. Whenever we speak, we're visualizing; it's almost impossible not to. That's why we gesture, why some people are said to 'talk with their hands'—they're gesturing to what they 'see' as they talk. If you talk about the person next door, you'll frequently gesture as if to the house next door, even if you're in an entirely different city talking about this person. Do you know what I mean?"

People nodded.

"So, we're visualizing, and we're feeling, and we have an intention behind our words, and the animals pick this up. Often cats and dogs, and birds, who live inside our homes, will actually understand much more literal language than we imagine. But even when they don't, we're communicating with them all the same."

It was like Shakespeare. Peyton had watched good actors like Dair and Craig and Malcolm perform in Shakespeare plays he'd never read. And because *they* knew what they were saying, and communicated it with much more than just the words, *he* knew what they were saying, even if he wasn't understanding it word for word.

Cassie turned to Peyton and said, "Shodan does *not* like the man you're staying with."

Peyton swallowed and felt as if the muffin he'd eaten were lodged in his throat.

"She knows the man is afraid of her, and he's afraid of you, too."

Peyton saw Dair look sharply across the circle at him. What man? he felt her thinking.

He almost couldn't hear Cassie's quiet voice over the whine that blasted to life in his head. Malcolm better be afraid, if he was still using. If he'd had anything to do with Craig getting heroin, Peyton would kill him.

Peyton breathed easier, and his mind wandered when Cassie moved on to other animals.

R.B. sat on his bucket, elbows on his knees, picking at his nails. It was hard to read his response to all this.

Peyton tuned back into the conversation, growing tired. He hadn't slept well all week.

One of the horsewomen leaned forward and said, "When you came to our barn, before, you talked a little bit about totem animals. You said the totems chose us, and I think I know what my totem animal is, but how do we know what the totem has to offer us? What it means?"

"Some people would say you have to intuit that from the animal, that you must interpret it for yourself. There are some books, though, that help point out what the various animals represent. I have a good one in the house, called *Animal Speak*. Let's break for lunch. I'll get the book out."

Cassie had already explained Peyton's totem to him once. She'd told him the wolf was connected to family and loyalty and often chose people learning to trust their intuition.

So much for his intuition, though. Not much to trust there. For eight years he'd believed everything Dair had said about Sylvan. To his credit, he'd known something was terribly wrong with the Sylvan story; he'd known that not talking about Sylvan was hurting Dair. His intuition had been correct on that, at least.

Everyone headed for the house, and Cassie invited people to let their dogs play either in the barn or in the backyard. Dair let Blizzard loose in the backyard, and Peyton unclipped Shodan. They rushed to each other, licking each other's faces. Peyton turned away and went into the house, feeling odd and out of place. He'd loved picturing Dair here as a child, but of course, he'd pictured both her and Sylvan in the yard, in the barn, in this house. Now it felt like the scene of a crime or a movie set of a home that wasn't real. And Dair had never slept here without him since he'd met her. Until now.

She stood in the kitchen, next to the horsewoman who'd asked about totems. People moved around them, making sandwiches from the meat and cheese trays, pulling drinks out of the cooler. The horsewoman looked at a book, probably the book Cassie had mentioned. She said something he couldn't hear and handed the book to Dair, smiling.

Dair took it and set it on the table, flipping to the back and running her finger down an index. Then she turned the pages, hungrily, needily, and stopped, finding what she searched for. She held the book at chest level and read, engrossed, not sensing him watching her. The blood ran from her face, and Peyton felt light-headed. She set the book down, leaving it open, and backed away from it. Then she turned and walked out the back door, into the yard. Peyton watched her weave her way through the dogs and out the gate, toward the barn. Instead of following her, he headed for the book she'd left behind.

It was open, and the page heading read "The Chickadee," as he'd suspected.

But he hadn't at all suspected what it said.

"Keynote: Truthful Expression." Goose bumps prickled his skin. He read on: "The chickadee can help you with the uncovering of mysteries of the mind. It can awaken understanding and higher truth. It can help you to perceive more clearly in the dark."

The next line made the hair on the back of his neck stand up. "To the Cherokee Indians, the chickadee is the bird of truth. It helps us to pinpoint truth and knowledge." He swallowed and skimmed through the page.

The paramedic showed up at his elbow. "Ooh, can I see that when you're done?"

"Sure." He hastily read the last paragraph: "Some people say, 'The truth hurts.' Those who have a chickadee as a totem will learn to express the truth in a manner that heals, balances, and opens the perceptions. Truth is shared in a manner that adds cheer and joy to your own life and the lives of others."

Peyton handed the book to the paramedic and suddenly couldn't breathe in the crowded, noisy house. He made his way blindly to the back door and burst out into the autumn air.

Chapter Twenty-two

The chickadee. The chickadee in her dreams. The chickadee that had literally flown into her life the year she'd started lying.

In a way, Dair found a totem book as silly as a horoscope. Couldn't she read into it what she wanted? And "Truth is shared in a manner that adds cheer and joy to your own life and the lives of others"? Telling the truth had done anything but heal and balance her life. And it certainly hadn't healed Peyton's.

That last, violent chickadee dream still gave her the creeps. But maybe the chickadee for whatever reason was getting more desperate.

She walked out to the now deserted barn. Her dad's truck still stood at the end of the drive, so he was here. He wasn't in his office or any of the exam rooms. He hadn't gone in the house, had he? She couldn't picture him mixing and mingling with all those people.

At the back gate of the barn, she looked out at the field. Sure enough, there sat her father by the creek, in a patch of sunlight. Snowflake's grave—a white stone the size and shape of a bread loaf—stood near the log where Dad sat. Dair had brought Snowflake home from her first Cincinnati apartment when she'd died. Snowflake had been over twenty years old.

Dair slipped out the gate and strolled up behind her father. Her shadow reached him first, and he turned, squinting into the sun, then smiled. She sat beside him on the log and held his hand, as she had as a little girl, sitting here at dusk, watching the deer or the muskrat mama and her round baby in the creek. She leaned her head against his shoulder, smelled the sunshine in his flannel shirt.

"What goes on in your marriage is none of my business," he said softly, looking out at the field. "But I love you. And I love Peyton. And I love the two of you together, and I'm sorry if that . . . can't be. I hope you find a way to fix this."

That was a lot for her father to say, she knew. She kissed his shoulder. "Thank you. I love you, too, Dad. I feel the same way about you and Mom."

He let go of her hand and put his arm around her shoulders. She liked that.

"I did a bad thing, Dad. I lied to Peyton."

He raised his eyebrows. "Peyton said you had a 'communication problem.'"

Dair snorted. "I lied a big, bad lie." They sat in silence. He didn't ask. She knew he wouldn't. "I don't want to tell you yet, because I want to ask you something, okay?"

He seemed surprised but nodded.

"I want to talk about what you said in there." She gestured over their shoulders, back toward the barn.

He dropped his chin to his chest and let go of her hand to pick at a bit of leaf on his well-worn jeans. Dair took his hand back into hers.

"I know you and Mom lost a baby." She felt him tense. "She told me about the wreck. And *why* she wrecked. This is really what's wrong between you two, isn't it?"

His body felt coiled beside her. He looked up at the sky, a thin blue today. "She says it's not."

"But it is, isn't it?"

He lifted a shoulder. "It was a long time ago . . . but it's hung around."

"So . . . how did it come up? I mean, I know it's none of my business, really." He'd been so respectful, not prying into what was wrong with her and Peyton, after all. "You can tell me if I'm just being nosy, but what made her leave you after all these years? I mean, after all that time not talking about it, what happened the day she told you?"

He let go of her hand and ran his fingers through his white hair, then leaned forward, elbows on his knees. Dair leaned against him, chin on his shoulder. "It was Bonnie's foal," he said in a tone that suggested he'd just realized it.

"Bonnie? The Clydesdale?"

He nodded. "This isn't *Bonnie* Bonnie, not the one you knew. It's one of her fillies. But Bob calls her Bonnie, too." He stopped, but Dair stayed quiet. She could see he was watching a scene in his head. After a moment he said, "Bonnie had twins this spring."

Dair felt the knot tie up in her gut, as it always did with that word. Habit now, even though the truth was exposed.

"I didn't know it at first," Dad said. "It took a while to get two different heartbeats."

His voice thinned, revealing more emotion than she knew he wanted to. "Cassie went with me for the foaling. And there were problems. . . ."

"Problems?"

"One foal was deformed. It . . . it didn't really have a face; it was round, not long like a horse head. It . . . it didn't have ears . . . and only had one eye, and . . ." He was using his hands, just as Mom had described. Dair knew he was seeing the foal right then, right there, before him on this dry, dusty grass, this parched and cracked creek bed. "And its forelegs ended at the knee."

She closed her eyes a moment. "Was it alive?" she whispered.

He made a move, not a yes, not a no. "For a few minutes," he said.

A hawk cried somewhere in the woods behind the field. "But, what did this have to do with you and Mom?"

He sighed. "Well, once the live foal, the healthy foal, was nursing, Bonnie kept trying to tend to the dead one, licking its coat dry. She knew it was dead; she wasn't trying to get it to its feet, and she'd ignored it until the healthy foal was nursing. Your mother was tending the dead one, too, rubbing it with a towel. It was laid out in the grass. I went over and was going to take the foal away. And Bob came over, too, just sort of looking at the foal. And I said that we shouldn't let Bonnie waste her energy on this. I didn't mean anything by it. I just meant that we had to remove the dead foal anyway, but . . . Cass stood up and kicked me."

"Kicked you?" Dair couldn't have heard him correctly.

He nodded. "Right in the shin. Hard. And she started shoving me and she said, 'Leave her be, let her do it,' and finally just sort of crumpled up in the field and cried. Bob—he didn't know what to do. He just sort of walked away from us, left us alone."

"Is that what you did after the wreck?"

He looked up at her. Surprised.

Dair made sure her voice was gentle. "Did you just leave each other alone?"

"I thought that's what she wanted," he whispered.

She wrapped her arms around him, and he put his hands on her forearms across his chest, welcoming her embrace. "Is that what *you* wanted?"

His back convulsed in one sob. He shook his head. To her surprise, he kept talking. "People knew she'd been drinking. No one knew about the baby. But they knew she'd been hurt. Everyone kept asking, 'How's your wife?' afterward. No one asked how I was . . . so I didn't really, either. I just wanted her to move on, be her normal self again. Her sober self."

"Did you ever fight about it?"

"God, no."

Dair wondered if maybe they should have.

She kept her arms around him and looked out across the rustling grass, sounding like whispering voices, like gossip in the wind. Leaves scratched along the creek bed, and something else, shinier—a snakeskin. Thin and crackly as paper, it rolled over and over in the breeze. Dair wondered if it hurt, shedding skin? How long did it take before the freshly peeled, raw self could tolerate exposure?

"You couldn't fight about the accident because that would mean fighting about her drinking, right? You'd have to blame her?"

He sighed. "It's an ugly thing, a drunk woman."

Shame coursed through Dair.

Dad went on. "People thought she was crazy. I—"

Dair knew what he was going to say. He'd been embarrassed. She'd misinterpreted his humiliation as a child. She thought he'd been embarrassed by the animal communication.

"I think you two have to talk about it," Dair said. "Maybe to a doctor, or a counselor."

"Dair, it upsets her to talk about it."

"Daddy, of *course* it does. It *should*. But . . . being upset and dealing with it has to be better than *this,* doesn't it?"

He put his face in his hands again, elbows on his knees. He'd done what he'd thought was right, of course. He'd spent his life calming wild things—Dair remembered him gentling a panicked, injured stallion with just his voice and hands; she remembered him crooning a thrashing deer with splintered legs into quiet, placid rest long before Dair was able to hand him the needle; remembered him convincing the screaming, foaming dog—its nearly severed foreleg dragging a steel trap by a tendon thread—to let him approach. She'd seen those animals' eyes. They'd known and understood that he intended to ease their pain and make things better. That's what he was good at; that's what he knew how to do. Prying at her mother's guilt and blame probably felt as unnatural to him as chasing after that pain-crazed dog, rattling and clanking that steel trap at it.

"Dad? Do you know that I drink, too?"

He made a small sound.

"I drink a *lot*. And I have for years. And I try to rationalize it and limit it, and I hide it and lie about it . . . and if only I'd *known,* then maybe—"

He raised his head, his face agonized.

"No, no. Dad, I'm not blaming you. Please don't think that. I don't blame you or Mom. I just . . . I think you were right—what you said in the barn today. Things could've been different." Dair knew now that her parents couldn't have united in their concern about Dair's own drinking without first dealing with her mother's. "Not just different for me, but for you and Mom. Will you *try* to talk about it? Please?"

He said nothing.

"Promise me," she begged.

He pulled her against his chest, almost roughly, and held her tight.

She hugged him back and, over his shoulder, watched the snakeskin tumble down the creek bed out of sight.

Dair drove back to Cincinnati, with Blizzard and Godot, for rehearsal. It amazed her that an entire week had passed since Craig's death. This time last Saturday they'd just found out on the news.

Saturday night. Oh, God, tonight was trick-or-treat, even though her birthday, real Halloween, wasn't until Monday. It stressed Blizzard out when the doorbell rang that many times. It was never a good night in their house. Captain Hook kept shrieking, *"Who's outside?"* all night long, and the dogs barked and barked and barked.

And Matt and Marielle weren't going to be home. Where were they? And what was Marielle hiding? She'd loved Craig—Dair knew Marielle hadn't lied about that. So why was she withholding information if she knew who killed him?

As Dair drove, with Blizzard draped on the front seat beside her, his snout on her thigh, Godot in his carrier in the backseat, Dair told them all about what she'd done and why Peyton had left. She drove with her left hand and kept her right on Blizzard's white, fluffy shoulder, except when she needed to turn or merge in traffic.

She talked on and on, tears streaming down her face, not caring who saw her or wondered about her talking to herself. She often practiced monologues as she drove or did vocal warm-ups on the way to rehearsal. This time she wasn't talking to herself. She talked to others, who stayed very still and quiet and listened to her story with rapt attention.

She combed her fingers through Blizzard's long white hair, and once she was silent for several minutes, he moved his head. Dair glanced down into his dark, brown eyes and got a feeling, a sensation of *It's hard, isn't it?* It was a feeling of total sympathy, understanding. And she knew he meant all of it, not just her and Peyton, and the lie, but the struggle to be better, to be "open," as her mother called it, to be alive on earth, really.

It was hard to leave the animals, to go to rehearsal. Dair felt the day had changed her, and she wasn't ready to let go of the feeling yet. Perhaps this was what people felt about religion. She felt as though she'd been born again.

She smiled. That phrase, *born again,* made her think of Peyton, not of Christianity.

Peyton might be right. That they returned in different incarnations. That they were meant to find certain people. Other beings, too. She knelt and hugged Blizzard.

But in her blood she felt no pulse, however faint, of a previous life. Her only memories were of this life. And she knew this life would be empty without Peyton.

Everything around her seemed to point to emptiness or absence, as if a set designer had been working with a design concept of loss: The flocks of geese and other birds were gone from the autumn sky, the trees had been stripped of leaves in the two nights she'd been gone, frost had blackened the asters and mums near the back porch.

And Peyton had been in their bed. She smelled him and saw his indentation in the mattress and pillow. It reminded her of walking in her parents' pasture and finding grass pressed into the shapes of sleeping deer. She curled up in the vague hollow he'd left and imagined that the sheets wrapped around her were his arms. "What am I going to do, Blizzard?" she asked. Blizzard rested his chin on the edge of the mattress and stared mournfully up at her with those liquid brown eyes until she got out of bed.

She was too aware of the Kahlúa in the kitchen, afraid even to open the cupboard to throw it away, in case in the process she guzzled the entire bottle. She went next door. She called, and she knocked, and she checked the basement window. Nothing. But Mr. Lively heard her and flung open his door.

"What the hell is going on?" he asked. He looked truly distraught.

"Who's outside?" Captain Hook called.

Mr. Lively shut his door and came down a few of his steps, gripping the banister tightly. "Marielle was here today. She carried things out. Boxes. Are they moving?"

The beak started against Dair's sore sternum. What was Marielle hiding, running from? She couldn't have harmed Craig herself. No . . . she was afraid of what she knew. Godammit, why didn't Marielle tell her? Maybe Dair could help.

"Where did they go?" Mr. Lively asked, concern in his eyes.

"She won't tell me," Dair said, feeling on the verge of tears. "She was scared. She said they were going to a hotel, but she wouldn't tell me which one."

"Why was she scared?" he asked.

"Because, someone is going around killing people!"

"But that happened a week ago. Why did they leave *now?*" Just as Dair had asked her dad today. What was "the moment before," the motivator?

Dair thought, and a slow tingle started in her hands and feet. "It was a picture," Dair said. "A photo of Marielle with Matt's dad. They thought maybe the intruder took it."

Mr. Lively frowned.

Dair told him about the photos at Gayle's. "Maybe the target wasn't Craig," she said, realizing it for the first time. "Maybe it's someone after Marielle. Oh, God . . . I wish they'd find Gayle."

"Or the boy," Mr. Lively said.

"What?"

"Sounds like the father is after the boy."

"W-what do you mean?" Dair asked. "Matt's dad died."

Mr. Lively's expression was one she'd never seen on him before. Utter surprise. Almost delight. "When did that happen?" he asked.

"Before Matt was born."

The delight vanished. "No, he didn't," Mr. Lively said, as if scolding her. "Marielle's moved twice, hiding from him."

"What?" His words nearly toppled her down the metal steps.

"Don't you people ever *talk* to each other?"

"B-but she told me that he died," Dair said, the tingle spreading as if her entire body had fallen asleep.

And she realized she'd believed it, as she told her acting classes, simply because an audience will accept anything they are not given a reason to disbelieve.

"How do you know that?" she asked Mr. Lively.

His expression was that of a person watching theater of the absurd. "She told me."

"So . . . it's true."

"Why on earth would I *say* it if it wasn't true?" he snapped.

Why? At least Marielle had an answer to that question.

Dair thought of the look of understanding Marielle had had at the table when Dair told her about Sylvan, the twin she'd never had. Just as Peyton, Craig, and Marielle—everyone, really—had believed her story about Sylvan, they'd all believed Marielle's story about Matt's dad. Why shouldn't they? When people confided their personal tragedies, it went against human nature to doubt them. Who went around making up heartrending stories like that?

Who indeed.

Marielle had said recently that Matt was becoming more like his father every day. What did that mean?

And Matt was right: Who else would want to steal that photo? But that didn't make sense. Why steal it and tip Marielle off?

"But . . ." Dair felt herself deflate.

And she finally understood what she'd made Peyton feel. You thought you knew someone, and suddenly you wondered if you knew anyone. God, she wanted to go back to that day in the park, the day she'd first met him.

Panic spilled onto Dair. She had to see Marielle. Dair wasn't sure exactly what she'd say to her, what she'd do, but somehow she had to convince her not to leave. Marielle could go to Dair's parents' farm. Dair would help her with anything. She just couldn't stand the thought of losing two more people she cared about.

"If she comes back while I'm gone," Dair said, "I want you to call me—"

"Where are you going *now?*" he asked, and she recognized fear in his eyes.

"I have to go to work, to rehearsal. Here, let me give you my cell phone number."

"I don't have a phone," he snapped.

"Oh." Dair thought about giving him her cell phone but knew it was unlikely anyone would answer the theater office phones on a weekend. "How 'bout I give you a key to our place? If Marielle comes back, you come downstairs and use our phone and call me."

He eyed the stairs. He'd have to leave his home, expose himself. "Do you want me to leave Blizzard out in the yard?" Dair asked.

His eyes flashed gratitude, but then he scoffed. "Why would I want that noisy oaf barking the whole time you're gone?"

Dair made a face at him, but his statement reminded her. "You know it's trick-or-treat night, right? He's going to be barking any-way . . . with the trick-or-treaters coming to the door." She looked at her watch. "Kids are out already."

"Oh, for God's sake!" He wrung his hands and rocked from foot to foot, reminding her of his parrot. "What a ridiculous tradition."

"Listen, I'll turn off the porch lights. Maybe that will keep people away. The yard is so steep, a lot of people won't bother if the light is off up top. I'll leave lights on back here, so you can see to get to our back door, if you need to."

He paused. "Oh, all right," he said.

She ran down the steps and through the house.

She made sure the porch lights were off and locked her screen door, turning out all the lights in the front of the house.

She left the lights on in the kitchen. Taped up a big piece of paper with fat Magic Marker letters pointing out PHONE with an arrow. She was sure Mr. Lively would be offended. He'd make some comment later about how he wasn't blind.

Then she jotted down her cell phone number and fished out a spare key.

She trotted up the stairs with the info for Mr. Lively. He opened the door as she was halfway up. He took the key and number with a curt nod. "The phone is right next to the coffeemaker," she said. "To your right inside the back door. You can't miss it."

He looked down the stairs into the yard and asked, "Are you letting that dog out?"

"Oh. I didn't think you wanted me to."

He sighed heavily, as if Dair were begging him. "Go ahead," he said. "If you must."

"Okay." She thought of her mother's magic touch with him and said, "Thank you."

He nodded again, beginning to shut his door.

"You call that number and I'll come home. I can be home in about ten minutes."

Dair ran back down the stairs and into her kitchen. She took Blizzard's bowl, got him dinner, and moved the bowl and his water dish outside to the porch. Before she let him out, though, she sat on the floor with him and told him out loud about the trick-or-treaters and that Mr. Lively was scared and wanted him out in the yard as protection. She was running behind, she felt rushed and out of breath, and she knew she wasn't communicating as well as she had with Mom's guidance. She took a deep breath and tried again. Blizzard walked to the back door. Dair didn't know if he just wanted his dinner or if he'd understood.

Dair got in the car again and drove to the Aronoff, already passing little bands of ghosts and witches and knife-wielding horror movie characters walking the sidewalks with their bags and pillowcases.

She'd forgotten that the touring Broadway revue had opened. All parking near the Aronoff had been taken by theater patrons, three parking garages blocked with "Full" signs, forcing her to search much farther away than usual. She circled blocks, she swore, and she ended up what felt like a mile from the theater, where she'd normally be too nervous to park and walk alone. It took her nearly ten minutes to get to the Aronoff, and by the time she did, she'd peeled off her fleece jacket and was out of breath and sweaty.

She jogged into rehearsal right at eight on the nose, which was not her style at all.

The stage manager said, "*There's* Dair," as if he'd been waiting. He wore a pair of little red devil horns on his head, and she saw the red cape draped across his chair. There were big Halloween parties on the riverboats tonight.

"We were worried," C.J. said, squeezing her arm. He wore camouflage fatigues and combat boots. He must have been heading to the party, too. Dair knew why they were worried.

"Anyone heard from Gayle?" she asked.

C.J. shook his head, as did several others near them. Anxiety hung heavy in the theater in spite of the festive costumes. It seemed absurd to go on rehearsing under the circumstances. One cast member was dead, the artistic director of the theater was missing and perhaps—as Dair had begun to fear—dead, too.

Malcolm looked better than he had at the funeral, but he still fidgeted. Dair watched him sitting on a rehearsal block, bouncing his knee, shredding the Styrofoam coffee cup he held. He had to be "the man" Shodan didn't like. Dair thought back to what Malcolm had said to her at the funeral. How else would he know that they had split up? He looked over at her, and that swatch of red spread across his cheeks. He looked away.

Mr. Lively's information festered away inside her. If Matt's dad was alive, had Marielle told Craig about him? Was that why Craig stopped by on Saturday when he knew Marielle was gone?

Dair remembered the image Slip Jig had shown to Dair's mom: the intruder looking at the class schedules on the fridge. He'd known Marielle would be gone Saturday morning. And that Matt would be alone. But Matt had convinced Mr. Lively to go with him to the zoo.

And really, Matt and Marielle had rarely been alone since that day, a week ago today.

Why had Marielle run from Matt's dad in the first place—was he some kind of stalker? Abusive? Were they even divorced? The crazy father perhaps explained why Craig had been killed . . . but not how Craig had ended up drugged over at Gayle's house or in a dress. And not why Gayle was missing. What if the two things were not connected at all? Was Dair simply trying desperately to analyze and categorize and connect?

Rosylyn began working act II, scene iii. Dair only walked on in this scene, so she sat in the wings—shaking her head no when Bethany passed around bags of candy corn—and watched Malcolm, his face focused as he listened to Rosylyn. Malcolm seemed obsessed with Marielle, always asking how she was, where she was going to be. But . . . that didn't make sense. Malcolm *couldn't* be Matt's father. Marielle had seen him, talked to him. She'd recognize him. But something felt wrong about his interest.

Jefferson, the actor playing Cassio, borrowed Dair's jacket, tying the black fleece sleeves around his neck to act as a cloak. Malcolm and Jefferson started the scene. Iago urged Cassio to drink. Cassio said, "I have very poor and unhappy brains for drinking. I could well wish courtesy would invent some other custom of entertainment."

Dair felt Cassio's struggle as Iago urged him to drink more. They held their prop cups, Malcolm holding the prop bottle of wine, and Dair longed for it to be real at the same time that she longed for Iago to leave Cassio alone.

Cassio tried again: "I am unfortunate in the infirmity and dare not task my weakness with any more."

Dair felt for him. Infirmity. Weakness. She had a weakness, didn't she? A weakness so strong, if that made any sense, that even water in a prop wine bottle made her crave the burn of alcohol on her tongue, the buzz of it in her brain.

She watched the scene as Iago got Cassio drunker and drunker and staged the fight between Roderigo and Cassio, waking Othello from bed. She went on, as Emilia, attending Desdemona as she, too, came from bed to see what was the matter, then went off when Othello commanded them all to bed, leaving poor Cassio onstage with the man he thought was his only friend left, never realizing that Iago had orchestrated the entire incident.

They ran the scene twice more, then the stage manager called a fifteen-minute break.

Their break came about the same time as the intermission for the revue. The lobby was crowded with theater patrons milling about, lining up for concessions.

Concessions. Dair eyed the little plastic glasses of white and red wine, heard people ordering Chivas on the rocks and gin martinis.

She turned away, adrift in this sea of noise. She weaved around people's elbows, squeezed between bodies, got bombarded with voices, little snippets of conversation, an overall roar of sound in the room, like waves pounding, emptiness and neediness tugging on her clothes, pulling her under, drowning her. She wanted to swim to safety, to flee.

She wanted to drink.

She stumbled for the side stairs that led up to the light booth in the big hall. Once out of the crowd, she gasped for air. A few theater patrons came down this staircase from the balcony, but most chose the grand, open staircase that led down to the lobby. She climbed and went through the small narrow hallway to the light and sound booth. She heard Andy's laughter before she saw him. The door to the booth was open, and he and Steve, the soundboard op—creatively nicknamed Sound Guy Steve—sat talking. Dair tapped on the door, pushing it farther open. They both looked up, saw her, and smiled.

"Hey," Andy said. "How ya doing?" He stood and hugged her, and that scent of warm apples soothed her somehow.

"I've been better," she said.

"Anyone at rehearsal heard anything about Gayle?" Andy asked. Dair shook her head and felt all of their worries crowd the room.

"This is getting scary," Steve said, shuffling the mini CDs in his hand. Steve wore a brown robe with a hood and had a fake lightsaber attached to his belt. It looked as though he'd be heading to the riverboats as a Jedi knight. "Everybody's talking like Gayle's disappearance is tied to Craig dying. It's like, is the theater cursed or something? Who's next?"

No one knew what to say.

"Want a smoky treat?" Andy asked into the fearful silence.

Dair nodded. "Desperately."

He checked his watch. "I got ten minutes." He leaned down to dig in his bag. Dair saw something black and hairy at the top; it looked like a dead animal.

"What the hell is that?" she asked.

Steve was looking at it with alarm, too.

Andy laughed and pulled out a wig. Once he held it upright, it looked fine. He stuffed it back in the bag and pulled out a packet of vampire teeth and white pancake makeup. "I'm going to the river-boats after the show. You wanna come with me?"

"Thanks, but I'm not in a party mood. I don't feel so hot, and we've got an eight-hour rehearsal tomorrow. I better not."

Actually, she couldn't imagine being in that loud crowd unless she drank.

"Let's get you a remedy," Andy said, finding his pack of cigarettes and pocketing a lighter. "I'll take these," he said to Steve, holding up his headphones and tucking them around his neck. "We'll just be out on the fire steps."

"Cool," Steve said, still shuffling his CDs.

They didn't speak until they'd made their way down the narrow hallway and out the door marked "Fire Escape." A flattened Coke can sat on the fire escape landing, and Andy used this to prop the door open, as he and others no doubt had done countless times before.

He handed her a cigarette and lit it, and she gratefully pulled the smoke down her throat, into her lungs. There was something ritual-istic about it that she needed, that comforted her.

She shivered in the autumn briskness and looked up at the fat moon, no longer full but still huge.

"So, what's going on? I haven't seen you in a couple days."

Dair nodded. "I went home, to my parents'." She said "parents'," even though technically she should say "my mom's" now. But there might be hope. For them, anyway.

"You and Peyton back together?"

She shook her head.

He shrugged. "It's getting around. People saw you arrive separately for the funeral and everything."

She nodded. "They all think it's proof I was sleeping with Craig."

"But what really happened?" he asked.

Dair inhaled, loving the mild buzz the nicotine produced. "It's a long story," she said, not wanting to tell him. He had a twin, after all, and she'd discovered that there was a kinship among twins, like cancer survivors or veterans. She'd gained access to a club, but she was an impostor. "Takes longer than an intermission to tell."

He snorted. "You okay?"

She shrugged. "I'm getting by."

"How's Craig's fiancée?"

A vague warning went off throughout her body. Suddenly anyone asking about Marielle felt suspect rather than supportive. She tapped her ash and said, "I don't know. She took off the other night and won't tell anyone where she is."

"Why?"

Dair searched his face. He seemed honestly concerned; he wasn't digging for gossip or information. "She seems really scared. I mean, someone's been coming in her house, Craig got killed, and now Gayle is missing. . . . I don't feel hopeful about Gayle, do you?" She looked at him, his face so worried. "I mean, do we think she just took off for some spa weekend and forgot to tell anyone? Forgot that a hundred people were coming to her house?"

Andy said, "No one says this, but . . . do you ever wonder if she staged it? The disappearance?"

Dair chewed her lip. "Yeah. Yeah, I have wondered, but Gayle thrives on attention. Hiding out, laying low, isn't her style, you know? The whole thing is so screwed up. I don't blame Marielle for being spooked. I'm spooked, too, but it's not my house that someone's breaking into."

"Jesus," Andy whispered. "How long has she been gone?"

"Since the night of the funeral." She didn't tell him Marielle had been home today, but mainly because saying it out loud scared her; Marielle couldn't be gone. Or moving.

Andy's headset crackled, and they heard distinctly, "Five minutes. The call is five."

"You gotta go," Dair said, taking one last pull off her cigarette before stubbing it out.

He did the same. As they opened the fire escape door and headed down the narrow hallway, Dair saw Malcolm step out of the light booth, Sound Guy Steve pointing down the hall toward them.

Her pulse quickened. Was he following her?

"Dair," Malcolm said. He panted, and she pictured him running up the stairs to find her. She checked her watch, thinking she was late. "Dair, your cell phone rang."

Oh, shit. She'd forgotten about it and had left it in her bag down in the rehearsal hall. "Did anyone answer it?" she asked.

He nodded, trying to catch his breath. "It was some old guy. He said to tell you to come home. He said for you to hurry, that's why I—"

"Oh, my God." Dair headed for the stairs, both men following her.

"What's wrong?" Andy asked. "What old guy?"

"The guy who lives upstairs." Dair caught herself pointing up, just as Mom had described in the barn that afternoon. She gestured up to the ceiling, visualizing Mr. Lively in his apartment above hers.

"He said, 'She's home,'" Malcolm said.

"Who?" Andy asked. "Marielle?"

Dair didn't answer. She ran down the stairs and through the thinning crowd in the lobby to the rehearsal hall.

Everyone was gathered around her bag, and Bethany held the phone. "Dair, your—"

"I know, Malcolm found me." She took the phone. All she heard was a dial tone.

"Is Marielle okay?" Bethany asked.

How did she know this was about Marielle?

Dair dialed Marielle's number. "Who answered my phone?"

"I did," Bethany said.

Marielle's phone rang. "What did he say to you?"

"He just said, 'She's home,' and I said, 'Who is this?' and he asked, 'Dair?' and I said, 'No, but I can go get her'"—Marielle's phone kept ringing— "and then he said, 'Just tell her to come home now.' He really stressed *now,* like it was urgent." Dair flipped her phone shut. Marielle's machine must be off, and she was ignoring the phone.

"I have to go," Dair said to Rosylyn. She grabbed her bag.

"Do you need us to call anyone?" Rosylyn asked, looking bewildered. "The police?"

"No. It's okay," Dair said, running from the room. Marielle didn't want the police.

As she burst out the door, she realized she'd left her jacket behind. No time for it now. On the street she looked around in a panic for her car. Where had she parked? *Shit.* She was *blocks* away tonight.

She took off running, her bag banging against her hip. Please, please let Marielle stay until I get there, she chanted as she ran. Dair's lungs wanted to burst by the time she reached her car. She dug in her bag for her keys. Shit. She scrambled frantically, feeling for them. Nothing. Shit, shit. She touched all her jeans pockets. Shit. She tipped her bag, ready to pour its contents out onto the sidewalk, but she told herself, slow down—*breathe*. She tried. She remembered getting out of the car for rehearsal. She'd been running behind, and it had been hard to find parking . . . she saw herself slip the keys into her jacket pocket.

"Shit!" she said out loud, running back down the street. She'd told Mr. Lively she could be home in ten minutes, but it had taken her nearly that long to make the trip from the goddamn car to the Aronoff.

Miserable and sweating, she reached the stage door and yanked but nearly plowed face first into the glass when the door didn't open. It was locked. No way. She banged on the door, loud and long, but no security guard appeared. Dair ran farther down the street to the lobby doors for Procter & Gamble Hall. An elderly usher stepped toward her as she burst through the doors. "I won't be able to seat you if the revue has resumed its second—"

"I'm in the *Othello* rehearsal!" Dair said. The usher winced at how loudly she spoke and put a finger to his lips to shush her. Her voice echoed in the now deserted lobby.

Dair ran past the box office and into the *Othello* rehearsal. They hadn't started working again. The cast and Rosylyn stood in the center of the stage, and Dair could see in their eyes that she'd been the topic of conversation by the mixture of alarm and sheepishness that crossed their faces when they turned to her.

"M-my car keys," she panted. "I—I left them in my jacket." She surveyed the theater wildly. "Where's Jefferson? He has my jacket."

"He's looking for Malcolm," the stage manager said.

"What?!" Dair was trying not to scream or shake anyone.

Before she could head back out to the lobby to search for Jefferson, Sound Guy Steve appeared in the doorway, panic on his face. "Anybody seen Andy Baker?" he asked.

"I was just talking to him," Dair said. "Me and Malcolm."

"He never came back to the booth," Steve said. "They're holding the show."

"You haven't started act two?" C.J. asked.

"He's missing?" Bethany asked, eyes wide. The way she said it immediately registered with the group. She didn't have to add "too" or "like Gayle"; they all did it mentally.

Steve shook his head, his arms braced in the doorway, blocking Dair's way. "You were smoking with him, right, Dair?"

She felt the collective gaze of the cast. She seemed to be the kiss of death for everyone. Steve looked into her eyes, and she remembered him asking, just minutes ago, "Who's next?"

"But, but, he was right outside the booth," she said. "When Malcolm told me about the phone call . . . Where *is* Malcolm?" With delayed hearing she registered what they'd said Jefferson was doing.

"What did they do?" Steve asked. "Where was Andy going when you saw him last?"

"He was going into the booth. I left them both and ran down here."

"Well, shit! I can't run the light board!" Steve left the doorway, to do who knew what.

"Oh, my God," Bethany said. "What's going on?"

Dair stepped into the lobby, half the cast following her.

"Did you *see* him go into the booth?" C.J. asked her.

"No, but I didn't stick around, I just ran back downstairs, I wanted to know what was wrong with Marielle. I—I just want my keys. I really have to go."

Jefferson bounded down the stairs from the booths. "No luck," he said. He still had Dair's jacket tied around his neck.

"I need my jacket," she said. She reached with what must've seemed like desperation. As he handed it to her, she heard the reassuring rattle from the pocket.

With her car keys firmly in her grip, she took off running again. They could think what they wanted of her, but she couldn't waste any more time.

Passing the deserted stairwell of Procter & Gamble Hall, Dair saw a plastic cup of wine abandoned on the banister. A whole cup; it looked untouched. The sweet rosy glow of white Zinfandel. She picked it up and downed it on the way out the door. One full cup, one smooth, soothing swallow.

With Peyton gone, this was the only security blanket she had left.

Chapter Twenty-three

Dair squealed onto her street, sending a little flock of trick-or-treaters scurrying. Marielle's car was nowhere to be seen. *Please don't let her be gone already. Please, please.*

Dair got out of the car, fumbling with her bag and jacket and keys, and ran up the steps and around to the gate. Blizzard howled and barked, but he wasn't out in the yard. Dair heard him throwing himself against the door, rattling the cat flap. Had Mr. Lively left him in the house? She left the gate open and ran up the steps to the wooden deck. The back-door knob turned in her hand; it wasn't locked, but when she opened it a crack, Blizzard leapt at it, throwing it open, making her drop her bag and jacket and her keys. She heard everything in her bag go flying—lipstick tubes, her phone, spare change. She barely had time to glance down and register that she'd lost the car keys when Blizzard advanced on her, teeth bared, barking and growling. "Blizzard! It's just me."

But he came at her, stiff-legged, his black lips curled back, his face almost unrecognizable.

Blizzard drove her off the porch, the long white hair on his back standing up like a porcupine. Once she was down the steps, she stopped, confused. Whose dog was this? When she stood still, Blizzard crouched down on the deck, growling low in his throat.

Dair looked past him through the open door into her apartment. Her kitchen light was still on. Marielle's half of the house was lit up, too. And she heard voices inside. Heard Marielle's distinctly, urgent and pleading.

Dair edged past Blizzard, heading cautiously for Marielle's back door, but Blizzard leapt on her from the porch, knocking her to the sidewalk, snagging the back of her arm with his teeth. She scrambled to her feet, sprinted for the back gate, and slammed it shut just as he threw himself against it, snarling like something rabid. "Blizzard!" she said, shocked.

Her own voice came back to her, mocking her tone: *"Blizzard!"* The voices inside Marielle's house rose sharply, then fell quiet. *"Blizzard!"* Dair's voice said again.

She turned, panting, not recognizing for a moment that the voice was Captain Hook's, because the sound didn't come from upstairs. She looked up at Mr. Lively's door, and her mouth stripped dry. His door stood wide open.

"Oh, God." Something scuttled to her right in the front yard, and she jumped, but only two little white-sheeted ghosts ran by, holding hands, both carrying plastic pumpkin buckets. They were followed by a taller scarecrow, obviously an older brother or dad, chaperoning.

Her heart thudded, sounding like the drums in Footforce, not like a little bird.

"Mr. Lively?" she called. No answer. She tried again, louder, calling over the fence, over the giant white dog growling on the other side. "Mr. Lively?"

No sound came from his open door or Marielle's side of the house. *"Papa?"* the parrot's voice called. *"Papa, where are you?"*

It was difficult to see outside the ring of the porch light, but Dair could just make out the parrot's white head in a bare tree, silhouetted against the moon. Where was Mr. Lively?

She eyed Blizzard, who crouched, ready to spring again.

"What's the matter?" she whispered. "What's going on?"

Only growling answered her. She wasn't getting in that back gate. Her cell phone still spun slowly on the patio, and her keys sparkled next to Blizzard's water bowl.

She turned and walked around to the front porch, still dark. The street moved, was alive with groups of kids, their laughter, their shrieks, the chorus calls of "Trick or treat!" echoing down the street. There was some safety in the number of people about, although it was surreal, all the ghouls and demons walking by.

She pounded on Marielle's front door and peered through the glass.

With all the lights on inside, Dair saw that much of the room was boxed up, bare. Mr. Lively had been right: Marielle was moving out. No one came to the door, though. Dair strained to hear something, anything, over her pounding heart, but she couldn't.

Dair's own screen door was locked, of course, so even if she had her keys, she wasn't going in that way unless she slashed the screen. And without the keys there was no point—the glass window of the door was too high up to reach through for the knob.

She backed away, off the porch. As she stood there, wondering what to do, the lights went off on Marielle's side of the house. Shit. She had to *do* something; she couldn't just stand there.

She *had* to be able to get to her phone, to her keys. What was wrong with Blizzard? It was as if he didn't know her. As if . . . Idiot, you idiot, Dair said to herself. Listen to him.

She headed back around the house, and Blizzard started in on a whole new barrage of barking at her approach. It was going to be tough to try to communicate. What did she want to ask him? And how the hell was she supposed to quiet her mind under the circumstances?

She stood, huddled against the side of the house where she could see him over the fence, and tried to visualize herself going in the back gate. She pictured herself walking up the porch to Marielle's door.

Blizzard growled at her. *No.* It was loud and clear, the impression that came back to her. He would not let her enter the house. And a rush of sensations and sounds hurtled at her from the white dog— commotion, wings flapping, doors slamming, angry voices, the musky smell of fear, the scent of warm apples.

The scent of warm apples. No. No, it couldn't be. If he was here, it was just to help, to find out what was wrong, why Dair ran away so quickly, right? Right?

"You have to let me in," she whispered to the dog, trying to picture herself entering again. "It's okay."

He growled.

But as she moved toward the gate, still hugging the side of the house, Blizzard abruptly stopped growling and turned toward the back doors. Dair heard a door open, and Blizzard disappeared from her view, sounding as though he'd disembowel whoever was coming out. Dair ran the remaining steps to the gate, to see who it was. Marielle's door stood open an inch or two, and Blizzard crouched on the porch, facing it, growling.

"Marielle?" Dair called.

Her hands shook as she reached over the gate for the latch. Maybe she could slip inside while Blizzard was preoccupied with Marielle's door. He wouldn't *attack* her, would he? But the back of her arm still stung from his bite.

A shadow passed in the sliver of light spilling out the cracked open door.

"Marielle?" she called, louder. "Matt?"

"Dair!" she heard Matt's voice call, but she swore it came from the house, not the tree. She heard footsteps and a thud. Matt was in there.

"Matt?" Dair called as loudly as she could. "Marielle? Goddammit. I'm calling the police if you don't answer me."

Blizzard still stood there, hackles raised, snarling.

"You guys, come on! What the hell is going on?"

"Hey!" the parrot called in Craig's voice, rippling her skin with goose bumps. *"What the hell are you doing?"*

"Can you guys hear me?" Dair called.

"Hey! Get the hell away from there!" Craig's voice screamed from the tree. *"What are you doing?"* Dair saw Captain Hook spread his wings in the tree, flapping them, and then he began to imitate someone knocking on a door.

The sound made her jump; made her look to the back doors in alarm; made the hackles stand up further on Blizzard's back.

At that moment Blizzard stopped barking and ran to the far side of the yard, looking down the side of the house, past the intruder's window, toward the front yard. Did he think someone knocked on the front door? Could she slip inside the house while he was distracted?

But as she reached over the gate to try, not knowing what else to do, she heard a man's voice in the front yard—a familiar voice—yell, "Ow! Shit!" then, "Matthew!"

She knew that voice. She knew, but she didn't know. She knew, but she *wouldn't* know. She would not allow herself to believe she'd been so duped, so gullible.

That anger, that betrayal, finally woke her body up. She ran to the front yard. Saw someone tall, with long black hair, hobbling down the stairs to the street. The figure lost the limp as the fleeing figure of Matthew gained speed ahead of him.

Dair was afraid of why she didn't see Marielle. She was afraid to think about where Mr. Lively might be and why Captain Hook was loose. She knew she should go in Marielle's open door and call 911.

But she was mostly afraid that 911 wouldn't matter if she lost sight of Matt. What would she be able to tell them?

Dair saw herself locking her car door that day, a week ago, on 75, above Clifton Avenue. She'd locked her door when she could've saved Craig.

Not this time. She wouldn't run that same scene twice.

She took off running down the steps.

Chapter Twenty-four

Peyton pulled onto his street, surprised that Dair's car was still there. She should be at rehearsal. Had they canceled again? Was there news about Gayle?

All the lights were off at Marielle's. Maybe this was good. If the day had taught him anything, it was that he and Dair had to talk.

The lie still amazed him, made him want to break things. He thought of their history with embarrassment, knowing that the lie had been there, with them, when they made love, when they slept, when they laughed. All of it. There'd been not one moment between them of total truth. Ever.

And he feared there'd be not one moment of total trust between them ever again.

Had there ever been? How many times did she pause over a bruise, or a strange mood, or any time he felt sleepy? He felt defensive every time he caught a cold and wanted to nap.

And did he trust her? Even before this? No, he'd known she lied. He was an idiot for believing she never lied to him. He'd figured she did . . . but he'd never dreamed it would be this, something this big. Something so important.

The whine sputtered feedback in his head. Shodan whimpered beside him.

"Okay," he said, getting out of the car. He wasn't sure what he was doing here or what he'd say. He felt Shodan's joy as she trotted up the steps toward Blizzard at the back gate. But something was wrong with Blizzard. The Pyrenees whined and howled, and Peyton recognized that Blizzard had been the sound he'd assumed was in his head.

"What's the matter?" Peyton said, cringing. Mr. Lively would be so pissed off at this racket. It was a bloodcurdling sound, sad and desperate.

He unlatched the gate to go inside, but the second the gate opened, Blizzard hurled himself through it, almost knocking Peyton down. Shodan tried to follow Blizzard running away but came up short on her leash with a yelp. Peyton felt horrible, as though he'd yanked her intentionally, but it all happened so fast, and then she pulled him with surprising force toward the front yard.

"Blizzard!" Peyton called. "Blizzard! Come!" But the dog was a white blur scrambling down the ivy-covered hill and sprinting up the street.

Peyton stopped at the top of the yard, digging in his heels, Shodan pulling his arm, wanting to follow. Where was Blizzard going? And with such purpose? Part of Peyton coiled, expecting to hear a horn, car brakes squeal, and the thump.

He looked at the house, the front dark. Didn't Dair hear him yelling? Was she drunk? Weariness draped over him. He didn't think he had it in him tonight to deal with that.

Rather than chase Blizzard, Peyton turned back to the house. If Dair wasn't drunk, she could help him. Maybe Blizzard would head for Burnet Woods, and if they went armed with treats, they'd snare him. "Come on," he said, dragging Shodan.

But at the gate, the whine screeched to full force in his head. He stared at their open back door. Dair's purse on the porch. Her phone, her keys, her money strewn on the ground.

He thought of Gayle's garage. Those keys. That shoe.

Peyton ran into the house, calling, "Dair? Dair!" He let go of Shodan's leash, and she ran ahead of him, trailing the leash behind her. Dair wasn't here. No sign of her. Nothing.

Marielle's. Please let her be at Marielle's. He shoved away the thought that there had been no lights on at Marielle's as he bolted out the back door, Shodan following him. Marielle's door stood open a crack, too, unlocked. Jesus, what was going on?

"Marielle? Dair?" Peyton turned on the lights, and blinked at the bare kitchen. For a split second he feared he'd entered the wrong home. He *wanted* to have entered the wrong home. He wanted his wife and his friend and her son to be safe while he stumbled in a panic through the wrong house. But it wasn't the wrong house. It wasn't.

As though he'd injected too much cocaine, his heart raced with a speed that hurt him. He moved through the hall toward the living room, his legs stiff, his feet numb as they touched the floor. He turned on the living room light.

Marielle lay propped against the wall. Her legs were straight out in front of her, and one arm lay draped palm up in her lap, her sleeve rolled up past the elbow. He recognized her posture, but his mind refused to accept it. He knelt beside her, lifted her chin. She was breathing, drying blood bubbling in one nostril, caked above her lip. Her eyes fluttered open, and he saw her constricted, pinpoint pupils, barely visible in the glazed green discs of her irises. He looked at her right arm, displayed in her lap, and there it was—the red line of the tourniquet still remained in her skin, a puncture mark in the luscious thick vein inside her elbow, and at her side lay the telltale shoestring and the syringe, its fine needle glinting.

The needle hypnotized him. He smelled the faint chemical odor and stared transfixed. In his mind he saw himself pick it up, tie off his own arm with this shoestring. He ached to perform the old ritual.

Marielle made a gurgling sound, and he tore his gaze from the needle in time to see her spit up. Her face muscles twitched and her eyes rolled back in her head, only the bloodshot whites staring back at him. Shit. He made it to the kitchen phone and dialed 911. It only rang once, but that ring seemed to last an hour as he pulled the cord as far as it would stretch to keep his eye on Marielle. He had time to notice her hand clench and unclench in her lap during that one ring. Time to notice the pieces of shiny gray duct tape on the shin of her jeans. Time to notice a ring of pink raw skin on her wrist. The roll of duct tape near the front door. Next to the pair of scissors. And the wadded-up ball of duct tape that he knew had been wrapped around Marielle's wrists and legs. All the boxes in the living room, wrapped in this same duct tape. Slip Jig, hair puffed out as though she'd been electrocuted, approached the shuddering, moaning Marielle.

"911," a voice said at last. "What is your emergency?"

"Drug overdose."

Shodan clicked into the kitchen and stared up at him.

The voice asked him to verify the address. He said it was correct. The woman urged him in a soothing voice to stay on the line, help would be there soon.

Shodan clicked past him and out into the backyard.

"Is the victim conscious?"

"No."

"Is the victim breathing?"

"Yes . . . but it's not right . . . she's convulsing. She threw up."

"Can you touch the victim from where you are?"

"No."

She began to explain what she wanted him to do, but Shodan barked at something in the backyard, and he heard Dair say, *"Shodan, hush!"*

He dropped the phone and ran out the back door.

"Dair?!"

Shodan looked at him. She wagged her tail and whimpered.

"Dair?" Peyton shouted.

"Blizzard! Blizzard!" Dair's voice called, only it was above his head. He looked up and saw Captain Hook silhouetted in the moonlight. What was he—? Peyton looked at Mr. Lively's door and saw it stood wide open. Some sort of fire started in his guts. He ran back into Marielle's, saw that her twitching had subsided but the bubbles of blood on her nostril still rose and fell.

"Sir? . . . Sir?" he heard faintly from the phone on the counter, where it had sprung back when he released the cord.

He picked it up and said, "There may be another victim upstairs in this house. I think there was an intruder. And there's two other people missing—a woman and a little boy—I have to go check on the man upstairs."

"Sir? We need you to stay on the—"

But he dropped the phone again and bounded out the back door and up Mr. Lively's steps three at a time. In the dimly lit kitchen he saw the old man sitting up, rubbing his head.

"Mr. Lively? Are you okay? Paramedics are on the way."

"Where's the boy?" he asked. Lines of blood ran down his balding head.

"I don't know. Marielle is next—"

"He took the boy." Mr. Lively reached for the countertop to haul himself to his feet, but Peyton tried to stop him.

"Stay still. The police and paramedics are coming. What happened?"

"My door was open. Captain Hook was—" The old man suddenly jerked to life. "Captain Hook! Where's—"

"He's right outside. He's in a tree."

"Captain Hook!" Mr. Lively shouted.

"Papa? Papa, where are you?" came the answer from the backyard.

"Come to Papa!" the old man shouted, again trying to stand.

"Wait, Mr. Lively, wait. What happened to you?" Shit, he needed to go check on Marielle, but he was afraid the man wouldn't stay still if he left him.

"He was in here, waiting for me. I was next door, talking to Marielle, when I heard Captain Hook outside. I *know* I shut my door, but there he was, out, loose, in a tree. I came up to get treats, to try to get him down . . . the son of a bitch came from behind the door . . . and . . ." Mr. Lively touched the wound on top of his head and winced. He brought his hand away from his head and stared morosely at the blood. If the old guy had fallen, there's no telling what he might have cracked or broken.

"Mr. Lively, I have to go check on Marielle. Please, *please* wait for me before you get up, okay? Please?"

"He took the boy, you have to go after the boy."

Where were the fucking sirens? "Stay still, please?" Peyton didn't know what else to do. He ran down the stairs. The parrot fluttered down from the tree and landed on the back porch. Shodan approached him, haunches low to the ground. Shit. That's all they needed.

"Shodie, come!" Peyton called.

"Shodie, come!" the parrot repeated, mimicking him, and Shodan continued to walk toward the bird. Shit, what should he do? Save the parrot? Check on Marielle? She might have stopped breathing. Peyton headed for Marielle's back door, but Dair's cell phone rang from the ground. The dog, the bird, and Peyton all turned to it, startled. Peyton picked it up and answered.

"Oh! Peyton? Hi, it's Cass. We just wanted—"

"Is Dair with you?"

Sirens finally sounded, edging into his hearing, the way the whine did sometimes.

"No. Why?" His panic was contagious; she'd caught it already.

"I don't know where she is. I think, I think she's in danger. Some-one attacked Marielle and Mr. Lively and—"

"What happened?" Cass asked, her voice rising high.

The sirens grew louder.

"The police! Only the police!" Captain Hook said, flapping his wings, taking to the air again, sending Shodan scuttling backward. Peyton ducked as the large bird rose into the air before him.

"What the hell?" R.B. asked. He was on the phone, too.

Shodan barked.

The sirens stopped in front of the house.

Peyton ran to the front yard, phone in hand, waving. "Back here!" he shouted. "Back here!" Paramedics came running up the steps.

He led the paramedics to Marielle, who was still breathing, her eyes still unresponsive, her skin gray.

"And there's an old guy upstairs who got knocked out."

"Drugs?" the paramedic asked.

"No. He got hit. An attacker. The same person who did this to her."

The paramedic scooped the shoestring and syringe into a plastic bag, his expression suggesting that this woman had clearly done this to herself.

Another paramedic left to check on Mr. Lively, while two contin-ued to work on Marielle.

Peyton showed the paramedic the stairs to Mr. Lively's and found police at the back gate.

One of the cops, a young redheaded guy, looked familiar. He was one of the officers who'd talked to them at Gayle's.

Cassie's voice squawked from the phone he still carried. "Pey-ton? . . . Peyton?" He held it to his ear, telling Cass and R.B. as he told the cop, "Dair's missing. I got home and her stuff is all dumped by the back door." He pointed, and the cop looked. "And then I found Marielle, and called 911, and I thought I heard Dair, but it was only the parrot." Captain Hook now strutted back and forth on a tree branch.

The cop's expression shifted, and he said, "Yeah, we heard him do that the other night. Totally amazing."

"So we gotta find Dair," Peyton said. "She left in a hurry, or was abducted, or something. Her phone was out. I mean, look." He grew desperate. "Her car's here. Her keys are on that porch."

"Blizzard! Shodie!" Captain Hook called in Dair's voice.

"Is that Dair?" R.B. asked. "Is she there?"

"No, it's the bird."

"Where's Blizzard?" Cass asked.

"Oh, my God," Peyton said, remembering. "He ran off as soon as I got home."

The cop looked questioning. "Someone else was here and ran off?"

Peyton lowered the phone and said, "The dog."

"Big white dog, right?" the cop asked, looking pleased.

Peyton nodded and continued telling Cass, "I forgot as soon as I saw the stuff. But he was waiting for me to open the gate. I mean, the second I did, he bolted. Cass, can you talk to him? Was he following her?"

"Ohh . . . I don't know," Cass said.

The cop looked at Peyton strangely. "You're still talking about a dog?" His pencil was poised over his notepad. Peyton ignored him.

"Cass," R.B. said. "Do it."

"Maybe he knows where Dair is," Peyton said.

The cop looked as though he couldn't believe his ears.

Peyton heard Mr. Lively shouting, "I don't need to go to the hospital!"

"Papa? Papa, where are you?"

"Can't you try?" Peyton begged Cass.

She was crying. "It's just, I can't . . . I'm scared, so I can't—"

"Try," he said. "Please!"

"She's off the phone," R.B. said. "She'll try."

The paramedic in Mr. Lively's apartment appeared in his doorway and shouted, "Ray? Ray? I need a hand up here!"

"I'll go tell them," the redheaded cop said, jogging into Marielle's apartment.

They had to find Dair. They had to. Who the hell was doing this?

The cop and another paramedic came back out and climbed the stairs to Mr. Lively's.

Two other cops appeared at the back gate. "Did you find the others?" Peyton asked.

The new cops backed away from Peyton, apparently frightened by his neediness.

"It's the police. Just the police. Don't get yourself riled," the parrot said. The cops looked up bewildered, hands moving instinctively to their guns.

"It's just a parrot," Peyton told them. "He got loose. Do you know anything about the others?" he asked again.

"Others?" they asked, pulling out their notepads.

"I got it," the first cop said, coming down Mr. Lively's stairs. "We got a 911 on an OD, and when I arrived, we found . . ." He talked in hushed tones when he got to the gate.

Into the phone Peyton said, "What's Cass doing? Is she getting anything?"

"Hang on, son," R.B. said.

"I can't concentrate," he heard her cry. She was too upset, too worried.

The paramedics began bringing Mr. Lively down his stairs on the stretcher. "This is horseshit!" he yelled. "You can't make me pay for this if I don't want to go! I need to catch my bird!"

"Papa!" The parrot spread his wings wide.

"Captain, you come down here!" Mr. Lively called. Then to the paramedics, "If you take me away, he'll follow the ambulance and we'll never find him. He'll get lost."

They set the gurney down on the porch.

One of the cops stood on a trash can and reached for the parrot in the tree.

Captain Hook spread his wings and shrieked.

"What are you doing?" Mr. Lively yelled at the cop. "Get the hell away from there!"

The cop jumped down from the trash can, and Peyton wasn't sure whether he was afraid of the shrieking bird or the shrieking old man.

"What the hell are you doing?" Captain Hook yelled in Craig's voice. Craig's voice, so real, so eerie, just faintly warped as on a tape recorder. It was like an injection of ice water booting through Peyton's veins.

"Hey! Get the hell away from there!" Craig's voice screamed from the tree. *"What are you doing?"*

One paramedic sighed. "If we catch the bird, will you go willingly to the hospital?"

"I don't need to go to the hospital!"

The paramedics stared at each other, shaking their heads.

Peyton heard car doors out front but assumed it was the ambulance or the cruiser until he saw Malcolm appear at the gate. "Hey, do you know where Dair is?" Peyton called.

But Malcolm didn't seem to hear him. Malcolm looked around the backyard, his face pale, taking in the cops, the paramedics. "What's going on? Looks like it's a good thing Dair got that phone call."

"What the hell are you talking about? What phone call?"

"Some old guy, the guy upstairs called her at rehearsal and told her to come home. I was just—"

"Why?" Any second Peyton was going to smack someone.

"Marielle came home," Mr. Lively said. "She was moving out. Dair wanted me to call her." He looked around the yard. "Where is Dair?"

"She's missing!" Peyton screamed. "Her shit is everywhere—her phone, her purse, her keys—"

"Oh, my God," Malcolm said. He looked at her keys on the deck, as if befuddled. "Where . . . ?"

Peyton brought the phone back to his ear. "*Please,* Cassie."

Malcolm's hands went to his jacket zipper. He zipped it up and down.

A radio squawked, and Peyton heard, "We have the woman ready for transport. You guys ready?"

One paramedic touched the radio at his collar. "We're coming." Then he turned to Mr. Lively. "Sir, you have to come with us now. These people will catch your bird for you."

"Who's being transported?" Malcolm asked.

"Marielle."

"Oh, my God, what happened?"

"She got shot up with heroin, which is exactly what I think happened to Craig."

Peyton felt as if he might start to hyperventilate.

Mr. Lively sat up, causing one paramedic to curse, and crooned, "Captain! Captain, come down here. It's time to go inside."

"Blizzard, hush!" the parrot called in Dair's voice.

Cassie gasped in Peyton's ear. He held his breath. "He's seeing train tracks," she said.

Peyton knew she meant Blizzard. "Train tracks?" he asked. *"Train tracks?"* There were no fucking train tracks around here.

Malcolm stared at him. "When?" he said. "When did this happen to her? To Marielle?"

"Just now. She still had a tie-off mark on her arm."

"Oh, shit," Malcolm said, turning even paler. He looked around him, as if looking for something nearby.

"Hey! What the hell are you doing?"

"And there's a big animal near him," Cassie continued. "He's afraid of it, too . . . he's afraid to cross the train tracks; he doesn't know what they are . . . but this animal . . . it's a bird . . . but it's big, it's really big. . . . "

"Captain Hook?" Peyton asked her. "Captain Hook is out in the yard. Is that the bird?"

"Peyton," Malcolm whispered, "Andy isn't missing."

Peyton had Malcolm talking into one ear, Cassie in the other.

"No, it's a really big bird," Cassie said. "Lots of smells."

"Andy?" Peyton asked. "Andy's missing?"

"No," Malcolm said. "He left. He was standing right next to Dair when I told her about the phone call."

"He has to cross the tracks or he'll lose her," Cassie said.

"Peyton!" Malcolm insisted, tugging his arm. "He heard me say it. He heard me say Marielle was home. I think he left right then, before Dair did."

"Andy?" Peyton asked.

"Andy?" the parrot called in Craig's voice. *"Andy? What are you—"*

It was as if a knife punctured Peyton's lungs and he couldn't get air.

"Andy?" Craig's voice repeated in anguished disbelief. *"Andy? What are you—"*

Cassie moaned on the phone. "It's hard. He won't hear me . . . and I'm not . . . oh, God . . . this bird, oh . . . oh, my God, it's a peacock, I think."

"A peacock?!"

"What are you talking about?" Mr. Lively asked, his eyes narrowed. Malcolm kept a firm hold on Peyton's arm. He glanced at the cops, then whispered urgently, "I bought from him, Peyton. I owe him money. He's got heroin. He could've done this."

"He *did* do this," Peyton said. Pieces were falling into place, but they didn't mean shit unless he found Dair.

The paramedics attempted to take Mr. Lively's gurney off the porch, but he sat up, forcing them to stop or topple him off the porch. "What are you talking about?" the old man insisted. "Train tracks and peacocks?"

Peyton didn't know how to explain what Cassie was doing, so he just blurted, "This is where we think Dair is. And maybe Matt." His mind whirred. Andy. The supplier. Pieces, but still . . .

"Mr. Lively, please!" the paramedic insisted. "We have to transport your neighbor. You don't want to jeopardize that woman's life, do you?"

Please let Dair be safe somewhere. Not drugged up. Not bashed in the head.

Cassie moaned again. "He's not sure which way she went. And there's so many smells. He's on asphalt; it's hard to scent her. . . ."

"I don't know what the hell you're doing," Mr. Lively said, "but you think they're with a peacock and train tracks?"

Peyton nodded. "And asphalt."

"It's the zoo," Mr. Lively said, throwing his skinny legs over the gurney. "They're at the zoo."

Chapter Twenty-five

Dair should have known this was where Matt would run, but she didn't like it. It was too big, too sprawling, with way too many places to hide.

The zoo at night.

There were nightwatchmen. Locks. A fence. But Matt, small and lithe as a cat, scrambled right up and over the tall chain-link fence, the three strands of barbed wire not slowing him a bit.

Adrenaline fueled the man chasing Matt, but the wire caught him, and Dair heard him curse. A long black wig hung trapped on the fence when the man dropped to the other side. Dair tried to use the wig to protect her hands from the barbs but still shredded her palms before getting over the fence herself.

Once inside the zoo, of course, she lost sight of both Matt and the man. The man.

Andy.

Andy, who had been here only two months. Who had "never met" Marielle. Who'd asked about her, whether or not she'd be here or there. Who had a deaf twin. God, Dair'd been so stupid.

She wasn't sure either Matt or Andy knew she followed them. Her breath sounded amplified, and she hovered near the Bald Eagle Eyrie, not sure which way to go. She heard nothing. Even the birds in the flight cage were quiet.

Where were the nightwatchmen? There were several here, on duty, she knew. Should she try to get into a building for a phone? Would the shattering glass give away her location? Did she care? Maybe it was better if Andy came after her, not Matt.

Just then she heard, "Matthew!" called again.

The voice came from her left, so she ran past the Reptile House, hugging the shadows, avoiding the soft white light that spilled from the exhibit buildings. She wished her breath and heartbeat would quiet so she could hear something besides her own *thunk thunk thunk*.

Dair darted across the open intersection, over the train tracks, then paused again, where there were decorative grasses to cover her. She crept along, listening for a clue. Something large moved in front of her in the darkness, and she froze. A resting peacock stood up and lifted its tail feathers. "Sorry," she whispered.

Hollow footsteps sounded to her right. Someone walked on the wooden bridge through the Gibbon Islands. Light, rapid steps—probably Matt. Dair didn't call out or step onto the walkway herself. The footsteps moved away from her, so she cut down the asphalt path, circling around the Gibbon Islands exhibit, hoping to see Matt on the other side.

Sure enough, there he was, his head of white curls bouncing on the path as he ran ahead of her. "Matt!" she hissed. "Matt! It's Dair!"

"Hey!" she heard someone call, then curse. It wasn't Andy. A watchman.

"Call the police!" she called over her shoulder as she ran. She couldn't stop to explain. She couldn't lose Matt.

Matt kept running, rounding Swan Lake and heading for the Vanishing Giants exhibit. Dair ran after him, knowing she was too loud, knowing that as she ran she wasn't keeping a watch out, but knowing she couldn't risk losing sight of him.

Dair caught up, grabbed him and hugged him close, both of them panting. "It's me," she whispered. "It's Dair." He hugged her tight enough to bruise.

She got her bearings in the dark. "C'mon," she whispered, tugging him down the brick path toward the Elephant House in the Vanishing Giants exhibit. Surely there'd be handlers inside and a phone. Holding hands, they cut across the elephant performance yard, behind the bleachers, and headed for the doorway, where a light was on. "Keep a watch behind us," Dair whispered as she reached for the doorknob. Damn. Locked. She raised her hand to knock on the glass, when Matt grabbed her arm, stopping her.

Someone was walking on the brick path toward the building. It could be a watchman, but . . . they crept out of the light and huddled against the building.

"Matthew?" Andy called softly. They were stuck. Dead end. Unless . . . Dair threw her leg over the wooden post fence of the okapi enclosure.

"What are you doing?" Matt whispered, grabbing her hand tighter.

"It's okay," she said, close to his ear. "The animals are inside the building at night. It's safe. He won't know that. He won't come into an exhibit."

The whites of Matt's eyes glowed in the moonlight, but he climbed over the fence. The dry grass crunched under their feet, making Dair wince, as they scurried through the shallow ditch of the safety moat. She pulled on his arm to slow him. "There's electric wire here somewhere," she said. She peered through the darkness for the wire she knew was four feet or so from the fence. The electric wire should be shut off at night, but she didn't want to count on it. She listened for its hum but heard only distant traffic on the street above. They stepped forward tentatively, holding hands. Matt squeezed her hand and pointed to where the wire glinted in the moonlight about two and a half feet off the ground.

Dair nodded. Although she was certain it was dead, they both crawled under it on their bellies and picked through the crackling, dusty grass to a low shrub. They sat behind it, holding hands, catching their breath.

She heard deep, bass barking. "Is that Blizzard?" Matt whispered.

She put a finger over her lips. It sure sounded like Blizzard, but he'd been inside the locked fence in the backyard. She hadn't taken her eyes from the brick path.

Craig's fiancée, what's her name? Marilyn?

"Matt? Who is he? Why is he following you?"

Matt put his mouth to her ear, and she smelled milk on his breath. "My mom lied," he said, anger under his whisper. "That's my dad. He's not dead. He looks just like my dad in the picture."

That picture. That stolen picture. Dair knew that the photo had been stolen so that she wouldn't recognize him.

"She lied. He was alive all this time, and she wouldn't let me see him. He said he's been looking for me a long time and he finally found us."

"When did he say that?"

"Tonight. He came over tonight."

Dair had led Andy straight to them.

"She said he was dead," Matt said. "I hate her."

"Shh." Dair didn't know what to say. "You don't hate your mom."

"She lied!" he said too loudly. Dair put an arm around him, a hand over his mouth.

"Matt. We're hiding in the zoo in the middle of the night. What's wrong with this picture? If you're so happy to have a dad, why are you running from him?"

He looked up at her, eyes glittering in the moonlight. "He . . . scared me. And he was mean to my mom. He's *crazy.*"

Dair nodded. Yes, he was. He'd been there, at Craig's death. Dair remembered Craig looking back across 75, at the hillside, up toward the houses. Andy must have been *chasing* Craig. He'd known it was Craig as they'd watched the paramedics load the body.

"But he's still my dad. I still had a dad; he wasn't dead. She *lied.* That isn't fair." His tears sparkled. Dair hugged him close to her, keeping her eyes on the brick path. She heard what sounded like Blizzard's deep bark even closer.

Had Blizzard gotten out of the yard? Followed her here?

So . . . Andy. Andy was Gayle's "mystery" boyfriend? If he had a key . . . knew Gayle's house . . . when Craig interrupted Andy breaking into Marielle's, had Andy knocked Craig out and dragged him to Gayle's? Her house was only a mile away, but . . . why? To kill him? What if—God, what if Dair had walked in on that? What if Craig and Andy had actually been in Gayle's house when Dair fed Tuxedo that morning?

Blizzard barked again. He was *here,* at the zoo. It was a questioning bark, not a threatening one.

And Tibaba, the elephant, answered him with a blast of her trumpet that made Dair and Matt hunch their shoulders.

Dair turned back to the path. Andy came into sight on the path, and Dair squeezed Matt's hand. Andy stopped at the Elephant House door then stood very still. He seemed to look right at them.

Blizzard barked again, very close. Andy turned toward the sound.

Tibaba trumpeted again. "Are you sure she's inside?" Matt whispered. Dair nodded. Andy didn't turn toward the elephant noise at all. He continued staring to his right. And sure enough, the white body of Blizzard came loping down that brick path. Oh, God.

Dair heard Blizzard growl from a hundred yards away.

"Hey there, Blizzard," Andy said. "Good dog, good boy. Hey now."

How did he know Blizzard's name? Had he heard her say it that day under the overpass on Clifton Avenue? Or had he been watching them all for the two months he'd been in Cincinnati?

Sirens sounded in the distance. *Please, please let the police be on the way.*

Dair tried to communicate with Blizzard, tried to visualize him *not* going to Andy.

But Blizzard turned toward her, ears lifted.

Shit. That wouldn't work. Dair didn't want the dog to give them away.

Dair couldn't breathe. She shouldn't breathe. She didn't deserve to. She was an idiot. How could she not have put this together?

Andy fumbled with something in his pocket, backing away from the dog.

The sirens were close but passed by, sounding as if they were heading up Vine Street.

Something glinted in his hand. What did he have? A knife? "C'mere," she heard Andy say. "C'mere."

Blizzard turned his attention back to Andy, his growl becoming a snarl.

"Matt," Dair whispered, "stay here. Promise me that no matter what happens you'll stay right here by this bush."

"But what are you—"

"I can't let him hurt Blizzard. I'll lead him away. You stay here, Matt. Don't come out until it's safe, no matter what happens to me."

"But—"

Dair crawled away from the bush, and both Andy and Blizzard turned toward her, Blizzard stopping his growling. Dair flattened herself to the ground and tried not to breathe.

"Matthew?" Andy called.

And Blizzard sprang. He leapt at Andy, but Andy heard it coming and swung the hand holding the unidentified object at the dog. Both cried out at once, Andy's yell low and primal, Blizzard's yelp high and surprised. Blizzard knocked Andy to the ground, then turned to his side, crying and snapping at himself. Dair stood and ran for the fence, but Andy scrambled to his feet and kicked Blizzard, hard, in the ribs; Dair heard the sound, felt it in her own side like fire. "Hey!" she screamed. Andy turned his attention to her, giving Blizzard the chance to move out of range, but Dair forgot the electric wire, which caught her at the knees and sent her skidding into the safety ditch, her head, one shoulder, one hip, and her knees hitting the ground with punishing thuds as she tumbled. She came to a stop and lay frozen. It took a moment to find air. Blizzard's yelps drove her on, forcing her up off the ground; but just as she pushed herself to sitting, she was yanked to her feet by the hair. Before she could scream, Andy stabbed something into her thigh. Sudden, sharp pain, like a snakebite. It stopped the sound in her throat.

She managed to pull against his hand in her hair to look down. A hypodermic needle. Warmth spread through her thigh and buttock, whatever he'd injected her with traveling through her like venom. Then he left the needle there, flopping in her jeans-clad thigh, and clamped a hand over her mouth and nose.

She was lifted and hauled bodily over the wooden post fence back to the brick path. All she could breathe was that hand, that skin . . . and the scent of warm apples.

She stopped struggling. For the moment. Saving her energy.

What had he given her? Heroin? But it wasn't in a vein . . . would it affect her?

"Shut the fuck up," Andy warned. "Don't make a sound or you're dead." Oh, God. What had he done to Marielle? Because of Dair he'd known Marielle was home.

Her eyes stung from this realization and from her smarting scalp, where he still kept hold of a fistful of hair.

He let go of her mouth and allowed her to turn to face him. He grinned and ran a hand through his hair. It shone white in the moonlight like Matthew's.

Blizzard still turned in circles, biting at his side, yipping feebly.

"Your fucking dog bit me," he said, twisting her hair again.

"What did you do to him?" she asked, watching Blizzard whirl and whirl, his breath in wheezy, high-pitched pants.

Andy slapped her hard, his hand covering what felt like one half of her face. Teeth rattled in her head.

"I said don't make a sound!" he hissed. He tried slapping her again, but she caught his arm with her hands.

"Stop it!" Matt shouted. Dair's heart sank.

Andy dragged her by the hair toward the fence, with one arm. She kept hold of his other and kicked him repeatedly in the shin—the needle bobbing, still embedded in her thigh—but he acted as if he felt no pain. That hot sensation still spread through her leg, as if spilled coffee seeped through her clothes.

"Matthew?" Andy called. "Matthew, buddy, where are you?"

"Stop hurting her!" Matt's voice called.

The elephant trumpeted again. Angry and bellowing.

Dair didn't look toward Matt. She didn't want to give him away. She watched Andy's face as he searched the dark habitat and kept kicking him, digging her nails into his arm.

"Is there an elephant loose out there?" he asked her, putting one foot on the fence as if he would climb over and drag her with him.

"Yes."

"Matt! You have to come out! The elephant could hurt you."

"The elephant is inside!" Matt said.

"No, it's not," Andy said. "Please. They're very dangerous."

"Dair said the elephant is inside."

"You bitch!" He yanked his arm free from her grasp and punched her in the ribs.

She cried out and bent over, only to be yanked up by the hair again.

"Stop it!" Matt screamed. She saw his white hair pop up from behind the bush. "Stop hurting her!"

"I'll stop hurting her if you come out," Andy said.

"Don't believe him, Matt," Dair called. "Don't come out."

"Do you promise?" Matt asked, walking from the bush toward the wire.

"Yes, I promise," Andy said. "I don't want to hurt anybody. I don't want to hurt you. I just want to be with you. Aren't you mad she kept us apart?"

Oh, God. Oh, God. Don't fall for this, Matt. "Matt, don't listen to him. He's a liar!"

Andy punched her again, but she'd anticipated this one and twisted away from the brunt of it, only getting yanked by the hair. Her scalp was going numb. She elbowed him in the gut, but he caught her arm and twisted it behind her back. He pressed her hard against the wooden fence, his whole body weight pinning her so she couldn't move her legs. This helplessness infuriated her.

Matt had stopped in his tracks. "You said you wouldn't hurt her."

"I said I wouldn't hurt her if you came with me."

"No," Matt said. "You said you wouldn't hurt her if I came out. I'm out."

"I meant out *here*," Andy said, gesturing toward the brick path.

"Don't do it, Matt," Dair said. "Don't come out here. I'll be okay."

"But—"

"Where's your mom, Matt?" she asked. "Did he hurt her?"

Andy twisted her hair, hard, forcing her to contort herself in a back bend.

"Matthew's *mother*," Andy spat out, "is the liar. She told you I was dead, Matt."

Blizzard's panting grew more pronounced, his circling more unsteady. He weaved, whimpering and biting at his side. What had Andy done? Given him drugs, too? But Dair didn't feel any affects from the drug herself, other than a hot heaviness in her thigh.

"Why?" Matt asked. "Why did she tell me you were dead?"

"How should I know? She was a selfish *bitch,* and she didn't want you to have a father. She wanted to be in charge."

"She wanted to protect you, Matt!" Dair yelled. Andy didn't punch her this time but clamped a hand over her mouth again, his thumb and fingers digging into her jaw so hard that she saw white light, his other fist still firmly embedded in her hair.

Marielle had been right to run. And she'd kept up a harder lie than Dair had. And for better reasons. But Andy . . . Andy was the best liar Dair knew, had ever encountered.

"She couldn't tell you about me or she couldn't marry Craig."

"Did you kill Craig?" Matt asked.

The grip tightened over Dair's mouth. "No, I didn't kill Craig. I actually *liked* Craig. Craig would marry your *mother,* and then she wouldn't want you anymore, and I could be with you."

This was so sick, so twisted. Please Matt, Dair thought, you're smarter than that.

"I didn't *mean* to kill Craig," Andy whispered to Dair so Matt couldn't hear him. "He just showed up at the wrong time. I took great pains *not* to kill him; I'm not a bad person. I only wanted what was mine. I only wanted him doped up, out of the way, until I got Matt. It would have fucking worked"—Andy yanked Dair's hair—"it only took me ten minutes to dump him at Gayle's. He'd have to explain the drugs and why he came to and found himself at her house, after me and Matt were long gone. But then . . ." Andy dug his nails into her mouth. "When I went back to your house, your fucking husband was there. And then Ella came home. And then *you* came home. What the fuck was I supposed to do with Craig *then?*"

Your husband came home. What? Saturday morning? Peyton had come by the house? And who was Ella?

Andy kept whispering, "I thought I had to kill him then. But I didn't. He killed himself. You saw it. I saw it. Twenty people saw it."

Andy tightened his grip before Dair could protest. "The dress was a perfect touch—I couldn't have thought of that myself. Ooh, was he a cross-dresser? Oh, my God, was he gay? And then you told me you'd *worn* the dress. So I told Gayle. It just kept getting better and better." He laughed. "Really, he was only too modest to make his escape naked. And still too high to think it mattered."

So Andy had stripped Craig. And once Craig died, he'd had to clean up Gayle's house. So the clothes had gone back to Marielle's. What did Andy care if it implicated Marielle.

Dair wanted to stomp on Andy's feet or kick him, but she was pinned against the fence. Her jaw hurt so badly that it was hard to move, much less contemplate inviting more abuse. And that heat was traveling up her back, into her shoulders and neck. Why was he telling her all this? Was he going to kill her?

Matt crept close and crawled under the wire on his belly. *No, no, no,* Dair tried to will him. *Stay away! Run away!*

More sirens sounded in the distance. Please, Dair prayed.

Andy must've put the clothes in Marielle's house Sunday morning when he saw Dair and Marielle leave with the dogs. Had he expected to find Matt alone? But Peyton had been there. Thank God. And Peyton had taken Matt next door to make pancakes.

Blizzard stopped spinning and now lay down and faced them, at attention, head raised. He breathed raggedly but seemed in less pain than before.

Matt approached the railing, several yards to the right of them. He stopped on the other side of it and said, "What were you whispering?"

"Don't move," Andy whispered to Dair, releasing the grip on her hair. "Understand?"

She nodded.

Andy let go of her mouth, and Dair called, "He killed Craig! And Gayle! Don't believe—"

The hand clapped back over her face, fingers grinding her cheeks against her teeth. She tasted blood. "I didn't fucking kill Gayle," he hissed. "*You* did, filling her stupid little head with crap about the dress and her house and who had keys. She was too stupid to put it all together herself—you had to tell her and *fuck everything up.*" Dair feared his thumb would rip through her cheek into her mouth. Little purple sparks danced before her eyes.

The sirens were louder, stopping on the street above them. *Thank God, thank God.*

Blizzard growled and moved closer, crawling on his belly. Dair tried to connect with him, as she had at the barn that afternoon—was that only that afternoon?—but felt only intense pain. Burning pain in her lower back. Was that his pain or hers? Oh, God. Gayle.

Matt put his short leg over the fence and slithered across it. Her heart pounded. *Don't come closer, Matt. Don't.* Blizzard growled again.

Matt looked at Dair, right in her eyes. *Run away!* she screamed inside her head. She visualized him fleeing, running out to the street, where all those trick-or-treaters roamed, where she heard car doors and hoped it was police, where someone would help him. She tried to ignore the scalding pain in her back and visualize this with all her might. Matt blinked. Then he looked up at Andy. He chewed his lip as he did when he was thinking something over. And then he turned and took off running.

Blizzard's deep, throaty growl turned into a snarl. Dair planted an elbow hard in Andy's belly and turned to wrap her arms around his waist, her legs around his thighs, miring him down with her weight. He tried to run. Blizzard's snarls filled her ears, and white fur filled her vision. She lost her grip and slid, but caught hold of one of Andy's thighs. Every second she held on to Andy was more chance for Matt to get away. Hauling Dair and the dog, Andy struggled forward, punching at them both. A blow to Dair's ear made her lose her grasp further, and she only had his ankle; her body dragged, the hypodermic scraping across the bricks. Andy jerked his ankle free of her grip and kicked her in the side of the head.

The purple sparks blurred into a solid white heat before her eyes. Then blackness. And a howling in her ears, like a pack of wolves.

Chapter Twenty-six

Cold seeped through Dair's jeans and sweater.

How much time had passed? Had she slept for hours?

She tried to pry her eyelids open but saw only moonlight, too bright, hurting her eyes and her throbbing brain.

Where was she? . . . It smelled . . . it smelled like a barn. . . .

Someone breathed heavily. As if they'd been running. They should relax. Just relax and lie down . . . like her. . . .

Dair opened her lips to call to whoever it was but found her mouth stripped dry. Her brain felt too big for her skull, as though it might start squeezing out of her ears. She moaned.

Another moan answered her, and she moved her head to find the source of the sound. Something large and white crawled toward her. She blinked, and it came into a hazy focus. Blizzard. Her dog, Blizzard, panting.

Dair sat up, head throbbing.

The elephant trumpeted in the Vanishing Giants building behind her, and the sound sliced into her swollen, aching brain like needles.

Needles.

She remembered. She was at the zoo. Dair looked down at her leg just as heat—intense, pleasant, almost sexual heat—rushed through her entire body. She sighed. Ahh . . . Her head felt so much better.

She reached, with hands that suddenly seemed to weigh fifty pounds, and pulled the needle from her thigh. She tossed it to the side and heard it clink on the brick path.

Blizzard reached her and licked her face. His nose was hot and dry. "Oh, sweetheart," she slurred, surprised by how difficult it was to move the muscles in her face. She tried to communicate with him, tried to be open, but some sort of song entered her brain, a soft, soothing lullaby. She couldn't hear or concentrate over it. And she didn't really want to.

Blizzard pushed her with his head. Okay. He was right. She should get up. She tried, but her hands and feet were so impossibly heavy and seemed to actually reach the bricks two full seconds behind when her eyes thought they had. The ground kept shifting beneath her. The lullaby entered her muscles, made her slow, made her sleepy.

Poor Blizzard crawled beside her, but his back end seemed useless; it dragged along behind him. Dair thought maybe she could carry him, but when she tried, the moonlit landscape spun in her vision, and Blizzard yelped anyway.

"I'm so sorry, baby." Her tongue felt thicker than she remembered, her lips fat and so dry. She tried to make Blizzard stay, but if she staggered on without him, he'd start to crawl, dragging his back legs. Dair sat beside him, stroking his long hair. "I have to get help for us." She wanted nothing more than to curl up to sleep, using Blizzard as her pillow, cozy and warm. The lullaby hummed sweetly in her brain and lulled her, but she knew Blizzard needed a vet.

"Stay. Please? Stay?" she begged Blizzard. This time he did. "Good dog," she said, her own voice sounding distorted. "Good boy."

She stood, looked at him over her shoulder . . . and stepped into nothingness.

She flailed in the darkness and fell hard. She heard a pop, like a flashbulb, although the light and heat seemed to be in her thigh. She lay still at the bottom of the four steps she'd forgotten in the path. Blizzard's head appeared at the top of the stairs. He whined.

"No, sweetie," she said. It was only four steps, but with his hind end, he couldn't do it. "Stay." She sat up, the lullaby's pace cranked high, like an ice-cream truck going fifty-five miles an hour.

Something went wrong between sitting and standing, though. There was something very wrong about setting her right foot down. The lullaby cranked to an unbearable volume and then stopped. . . .

And Dair dreamed her old cat, Snowflake, came to her, her long white hair tickling Dair's face, her warm breath tickling Dair's nose. In the dream Dair said, "I can't get up."

"No," Snowflake said. "You stay. Good girl."

She lay on Dair's chest, as she always did. Her purr vibrated through Dair's torso. "A chickadee burst out of me," Dair said to her, stroking her hair.

"I know," the cat said. "I caught it."

"Oh, no, what did you do with it?"

"I ate it."

"Ohhh . . . no, Snowflake. I needed that bird."

"Not anymore," she said.

Dair sighed and let the purring heal her sternum and all the splintered bone.

"There's something else in you," the cat said.

"What?" Dair asked.

Snowflake didn't answer.

Dair forced her lids open and looked into those glacier pool eyes. "A baby?" she asked. She couldn't think of anything else.

Snowflake nodded and licked one front paw. "That's why you don't need the bird."

"But . . . I don't want . . . that's not . . ."

"Shhh," Snowflake purred, stretching out the paw and shutting Dair's eyes.

"But, I—"

"Shhh," the cat said again, putting a paw on Dair's mouth.

Snowflake's purring blended beautifully with the lullaby, which had returned to a normal, soothing speed and volume.

An image of herself floating at the edge of a swimming pool entered Dair's brain. She let go of the wall and drifted away.

Chapter Twenty-seven

Peyton ran down the street toward the zoo, the police cars already passing them, lights on. Groups of kids dressed as ghouls and monsters parted for them. Wasn't it late for them to still be out? Shouldn't they be home?

Then he felt it.

A sensation like the earth opening beneath him, like finding himself above a wide-open expanse of air, free-falling.

Dair was hurt.

The sensation was worse than when she'd told him there was no twin. It was worse than realizing he'd believed in something nonexistent for eight years.

None of that mattered.

The only thing true was that he loved that woman.

She was a liar. And an alcoholic. And he didn't want to live without her.

He ran.

He thought he hallucinated when he recognized Matthew running toward him from a cluster of cops at the Erkenbrecher Avenue pedestrian gate. "Peyton!" Matt yelled. Peyton swooped him up into his arms. He kissed the boy's sweaty blond curls.

Peyton asked, "Where's Dair?" at the exact second Matt said, "Dair's still in there!"

Peyton looked at the assembly of cops, bits and pieces of their conversation reaching his ears. "Nightwatchman . . . call about an intruder . . . drug overdose . . . connected to the man in the dress." It would take forever for the two groups to make each other understand the connection. Peyton didn't understand it himself.

"My wife is still in there!" Peyton yelled.

Matt said, "They were at the Vanishing Giants. I'll show you."

"No," a cop said, trying to block Matthew. "You stay here. Was the man armed?"

Matt let go of Peyton's hand and ducked around the cop. Matt ran, and Peyton followed.

The cop cursed but followed, too.

Matt stopped at an intersection where the asphalt path branched into a brick one. Peyton caught up to him. Matt peered ahead of them into the darkness and said, "She was right—" when Peyton sensed someone else, something predatory, moving for them, to attack.

Peyton turned his head and saw the man lunging from behind tall decorative grass, reaching for Matthew. Peyton recognized him. He'd been vaguely familiar to him because of Matthew's photo. Nine years older, without a beard, but still pretty much the same man.

This same man had killed Craig. Had harmed Marielle and maybe Dair, too.

The man was already off balance, as an attacker always was. As if he'd rehearsed it a million times, Peyton placed his hands on Andy's closest outstretched arm and redirected Andy's energy, using Andy's own lunge, his own speed, his own desperation, to send him forward and down.

As Andy fell, Peyton kept Andy's fragile arm in his grasp and had one split second to review his options. He could direct his own energy to fall with Andy, snapping his spine with his knee. He longed to feel Andy's vertebrae pop under his kneecap. He hungered to aim high, the base of his neck, to insure paralysis if Andy survived. He could aim for a kidney instead, his entire body weight concentrated into six inches of force.

A split second. No more. Peyton's body responded with its training, with what he had practiced. It was as if he watched himself control Andy's descent. Peyton sent him, none too gently, to the asphalt face first. But Peyton remained standing.

He kept Andy's arm locked behind him, in excruciating pain. Pain that would end the second Peyton released him.

He took a deep breath and looked at the cops now surrounding them. "I got him," one cop said, kneeling down to cuff Andy. Peyton let them take Andy's arm and walked away from him, back up the path in the direction he'd been heading.

"Dair's still here somewhere," he said, breaking into a run again.

Dair heard Peyton's voice. Maybe she would dream of Peyton, too. How nice.

"Dair? Love? Talk to me." He was crying. Oh, she'd made him so sad.

Dair pried open her eyes, even though she still felt Snowflake on her chest and knew the cat would close them. Snowflake didn't, though, and Dair stared up into Peyton's face.

"I'm sorry," she whispered.

"Oh, God." He leaned down and kissed her. "I love you, Dair." He kissed her forehead, her nose, her lips. What a nice dream. Dair thought she'd reached up to touch him but found her fingers still entwined in Snowflake's hair.

Peyton moved out of her vision, and Dair winced in the moon-light until he returned.

"Don't move, love," he said, touching her forehead, looking at a spot just above her left ear. "Stay still." Then he looked up, away from her, and shouted, "Over here! Hurry up!"

"Call my dad, Peyton. Blizzard's hurt bad. He's up there. I told him to stay—"

"Blizzard's right here," he said, wiping his eyes.

Dair turned her head to the side and twisted her neck to look down at her chest. Sure enough, the long white hair she stroked was the Great Pyrenees's, his head and one paw draped over her torso, huddled against her side.

"His nose is hot. He needs a vet."

"Shh," Peyton said, just as Snowflake had. "I'll take care of him."

"Let's move the dog," an unfamiliar voice said.

And in her peripheral vision Dair saw someone helping Blizzard off her.

"Oh, God," Peyton said, lifting one of her eyelids, bringing his eyes close to her own. "She's on heroin, too."

"I am not!" Dair protested. It was one thing for him to call her a drunk, but . . . but then she remembered. . . .

And Peyton's face stayed with her while they put a brace around her neck and a board got wriggled under her. And then she was lifted up up up toward the moon. She giggled.

"Guess she doesn't need a painkiller, does she?" someone said.

"Nope," Peyton whispered, stroking her hair back. He kissed her forehead again.

"Her vitals are good," another voice said. All these voices hovered around her, thick and lazily. They complemented the lullaby that still serenaded her in the background. "She's not in overdose, just high as a kite."

Suddenly Dair's view was not the moon, but a flat white ceiling. Doors slammed.

"Peyton? I'm not dreaming, am I?"

"Nope."

"Where are we going?"

"To the hospital, love. We think you broke your leg."

"Matthew's okay?"

"Yes. They took Marielle to the hospital already. Mr. Lively, too."

"Blizzard's hurt," she said, the tears scalding her cheeks.

"Shh," Peyton said, taking her hand. He was crying, too.

"It wasn't Malcolm."

He nodded. "I know."

"Andy was Iago. He was good."

"Hush, love," Peyton said.

"And I think I'm pregnant."

"What?"

"That's what Snowflake said. Remember my cat? She told me that, just now, at the zoo."

He shook his head and laughed.

He kissed her hand. "Relax," he said. "Enjoy the ride, love. Enjoy the ride."

And Dair did.

Chapter Twenty-eight

Dair vaguely remembered parts of the hospital. She couldn't keep track of people. One minute Peyton held her hand, but the next time she looked he'd be her mother. She'd blink and it was her dad, rubbing her feet because she said they were cold.

They cut her clothes off with scissors, but she didn't care. They X-rayed her for what seemed like the entire night, but that was just peachy. Whatever they needed to do, she didn't want them to mind her. She just floated along on her comfy raft of serenity and calm.

Eventually she woke up. Really woke up. In a recovery room, in a circle of beds surrounding a giant station of desks. With a trashed throat and a groggy postanesthetic hangover. She was certain someone had beaten her with a baseball bat. She groaned.

A nurse rushed over to her. "Hello there, Dair," she said. "How are you feeling?"

Dair opened her mouth, but her voice wouldn't even work. It took three tries to croak out, "Like shit."

The nurse smiled. Her name tag read "Emilia." Dair blinked and wondered if she were truly conscious yet.

"What . . ." She tried to clear her throat. "What happened to me? Did I break my leg?"

"Yes," Emilia said. "You broke your right femur. At the hip. The ball of the ball-and-socket joint broke off."

Dair reached under the thin sheet and felt her leg. "Why don't I have a cast?"

"You have a pin in your hip. A cast isn't necessary."

Dair moved her hand to her hip. Felt the gauze and tape.

"I need to have a pregnancy test."

"Well . . . I . . . I suppose we can—why don't I get the doctor?"

Dair grabbed the nurse's wrist. "I have a baby inside me. That's what she said."

Emilia opened her lips in surprise, paling just a shade. "That's what who said?"

Dair opened her mouth to speak but remembered the dream and was suddenly mortified. "I—I'm sorry. I feel really—" She brought a hand to her head and noticed her palms were raw and scraped.

"You were given heroin," the nurse said. "Do you remember that?"

Dair nodded and touched her thigh, still able to see the needle flopping there in her memory. "I need a drink," she said.

Emilia smiled and said, "How about some ice chips?"

"Oh . . . okay." What she'd really meant was a vodka and cranberry juice.

"And I'll get the doctor. And your husband." She walked away, and Dair shifted, wincing. She lifted the sheet again and pulled up her blue-dotted hospital nightgown to look. Hieroglyphs of purple-and-red bruises mottled her legs and what she could see of her belly. Her right upper thigh all the way up to her waist was bright red-dish orange, and the bite of Betadine or iodine reached her nostrils. And in the middle of all that orange, the hip joint in question was covered in gauze. Not even a big piece of gauze. They'd put a pin in her hip and that was all the damage done? That little six-inch square? But on her belly, inside her hipbone, was another incision, this one only an inch long, stitched and held closed with thin white strips. Dair touched it with her fingertips and felt frightened for some reason.

"Hey, love," Peyton said, sitting beside her. He hadn't shaved, and his eyes were bloodshot. His clothes looked as though he'd slept in them.

"I'm sorry," Dair said.

"Shut up," he said gently.

"Do you know what this is?" She showed him the incision.

"Um . . . not yet . . . they found something in X ray and . . ." He paused.

Dair looked up for Emilia and saw her talking to a young, petite woman who was writing something in a chart. At the nurse's words, the woman—apparently Dair's doctor—lifted her head, saw Dair watching her, and smiled. The doctor had short brown hair and tiny green-framed glasses. The doctor walked toward Dair with the nurse.

Dair heard Emilia say, "Do you think she could have subconsciously heard us? While she was under?"

"Hi," the doctor said to Dair. "I'm not sure you remember me, although we talked last night." She reached out to shake Dair's hand. "I'm Dr. Burkett. I'm your orthopedic surgeon."

"What's this?" Dair lowered the sheet to show the mysterious incision.

"Ahh," Dr. Burkett said, pulling up a stool beside the bed. "That's very interesting."

Panic backed up in Dair's throat. "But *what is it?* It's not part of the hip surgery?"

Dr. Burkett raised her eyebrows at Dair's urgency. "No, it's nothing to worry about at all. Please understand that. When we X-rayed your leg we saw what we thought to be some sort of tumor or cyst."

Oh, God. "A tumor?" Dair whispered.

"Hey . . ." Dr. Burkett squeezed her hand. "It wasn't a tumor. We *thought* it was; it stood out so clearly in the X ray. And we got your husband's permission to biopsy it while you were under, and since it was so isolated and self-contained, we simply removed it—"

"What was it?" Dair asked.

"Okay!" The doctor held up her hands. "We just found out about an hour ago. It's called a teratoma."

"Teratoma." The word prickled in Dair's mouth. It sounded like poison.

"The lab biopsied it and found it to be made up of bits of hair and teeth and fetal bones."

Dair looked at the doctor's face and thought she was speaking a foreign language.

Dr. Burkett straightened her glasses. "Teratomas are cysts that are remnants of a vanished twin. They're really very fascinating."

Dair blinked. "A twin?" She looked at Peyton, who appeared paralyzed, staring at Dr. Burkett in awe as if she'd just cured Dair of cancer. "I—I don't understand. Was this *my* baby somehow? Some weird sort of pregnancy thing?"

"No, no, no. It's *your* twin. You were a twin for a time in the womb, and for a hundred different possible reasons, you absorbed the other twin and were born a singleton. It happens all the time."

A twin. She'd been a twin? "Oh, my God," Dair whispered.

The doctor's eyes shone, and her face was animated as she went on, "It's called 'vanishing twin syndrome' or 'vanishing twin phenomenon,' but a lot of doctors agree those are misleading names. It happens for too many different reasons to be considered a syndrome. And it's far too common to be considered phenomenal."

"Oh, my God," Dair said again.

Dr. Burkett flipped through her chart. "In one study I looked up, forty-four twin pregnancies were detected between five and six weeks, but only two of those forty-four delivered twins. Three sets lost both, and the rest delivered singletons."

"Peyton?" Dair reached for him. He grabbed her hand in both of his and pressed it to his cheek. And the strangest muddle of emotions somersaulted in Dair's still hazy, anesthetized brain. Guilt. Almost embarrassment that this was true. That Peyton might let her off the hook. She hadn't known this. She'd lied.

Dair looked into his face, which seemed elated somehow. He exhaled, and his shoulders dropped. Dair could almost see tension draining from him, as if he'd been massaged, or the way she felt when she took the first long swallow of rich Merlot. . . .

And she felt that way right now, that warm tingle beginning, that softening effect. She didn't understand Peyton's elation, but she felt it, too. This news felt like relief. There was a reason. There was a reason for the emptiness.

Peyton kept Dair's hand against her cheek and closed his eyes. Dair drank in his touch, his love, this affection. She was parched for it.

Dr. Burkett smiled warmly at them. "As for your other injuries," she said, "you're a lucky woman." She told Dair about her hip pin, how she'd need crutches for six weeks and physical therapy.

Dair was amazed to discover it was nearly midnight. But of the next day. Sunday. Dair found herself remembering the rest of the last week, the last day, in fragments, asking questions abruptly.

"Matthew?" Dair asked.

"He's fine," Peyton said, wiping his eyes. "He stayed here with me last night. He's with your mom now."

"Marielle?"

"She's here. She's fine. She should get released today."

Dair tried to remember the evening. All that had happened. "Did they catch Captain Hook?"

"Your mom did."

A memory knocked into Dair's addled brain. "Oh, God. Blizzard! How's Blizzard?"

Peyton bit his lip, and his face twitched. He shook his head.

Dair felt she was floating away from this bed, tethered to it only by his hands, which still held her own. "No, no, no, no, no," she breathed. "No."

Peyton nodded and closed his eyes a moment.

Dair shook with sobs, each one sending a stab through her hip. Dr. Burkett wandered discreetly away. Peyton held Dair's hands while she cried.

"Your dad did everything he could . . . but, but he had to put him to sleep."

"Dad did it?"

Peyton nodded. That was something, some odd kind of comfort. Blizzard knew him, at least, and Dair knew her father would have been soothing and loving.

She tried to remember. She felt Blizzard's head on her chest. Her hands in his long white hair.

"Did . . . did Blizzard get drugged, too?"

Peyton shook his head. "But he got stabbed with a needle. It punctured some . . . some organs. Your mom helped figure that out, where he hurt, what to test, because they couldn't find a wound. His kidney was torn. He—your dad said he was in a lot of pain. . . . It—it was the right thing to do."

Dair closed her eyes, squeezing the tears out the corners. "He saved me. He wouldn't let me in the house because . . . of Andy." It was hard to say Andy's name and picture the person she thought she knew. "Andy was waiting for me, I'm sure. He—he knew I was coming. I told him she was home. I—I led him straight to her. I—"

"Shh, Dair," Peyton said, stroking her hair. "It's all okay, now. It's okay."

"But, Blizzard . . ."

"I know, I know."

Dr. Burkett returned with the nurse, explaining it was time for some meds.

Dr. Burkett cleared her throat. "Now, I understand you want a pregnancy test?"

Dair looked at Peyton. "Yeah, you said that last night," he told her. He shook his head, confused and somewhat concerned. "Do you really think—"

"No. Never mind. I think I . . . I misunderstood what . . . what was said to me."

Both Peyton and the doctor looked bewildered.

Dair shook her head. "I was . . ." How to explain it? "I was high."

They nodded, and that was the end of it. Dr. Burkett made Dair get up, claiming the sooner she started to move, the better. Dair found this hard to believe, as moving was slow and excruciating, even with two nurse escorts. The crutches hurt against her bruised ribs, and a fire burned in her hip joint. Once she made it to a bathroom, she hung her IV bag on the doorknob and gasped at her reflection in the mirror, not recognizing herself at first. She looked as if she'd gone through a windshield, her face was so discolored and swollen. And part of her head was shaved, with some tiny black stitches on the sickly white skin of her scalp. She looked made up for Halloween. Once she went to the bathroom, they moved her to a regular hospital room. Peyton slept there with her.

And if she had any dreams, she didn't remember them.

Chapter Twenty-nine

When Dair woke up Monday morning, Peyton was gone.

Dr. Burkett came to check on Dair and made her get out of bed. Dair felt swollen and torpid, and the hieroglyphs of bruises had blossomed into new configurations, leaving an entirely new message behind.

"You'll feel better," Dr. Burkett said simply. "C'mon."

Dair didn't believe her. Her mouth, her muscles, her memory, all craved some cold, clean vodka, a relaxant that had worked wonders after long, physical rehearsals.

But she allowed herself to be bullied out of bed. Dr. Burkett prepared to leave Dair with a nurse, but Dair said, "Wait. Could I talk to you a minute?"

Dr. Burkett looked at her watch, then smiled wickedly. "Sure. But you'll have to walk with me."

Dair lumbered alongside the trim doctor, hating the easy, comfortable way she clomped along in her stylish leather clogs. Dair wore an ugly brown slipper-sock on her left foot. Her right foot was swollen and purplish.

"This teratoma . . . ," Dair said. "My twin . . ."

Dr. Burkett slowed, appeared interested. "Yes?"

"What would make one twin survive over another?"

"Oh. Well. Twins are difficult. There's competition for space and nutrients."

Dair stopped, wincing, her sore ribs throbbing against the crutches. "So, how . . . ?"

Dr. Burkett smiled. "There's competition," she repeated. "Only one usually wins."

Dair opened her mouth, a dawning breaking over her. "I killed the other one?"

"No. Oh, no. You mustn't think of it that way." Dr. Burkett guided Dair to a bench near an elevator. Dair lowered herself with some struggle, her hip sending scorches of pain up all the way through her shoulder. The nurse hovered nearby.

"It's very common when a twin dies for the survivor to feel life-long feelings of guilt. They suffer depression and sadness."

"But I didn't even know I was a survivor."

The doctor put a hand on Dair's shoulder. "There are support groups for lone twins, and many of their members are people who never knew their twin, never even knew they were twins until they were about to get married, or were expecting their first child and were told, out of the blue, about their stillborn twin. And for most of these people, they say the news came as a—"

"A relief," Dair said.

Dr. Burkett's face brightened, as if curious.

"I've missed her my whole life. But I never understood it. That sounds so insane, but . . ."

"It's not insane. And you share those feelings with a lot of people. Here, you keep walking. I'm going to bring you some of that information. Okay?"

Dair nodded and let the nurse help her up from the bench. This nurse was stray-cat thin with overprocessed hair but a kind face. Dair continued her slow, stabbing way down the hall. The thin nurse was not talkative, and Dair let her mind wander to her twin. Would they have been friends? Shared talents? Would they have looked alike? Would her sister have been a liar? Would she like to drink?

Would Dair have needed to drink if she'd had her sister?

"I—I want to go back," Dair said, the pain like barbed wire cutting into her hip.

The thin nurse shook her head. "We have to go all the way around," she said, pointing to a hallway just ahead of them. "But we can't turn back."

Dair wondered what the woman would do if Dair simply refused. If she sat down and stopped or turned around anyway. They couldn't *make* her. But she kept putting her left foot down, adjusting her weight on the crutches, hefting herself forward, landing on the left foot again. One foot. She would focus on one foot at a time.

And miraculously, they limped their way back to Dair's room just as Dr. Burkett came breezing down the hallway, in her cute little clogs, on her fit, strong legs. Dair thought about tripping her across the shins with a crutch.

"Here you go," she said, handing Dair a small stack of papers printed from the Internet. Dair wondered how she was supposed to hold these papers and keep crutching.

Dair leaned on her crutches and looked at the papers. "Look," Dr. Burkett said, pointing to a passage she'd starred with a green pen. "Early twin loss can be a strong influence on thoughts and preoccupations. There's a bunch of accounts in there of people who believed they were born twins even without any medical proof of twinship. They all talk about depression and emptiness and the feeling that someone else is out there."

Dair shivered as a hand touched her between the shoulder blades. Peyton stood beside her. "There you are," he said. "I've been looking for you."

She blinked, confused, but he went on, "Your mom and dad are here, but when you weren't in your room, we worried that you'd been moved or something."

"Oh." She took a deep breath, her sore ribs protesting. "No. I was being forced to march through the hallways against my will."

The thin nurse squinted, but Dr. Burkett laughed. "I'll check in on you later—"

"Wait," Dair said. Dr. Burkett stopped, and Dair wished she were closer so she didn't have to speak loudly enough to include the thin nurse and Peyton. But she didn't have the strength to move closer herself. "Um. I was wondering if I could talk to you . . . or someone else, about some things. . . ."

"A counselor?" Dr. Burkett asked without judgment.

Dair's face burned anyway. She nodded.

"About the twin issues?"

Dair nodded and whispered, "And . . . some other stuff, too."

Dr. Burkett looked to Peyton a moment, but Dair couldn't turn around to see him; it took too much effort. The doctor looked back at Dair and stepped closer. She looked at her watch again. "I'll come back this afternoon, okay? I think we have some programs you might find . . . very helpful." And she clicked away down the hall.

Dair turned her head to face Peyton.

"What 'programs'?" she demanded.

Peyton shoved his hands in his pockets. "They, um, have a good, you know, substance abuse program."

Dair stared at him. "You *told* her?"

"I had to, Dair. They asked questions, and I had to answer. If I didn't, for anesthesia and stuff, it could harm you. It can affect medications and things."

"Here," she said, thrusting the papers at him. "Hold these, okay?"

He took them but didn't look at them. He kept staring at her. She softened. "Thank you," she said. He looked as if he weren't sure she meant the rehab program or the papers. She wasn't sure, either.

She let the nurse guide her into her room.

Mom and Dad sat at the foot of Dair's bed. On Dair's breakfast tray, a white candle stood in a muffin. Mom jumped up and lit it when Dair came into the room.

"Happy birthday!" Mom said.

The nurse helped Dair settle herself back in bed. Sweat stood on Dair's lip from the effort, from the pain. It was her birthday. She should have champagne on her birthday. A mimosa, perhaps, with this weak-looking orange juice.

"Make a wish," Mom said. The candle's flame sputtered.

Dair stared at the flame. What could she wish for? That her twin had lived? That her parents had told her about her mother's drinking? That she'd never lied? That Peyton had never left? That she'd never ignored her ability to listen to animals?

Sudden sorrow grasped her tender, bruised ribs, and she blew the candle out. She stared at the little curl of white smoke rising from it and said carefully, trying not to cry, "Peyton told me . . . about Blizzard."

She lifted her head to her parents, who both nodded with sad eyes. "Dair," her dad said, "I did everything I could."

She nodded. "I know. I know you would. I just wish I could've been there."

Mom moved to sit on the edge of the bed, facing her. She reached out and tucked Dair's hair behind her ear. "He understood," she said. "I was there. He wanted to wait for you, too, but he was in so much pain."

It hurt Dair to even imagine his suffering.

"He said he already said good-bye to you . . . but . . ." She cocked her head.

"What?" Dair asked.

Mom sighed. "I was a mess, so I might not have been receiving clearly, but—he didn't think you . . . recognized him?"

Dair nodded. "I did. I knew who he was."

A knock at the door turned their attention. Tall blond Detective Monty stood at the door. "Oh, I'm sorry, I . . ." Monty paused, did a double take. "Oh, it *is* you."

Dair knew how hideous she looked. She touched her head, felt the bald spot, the stitches, the bumps and ridges where there usually weren't any.

Monty entered the room. "Do you feel up to answering some questions?"

"Sure," Dair said. Why did this guy only ever see her at her worst? At least he'd seen her in a show once.

Craig. She'd been in that show with Craig. She had an image of Craig waking up in Gayle's house, naked, confused, high. . . .

Peyton moved to give the detective his seat, his movements stiff and self-conscious.

Monty opened a notepad. "First of all, I'm glad you're okay. Very glad."

Dair admired how he said that so sincerely. Why should he care?

"We're just trying to fill in some gaps in the statements. Get a handle on some time frames, make sure we have an accurate account."

Mom and Dad stood. Dad said, "We'll step out for a minute."

Monty nodded at them. Then he looked at Peyton. For a moment Dair thought Peyton was going to leave, too, and terror seized her. Peyton looked at Dair, then sat in the seat her dad had left vacant.

Monty cleared his throat. "Do you recall what time you arrived home Saturday night? Once you got the call from Mrs. Marshall?"

"Mrs. Marshall?"

He shook his head. "I mean"—he turned back a page in his notepad—"I mean Ms. Evans, your neighbor."

"Marielle?"

Monty nodded.

"Her name is Mrs. Marshall?"

Dair looked at Peyton. He looked flabbergasted as well.

"Yes, her legal name is Ella Marshall."

Dair blinked. "Is, is she in trouble? Is she going to—"

"She's going to be fine," Monty said. Again his sincerity impressed Dair. "But it's complicated. It's a case of kidnapping, but—"

"But justified kidnapping!" Dair sat up straight, and her animation sent a lightning bolt of pain through her right side. She gasped and grabbed a handful of blanket in her fist. "Andy's crazy. The man's a psychopath. If she kidnapped her son to keep him safe, then she was right and he—"

"Hey, hey, hey, slow down," Monty said. "Your friend Marielle is going to be fine. Her husband is in custody. He's got a manslaughter charge, a murder charge, drug possession, assault—"

"Gayle?" Dair asked. She couldn't breathe for a moment. She remembered Andy's thumb digging into her mouth, the taste of blood. Peyton moved to sit beside Dair on the bed. "Did you find Gayle?"

Monty nodded. "We found her body."

Dair stared at him until he went on.

"She was in the trunk of Mr. Baker's second car. A car registered to a Drew Lancaster, in storage. We found receipts that led us to it in Mr. Baker's apartment. And Mr. Baker, whose real name is Drew Marshall, was carrying ID—complete and total ID—for Drew Lancaster, of Kenai, Alaska. We think he would've dumped Ms. Lyons's body, taken off with the boy, and would've been gone without a trace. Literally. There was nothing to connect Andy Baker to the boy. Or to, um, Marielle, your neighbor. I believe that was his plan. And it's unfortunate what happened to prevent that, but it did prevent it."

Peyton cleared his throat. "Matt was never alone after we found out . . . about Craig. He was with us, or he was gone, with Marielle somewhere else."

Dair saw the schedules on Marielle's refrigerator. Remembered that small window of time that Matt had left the house with Mr. Lively.

She tried not to think about Matt being home, answering the door when Craig came with the flowers.

Dair told Officer Monty what she could remember about times, about the phone call at the theater, all about the bizarre week that they'd just lived through.

"Hey," Dair said. "Why did Malcolm have a key to Gayle's house?"

Monty looked at Payton and smiled a tight smile. He snapped his notepad shut and said to Dair, "Thank you. I'm going to get out of here and let you rest. You . . . um, you take care. I hope I see you on-stage again soon."

Dair laughed. How could she be in *Othello* on crutches? There was no way. That production was cursed. They might as well be doing *Macbeth*.

Monty left the room, but Dair's parents didn't return. Peyton sat on the bed beside her, watching her, waiting.

"Can I ask you that?" Dair whispered. "Do you know why Malcolm had a key?"

Peyton nodded. "Malcolm went into a rehab in September. He didn't have—"

"Rehab? He's a . . . junkie?"

Peyton flinched. "Yup. Just like me."

Dair blinked. Malcolm wasn't anything like Peyton. "He used heroin?"

Peyton nodded. "Gayle gave him a place to live when he got out. Until he saved up more money."

Dair stared.

"I know," Peyton said. "Gayle Lyons. Whoever would've thought?"

Gayle's fierce loyalty, her determination to protect Malcolm, shamed Dair, who had completely misinterpreted Gayle's intentions. She lifted one of her scraped hands and wiped her swollen cheek. Was anyone who she thought they were?

"So . . . last Saturday, what were you doing with Malcolm? Why did you come back early? Andy said he saw you at our house."

Peyton reached out to her, touched her bald spot. He didn't look into her face while he spoke. "I went to one of Malcolm's meetings at NA. He asked me to be there when he, you know, where he tells his story to the group? I'm his . . . I said I'd be his sponsor."

Dair's chest expanded, her bruised ribs ached, but the soreness felt exquisitely sweet. "Why didn't you tell me?"

Peyton made eye contact with her then. "'Why didn't you tell me?'" he repeated softly. "Hmm. There's an interesting question."

Dair's stitches itched with the heat that coursed through her face and exposed scalp.

He smiled ever so slightly, the grin unfurling only halfway. "I didn't think you needed to know that about Malcolm. It would've made you not like him."

Dair didn't know what to say. She wanted to say, "No, it wouldn't," but she was trying not to lie. She was trying to examine every statement that formed in her brain before she allowed her mouth to utter it. Lying was so habitual, it took that sort of effort. More effort than walking with crutches.

"It felt important to me," Peyton said. "It's the twelfth step, you know, to carry the message."

"But . . . ," Dair said. "You could've said you were *someone's* sponsor—you didn't have to give me a name. I—I think I would've been happy for you."

"You're right. But . . ."

"What?"

"It was a good excuse to check on . . . some things."

Dair swallowed. "Things?"

Peyton's shoulders slumped. "Dair, your drinking . . . it's been . . . out of control for a while. I—I just thought, I don't know, since I was coming back early anyway, I wanted to see . . . how much damage control you had to do before I got back. How many bottles were gone."

Dair felt as if the bed had been wheeled out from under her.

"But I felt terrible," Peyton said. "Because I know. It's hard . . . not to feel trusted."

"I know," she whispered.

Peyton picked at her pale green blanket for a moment.

"What are we going to do?" Dair asked.

Peyton looked at her a long time, combing back her hair, touching one of her eyebrows. She had to look horrible, like some creature just spawned. This moment felt so fragile. She didn't know how to behave with him. Here he was touching her, tending to her. Last night he'd said he loved her. Yet he didn't trust her. She didn't even know if she was allowed to touch him back.

"I don't know," he said.

That answer was better than the one she'd expected. Hope sparked feebly within her, like that lonely little birthday candle still standing in her breakfast muffin.

Chapter Thirty

L ater that day Peyton and her parents took Dair home. It took ambulatory care to get her up the steep front steps. Now she was marooned at the house. She moved clumsily on her crutches. There was no way she'd be in *Othello* now. And to be honest, she didn't care.

To be honest. Strange territory for Dair.

Marielle and Matt were not at home. No one knew where they were.

For an hour or two, there was a flurry of comforting activity. Mom and Dad helped prepare the house for Dair's convenience, and Mom even took inventory of the kitchen cupboards and fridge and went grocery shopping for her.

But when Dad brought Blizzard's body home from the emergency vet clinic, Dair's mom found Dair in the living room and said, "We're going to give you and Peyton some time alone. I'm sure you need to talk."

No, don't go! Dair's mind screamed. But she swallowed and nodded. "Are you guys going home together?"

"Yes, we drove in together."

"So you'll have some time alone, too, right?"

Mom pursed her lips at Dair but smiled with her eyes. "Good luck. I love you."

"I love you."

Hugging was difficult, but Mom held Dair's face in her hands a few minutes before she and Dad got in the truck and drove away.

Peyton seemed afraid to be alone there, too, and busied himself burying Blizzard.

Dair stood on the back porch, leaning on her crutches, while he dug a grave in the corner of the yard.

Dair wanted to go to Blizzard. She wanted to unwrap him from his baby blue blanket and bury her face in his sweet-smelling fur, but she stood on the porch and watched. Only his face was visible from where she stood.

Godot *ca-clunk*ed out of his cat door, rubbed against Dair's shin, and sat at her feet.

Shodan whined inside the kitchen, so Dair opened the door and let her out, too.

Shodie trotted down the stairs, sniffed at Blizzard's body, licked his snout once, then moved away, snuffling about the yard as usual.

Dair tried to face her sorrow, but the thought of losing her friends, both Blizzard and Craig, even Gayle, and now perhaps Peyton, felt like deeper, more damaging incisions than the surgery. There was only one way she'd learned to deal with sorrow.

And the craving washed over her with an intensity that took her breath away. She still had Kahlúa. In her kitchen.

She turned her head to go inside, but Mr. Lively's door opened. The old man stepped out onto the metal stairs. He had white tape on his bald head, and one eye sported quite an impressive shiner. Before Mr. Lively could speak, Captain Hook fluttered out to the railing.

"Blast it," Mr. Lively said, hands in front of him, waiting for the parrot to settle so he could grab him. Dair had a feeling Captain Hook had enjoyed his little adventure.

"Shodie!" Captain Hook called in Dair's voice. Shodan lifted her head to him and wagged her stump. Then she looked at Dair. She knew the difference.

Peyton stopped digging and looked up at the bird.

Godot flattened his ears, scowling up at the parrot, and stalked back through his cat door into the house.

Dair watched the parrot shuffle from foot to foot, craning his head, looking with one yellow eye and then the other down at Blizzard's body.

Mr. Lively carefully reached out and took the parrot in his hands.

"Blizzard," Captain Hook called in his own childlike voice. *"Those damn dogs!"*

Mr. Lively cleared his throat, and said in a thick, odd voice, "I'm glad you're well. It's a shame—a shame about the dog." Without even waiting for her response, he carried the bird into his apartment and shut the door.

As soon as Peyton resumed digging again, Dair crutched her way through the back door and into the kitchen. She balanced on her crutches and opened the cupboard to reach for the Kahlúa.

It was gone.

Shit. She looked around, looked in other cupboards, wincing at the strain on her sore and damaged body. It was gone.

No, there it was, right on top of the trash, in plain sight.

Empty. Dair opened it, hoping for a drop or two, even the fumes, but the bottle smelled only of dishwashing detergent; it even had suds in the bottom.

Mom. While Mom futzed around in the kitchen this morning, had she done this? Or had Peyton?

Dair's skin itched. She wanted to kick the cupboard. Hurl the bottle.

Cursing under her breath, she made her tottering way back out to the porch. Peyton kept digging at the hard, dusty ground. He had to slam the shovel, like bashing into concrete, to get even a few inches of give in the parched, dry earth. Dair longed to do something that violent herself. It looked like something to lose yourself in.

Shodan raised her head, ears lifted, and Dair followed her gaze toward the back gate. No one was there. But even as she thought that, Marielle and Matt appeared. Marielle paused, seeing them, but Matt called, "Hey, Dair!" and opened the gate.

Peyton stopped shoveling and turned around, too.

Matt ran up onto the porch but stopped short in front of Dair. His gray eyes widened. "Oh, man," he said in awe. "You look really, *really* bad."

Dair had to laugh. "I feel really, really bad."

Marielle and Peyton both slowly approached the porch.

Marielle looked smaller than Dair remembered her. She'd lost weight this week, enough to notice. Her blond hair was pulled back in a ponytail, highlighting her pale face, dark shadows ringing her eyes, but she was mysteriously radiant. She seemed relaxed, present in some strange manner that she'd never been before. "Oh, Dair," she whispered, taking in Dair's appearance. She covered her mouth with her hand and shook her head. She raised her hand, touching the spot on her own head where Dair's was shaved and stitched. "I'm so sorry," she said. "I'm so, so sorry I put you all in danger. That . . . I lied to you."

Matt looked up at his mother, his face sullen, and moved past Dair into the house.

Marielle sighed and said, "We have a lot of work to do."

Peyton sat on the top step of the porch. "I know what you mean."

Marielle looked at him, then at Dair. "Jesus," she said. "Maybe we should have a cookout so that everyone in the house can get to know each other."

Dair's heart lifted when Peyton snorted. He didn't laugh outright, but he responded.

Dair smiled at Marielle, grateful.

Something flowed between the women again, as it had when Dair had first told her about the lie. Recognition. Admiration.

"You don't look like an Ella," Dair said.

Marielle tilted her head. "You don't think so? Hmm. I like Marielle better, actually."

Dair wondered if she meant just the name or the whole person.

"I'm sorry," Marielle said again. "That I couldn't tell you. I can't ever begin to—"

"You had a reason," Dair said. "For God's sake, you had a good reason."

Peyton squinted up at her through the late afternoon light.

They stood, silent and uncertain, strangers, all of them, after all this time.

"Did Craig know?" Peyton asked Marielle.

Dair held her breath at the mention of Craig's name.

Marielle's mouth quivered. "Of *course*. I couldn't marry him without him knowing the truth. I couldn't do that to someone; I would never—" She stopped, looking at Dair.

Dair wanted to crawl into the hole Peyton had chipped into the ground. She couldn't look at Peyton.

Marielle shrugged. "I'm going to go try to salvage life with my son."

As she stepped onto the porch and past Dair, Dair said, "Are you still moving?"

Marielle shook her head. "No, you're stuck with us." She looked at Peyton and said, "I hope you're both stuck with us," and went into her house.

And once again, left alone, Dair and Peyton were awkward, fumbling. They both stood and stared at their feet. Dair's arms ached from being on her crutches too long.

"Well," Peyton said, "I better keep at this."

"Yeah," Dair said too brightly.

She watched him work for a while, hammering into the ground, the dust nearly obscuring him. Her head throbbed with every stab of his shovel. Her skin called out, like the ground and the trees, for sustenance, for moisture.

She had nothing. Not a goddamn thing to drink.

But . . . Dair turned her head to Marielle's back door. She did. Unless she'd packed it.

She crutched her way into Marielle's kitchen. Peyton never looked up. Dair stood still and listened. She heard voices upstairs. Gentle voices, not arguing. "Marielle?" she called too quietly to be heard.

When the voices continued, Dair swung her way over to the fridge and opened it. Sure enough, the bottle of Chardonnay Marielle had opened last Saturday was still there, untouched, on its side. Dair reached in and pulled it out.

She set it on the counter and admired it a moment.

With one finger she wiped a line in the condensation on the bottle, wrote her name in that beautiful dew.

Then she clutched the neck of the bottle in her fingers, enclosing it in her grasp of the crutch, and hobbled out the door.

She stood on the porch, feeling bold, daring. There she was, in broad daylight, only fifteen yards or so between her and Peyton, holding a bottle of wine.

He kept hacking at the ground.

Thunder rumbled, far off. Dair looked up at the still sunny sky, knew that the storm, when it came, would be violent.

She went inside her own kitchen.

Her skull ached as if it would explode. She opened the cupboard and took out a glass.

She poured herself one glass and, balancing on one crutch, set it on the table. She corked the bottle, put it in the fridge, then hobbled to a chair and lowered herself to it with a whimper. She took a moment, gathered herself, then lifted the glass and smelled the wine. The aroma alone eased the pressure in her head.

She waited for some sort of sign. None came. So she took a sip. Cool, alive on her tongue, familiar, comforting. She took another sip. She savored each one, rolling it on her tongue, swishing it through her teeth, until the glass was empty. Although she felt better, the broken ribs of her sorrow still ached.

Another glass would do it.

She struggled to her feet on her crutches and returned to the fridge. She took out the bottle. She uncorked it.

But she didn't pour.

Another glass wouldn't do it. And neither would a third, although the second glass would convince her to try. If she poured again, she'd drink until the bottle was empty.

Her ribs ached even more, and she half expected the *thunk thunk thunk* of the chickadee beak. But the chickadee was gone. And Dair knew why.

"Hey, Peyton?" she called through the open screen door.

He turned to her, panting and sweaty.

"Could you come inside a minute? I need to talk to you. Please?"

He lifted the bottom of his T-shirt to wipe his face and nodded.

Dair sat at the kitchen table and waited. And Peyton came in, dirt under his nails and sweat soaked through his shirt.

He looked at her, questioning, and she turned her head toward the bottle on the counter. He took in the bottle, the glass, and sighed and sat down. He reached for her hands, and she gave them, smelling the dry dust on his own.

"I—I need help," Dair said.

He nodded.

They stared at each other a moment. Dair asked, "What's wrong with me?"

He took a deep breath and said gently, "You're an alcoholic, Dair."

She blinked. "I'm—but . . . I—I . . . I'm not . . . am I?"

He nodded. "Yes. You are. You know you are. Tell the truth." He un-furled a rueful grin. "For once in your life, tell the truth."

Dair bit her lip. "I am," she said. She thought her ribs cracked at that moment. There was exquisite pain and then release.

She must've paled or gasped . . . or something, because Peyton leaned forward. "Are you okay?"

She nodded, eyes bulging. She crinkled her nose. "That hurt."

He nodded again, his eyes full of recognition, understanding.

"I—I don't know what to do," Dair admitted. "Will you help me?"

His Adam's apple bobbed as he nodded. His eyes glittered.

She kissed his dirty hands. She laid her cheek upon them. "Thank you."

"Thank *you*," he whispered.

Without lifting her head, Dair said, "I'm so sorry I lied."

"You didn't lie," he said simply.

She winced.

"But you meant to."

She was glad he'd said that. It was true. Her intention had been to lie. "Yes," she said.

"But it wasn't a lie, and that's important." He stroked her hair. "That's important—you should look at that, see what you're supposed to learn."

Distant thunder rumbled again.

What had she learned? She'd found the answer to one sense of emptiness but had opened up another emptiness by driving Peyton away.

"I love you," Dair whispered.

One tear wiped a clean white line down Peyton's dusty face. "I love you, Dair." He leaned across and kissed her on that bald spot. "But I feel like . . . like I need to get to know you."

Dair nodded. "Me, too." She knew Peyton understood that she needed to get to know herself.

"And that's gonna keep you busy for a while," Peyton said. "I've been there. You don't need other things to worry about; you—"

"But you said you'd help me. You can't leave, please don't—"

"Shh," he said. "I will help you. Just because I'm not going to live here right now doesn't mean I never will again."

"You'll wait for me?"

He laughed. Laughed out loud, that smile unfurling as she hadn't seen it since a week ago Saturday. "You make it sound like I'm going off to war or something."

"I feel like *I'm* going off to war," Dair said. "If I go into this program tomorrow, if I . . . Peyton, I don't know if I can do it. I don't know what's going to happen to me."

"Well . . . we never know, do we?" he said, still smiling. "I mean, nobody knows that."

Dair sighed. "Shouldn't you stay here with me, though? I mean, to make sure I don't drink anything?"

Peyton shook his head. Shodan scratched at the door, and he stood and let her in. "Nope. That's not how it works. If the only thing stopping you is me policing you, then it'll never work."

"Well, that's the only thing stopping me," Dair said sullenly. "I just stole this from Marielle."

"It's not the only thing stopping you." Peyton remained standing and crossed his arms. "There's still wine in that bottle. You called me in here. It's not like I caught you."

Dair thought about that. "You wouldn't stop me if I wanted another glass?"

He narrowed his eyes and admitted, "No."

"Well, then pour me another."

"No. You'd have to do that yourself."

They stared at each other a moment.

"What do you *want,* Dair?" he asked.

"I want to live with you again," she said.

He nodded. "Well, I want that, too."

They stared again. It was that simple. They'd said all they needed to say.

A crash of thunder, closer, followed by a pop of lightning, made them both jump.

"I'm going to bury Blizzard before it pours," Peyton said.

Dair nodded and hobbled to the door, watching Peyton through the screen. Godot curled around her legs and crutches. Shodan lay under the kitchen table.

Dair watched Peyton lower the dog's body, filling the hole, just as the first few drops hit the ground. The dampening of dry grass and pavement rose from the dust and filled Dair's nostrils. A sound, like a sigh of relief, seemed to come from the earth. Dair closed her eyes and drank it in.

ALSO AVAILABLE FROM WARNER BOOKS

TRAVELING LIGHT
by Katrina Kittle

Everything is going wrong in Summer's life. A dancer recovering from the injury that ended her career, she's grown detached from her lover, and her cherished brother is slowly dying. But when Summer strives to fulfill the promise her brother exacted from her long ago, she meets her greatest challenge—and realizes how truly fortunate she really is. From an exciting new voice in contemporary fiction, this is a deeply moving love story that touches our deepest fears and truest longings.

"Wonderfully moving...hard to put down and harder still to forget."

—*Booklist* (starred review)

WAIT AND SEE, ANNIE LEE
by Michelle Curry Wright

With a deft feel for dialogue, a lively eye for human comedy, and a loving portrayal of eccentric characters, Michelle Curry Wright is one of the most delightfully fresh new voices in fiction today. Her new novel depicts a thoroughly modern woman with an old-fashioned yen for a baby, a woman whose imagination may be the most fertile thing about her. With a little derring-do, Annie Lee conceives a whole new world of possibilities, including the most far-fetched of all: that sometimes the quickest way to get your wish is just to wait and see...

"A deliciously funny novel featuring a delectably engaging heroine."

—Caroline Leavitt, author of *Coming Back to Me*

more...

WHO WILL RUN THE FROG HOSPITAL?

by Lorrie Moore

One day Berie Carr, a middle-aged woman, realizes she no longer loves her husband. Her thoughts return to a small town in upstate New York, to her childhood and the deep friendship she shared with a girl named Sils—Sils, who always a little older and a little faster. Lorrie Moore's achingly beautiful novel explores what it means to be a child and then a woman, a friend, and then a stranger— and to be both bound to your past and separated from it forever.

"Exquisite…exhilarating…balanced adroitly on the fine line between laughter and tears."
—*Chicago Tribune*